PRAISE FOR

"A vivid, evocative journey...This compelling debut is a story for our current world."
—Kimiko Guthrie, author of *Block Seventeen*, on *Reset*

"A collision of our era's catastrophes fuses a new world, becoming something rich and strange."
—Kim Stanley Robinson, Hugo Award–winning novelist, on *Preset*

"Crisp, stylish prose and a story about love trying to withstand the rigors of time. This is a book subtle in its intensity, lush and beautiful, while carefully exploring what it means to be human and what we are to each other. Evocative and literary, I highly recommend it."
—David R. Slayton, author of *White Trash Warlock*, on *Reset*

FREE
SET

BOOKS BY SARINA DAHLAN

THE FOUR CITIES

Preset
Reset
Freeset

SHORT STORY COLLECTIONS

Shadow Play

FREE SET

A NOVEL

SARINA DAHLAN

BLACK STONE
PUBLISHING

Copyright © 2024 by Sarina Dahlan
Published in 2024 by Blackstone Publishing
Cover design by Alenka Vdovič Linaschke
Book design by K. Jones

All rights reserved. This book or any portion
thereof may not be reproduced or used in any manner
whatsoever without the express written permission
of the publisher except for the use of brief quotations
in a book review.

The characters and events in this book are fictitious.
Any similarity to real persons, living or dead, is coincidental
and not intended by the author.

Printed in the United States of America

First edition: 2024
ISBN 979-8-212-63135-8
Fiction / Science Fiction / General

Version 1

Blackstone Publishing
31 Mistletoe Rd.
Ashland, OR 97520

www.BlackstonePublishing.com

*My eternal gratitude to allies
and those who serve as bridges
—for without you this world
would be a much darker place*

On the edge of a cliff,
hidden by jagged peaks
and a northern forest of pine,
lives Old Mem.
Her face,
empty of lines,
holds secret lives within.
Her soul,
stolen in slumber,
awaits deliverance.
Look homeward, angel,
and breathe life everlasting.
—Anonymous

CHAPTER ONE

ARIS

February 14, 2233
(34 days before Tabula Rasa)

Through a broken window of a broken building, Aris sees the night sky. Dots of stars sprinkle it like sugar on a cake—more stars than she's ever seen, more than it would take her an entire lifetime to count. Her winter jacket is no match for the cold. There's an edge of otherworldliness to the freezing desert air, making her wonder whether she is inside a dream. *Maybe.* She's exhausted enough. It must be close to midnight by now. She leans against the body next to hers, his warmth trying and failing to replace the fire they could not start.

"We need to separate," he says, his words puncturing both the darkness and her heart.

"Why?" She knows but asks anyway.

"You need to keep going north. I'll lead the drones away. You heard them last night, didn't you?"

For a month, to stay out of sight, they have been sleeping during the day and traveling under the cloak of darkness. The journey took them past weed-filled farmlands and broken-down gas stations, dead towns with characteristically American names and drained lakes that once fed thirsty coastal cities.

Now, with drones flying at random hours of the day, it is becoming nearly impossible to move. Elara is far behind them. Their destination is somewhere ahead. They are stuck in the middle of a treeless desert, danger circling closer and closer. Had they not found this long-abandoned building, it would have been the end.

"I don't want you to," she says.

"I know, love. I don't want to either. But I have to so you can make it. What we're doing is bigger than the both of us, you know that."

That's Metis—selfless to the end.

"We don't even know where it really is," she responds. "What if it's not where we think it is?"

"Just follow the train tracks like we planned. They run north–south. The Four Cities are in the south—we've determined that. Which means something else is in the north."

Something can mean anything. But they have been operating on the promise of "something" for so long the word has become the mantra of their survival.

I can see something *glittery ahead—maybe it's water.*

There's something *over there! I think it's shelter.*

"Do you really believe our memories are there?" she asks.

"That's what the legend says," he replies.

> On the edge of a cliff,
> hidden by jagged peaks
> and a northern forest of pine,
> lives Old Mem.

The legend of Mem first came to them as a poem. The Crone believes that, like most myths and legends, it grew from humbler stories—stories told by past Resistance members who may have found Mem, ones that were told and retold thousands of times over the past two hundred years. *Through time, past memory erasure.*

Once Aris and Metis knew what to look for, they kept seeing clues everywhere. In notes written on the margins of old books. In songs and words hidden in paintings found in museums. All of them pointed in one direction: north. Despite the clues, she knows this is still the wildest of guesses. But it's what they have.

"You will find it," Metis says. "I have faith."

"But what good will finding it be if you're arrested? They're going to erase your dreams."

She shudders at the thought of the Interpreter's icy blue eyes. Absinthe had reminded her what the woman is—a murderer of dreams.

"I'll be fine," he says. "Remember what the Crone said? Since the Planner values my ability to create, he won't let the Interpreter erase my dreams. That's why I get to keep my name and our house every cycle. I'm protected by my music."

Metis is just trying to make her feel better, she knows, though there is truth in it. The Crone reasoned the System gives him only one name to track his body of work through all the cycles, but the house is more likely for practical reasons. Being a pianist, he needs a piano in his house, and there aren't that many in the Four Cities. Moving it from home to home isn't easy. Metis doesn't need to move, he just needs to think he did.

"How am I supposed to be okay with letting you go?" Aris asks.

"There's no letting go. We're forever."

He leans in and kisses her, his mouth hot against her cold lips.

Forever. She hates the word. Hates it for all its failed promises. Hates it for how much she loves hearing it from him.

He trails his lips across her cheek to her ear. She presses her body against his. She wants—*needs*—to brand this moment into her memory. Her hand digs into her pocket and pulls out a glass vial. Seeing what she's doing, Metis reaches into his jacket and does the same. The green liquid gleams in the moonlight.

Her eyes drink in all of him, memorizing every detail. He does the same. He mouths "I love you." She returns the words, fragile as a butterfly, in a whisper. They open the vial tops and flick the green liquid down their throats.

It feels like a ball of air exploding inside, followed by a tingling sensation traveling throughout her body. His lips are on hers at once. She tastes the green herbal tang of hypnos with the sting of alcohol.

His fingers move to her coat, and she hears it unzipping. Cold air seeps in through the opening, and she shivers from it and desire.

"Don't let me go," she says.

"I couldn't even if I tried," he replies.

"Promise?"

"Promise."

Hope—whatever is left of it—flutters inside her chest.

CHAPTER TWO

METIS

February 19, 2233
(29 days before Tabula Rasa)

Metis wipes his face with the only clean part of his sleeve and crawls from under the rock overhang. It has been five days since he separated from Aris. *Five excruciating days.* Why did he think it was a good idea? Now she is out there in the unforgiving desert, alone. This is all his fault.

But she's not alone. The Crone is with her.

"She's safe and on her way to Mem," he whispers to himself. She has to be.

His plan is working. He has been leaving a trail of dying campfires as he zigzags his way south, and the drone has been following. As long as it is following him, it's not following her.

Crying doesn't help his thirst. The last creek he saw was a day ago. There's only enough water in his bottle for one more drink. All morning, he has been talking himself out of draining it. Every hour becomes every half hour. Every half hour becomes every fifteen minutes. If he was not thinking of Aris, he was thinking of drinking that damn water.

The sun is finally making its way toward the west. It's time for him to move. The last campfire he left was hours east of here to misdirect the drone from his destination—Elara. With luck, he will get to it before nightfall. There, he can disappear with the help of his network of Dreamers and wait for Aris's return.

She will *come back.*

He looks up. There's no trace of clouds in the cerulean sky and no sign of drones as far as he can see. Perhaps they've moved east as he had hoped. These pesky fliers used to patrol only city blocks late at night. Must be because of all the disappearances. He and Aris are not the first to vanish from the Four Cities, and he doubts they will be the last. More and more have left.

Most of them he learned of through whispered rumors. Many were Dreamers, but not all. He doesn't know where they went, or if they were ever found. The System has done its best to keep it a secret. Only the disappearance of a well-known citizen would need explanation. He wonders what the System is telling people about him.

Metis, celebrated pianist, has been undergoing treatments at a Callisto hospital since the new year. All future concerts are canceled until further notice.

Piano virtuoso Metis retires from music after series of mental breakdowns.

Would they have realized by now that he's a Sandman? A missing pianist isn't as great a threat as the missing leader of the Dreamers. He pushes the worry from his mind. There's nothing he can do about it, and he needs the space for what he can actually control.

After a while, he comes upon a cluster of tall cacti with red fruits. His heart leaps. He runs toward it. He breaks off a stick from a scrub oak and sharpens it with a knife the way Aris taught him. He pierces the point into the middle of a ripe fruit before cutting it off the plant, avoiding the spines. They hurt for days if they get in his fingers. Slowly he peels off the thick skin with the knife, exposing the fruit's white flesh and tiny black seeds. He takes a bite off the stick. It tastes to him like a mix between watermelon and kiwi.

The land here is less desolate and inhospitable than that up north. He gave Aris most of their food. That should just last her a few more weeks. Once she's in the mountains, she should find wild edibles in the forest of pines.

Please make it to Mem.

There, the legend says, she'll find the erased memories of every citizen of the Four Cities.

"How do you think they're keeping our old memories?" Aris asked.

Her hands were busy folding and refolding clothes and stuffing them into her backpack. They had decided on two of each—underwear, shirt, pants, socks—one to wear and one to wash. The rest of the space was needed for food and water bottles.

"I don't know. It can be anything," he said.

"Maybe a big machine we can walk into and come out the other side of with all our old memories?"

"Like a digital version of the spring of Mnemosyne?"

A corner of her lips turned up. Just as quickly, her smile faded. "Do you really think there's something in the north?"

She had been asking this same question over and over the closer they were to leaving—so often that it was becoming a tic of sorts. But it was her way of processing fear, and so he always answered.

"There's something in the north. I'm sure of it."

"Do you think we'll have enough food?" she asked.

"Yeah. I think we're as prepared as we'll ever be."

Their strategy was to bring packets of camping food—bought over months to not draw attention from the System—and supplement it with whatever safe plants they could harvest using Aris's field guide. For water, he knew from having to get it fresh for Absinthe, that there'd be enough snowmelt this time of year in the desert.

He reached over and touched her hand. It was cold. "I know you're afraid."

She pulled away. "I'm not afraid. I'm just worried. There's a difference."

"It's okay to be afraid. We're leaving our home. We'll be traveling in the wilderness with not much food."

For the first time, they'd know what true hunger felt like.

She rolled her eyes. "You're doing a great job selling this trip."

"I don't want to sell you a fairy tale. This is going to be really hard—probably the hardest thing we both will ever do."

Her eyes flashed. "I know that. And I know what I'm doing it for."

Tabula Rasa was coming, and they needed to find a permanent solution to their problem—one that did not involve drinking poison or jumping off a cliff like many had done before them.

He grabbed her hand and squeezed gently. "We'll be okay."

"How do you know?"

"Because we want to be. Because we have to be."

There was no other choice.

Hours pass, and the sun is finally making its way to the horizon, bleeding yellow into blue. The thirst inside reignites, and this time he gives in to the fire. He uncaps the top of his bottle and drinks deeply. The water is cool and tastes almost sweet, unlike the slightly salty taste of the water in the Four Cities. He laps up the last drop, lowers the bottle from his lips, and exhales. There is another creek near the tunnel to Elara. He just has to make it there.

His stomach growls, reawakened by the water. He finds a spot under a scrub oak with a rock flat enough to sit on. His backpack is nearly empty of food. He pulls out a pouch of premade camping meal and eats directly from it. It feels like sand down his throat. The little bit of liquid in it is not enough to quench his thirst, but it will have to do for now. Once he's done, he cleans up and continues trekking.

What he worries about is the growing cramp in his left calf. He doesn't want to sleep outside for another night if he doesn't have to. He pats the last vial of Absinthe in his pocket—a talisman to ward off hopelessness—and continues forward.

The land begins to transform, scrub and cacti giving way to leafier plants. Ahead, he sees a line of small trees—a sign of water. That could be the creek near the tunnel to Elara. His heart leaps.

He increases his gait, dragging his crampy left leg behind him. He is going to make it. He'll refill his bottles at the creek and will make camp inside the tunnel tonight. Then it's just twenty more miles to downtown Elara. He can do that in just five hours.

From the periphery of his hearing comes a low hum. It sounds like the wind blowing from the east. But the air is still. The sound keeps growing, coming from behind.

He realizes what it is: a drone. They probably figured out his campfires were a ruse. He whips his head side to side, searching for something to hide under. He sees a few scrub oaks nearby, smaller than the one he ate under. That's not going to work. He looks back at the line of trees.

I can make it.

He takes off running at full speed, ignoring the shooting pain in his leg. The humming grows behind him. He keeps his eyes on the line of trees, his lifeline. He just has to get there. Almost. So close.

CHAPTER THREE

CASS

February 22, 2233
(26 days before Tabula Rasa)

Once, the mountain range had a name. Maybe it was Blue Giant for its color or Sleepy Dragon for the long bladelike crests along its back. Whatever people called it, the name had died long ago along with the Old World. In that world, Cass was told, lived the memories of eight billion people—lost like kites cut from their strings. A year from now, her memories, too, will join theirs.

Playful shrieking below her fourth-story window breaks her gaze. Children, elementary schoolers from their red shorts, are running around the lawn playing a game of tag. Cass misses being that age.

A knock comes at her door, followed by the sound of it opening as Bastian strolls in.

"Usually, people wait to hear an invitation before entering someone else's room," she says.

"Happy promotion day!" His voice is too cheerful for the occasion.

She grumbles. "There's nothing happy about today."

"Not even the feast?"

Tonight, the Food Hall will be transformed with flowers

from the garden and branches from the forest. The feast will be the best from the kitchen, with a long list of favorites. There'll be a centerpiece made of dessert—a backdrop for hugs, well-wishes, and congratulatory words.

Bastian drops onto her bed and leans against the wall. "What are you doing?"

"Mourning." She returns her eyes to the mountains, gauzy now from clouds moving in from the north.

"We're going to be okay, you know," he says.

"You're it!" a small voice yells from outside.

"What if they separate us?" she whispers. Since they were five, she has always had Bastian, and he her. Without him, how will she be?

"They're not going to. The decision is based on our propensity models, and we're practically the same."

Bastian is right, she tells herself. They are good at the same things, like the same subjects. Wherever there is Bastian, there is Cass—and it has been that way since she could toddle behind him in line. They are so similar and inseparable their classmates call them Castian, as if they were one person. It would be a mistake for the System to break them up now.

"What if they assign us both to Tabula Rasa instead of College?" she asks.

"Then we'll have each other to go through it with."

"What if your future you doesn't like my future me?"

"Cassiopeia," he says sternly, "I'm a hundred percent certain I will always like you. Besides, we still have a year left."

A year before they become full-fledged adults. A year before they have to leave the Center for Discovery and Learning forever. A year before their names disappear like that of the mountain range.

"What if—"

"We're going to be okay," He sounds slightly less certain this time. "And after this, we have a whole month off from school."

"Twenty-six days," she mumbles.

In twenty-six days, the seniors will turn eighteen and leave the CDL for Tabula Rasa. Until then, the Matres let all the students enjoy their last days together without the distraction of school.

"Okay, we have a whole twenty-six days," Bastian says. "Imagine all the fun we can have together."

The bell rings, startling her.

"It's time for the senior graduation and junior promotion ceremonies," the Head Matre's voice announces through a concealed speaker. "High school students, please proceed to the Grand Hall in an organized and timely manner."

She sighs and stands up. "We have to go."

"Wait." Bastian holds out a palm, and in the middle of it coils a string of small stones. "Your present."

"But I didn't get you anything."

"It's okay. I made one for me too." He pulls up the sleeve of his shirt and shows the same bracelet around his wrist.

She holds out her left arm, and he ties it on. The stone beads are in various shades of gray and amber. Bastian must have stolen them from the jewelry-making class they had taken earlier this year.

"It's beautiful," she says. "Thank you."

"Happy promotion day," he says. This time she smiles.

They exit her room to the busy corridor of their dorm floor. It's full of subdued faces, no one joking or yelling like usual. She catches a glimpse of the red-rimmed eyes of Penelope, whose final-year boyfriend is leaving next month for Tabula Rasa. Cass tugs at Bastian's arm. He turns to her.

"How are you fine?" she asks.

"Because I really think we're going to be okay," he says, his face oddly serene.

"How do you know?"

"I had a dream last night. In it, we were happy."

Sarcasm perches at the tip of her tongue, but she swallows it. She can use his optimism at this moment. They descend the spiral staircase and cross the courtyard of potted giant ferns before entering the main hallway. Paintings climb up both walls all the way to the vaulted ceiling.

Cass eyes her favorite as she passes—a blue ocean with an orange sun setting right into the water. She has never seen the ocean in real life since the CDL is deep in the mountains. If the Matres hadn't told her it was a real place, she would have thought it was made up.

Once they are outside, they follow a path across the campus grounds to the Grand Hall. The Matres said it used to be a chapel where the Old Word folks performed religious rites. To Cass it looks like an exotic castle she read about in a fairy tale when she was little. In front of it, students line up alphabetically and by year. Cass follows Bastian and enters through the arched doorway with their class.

They make their way to their assigned seating in the row closest to the stage and the elaborate gilded altar behind it. Cass sits to Bastian's right and leans over to steal a look at the outgoing senior class across the aisle. Instead of their normal uniform of black pants and white shirt, they wear all white—now painted rainbow hues by the light. Unlike their cheerful clothing, their faces are sober.

Next year, she and Bastian will be there.

Matre Selene sits perched on a chair in front of the piano next to the stage. Cass catches her kind eye, and she smiles. She is Cass's counselor and her favorite Matre. She is a favorite of many students.

The first note rings, and a procession of Matres enters the

Great Hall. Save for the lines on their faces reflecting their different ages, they are identical—tall, blond hair, pale skin. The only way Cass is able to tell most of them apart is by their name tags. At the end of the aisle, they step onto the stage and line up in a row in front of the altar.

Head Matre Hera enters the hall, and a special kind of hush settles over the crowd. While she dresses in the same uniform as the others, she does not have a name tag. Instead, she wears a necklace from which hangs a gold key. No student knows what door it unlocks.

She comes to a stop in the middle of the stage. Her long white dress and platinum hair blend with the backdrop of Matres and the gold altar like one glowing entity. The piano music ends.

"Welcome to the graduation ceremony," the Head Matre says. "Today we partake in a long-held tradition to celebrate our senior-year students before they leave the CDL and enter their next phase as adults."

She turns to the graduating class.

"For almost eighteen years, the CDL has been your home, and we your family. In a month's time, you will leave the safety of this place and enter a brand-new world—a world of endless possibilities. Whether you will go on to Tabula Rasa or College, what you make of your new life is yours."

She drags in a long breath before continuing.

"After Tabula Rasa, you'll be given a new name and a new life. For over two hundred years, this has been the way people in the Four Cities have existed. Still, I and every Matre here want you to know—in whatever way you may retain it—that you were raised with love. That love will be a part of you throughout all the cycles to come."

Some of the Matres behind her shake with emotion. The more composed ones dab their eyes.

The Head Matre turns her gaze to Cass's class. "Juniors, you are now the examples for the younger students. It's an important responsibility, one I hope you will take seriously."

Cold shoots up her spine, and she reaches for Bastian's hand. He squeezes hers and gives a reassuring smile.

"Now, we will begin the Calling of Names of those entering Tabula Rasa. When I say yours, please come up to the front."

"Alastair," Head Matre Hera calls.

Everyone repeats his name. The sound bounces against the stone walls of the Grand Hall before tapering off. A tall senior with pitch-black hair sitting at the end of the first row stands up. Cass knows him as the captain of the track and field team. He walks to the front of the room and stands in front of the stage.

"Alomena."

The names continue. Finally, the first two rows of the senior pews are empty.

"This concludes the Calling of Names for those getting Tabula Rasa," the Head Matre says.

Claps erupt throughout the Grand Hall. Cass knows without counting that there are 125 students standing up there—half the graduating class. It is always this number. Together with the graduates leaving College this year, they will make up the 250 new citizens joining the Four Cities to replace the average yearly dead.

Music sounds from the piano again. The Head Matre bows her head and laces her hands together. A short moment later, the music ends and she looks up.

"Now we begin the Calling of Names for those going to College. Your propensity models have determined the areas of study you'll be focusing on. Remember the discipline you learned in your years here. It's hard work and perseverance that will take you through tough times. You may at one point or another find your new experience intimidating and overwhelming, but know you have been well prepared for it. Know you will succeed. When I call your name, come line up in front of your classmates."

Again she starts with the *A* names and works her way through the remaining seniors until the last of the students joins the line.

"We have now concluded the Calling of Names," the Head Matre says.

Clapping rings out.

"Tonight will be the graduation party. Matre Tryphena has outdone herself on the feast in the seniors' honor. But before that, we have the promotion ceremony for the juniors."

Cass braces herself. This is when she and Bastian, together with the rest of their classmates, will receive their assignment—College or Tabula Rasa.

Suddenly the door at the back of the chapel opens with a loud clang, startling her. She turns to look behind her and sees a line of police officers walking down the aisle. The sound of their steps reverberating against the stone floor of the Grand Hall sends chills up her spine. They are not supposed to be here until the day before Tabula Rasa! What are they doing here?

They come to a stop at the stage and line up in front of the senior class, blocking them in. These men are all identical—the same dark hair and eyes, wearing long jackets and wide-brimmed hats. But like the Matres, their differences are more apparent when they form a line.

One walks up the steps and approaches the Head Matre. She draws herself up to full height and squares her shoulders.

"What's the meaning of this?" Her tone shifts from warm to cold.

"Head Matre Hera. It's Scylla," Cass hears him say.

"Why are you here?"

"I apologize for the intrusion, but the Planner requires the children in Callisto right away."

"They're not supposed to leave for almost a month. Why?"

"I'm afraid I don't know."

"But they have a feast to attend. And they need to have time with friends. The Planner agreed to this."

"I'm very sorry."

"They can't leave!" Her voice is half demand, half plea.

"The Planner asked me to remind you that, since they've graduated, they now belong to the System and not the CDL."

The Head Matre's face reddens. She looks back at the line of Matres. The expressions on their faces range from anger to confusion to dread. She turns back, casting her eyes on the upset students.

The officer steps closer and leans down. "More police are waiting at the train station. Head Matre, please. The Planner doesn't take no for an answer—you know this."

At those words, her shoulders slump. She nods.

"Seniors, the Planner requires you in Callisto," she says. "Please follow the police to the train station."

Murmurs of confusion and cries of shock come from all around Cass.

"I'm very sorry," the officer says.

The police begin walking down, and the line of students follows them. They look to each other and back to the Matres, varying degrees of fear on their faces.

"Remember you are loved," the Head Matre calls out behind them. For a split second, her face crumples before she regains composure.

"Thank you, Head Matre," Officer Scylla says. Then he hands her a bundle.

"What's this?" she asks.

"It's the assignment for the junior students."

Cold expands in Cass's core.

"But we already have them from the students' propensity models," the Head Matre says.

"This is from the Planner."

Her eyebrows knot. "This isn't right. It's not how we've done things in the past. What's going on, Scylla?"

He does not answer. Instead, he inclines his head and steps off the stage. Cass follows him with her eyes until he disappears through the door. She turns back and sees the Head Matre standing stupefied on the stage. Cass's breath catches in her throat.

Matre Selene gets up from the piano and walks to her. "What's happening?"

"We just lost our children . . ." the Head Matre says, and startles as if she had just broken from a trance.

She collects herself and hands the bundle to Selene, who distributes them among the Matres. The line of Matres breaks apart—each delivering the envelopes in their care to the students whose names appear on them. Matre Selene hands Cass hers. Her hands shake as she receives it.

"We're going to be okay." Bastian smiles, though weakly, his envelope trembling in his hand. "Ready?"

She isn't but nods anyway. She stares at the envelope as if it is catching fire. With unsteady fingers, she breaks the wax seal. The cracking sound joins others like it, echoing inside the cavernous space.

Please don't be Tabula Rasa.

She unfolds the paper.

College.

She sighs and turns to Bastian. "We have a few more years."

Her best friend is stock-still, eyes fixed on his paper. His blanched face makes her heart drop to her stomach.

"What does yours say?" she whispers. It can't be the worst scenario she had imagined. It just can't. The decision is based on propensity model, and they are too similar.

He hands her the paper, his lips quivering.

Tabula Rasa.

CHAPTER FOUR

ARIS

February 22, 2233
(26 days before Tabula Rasa)

She feels like a string pulled taut. Her feet are shredded. Her leg muscles burn from carrying her forward for hours on end uphill. She's been following the train tracks—traveling longer and farther, stretching her rations, sleeping less. But she cannot stop. There's a tunnel ahead, and she needs to get to it.

The ground begins to tremble. She scrambles down the embankment to the nearest tree. The rumbling grows louder. Sand and bits of gravel vibrate at her feet. The high-pitched sound whooshes by like an unexpected torrent. Wind rustles trees and bushes, whipping the leaves.

The train roars past—a blur of white—rattling the tracks and throwing loose dirt into the air. Aris presses her body against the bark of the tree she's hiding behind, hands shielding her ears. Two hours ago, this same train came through, startling her out of her skin. It was heading north then, and now it's returning south—toward the Four Cities. Since she began following the tracks almost a week ago, it's the first and only train she has seen. Metis has been right all along.

"Look." He handed her a book. The title read Look Homeward, Angel—by Thomas Wolfe.

The paperback cover appeared faded, old. "Where did you get this?"

"I stole it from the main library."

"You stole it? Is this from before the Last War?"

"Yes. It was printed in 2006."

"Metis, these copies are precious!"

"I know. I'm not doing anything bad to it. I will return it, but I wanted you to see it."

She didn't like it when Metis broke the law. Being the Sandman, he may already be on a watch list.

"What am I supposed to see?" she asked.

"Look homeward, angel, and breathe life everlasting," he said. It was a line from the Old Mem poem. "See the cover?"

On it, a man was standing in between train tracks, facing away. In his left hand was a suitcase. Around him, a landscape of trees veiled in fog.

"I think it's a clue," Metis said, his eyes dancing with excitement. "I think the poem is telling us to travel north on train tracks."

"But there are no trains that go outside the Four Cities."

"Before the Last War, there was a world beyond this place."

The hair on the nape of her neck stood up.

"We have to find a way to keep each other," he said. "Tabula Rasa is coming. I can't keep losing you."

The desperation in his voice squeezed her heart.

She climbs back up the embankment and runs toward the tunnel. The pitch-black hole pierces the side of the mountain—so dark it seems to be throbbing. She can't see even a pinprick of light on the other end. It probably cuts all the way through the mountain. With a dense forest all around and the desert behind, this is her only way to what is on the other side.

She looks up. It's still day. She opens her backpack and pulls out the book—*Love in the Time of Cholera*—and reads the passage she has committed to memory. The glowing form of the Crone appears.

"Before you say anything, it's not dark yet, and we're under the cover of trees, so no one will see you," Aris says.

The glowing woman studies her surroundings with interest. "We're in a pine forest."

"Yes."

"A train just came out of there." Aris points at the black tunnel.

"Do you think it's—"

"Yes." The word lifts her heart. "We're close to Mem. I can feel it."

A smile curls the corner of her lips. The gamble she and Metis made to separate is going to pay off.

"I'm going in." Aris looks at the Crone. "I could use your company."

The glowing woman glides into the tunnel, brightening the dark. Aris turns on the light embedded in her jacket and wraps her hands around the straps of her pack. There will be no creek or plants she can harvest, but she has enough water to last her a day and food for a few more. More delays, and she will run out of everything. She has to do this.

Her heart tugs. She turns to look over her shoulder. Somewhere across the vast desert is Metis. Is he safe? She closes her eyes and imagines his face. He is in front of the piano, hands on the keys. A song rises from it—their song, the one that brings her again and again to him.

There's no letting go. We're forever, his voice comes to her.

Her eyes burn. She drags in a steadying breath, turns back, and walks into the unknown.

CHAPTER FIVE

METIS

February 23, 2233
(25 days before Tabula Rasa)

A knock comes at the door. "It's just me."

Metis opens his eyes and sees a familiar face. Relief floods his chest. Cole smiles widely, his pearly teeth a contrast to his dark brown skin.

"I brought you soup in case you were hungry." He sets a steaming bowl on the bedside table.

At those words, Metis's stomach growls.

"And a towel," Cole adds. "You look like you could use a shower and a good scrub."

Metis laughs. "Yes to all the above. How long was I asleep?"

"Two days straight."

"I guess I was tired."

"I'd say."

"Does anyone else know I'm back?"

"Not yet. I didn't know what to tell them."

"Good. Don't."

"You've been gone for weeks," Cole adds. "I thought you were never coming back. Where did you go?"

"I just got lost in the desert." The lie comes out smoothly, the way he and Aris had practiced. It's best no one knows what they are trying to do. Not yet.

The look in Cole's eyes says he knows Metis is lying, but to his credit, he does not press him further. He's always been good that way. All Dreamers are used to keeping secrets.

Suddenly a shooting pain hits him squarely between the eyes. His vision becomes blurry. Metis blinks to clear it. His head throbs even more. The room begins to sway. Nausea rises. He leans back and closes his eyes.

"Are you okay?" Cole asks.

"A headache."

"Let me get you something for that." He walks out of the room and, a moment later, comes back with a pill and a glass of water. "Here, take this. It'll help with your headache."

Metis picks up the tiny round white pill from Cole's palm and swallows it down with water. The pinching eases. He closes his eyes and rests against the bed.

"I have a few errands to run, so make yourself comfortable. There's more food in the fridge. We can talk later, when I get back."

"Thank you."

A minute passes, and his headache disappears, replaced by a dull calm. Metis looks over at the soup Cole brought. White steam curls from it, a finger beckoning. His stomach still feels queasy, but he should eat something. He picks up the bowl. It looks like potato and leek soup. He spoons in a mouthful and finds it delicious. The soup glides down his throat, warming his stomach and making him feel better. He hasn't had any home-cooked food inside him for so long.

After he finishes, he begins assessing himself. Sunburned skin. Stained and dirt-embedded fingernails. Clothes he hasn't changed in days. He touches his hair. It feels greasy and matted.

He is in desperate need of a shower. Why did Cole even let him sleep on his clean bed?

Metis finds the bathroom across from his bedroom. He sheds his grimy clothes and turns the faucet to the hottest setting. The scorching water eases the knots in his shoulders and washes the dirtiness down the drain. He scrubs every inch of his body. In the desert, he and Aris only washed whenever they came across a creek. The water was always freezing, coming from melted snow.

After five minutes, the water automatically turns off. He steps out of the shower and towels himself dry. His eyes travel to the mirror. It's completely fogged up, white. *The emptiness.* It reaches out its tendrils and coils itself around him. His entire being feels hollowed out.

"Welcome to your new life," a voice said, monotonous and inhuman.

His eyes flew open, and a blinding whiteness punctured his vision. The light came from above. The entire ceiling glared with the glow of a hundred suns. His eyes began to burn. He shielded them with a hand.

He sat up. His surroundings began to take shape. A long row of beds opposite. More beds extended to his left and right. He looked down. He, too, was on a bed. It, too, was white. So were his clothes. And the walls of this cavernous space. Everything was an intimidating, soul-crushing absence of color. It felt of loss—of what, he could not exactly pinpoint. It threatened to swallow him with its nothingness.

Where am I?

A spot behind his eyes pinched. His vision became blurry. He blinked to clear it. All it did was make the pounding inside his head hurt even more. The room began to sway. He leaned back against the headboard and closed his eyes.

The black behind his eyelids was a reprieve. But it was only temporary. In the dark, he became acutely aware of the hollowness in his stomach—no, at the center of his being. An emptiness. It consumed him, making him feel as though he was about to disappear. He grabbed the bedding, holding on. But the tighter he gripped, the harder he tried, the more the emptiness grew. The thumping of his hammering heart filled his ears. Impending doom bitter at the tip of his tongue.

His chest suddenly constricted. The tightness traveled up his esophagus, and his breath caught. His eyes flew open. He pawed his throat, trying to drag in air. The intake of breath stopped halfway down his plugged airway. He felt as if he was drowning. He needed help. He never thought death would be so bright.

With all his strength, he forced air from his throat. The scream sounded between a deep bellow and a strangled cry. Not exactly human. It frightened him.

A split second later, from the surrounding beds, bodies sprang up with a chorus of cries in various pitches.

"Help!" he yelled into the choir of despair.

"Help! Help! Help!" his plea echoed back. No one here could give it. Everyone needed it. They were all drowning.

On their faces was the same expression. Stunned. Squinted eyes. Disquieted upturned lips. They looked as if they had just been struck with no provocation. Some wept into their hands. A few rattled their beds in anger. A man nearby screamed a cry of agony, of sadness. A drop of warmth touched his hand. His own tear. The swell of sorrow pounded down unrelenting until he was nothing but a shaking, sobbing mass.

He felt the weight of a stare on him. He looked in the direction and saw a vision of long brown hair and golden skin. She was here. He was going to be okay.

But she's not here.

His breathing hitches. Panic grips him, and he grabs on to the counter. His body begins to shake. Aris isn't here. She isn't here, and he had left her alone in the wilderness. What was he thinking? What if they never see each other again? What if something happened to her? What if the legend of Mem is nothing but fantasy created by those who needed the fairy tale to survive the cruel reality of memory erasure? What if he had just made the biggest mistake of his life?

CHAPTER SIX

CASS

February 24, 2233
(24 days before Tabula Rasa)

Cass leans back on her elbows. Their rock—the one they found the first day they were allowed to hike alone in the forest when they were eight—is still warm from the sun earlier. It sits on the edge of a cliff overlooking a valley. She's pretty sure this is her favorite spot in the world, even though she hasn't seen the rest of it.

The view doesn't look like much now, veiled by a thin layer of fog. But on a clear day, she can see the entire valley and the rolling mountains beyond. As they move into spring, it will be covered by wildflowers in all shades of wonderful. Then summer will come, bringing with it bone-drying wind from the desert, leaching the valley of vibrancy and turning it back to boring brown. In the winter, it will be buried under several feet of snow, making the land look like a blank page. Then the cycle will begin again.

"What do you think is on the other side of the mountains?" Bastian asks.

This is an old game, one they've been playing since they were young. The objective is to tell the wildest story one could concoct. He must be upset.

"A colony of human-bird hybrids," she says, appeasing him.

"I wonder if their body color matches their wings."

"Maybe," she says. "Or they could be like robins, with orange bodies and gray wings."

"How did they become human birds, you think?"

"The nuclear fallout after the Last War."

"Tough luck."

"Actually, I wouldn't mind having wings," she says.

Her mind flits to her favorite painting—the one of the ocean. It exists in real life, the Matres said. It's out there somewhere, and if Cass had wings, she could get to it—or to anywhere she wants, not just to the places she's allowed.

"What if there's a giant crater behind the mountains, and in it lives a shadow monster that eats time?" Bastian asks.

"Makes sense," she says.

Since the graduation ceremony, her days seem to stretch on. Usually, the month between graduation and Tabula Rasa is a time for friends to spend together in childhood nostalgia. At the beautiful feast, they'd celebrate and laugh and swap stories. But with no guests of honor in attendance at the last one, the feast ended up feeling like a Ceremony of the Dead. The chocolate fountain was barely touched. The music subdued. The Matres were grief-stricken. That sadness has bled into every moment after.

To make matters worse, her room shares a wall with Penelope, a heartbroken girl who lost her boyfriend to Tabula Rasa. The sound of her crying herself to sleep every night makes Cass want to scream and bang the wall. But that would be pointless. She's not the only one crying.

"What if we go to the other side?" Bastian says.

"Over the mountains?"

"Yeah."

"Those jagged mountains with steep sides across the valley?"

"It's just a thought."

"It's a nice thought." *Silly, but nice.*

They drift into another heavy silence.

"Why do you think the police came to take the seniors early?" Cass asks after a while. "If the Planner made an agreement with the Head Matre, why did he go back on it? And why did he give us a new assignment?"

She had asked these questions of Matre Selene, but her counselor did not have an answer.

"I mean, it doesn't really matter, does it?" he says. "The Planner didn't like the agreement or the old assignment, so he changed them."

This simplest explanation makes the best sense. The Planner is all-powerful. Someone all-powerful can do whatever they want.

"It's the same reason we're no longer split in half," Bastian adds.

Instead of 125 in each group, there are now 170 in Tabula Rasa and only 80 in College.

"So there's nothing we can do?" she asks.

"If the Head Matre can't do anything, what can *we* do? We're just kids."

The sound of a bell tolling comes from the direction of the CDL.

"Dinnertime," Bastian says.

"I'm not hungry."

"Me neither."

"Let's stay out here a while longer."

"Okay."

The fog below shifts color as the setting sun paints it gold. Soon, darkness will come, making the cliff a dangerous place to be for those unfamiliar with the path.

Bastian lies down, eyes on the sky. "Did you notice they split up all the best friends?"

"What do you mean?"

"Us. Eugene and Linus. Rhode and Suri. Cleo and Tia. None of them are going to College together."

"I hadn't noticed." Cass has been too distraught to connect the dots.

"Don't you think it's strange?"

"Yeah, I suppose so."

"It's like they're doing it on purpose," he says.

"But why?"

"Because the Planner wants it that way."

"Why would he want it that way?"

Bastian shrugs. "Maybe he doesn't want us to have friends. I mean, aren't we all being prepared for a memory erasure anyway?"

"Right, so why bother splitting us up now?"

His shoulders tighten. "What if . . ."

"What?"

"Never mind."

"You can't do that."

"I was just thinking that having friends wouldn't matter if the memory wipe were thorough. The only way it would matter is if it's not."

She leans in and whispers. "You think we can remember friends even after Tabula Rasa?"

Bastian gives an uneasy laugh. "I know it's silly. Like I said, never mind."

He stands up. "Maybe we can just grab a little something from the Food Hall in case we get hungry later."

She raises both arms, and he pulls her from her seated position. They hop off the rock and make their way to the main trail.

Around them stand skinny conifers in huddled layers. Cones and needles litter the ground, softening their steps. They've seen no one else on the trail. All are at dinner.

In the distance, the CDL looms against the mountains. With spires, a portico, domes, and a tall bell tower in pale stone, the place looks like an exotic castle in a fairy tale. Except it's not. The Matres told her it was the most opulent inn in California during the early to mid-1900s but had fallen on hard times before the Planner rescued it after the housing market collapsed in the early 2000s. And for two hundred years, it's been home to the created children—like her, like Bastian, like everyone here.

The original owner was obsessed with architectural styles with odd names like Spanish, Moorish, Mediterranean, and Gothic. But rather than clashing, the mix of curved walls, vaulted ceilings, colorful tiles, and round-top windows work in ways Cass finds beautiful.

Their trail merges with the stone pavement, and Cass and Bastian arrive at an arched gate pierced by six openings where bells hang. *The Gate of the Six Bells.* Its name isn't the most imaginative, but it was coined by students years ago and has stuck.

Bastian stops abruptly. "What's that over there?"

"What?"

"Over there." He points toward the wall of ivy.

"I don't see anything."

"There's something lying in the bushes." Bastian moves to walk toward it, and she grabs his arm.

"What are you doing?" Cass asks.

"I want to see what it is."

"No, you don't."

"Come on. There's nothing to be afraid of. It's still daylight."

"Barely." The sky is pale yellow blending into deepening blue.

"And if it turns out to be dangerous, we'll just run."

She rolls her eyes. "That sounds fun."

He pulls her forward, off the cobblestone path, zigzagging toward the massive wall of ivy through the dense vegetation of the untended grounds beyond the campus.

As they come closer, Cass can see there is indeed something in the bushes. It can't be a large animal. All of them went extinct after the Last War. They, too, could no longer bear young. The only reason humans survived is because of the Planner.

"I think it's a person," Bastian whispers.

"Who?"

"I don't know. It's no one I know. It's not a Matre either."

Matres are difficult to miss, being so tall and dressed entirely in white.

"You stay here," he says. "I'm going to take a closer look."

"I don't know if that's a good idea. Maybe we should just get someone."

He doesn't listen. *Of course.* He untangles his hand from hers and walks toward the bush. There, he lowers himself and sits on his haunches. Cass watches as he gets on his hands and knees and, idiotically sticks his head under the bush.

What are you doing?

Suddenly he screams.

"It's got me!" He's thrashing on the ground. Something has seized him. "Get a Matre!"

She can't move. Her entire body is frozen in place.

"Cass!" he yells.

At hearing her name, her limbs thaw. She whips around and runs as fast as she can to the Administrative building. At the front steps, she almost runs into a Matre coming out.

She grabs her arms. "Matre Selene! I need your help."

"What's going on?"

"Something's got Bastian!"

"Where?"

Cass leads her past the gate and off the cobblestone path to Bastian. Her friend is no longer on the ground. Instead, he is standing stock-still in front of the bush.

"Bastian! Are you okay?" Matre Selene asks.

He turns around slowly, his face leached of blood.

"She's from the outside," he whispers.

"Who?"

"The woman in the bush."

Cass feels the hair on her body stand on end.

CHAPTER SEVEN

ARIS

February 25, 2233
(23 days before Tabula Rasa)

A melody dances at the edge of her hearing. Metis must be awake. She strains her ears to listen, but like a startled songbird, it flits away and disappears.

Aris's eyes flutter open to a washed-out sky, the cool white of a melancholic spring day. She must have fallen asleep in the garden again. She's not yet ready to wake, so she closes her eyes, turns on her side, and curls up on the grass. Except it's not grass. It does not have the same soft coolness or smell as sweet. And where are the birds? It's so quiet she can hear her own breathing. Everything feels wrong. She pushes herself up.

Her surroundings begin to take shape, and she realizes she is not outside but in. The cavernous space has a ceiling that shoots up at least two stories. Under her is a white bed, the kind one finds in a hospital.

But she is not in a hospital. All around her stand towering bookcases in color-coded blocks. Bright blue like the summer sky. Orange, the sun. Vibrant greens. Subtle browns. They stretch in long rows for as far as the eye can see, each radiating from a central point—hers.

Where am I?

Her last memory is of an empty train station. And before that, the seemingly unending tunnel. She had run out of water sometime midway through it. At the thought, thirst burns her throat. She spots a table nearby with a carafe of water and a glass beside it. She eases herself off the bed, and her bare feet touch cold floor. She looks down and sees that she is standing on a circular black-and-white tile mosaic.

She takes a step and wobbles. She steadies herself. Carefully, she teeters to the table. With shaky hands, she picks up the carafe and drinks directly from it. She drains the entire thing but is still thirsty. She looks around for signs to something—*anything*—that will lead her to more water, but there are only books.

"Hello?" she yells, the sound scraping her esophagus. "Anyone?"

Silence.

She walks forward, toward an aisle. It has books with red bindings on the left shelves and yellow on the right. A series of zeros and ones are etched on the spines like train tracks. She pulls one out. The heavy tome is as thick as four of her fingers. She opens it. The first page is white: no letters, no numbers, no pictures—nothing. She flips through it and finds all the pages blank. *A journal? What is it doing here?* She checks another book. Again, it's empty.

She needs words, some kind of explanation as to where she is. Her eyes search and find them on the wall above her.

I have always imagined Paradise as a kind of library.
—Jorge Luis Borges

Is this heaven? Does that mean she is dead? But isn't heaven just a concept made up by those in the Old World? Also, her back aches. She must not be dead, she decides. A pain message requires nerve cells that release neurotransmitters when stimulated. When the body dies, the brain shortly follows. A dead person with a dead brain will not have functioning pain receptors and so cannot feel pain.

She reaches behind and massages a spot on her shoulder blade. From the corner of her eye, she notices a movement. She turns toward it and sees two figures in white dresses approaching her. Aside from their obvious age difference, they appear identical. But no one, aside from the policemen, is supposed to be biologically related in the Four Cities. The random mixing of DNA ensures that. Maybe she *is* dead, and this is heaven.

"You're awake," the younger one says.

"Who are you?" Her voice comes out sticky. She clears her throat.

"We've yet to officially meet. My name is Selene, and this is Head Matre Hera."

She looks from one face to the other, feeling as though she's in a dream. "Where am I?"

"You're at the Center for Discovery and Learning. What we call the CDL. We found you collapsed in a bush outside."

The CDL . . . She knows of this place. It's where all the created children are born and raised. It's the place she grew up—where everyone grew up—though she has no memory of it.

"Are you from the Four Cities?" Selene asks.

Aris does not answer. She doesn't know whether she can trust these people. What if they have the police waiting outside this room?

"You're not supposed to be here," the older one, the Head Matre, announces. "This place is forbidden to those from the outside."

"How did you get here?" Selene asks.

Aris, again, says nothing.

The Head Matre looks at her with annoyance. "If I can't assess how dangerous you are, I will have to call the police to make you talk."

"How do I know you don't already have them here?" she says.

"Do you see one?"

"No."

"Then they're not here. Believe me, I don't want them here, but I will make a call if you'd rather talk to them."

"No!" The police will take her right back to Callisto, and her and Metis's sacrifice will be for nothing.

"Then I suggest you talk."

Aris swallows. "I'm from the Four Cities. I didn't know I was coming to the CDL. And I walked the train tunnel to get here."

Head Matre Hera's brow furrows. "You walked the tunnel? How many days did it take?"

"I don't know. All the hours blended together. Two days maybe?"

"You walked for two days inside a dark tunnel, not knowing what would be on the other side?"

"Yes."

"That's extremely foolish."

Of course it's foolish. To have left the comfort of home, to have risked starvation and thirst, to separate from the love of her life. It's the stupidest thing she has ever done.

"If you didn't mean to come to the CDL, then where were you trying to get to?"

The Head Matre's penetrating eyes tell her there is no other option but to answer.

"I-I was looking for a place called Mem."

"What's that?" Selene asks.

"It's . . ." Aris searches her brain for a lie but comes up empty. "It's . . ."

"I'll know if you're lying," the Head Matre says, and Aris believes her.

"It's a place where I can find the erased memories of every citizen of the Four Cities."

"It doesn't exist. I've never heard of such a place," the Head Matre says.

"It's a legend that's been around for hundreds of years."

"A legend? You risked your life for a fairy tale?"

Aris's eyes burn. This woman has no right to reprimand her. She has no idea what she had to give up.

"It isn't a fairy tale! People left clues everywhere. In poems and stories. In paintings and music."

"What people? And how would they have remembered? Tabula Rasa erases everything."

Aris realizes she may have said too much.

"I-I don't know. All I know is it's real."

"Fairy tales are for children," the Head Matre says.

A knot forms in her throat, and she swallows it down. "Are you going to turn me in then?"

Selene places a hand on her shoulder. "Of course not."

"Though we should." The Head Matre's intense eyes make Aris feel translucent.

Selene gives her a weak smile. "You've put us in a tough position. The only way in and out of this place is through the tunnel, and the police control the train. If they find out you're here and that we're allowing you to stay, we would be in a lot of trouble."

"Our next scheduled visit from the police is in a month. It will be best if you're not here," Hera says, her words sounding like a command.

Aris steels herself. "I won't be here that long. Tabula Rasa is coming in less time than that. I'll leave as soon as I can."

The Head Matre nods. "Alright. For now, you can stay here. And you will take all your meals here."

Selene lifts the basket in her hand.

"I can't leave the library?" Aris asks.

"The CDL is a school. We don't want the students to know you're here. For as long as you're our guest, I trust you will keep a low profile and stay out of trouble."

Aris nods. It doesn't seem she has a choice. Considering her situation, it could be a lot worse. At least they don't want the police to see her here as much as she doesn't.

"I'm sorry for troubling you. Like I said, I didn't mean to come here. I just need to find Mem. I have to keep going north."

"There's nothing north of here but the wild," Hera says. "You'll die out there."

Aris's heart sinks. Suddenly she wants to cry or scream or both.

"Head Matre . . ." Selene says in a soft voice.

"Fine. Maybe we don't know a hundred percent," Hera concedes.

"We've never been outside the CDL," Selene adds.

"What do you mean?" Aris asks.

"We're not allowed to leave."

"Ever?"

"No. We're Matres. Our job is to take care of the children. Our place is here with them."

With the police controlling the only way in and out of the CDL and the Matres not being allowed to leave, this place sounds to Aris like a prison. The sooner she can go, the better.

Selene places the basket on the table and begins pulling out containers. "I'd like to know more about this Mem legend. Maybe we can help."

Can't hurt. Can it?

"I can recite you a poem about it," Aris says.

The Matre smiles. "I like poetry."

Aris clears her throat.

> "On the edge of a cliff,
> hidden by jagged peaks
> and a northern forest of pine,
> lives Old Mem.
> Her face,
> empty of lines,
> holds secret lives within.
> Her soul,
> stolen in slumber,
> awaits deliverance.
> Look homeward, angel
> and breathe life everlasting."

Selene and the Head Matre turn to each other. In their eyes is an expression Aris cannot decipher.

"Do you know the place?" she asks.

Head Matre Hera points to the floor.

Aris hadn't noticed before, but around the edges of the black-and-white mosaic design she's standing on are words. She walks around, reading them one by one.

> Welcome home, angels.
> Here, you live forever.

"I think you've found Mem," Selene says.

CHAPTER EIGHT

METIS

February 25, 2233
(23 days before Tabula Rasa)

Cole pours him another glass of wine. Metis takes a long, lingering sip. The dark cherry liquid reminds him of sitting on a plush couch beside a stack of books and a warm fireplace, Aris next to him. His heart aches.

The last time they were home, he played her a song, *Luce*. It's her favorite. He hasn't touched a piano since. His music was their sacrifice to a new future, but it had to be done. He misses the piano—its shiny form, the black and white keys existing in perfect order and harmony, the melody it sang for him in the middle of the night when sleep eluded.

"Dinner was excellent. Thank you," Metis says.

They started with a gazpacho made of peas, cucumber, and mint. The main was pasta primavera with sliced asparagus stems in a light coconut cream sauce served alongside grape tomatoes roasted on the vine. Everything tasted professionally prepared.

"How did you learn to cook like this?"

"There are thousands of recipes in the data bank. I just pick a new one to test every day."

"I'm really going to miss your food when I leave."

"Tired of me already?"

"I don't want to overtax your goodwill."

He has been here four days, counting the two he was dead to the world. The police are probably looking for him, making it all the more difficult to hide him in this small house. Good friend or not, it is an imposition.

Cole waves a hand in front of him. "Oh please. I like the company. Elara can be too quiet. People here tend to keep to themselves."

Metis takes another sip. The liquid dances in his mouth.

"Besides, where are you going to go?" Cole asks. "The System thinks you've disappeared."

The cave would have been perfect had the police not known about it.

"I don't know," Metis says. "Tabula Rasa is almost here. All of this won't matter much after."

Cole leans back on his chair. "Do you know a strange thing I heard?"

Metis looks up from his glass.

"People say the Book of Crone is missing."

Metis feigns surprise. "She's not at the cottage?"

"I thought *you* had her."

"No. The Crone doesn't leave the cottage. That's the rule." It's not a complete lie. It was the rule . . . until the Crone herself asked him and Aris to take her with them to Mem.

"The place has been turned upside down. No one is allowed near," Cole added. "And now everyone's wondering how to get more Absinthe."

But that can't possibly be right. Metis had made enough to last the Dreamers through the rest of the cycle. Why would Cole say that? His spine tightens.

"When was the last time you took it?" he asks.

A pause. "Just this morning."

"And have you been taking it every two days like you're supposed to?"

"Of course," Cole says.

Absinthe can only be taken once a month. Any more, and one risks overdosing. Every Dreamer knows that. He studies Cole. The man looks calm—way too calm. If he were overdosed, he would be too jittery to sit still on his chair. And instead of holding a civilized conversation over a glass of wine, he would be talking nonsense. *Something is very, very wrong.*

"I can make more for you if you want," Metis says. "I just need to get some ingredients."

"Would you do that for me?"

With just twenty-two days left before Tabula Rasa, there's not enough time to make a proper Absinthe. But that's not for Cole to know.

"Of course, what are friends for?"

CHAPTER NINE

SCYLLA

February 26, 2233
(22 days before Tabula Rasa)

Scylla braces himself and walks into the room. It doesn't seem to matter how many times he's been here, he still gets the same fluttering, nauseating feeling in the pit of his stomach. On one side of it are now two chairs, recently added. Two bodies sit on them. He glances from the blond woman to the man with black hair. On their heads are copper helmets. Both are connected via colorful wires to a white box that sits on a table between them. Their eyes are closed.

His throat narrows. He peels his eyes off them and makes his way to the wall-sized monitor at one end of the room. He places a palm on the panel on the wall. A moment later, the monitor flickers and the ancient face of the Planner appears on the screen.

"Scylla," the man says.

"Sir."

"What do you have for me?" His brown eyes, sharp as arrows, make Scylla feel like a target.

He pulls his shoulders back and steels himself. "I regret to report we still cannot find the Book of Crone, sir."

"What!" His voice echoes against the walls. "How many people do you have looking?"

"Half the force, sir."

"A hundred policemen, and no one can find one single book?"

"My brothers are doing their best out there, but they have a lot of land to cover," Scylla says. "They just need more ti—"

"Need I remind you again, Scylla? When you're working, they're not your brothers but police officers under your command."

He finds it harder to breathe. "No, sir, you don't need to remind me. I apologize."

"I want you to use the entire force for the search."

"All the policemen? But we're also dealing with the missing people." The number keeps growing the closer Tabula Rasa gets.

"What's your primary purpose?" the Planner asks.

"Sir?"

"Tell me!" his voice booms.

"To keep peace in the Four Cities, sir."

"You just failed your reason for being."

The words feel like a blow. Scylla wants to burrow inside himself.

"There's no peace as long as Eleanor is missing!" the Planner screams. "Do you have any idea what she's capable of, huh? You think she's just a harmless presence inside a book?"

"No, sir."

"She has the power to undo everything."

"We'll find her, sir. She has no reason to leave Callisto. Her Dreamers need her."

"Use the droids too. I need Eleanor found! Do you think you can handle this?"

"Yes, sir."

"Good, because I don't want to have to replace you."

A sharp pain pinches his heart. He needs this job, or rather the access it offers. "No, sir."

"Now, go do your job."

Scylla nods. He hurries to the exit, this time ignoring the two figures on the chairs as he passes. As soon as he closes the door behind him, he tastes blood. He bit the inside of his cheek sometime during the meeting.

With a heavy sigh, he leans against the door. Since being assigned as lead officer four years ago, he had learned from his predecessors that half the job is to deal with the Planner's mercurial moods. They have become less predictable over the years and grow worse the longer his wife is missing.

Despite their tumultuous relationship, she is a stabilizer in his otherwise infinite existence. She is the only one he listens to, the only one he considers his equal. Without her to refill the cracks in his barely human facade, they will only widen. The Four Cities need her back.

Where are you?

The last time he saw her, she was in her cottage, as she has been for over a hundred years. Her back to him, she was looking out the window of her loft to the overgrown backyard. She refuses to allow anyone to fix up the place. Walls lean and the roof sags, peeling wood swollen from mist and rain. Most of his brothers hate this place, but not Scylla. He likes it. To him, it smells sweet and earthy, with a hint of nostalgia—like the disintegration of time itself.

"I'm tired, Scylla," she had said then. "Forever is too long."

One of his brothers approaches. Scylla straightens.

"There you are!" Luke says. "We need you in the conference room."

"What's going on?"

"Emergency meeting. We just found that couple from Callisto who disappeared a week ago."

He follows Luke down the curved hall. Police Station One is the shape of a doughnut, with a courtyard in the middle. The conference room is located on the inner side of the ring. Everyone who is not out in the field is here. All eyes turn to him. Scylla takes his seat.

Gordon is standing at the head of the room. Behind him is a large screen. He clears his throat.

"As you may have heard, our drone found Mila and Willow—both citizens of Callisto—who went missing last week. Let me warn you: these images are disturbing."

A bird's-eye view of the desert appears on the screen. A swath of brown so barren there is not even scrub. The image zooms in until it centers on two bodies, the midday sun glaring off the exposed parts of their skin. They are lying side by side on the sand, hands clasped, eyes closed as if in slumber. Scylla's heart drops to his stomach.

"We first received a missing person report for Willow. Her coworker called in to say she received a strange message on her watch the night before. Two days later, the report for Mila came in. Upon further investigation, we learned both have been linked in a romantic relationship with each other for the past year. Per protocol, we ran blood tests." Gordon paused. "Both bodies came up positive for Absinthe."

Murmurs come from around the room. The Crone's drug, which her followers claim makes dream memories more vivid, has been discovered in the blood of many they have rescued or recovered from the desert.

"Is this a repeat of what happened last cycle?" comes a question from the back.

The field of lifeless bodies in white.

Scylla shakes off the image. "Did you find anything else in their blood?"

"No, they're clean otherwise."

"Then it's not the same," Scylla says. "The case in Elara last cycle was a planned mass suicide, and cyanide was also present."

"So they just got lost in the desert?" someone else says.

"Both died of extreme dehydration," Gordon says. "This location is two days' walk from the nearest water source."

"Maybe they lost their bearing while hiking and accidentally headed deeper into the desert," another says.

Except it wasn't an accident. There have been too many missing people for it to be a random coincidence. These were runaways.

"How can they get lost? Watches give them directions to anywhere," another officer says.

"They weren't wearing watches," Gordon says.

"Why the fuck would they do that?" one asks.

"We should have Communications send a message out to every citizen reminding them to wear watches when they go out hiking," another officer suggests.

"Do that," Scylla says. It's like putting a bandage on an arterial hemorrhage, but it's a good idea nonetheless.

"What should we do about these two?" Gordon asks.

"Stick to protocol," Scylla says, hating the words as they come out. "Report Willow and Mila as accidents, and send letters to their places of employment. Mention nothing of Absinthe in their blood. Bring up the map again."

The image on the screen changes to a map of the desert. On various spots are red dots marking the locations where runaways were found—most of them dead, a few alive.

"So far, the majority were found outside Elara," Gordon says.

Since it's the farthest city from Callisto, it seems to be the preferred launching point. From this image, it's painfully obvious. Not to mention that interrogations of the survivors had revealed that these trips were planned out as a way to escape Tabula Rasa—not realizing there is no running away from something embedded within their DNA. Despite all the policemen knowing this, they cannot say it aloud. To do so would be to question the Planner's utopia. And no one questions him.

"Divert more drones to the desert near Elara," Scylla says.

"What about the other open cases?"

"How many now?"

"Eighteen. We just received two more calls yesterday."

They've been getting about two calls each day for the past week. If this keeps up, with twenty-two days left before Tabula Rasa, and counting those they had already lost, they will be 73 people over the average projected death rate of 250 per year—a 29 percent increase. This may not seem significant when compared to the total population of 250,000 across the Four Cities, but the System and the complex predictive models it relies on require a delicate balance.

Even though the Planner will not admit it, this is the reason he removed the graduating seniors from the CDL a month early and why he is sending more children into Tabula Rasa instead of College. The next step, Scylla predicts, will be to ask the CDL to produce more created children. The System needs to replace the dead and the missing.

"Until we find them, dead or alive, we continue looking." He stands up and squares his shoulders, preparing himself for what he has to say next. "I also just received a new direct order from the Planner. We need all officers to search for the Book of Crone."

"But we already have a hundred officers on that case."

"He wants everyone to look for her."

"What about everything else we have to do?"

"It all has to get done," Scylla says. "There'll be no days off until further notice."

CHAPTER TEN

ARIS

February 26, 2233
(22 days before Tabula Rasa)

Aris glares up at the lit ceiling of the library. She wishes there was a way to turn off this perpetual day that drags time on unendingly. She's been here less than twenty-four hours, but already she feels haggard and about two hundred years old.

Stacks of books in various shades surround her. She has been trying to decipher them one by one. One thousand one hundred and seventy-two so far, hundreds of thousands more to go.

Of those she has gone through, she has counted 250 in each color. The numbers on the spines consist of two sets of zeros and ones. The first set is the same for each color, and the last set ranges from one digit to eight, increasing exponentially.

100010011101-1
100010011101-10
100010011101-11
100010011101-100 . . .
100010011101-11111010

Aside from these clues, they hold close their secrets. How are these empty books supposed to give back her past? *Can* they even? Metis's face comes to her, alone in the dark. Her heart squeezes, and her eyes burn. Their future—all the Dreamers' futures—rests on her, and she is no closer to an answer to their very imminent problem.

She screams her frustrations. The sound echoes around the cavernous space. The tightness in her chest loosens.

The Crone glides over from wherever she had disappeared to. "Feeling better?"

Aris looks at her. "Slightly. My throat hurts now though."

"You win some, you lose some."

"I don't feel like a winner." Aris points at the book on her lap. Its cover is the same bright purple as a lilac flower. "Why are all of them blank? Every single page of every book I've looked through. Nothing."

The glowing woman lowers herself to the ground, her long gown pooling around her like liquid clouds. "Knowing Eli, there's a reason for everything. We just don't know what it is yet."

"What's the reason for each color then? And these titles that are not titles at all?"

"Categorization and identification."

"Yeah, but how are we supposed to know what they mean?"

"I've been trying to figure that out. What I can say is this is very Eli." The Crone runs a translucent palm over the topmost book on a stack, lingering over the cover, unable to physically touch it.

"He had this record collection, a whole wall of them. It started out as those his mother had given him and grew over the years. I don't even know how many. Hundreds, a thousand . . . He never threw anything away, not even the ones so scratched up they'd skip every time he played them. These books are like those records. Despite distrusting humans with our own individual memories, he cannot bear to let them—as a collective—disappear forever. He can't let go."

She stands and glides to a shelf, examining it. "It makes perfect sense he would keep the erased memories inside books."

Aris agrees. After all, he keeps his own wife in one. Even though by doing so, he allows Absinthe to exist.

"Gotta give it to your husband for being poetic even while being a manipulative, controlling sociopath," Aris says.

The Crone laughs. In this space, the sound reminds her of the wind blowing.

"These are nothing like your book though," Aris adds.

"Consciousness and memories don't work the same. You are still encased in your own skin, whereas I'm not." She swipes an entire hand through a row of books.

From the far end of the room come footsteps. *Another feeding.* It must be dinnertime.

The Crone glides away through a shelf. She does not want to be seen by those at the CDL, not knowing how much loyalty the Matres have for their Planner. As soon as Eli realizes she's missing, he will be tearing through this land, searching for her. So far, the women can be trusted not to turn Aris in to the police. But does that extend to the Planner's missing wife with memories older than the Four Cities itself?

Aris gets up and walks to the black-and-white mosaic floor, where her bed sits near a table and two chairs. This spot has become her living area. From one of the aisles, she sees a Matre emerge.

"Did you say something?" Selene asks. "I heard you talking."

"Sometimes I talk to myself."

"I brought you dinner." She sets a basket on the table. "Tomato bisque with fresh basil."

Selene begins pulling things from the basket—a generous

container of hot soup, a spring salad, two bread rolls, utensils, and bottles of water. She opens the container, and a delectable scent rises from it. Aris's mouth waters. As much as she despises being locked up in here, at least the food is good. She sits down and begins spooning the bisque into her mouth. The warm liquid coats her throat, soothing it.

She looks up and sees the Matre's eager expression. "It's delicious, thank you."

Selene smiles. "We have a saying here: 'Porridge for cold nights. Soup for stress at its height. Tea for heartaches.'"

"It's a good saying." Aris takes another spoonful.

"How are you holding up? It must feel claustrophobic being inside the library all day."

"Excruciating."

The Matre's eyes gentle. "I know it's frustrating being stuck in here. Head Matre Hera may be tough, but it comes from a good place. The safety of everyone at the CDL is her first priority."

"As soon as I figure out the books, I will leave. I promise. I've been going through them but still don't know why they're all blank."

"I wish I knew. The police transport them in and leave them. And once in a while, they bring in a large machine and spend a whole day in here. They don't tell us anything. Just show up, do their job, and leave."

The muscles in Aris's entire body tighten. "The police have full access to this place whenever?"

"Not fully. We do have boundaries, and they respect them as long as we do what we're supposed to."

It's easier for her to be found here than she thought. And if the police see her, she'd put the Matres in jeopardy for housing a runaway. The Head Matre has every right to not want her here.

"I *am* the danger," Aris whispers.

Selene stretches an arm across the desk. "You're not the danger. It existed before you. You just brought it to the forefront."

Still, guilt rakes its claws on her. "I'm really sorry."

The Matre looks at her with sympathy.

> "In the desert of your soul
> darkness shakes stars
> from your tree of hope.
> Kneel down on the
> freshly turned earth
> and gather the fallen.
> In your cupped palms
> paradise rises."

Aris cannot help but smile. "Did you just make that up?"

"No, it's a poem by R. S. Raviya. She lived in early twentieth-century Indonesia and wrote about love and the magic of life. You seemed like you needed to hear it." She opens the basket. "I brought you something else."

She pulls out a bundle of flowers. Yellow black-eyed Susans, pink primroses, purple stalks of lavender, red poppies. She arranges them in a glass with water and places them in the middle of the table.

"These are beautiful." Aris hasn't seen flowers this colorful since last spring.

"They came from our gardens," Selene says. "We have several at the CDL. A flower garden. An herb garden with medicinal plants. A Shakespeare garden, where all the plants have lines from different plays. A vegetable garden that always has something new growing. An experimental one, where we try different hybrids. My room overlooks a rose garden that smells amazing. I'll bring you some roses tomorrow."

The Matre has a sweet innocence different from anyone Aris has encountered. It must be from living such an isolated life.

"Thank you," Aris says.

"I thought they might help."

"They do. You're very perceptive."

"It's my job. I'm a counselor."

"You are? What do you do for the students?"

Her face lights up. "I give them guidance outside the classroom. My job is to advise them and prepare them for their new life after they leave the CDL. It's an interesting job, and no day is the same. Students come to me for all kinds of things. Relationship problems, issues with friends, school stress."

"You love your job," Aris says. It's obvious.

"I care for the children very much. We all do. You can't help it, raising them since they were babies."

A thought strikes her. Why hasn't she realized this before? "You don't go through Tabula Rasa?"

"No, our memories are continuous. We need them to be able to take care of the children until they turn eighteen. Imagine the students having to remind me they're my students every four years."

An uninterrupted life. This is what Aris will have once she has all her memories back. She will never have to give up her memories of love again. No one else will either.

She takes a bite of a bread roll. It's still warm and tastes of home. An image rises. Her and Metis sitting at the dining table, holding hands. Them curling up on the same chair, reading from the same book. Just a simple, unbroken life. A knot forms in her throat. She clears it.

It will all be worth it—she clings to that hope.

"I have an idea," Selene says. "If you want, I'll ask the Head Matre for permission to walk you in the forest at night, when no students are awake."

"Really? I'd like that."

"Really." The Matre stands up, a wide smile spreading on her face. "If all goes well, I'll see you later tonight."

She turns and walks off. The soft echo of her steps moves farther and farther away.

"She's a nice one," the Crone says from beside Aris.

"She is. Where did you go?"

"Around." She drifts to the table and leans down, her face touching the flowers.

"Can you smell them?" Aris asks.

"No. Just an old habit," the Crone says.

"What's it like being a consciousness without body?"

"Like you being locked inside this library: excruciating."

Aris imagines herself sitting on the floor of the library, looking through books for eternity—an unending life trapped inside an empty existence. She shudders.

"I have to say it's clever," the Crone says.

"What is?"

"To hide memory books among those who have no use for them in a place no one outside can remember. Very Eli."

Aris looks at her from the corner of her eye. "Careful. You sound like you admire him."

"Oh, but I do. He *is* a brilliant man."

"I can't believe you still love him."

"Love doesn't go away—you know that."

"But Metis is a wonderful person."

"So was Eli. We are all capable of loving and hating someone in equal measure at the same time." She smiles sadly. "I hope you will never have to experience this."

CHAPTER ELEVEN

METIS

February 26, 2233
(22 days before Tabula Rasa)

Tonight's dinner is roasted portobello mushroom steaks stuffed with a mix of cheese, thyme, and garlic with a side of creamy pasta. Aris loves mushrooms. Whenever a fresh case became available at a specialty store, she'd risk putting on her watch to trade points for them. Not many things would make her do that.

What is she eating tonight? A knot forms in his throat. He swallows it and composes a smile.

Be relaxed, be gracious.

"You really are spoiling me with all this food," Metis says as he cuts another piece and puts it in his mouth.

It does taste good, and he is going to miss hot home-cooked meals. But the sooner he leaves, the better. Since their dinner last night, the feeling of unease inside him grew to become something he can no longer ignore. Outwardly his friend is himself, but there's something off about him Metis cannot put a finger on.

"It's nice to have someone to cook for," Cole says from the chair across the dining table. "People in Elara like to keep to themselves. It can be lonely."

"Where's Gia?" Metis asks. He thought Cole's girlfriend

would be here. They were always inseparable. Like him and Aris, they found each other early in the cycle.

"Back at home."

"What happened?"

"I don't know. What happened with you and Althea?"

The hair on the back of his neck stands on end. Aris hates the name her AI gave to her at the Waking, saying it feels like wearing someone else's skin. As soon as she learned her old name, she abandoned Althea, only using it when she needed to deal with the System. To the Dreamers, she is Aris.

"You haven't touched your wine," Cole says.

"I will. I'm just enjoying the food." His hands are shaking. He moves them under the table and presses them palm down against his lap to stop the trembling.

Cole takes a sip of his wine as if to show it isn't poisoned. "I've been meaning to tell you, some of us are meeting tomorrow."

"Who?"

"Tyra, Copley, Willow, Mila. You know, the usual suspects. I'm sure they'd love to see you."

Dreamers are not allowed to meet outside the official gatherings Metis normally led. That's always been the rule. It's too risky—and more so with the heightened police activity. Besides, there is no reason to meet since he had already given each Dreamer a supply of Absinthe before he left.

What's going on?

His insides are roiling. He wants to get up and run out the door, but his backpack with everything in it is in his room. He digs his fingernails into the flesh of his palms to focus. He needs to stay calm.

"I'll have to pass. I'm trying to keep a low profile," he says. "You haven't told them I'm here, have you?"

"No, of course not. Your secret is safe with me."

Metis is no longer hungry, but half his food is still on the plate. He doesn't want to arouse suspicion, so he picks up his utensils, cuts out a piece of mushroom, and puts it in his mouth. It was now rubbery and bland. His taste buds have stopped working.

"What are you meeting about?" he asks in a cool voice.

"The Crone."

His heart jumps. "Why?"

"Because she's missing." Cole leans in, his eyes penetrating. "You don't seem worried, considering you were her Sandman."

Metis steels himself. "Tabula Rasa is coming soon. We won't need her until the next cycle."

"But what if she's gone forever?"

"She's been around for two hundred years. She can't be gone forever."

"Then where do you think she is?"

In the forest of pine. "I don't know."

A shooting pain hits him in between his eyebrows. His utensils clang against the plate. He drops his head into his hand. "Ow."

"Are you okay?"

"A headache." His eyes water from the pain.

He hears Cole's chair scraping against the floor. A moment later he sees a white pill and a glass of water on the table in front of him.

"Here, it'll help."

It's the same painkiller he gave him yesterday. But now Metis is not sure if he should take it. Cole stares at him expectantly. There's no way to decline it without more questioning. Metis looks back at the pill. It did help with the headache. He picks it up and swallows it down with water. The pain eases.

"Thanks," he says, massaging the middle of his forehead with his fingers.

Cole returns to his chair, a glass of wine back in his hand. "You should rest. I'll clean up."

Metis gets up and walks to his room, feeling strangely like he's in an avant-garde stage play. Everything inside his body is telling him he can no longer stay here. He closes the door and begins packing everything he owns into his backpack.

He had hoped his network of Dreamers could help him disappear, but with Cole the way he is, he can't trust him. One major problem he has is food. Earlier when he quickly searched through Cole's cabinet, he saw no canned or camping foods. There were not even dry ingredients.

Metis doesn't have his watch to buy anything, and even if he does it would be tracked. The idea of scrounging leftovers from trash cans at night does not appeal to him though he may have to resort to it if he becomes desperate enough.

The door opens without a knock.

"Where are you going?" Cole asks. His tall frame dominates the threshold, blocking it.

Fuck.

Metis straightens, readying himself for a fight.

"I've decided to get the ingredients for Absinthe tonight," he says in as calm a voice as he can muster.

"But it's late. If you tell me what they are, I can get them for you in the morning."

He zips up the pack and puts it on. "It's okay. It'll be easier for me to do it. I'll be back in a few hours."

"Are you sure? The police are looking for you."

"That's why I'm going at night."

He walks to the door, facing Cole. The man studies him, his blue eyes piercing. Metis cannot recall them being blue.

"I need to get through."

"It's dangerous out there. I think you really should wait until morning."

"I'd like to go."

"But—"

Heat travels up his neck to his ears. He draws himself up to full height, his eyes almost lining up with Cole's. "Are you keeping me hostage?"

"I'm just worried about you, that's all." The man steps aside. "I'll leave the porch light on for you."

Relief washes through him. A part of Metis thought he might have to fight the man. "Thanks."

He walks out and Cole follows.

"Everyone will appreciate this," he says. "We need Absinthe."

"Okay. I'll see you later."

"Alright. See you later." He waves at him from the porch.

Outside, all the windows of the surrounding houses are dark. Metis looks down the hill toward main street but cannot see its lights. The only bright thing around is Cole's porch. Elara has always been a sleepy town compared to the other three cities, but this is too quiet.

Metis hesitantly walks forward, using the moonlight as a guide.

He hasn't fully thought through where to go. At this point there are not many options. The police will have their eyes on the Crone's cave and his house so those are out of the question. Hiding around here will eventually draw someone's attention. Plus, he doesn't want to be anywhere near Cole. The abandoned tunnel is the safest place for him to hide, he decides. If he walks to the other end, he will have a creek nearby. He can also harvest edible plants from the desert. And when Aris returns, he will be right there to greet her. The thought warms him.

He tips his neck back. The sky, instead of being dotted with stars, is a flat, black expanse. The moon is gone. *Something is wrong.* Fear clutches his spine and wrings every trace of warmth from his body.

"He knows," a voice—a woman's—whispers.

He whips his head from side to side. "Who's talking?"

Silence.

The night presses in all around. He looks back up the hill toward Cole's porch. It's still lit—the only light in existence. It begins to move farther and farther away.

What is this place?

He runs downhill as fast as he can. Something grabs hold of him, a vice constricting. The tightness travels up, a hand around his throat squeezing. He paws at it, trying to drag in air. The intake of breath stops halfway. He is drowning in this nothingness. Aris's face comes to him.

Please let me see her one last time.

With all his strength, he screams. Darkness swallows him, black.

CHAPTER TWELVE

ARIS

February 27, 2233
(21 days before Tabula Rasa)

Today is tomorrow.

Metis used to say that whenever they were up in the witching hours—talking, touching, treading quietly toward dawn. She misses him with her entire being.

Less than a week.

Based on her calculation—which is more like a guesstimate—she has to leave in less than a week to get back to him before Tabula Rasa. Since she now knows the way, it shouldn't take her as long to get to Elara as it did to get here. Still, it will take more than two weeks. If she doesn't rest during the day, she can travel in less time. She's not sure how she can do it safely. Between the police, the speed train, the drone, and the desert, she'll be lucky if she can return at all.

The midnight sky is a respite from her own thoughts and the library. Sounds come from all around them. Wings flapping. Rustling movements of small nocturnal animals. The soughing of the wind through the trees. The forest is far from asleep.

The moon is just a tad less full—the beginning of the waning gibbous phase—bright enough for her to see where she is going. Aris sucks in the cool air greedily through her nose, filling her lungs with the soothing scent of pine. Selene is walking beside her. The light of the lantern in her hand illuminates her white dress, reminding Aris of the Crone.

"It's strange. I don't have a memory of this place, but it feels familiar," she says.

"I don't think it's strange at all," Selene says. "It was once your home for eighteen years. Our mind isn't the only way we remember."

Aris imagines her childhood at the CDL. As a baby being cradled and fed by a Matre. As a toddler skinning her knees and a Matre cleaning her wounds. As a teenager with her first crush and a Matre counseling her on love.

"Did you grow up here too?" she asks.

"Born and raised."

"How long have you been here?"

"Twenty-five years."

"I don't know how old I am. No one does in the Four Cities."

"What's life like there?"

"In some ways, it's good. We're never hungry, there's always food. We have a house. We have a job. Life is, I suppose, comfortable." Sadness tugs. "But the best prison is a comfortable one."

"Is that how you see yourself, as a prisoner?"

"I escaped here, did I not?"

The Matre looks down. She's probably thinking about the children she loses to the System each year. Aris feels a pang in her stomach.

"But like I said, it's not all bad," Aris changes the subject. "All the cities are different. Each has its own personality. Callisto is crowded and has the best restaurants. Europa is great for wandering—so many wonderful coffeeshops and bookstores.

Lysithea has gorgeous architecture. And Elara . . . the sky there is big and beautiful."

"All named after Jupiter's moons," Selene says. "Callisto is the capital, the first one created."

"That's right."

"I don't know much outside of what I read and what the children told me."

"It's big and busy. Most people live and work there. The buildings are so tall, you can't even see the top of them when you look up from the street. And in the middle of the city is Central Park."

"The children like going there for field trips."

"It has most of the museums and entertainment venues. It can be quite fun." For a second, she misses it.

"What kind of entertainment do you have?" Selene asks.

"Plays, old movies from before the Last War, musical performances."

A smile brightens the Matre's face. "I'd love to see those! Is that where you live?"

"No, I live in Lysithea. It was the third city built. Smaller and quieter, but it has many art museums and a cute park. Our home is a beautiful blue house with a wraparound porch and a view of the Lysithea Valley. I have a garden behind it. And there's a special room in the back just for a piano. It's my favorite place in the world."

"Do you play?"

"No, my husband. He performs at Carnegie Hall—I mean, *used to*," she corrects herself.

Selene's eyes widen. "You have a husband? I thought that only existed in the Old World."

Heat travels to her cheeks. "I know it sounds old fashioned—nobody gets married anymore. But he's kind of the old-fashioned type. He likes to read books from before the Last War."

"In this marriage," Selene says,

> "you are not mine
> and I am not yours
> for there is no possession.
> In this marriage
> you are not there
> and I am not here
> for there is no distance.
> In this marriage
> we traverse mountains and oceans
> through monsoon rain and fire.
> In infinite love
> In eternity
> In oneness."

Aris smiles. "Is that another R. S. Raviya poem?"

"Yes."

"Did you memorize all of them?"

She laughs. "Just my favorites."

Aris realizes that despite having just met Selene, she really likes her. The woman is sunshine. She will miss her.

She decides she can trust her. "I'm Aris."

The Matre beams. "Hi, Aris. Thanks for entrusting me with your name."

"Thanks for not pressing me for it."

"Would you have told me your real name if I did?"

"Probably not."

Selene laughs. "Where's your husband now?"

"We had to separate so he could lead the drones away and I could get here."

"You sacrificed being together?"

"But we will reunite. I'm going back to him as soon as I figure out the memory books. With them, we can have a future where we won't ever have to worry about being separated from who we love again."

Silence hangs between them like a thick curtain.

Have I said too much?

"I'll do what I can to help you," Selene says after a while.

Aris turns and finds her looking right at her.

"Really?"

"Really," the Matre says with a smile. "Love is a gift."

Her eyes burn, and a knot forms in her throat. She clears it and changes the subject. "So what's your favorite place in the world?"

The Matre tilts her head. "I can show it to you, though it's probably not the prettiest right now."

"I'd love to see it."

Selene leads her off a small path. They walk through a thicket of trees until they reach a clearing at the edge of a cliff overlooking an expansive vista. Below them is a dark valley, and beyond it, mountains stretch back in layers toward the horizon.

"It's beautiful," Aris says.

"It's a lot more beautiful during the day," the Matre says. "This is where we hold the Ceremony of the Dead."

Selene's gaze is fixed on the landscape below, in her eyes a distant empty look.

"Usually it's for the Matres who've passed from old age like the previous Head Matre, but once a year we hold one for the children who die in their first Tabula Rasa."

Aris feels cold all of a sudden. She hugs her arms to her chest. "Some of them died? I didn't know Tabula Rasa can kill."

"I can't imagine the System would want you to know. When you tinker with the mind, bad things can happen. The police don't give us many details. I don't think they know either, except that sometimes the process causes the student's brain to stop working and they never wake up."

Melancholy hangs heavy, like thick winter fog.

"How many?" her question comes out a whisper.

"About two to three a year. The morgue in Callisto processes the bodies, and they return as ashes in small white boxes. The entire school would gather here to remember them. Those who want to, take turns saying a few words about the dead. What they were like, what they will miss about them."

Aris's heart skips a beat. "The children know who's in the box?"

"Yes."

"So they know Tabula Rasa can kill?"

"Yes."

"H-how are they okay with it?"

"Nobody is okay with it, Aris. It's just a part of life."

"But why would the System want the children to know?"

"It's not the System. The Head Matre had requested it."

"The Head Matre?"

"So we can honor the dead," Selene says.

"And the Planner lets her?"

"She tells him all the children will eventually forget through Tabula Rasa."

But they will not all forget—not everything.

Aris looks out into the dark.

The Head Matre . . . She wants them to know. She wants them to see.

"Are you ready to head back?" Selene asks. "I have one more place to show you."

They loop back toward the CDL. The path merges with the main trail, and they walk until they reach a gate with six bells. Here, the path of dirt and gravel transitions to cobblestone.

Selene points to the right of the trail. "That's where we

found you. You had collapsed from exhaustion and dehydration under a bush."

"I don't remember how I got there," Aris says. "I just remember walking the tunnel."

"I'll show you."

They turn right off the trail toward a massive wall covered in ivy. Selene pulls out a key attached to a long gold necklace from around her neck. She steps forward and looks as though she's about to walk into the ivy wall. Then she disappears into it.

Where did she go?

The Matre peeks from behind the ivy. "Are you coming?"

Aris follows and realizes it's not one but two layers of walls, an optical illusion. In between them is a narrow walkway.

"You had accidentally stumbled upon our secret passage to the train station," Selene says.

They walk until they reach a door. The Matre inserts the key into the lock and turns the knob to reveal a set of stairs going down. They descend several flights of the concrete steps until Aris's knees hurt. At the bottom is another door. Selene opens it and a stream of bright light breaks through, severing the dark in two.

They are inside a train station. Everything here—the tile floor, the walls, the columns, the ceiling—is white. Her brown complexion and hair stand out in stark contrast. They walk onto the platform. Where there is supposed to be a train, the tracks are empty.

"Where's the train right now?" Aris asks.

"In Callisto. It only comes when we need to transport the children there."

Aris walks to the edge of the platform. The tunnel is pitch black. She had walked through that to get here, and it will be how she'll leave.

Selene comes to stand next to her. "How long will it take you to get back to where you need to go?"

"At least two weeks, I think."

Her mouth gapes. "Two weeks? Through the wilderness?"

"Yeah."

"What's it like?"

"At the end of the tunnel is a pine forest. It's not that different from the one around here. But once you get out of the mountains, the land becomes a vast desert. There are no pine trees—just scrub, cacti, small plants, and some oaks."

"What did you eat as food?"

"Pouches of camping food. I have enough to last me a week. I'll also be able to forage some edible plants along the way to supplement."

"So you'll need more food. What about water?"

"Fortunately, I was able to find creeks and rivers along the way. I'll just follow the same path."

"Sounds like a dangerous journey."

"It is."

"The train only takes a few hours," Selene says.

"Well, at my best I can do four miles an hour. The train can go as fast as two hundred."

"You'd be much faster with the train."

"Yeah, but the police control the train."

"They do . . ." Selene gives her a careful look. "But they can't pay attention to everything when they have hundreds of children to manage on field trips."

Aris blinks, realizing what Selene has been trying to tell her.

A sunshine and a daredevil.

"You want me to sneak onto the train?"

The Matre shrugs. "It's a possible option in case you're desperate for time."

"But how will I do that without being seen?"

"I don't know, we can figure it out. Like I said, it's just a thought."

Instead of leaving the same way they came, they exit out a wide automatic glass door leading to a brightly lit staircase with a ramp next to it.

"This is our normal way in and out," Selene says.

"I wonder why I didn't go out this way. Seems more obvious."

"Maybe that's why. You probably didn't want to be seen."

"The police don't know about the other entrance?"

"No."

"So many secrets."

"Aren't they the Four Cities' lifeblood?" Selene says.

Aris smiles. She's liking the Matre more and more.

At the end of the ramp is a wooden door with black ironwork, a relic from another time. Selene pushes against it with her entire body, and they exit.

Aris's breath catches at the sight. In front of her stands an edifice that looks as if made of pure magic. The intricate and ornate facade is decorated with realistic-looking stone flowers and vines climbing up the sides. Spiraling columns stand like protectors. A round stained-glass window hangs above a massive and elaborately carved wooden door that looks big enough for a giant. The building could have sprung from a fairy tale.

"We call this the Grand Hall," Selene says.

"It's beautiful," she says and feels the word lacking. "It must look even more amazing in daylight."

"This is where we hold important ceremonies."

"Like what?"

"Promotions, award ceremonies, funerals of the Matres, senior graduations. This is also where we say goodbye to them before they leave for Tabula Rasa." Selene's voice is tinged with sadness. "The location right across from the train station makes it convenient."

Aris's heart squeezes at the thought. "How do you handle losing them to Tabula Rasa every year?"

Selene's lips turn downward. "We just do. What choice do we have?"

The Matres' existence is one of servitude, born and lived for one purpose—to raise, love, and educate the children for the System. The System imprisons everyone.

Guilt pricks. "I'm sorry you were forced into this life, having to take care of all of us. It isn't fair."

Selene blinks. "If you think we resent the children, we don't. It's not their fault. Like you, we try to find the good in all the bad. For me, the good is the children. Even knowing the day will come when we have to let go of every child we've brought up, I would never trade knowing and loving them."

Warmth envelops her. "I guess it's the same thing with us. Even knowing Tabula Rasa will take away all our loved ones and every relationship we've ever forged, I'd never trade loving."

The Matre turns off her lantern and plunges them back into darkness.

"Thank you for taking me out," Aris says as they weave through the grounds, keeping to the shadows. "I'm glad the Head Matre is open to me leaving the library at night."

"Head Matre Hera is really a kind person. Strict, yes. But kind."

"She's protective of the children."

"Very much so. A lot rests on her shoulders. There are four thousand five hundred students at the CDL."

"That's a lot of kids."

"You've only seen a small fraction of the CDL. We have a

nursery, elementary school, middle school, and high school all spread out across this crest—each section with its own designated Matres."

Inside, the foyer of the Administrative building is still empty and dark like before. They turn down a long hallway. On both sides are closed doors to offices with names of Matres on them. The last door on the right belongs to Head Matre Hera.

Selene opens it without knocking. The Head Matre is not here at this hour. They walk toward a wall decorated with a large map with the word "Eastern Sierra" on it. Selene pushes against the map, and it swings like a door into a small space. Another secret passage.

They step inside, and beyond it is the metal door of the elevator. Selene pushes a button on the wall next to it, and the door slides open. They enter and descend. A moment later they arrive at the library.

With over three hundred years of history, the CDL is not short on surprises. Before their walk in the forest, Selene showed Aris a network of hidden pathways to keep her out of sight. There are bookcases that, when pushed, become doors connecting rooms; a mazelike corridor that appears endless until it deposits you into the opposite side of the building; and staircases that lead to unexpected floors.

"You spoke earlier about the police taking the kids on field trips using the train." Aris says. "How many kids exactly?"

And would there be enough for her to hide in.

"Two hundred and fifty," Selene says.

Two hundred and fifty. Wait. "Every time?"

"Yes."

"Why that number?"

"That's how many kids we have in each grade."

"Every grade?"

"Yes." Selene looks at her curiously.

"It's always been this number all the way from kindergarten to high school?"

"As far as I know. And I'm sure our record would confirm."

"Record?"

"Of all the created children."

Aris's heart leaps. "You have a record of all the children born here?"

"Yes."

"By year?"

The Matre's brow furrows. "Yes. That's how we keep track of them."

Two hundred and fifty books in each color. Two hundred and fifty students in each class. Two hundred and fifty lives.

CHAPTER THIRTEEN

CASS

February 27, 2233
(21 days before Tabula Rasa)

"I guess the Matres are letting the Outsider stay," Bastian says from next to her, voice too excited for having been hiding in this bush for hours. "See, I was right! She's still here."

Cass rolls her eyes. "Wish you could have been right yesterday. We waited for hours."

After hiding under this bush for what felt like half their lifetime, they finally spotted the Outsider with a Matre. Both left for the forest, and were gone for a while before returning to the Administrative building.

"Aren't you glad you came back?" he asks.

"Didn't think I had a choice. You kept pestering me."

He ignores her comment. "Which Matre do you think that was?"

"It has to be Matre Selene."

She was the one Cass went to for help. Besides, she and the Head Matre made them promise not to say anything to anyone on the threat of detention for the rest of their time at the CDL. The news of the Outsider is not something they want known.

"We should have followed them into the forest," Bastian says.

"How? We would have been spotted. It's so quiet out there."

"What do you think they were doing?"

Cass shrugs. "I don't know. Your guess is as good as mine."

"Do you think they're going to let the police know?"

"Doesn't look like it." She and Matre Selene appear to be friendly with each other. "But we can't leave now. She's going to come back out, and we're going to get caught."

He makes a face. "We're going to sleep on the dirt all night?"

"This was your idea! Let's follow her, you said. We need to find out what's going on, you said," she mimics his deep voice.

"But we need to find out what's been happening."

"Do we though? Do we?" She is so tired she could cry.

"Something strange is happening," Bastian says. "How do you not want to know what it is?"

Cass huffs. "Do you have any idea what would happen to us if we're caught? We'd get detentions! We'd lose all of our senior privileges! We won't even be able to set foot outside our dorms except for class. If you think we have it bad now."

"It won't be that bad," Bastian mumbles.

"Ugh. I don't want to talk to you right now."

After a while, he turns to her. "Can I talk now?"

"Can I stop you?"

"How do you think she got here?" he asks.

"Well, she didn't take the train in."

"You think she walked here through the wild?"

"She must've. But I don't know how. It's too far to come all the way from the Four Cities. Even the speed train takes hours."

"What if she's not from the Four Cities?" he whispers.

Goose bumps run across her arms. "You think she's from the north?"

"Why not? We've always wondered if anyone out there survived the Last War. What if they did?" he says.

"But how did she survive the Last War? All that terrible stuff in the air."

"I don't know. Maybe she developed lungs of steel."

"Okay . . . say she's from the north, why do you think she came?" she asks.

"Maybe to establish contact? Maybe there's a whole community out there."

"Why would they wait all this time?"

"No idea. Maybe they're more primitive since they don't have advanced technology like the Four Cities do."

A thought comes. "Do you think she has all her memories?"

Bastian's eyes widen. They both grow quiet. Of all the times she and Bastian played their "what's in the north" guessing game, never once did either of them suggest that those on the other side of the mountains would have all their memories.

"We have to talk to her," her friend says.

"What? Why?"

He looks at her as if she does not understand what he just said. "Because she's from the outside. Because she could have all her memories. Because she made it all the way here somehow, surviving the wild. Because she might know how to get us out so we can stay together."

Cass stares at him. Warmth floods her body. Why didn't she think of this before?

"Okay," she says.

"Okay," he repeats.

Matre Selene steps out of the Administrative building.

"Shhh!" Cass says.

They flatten themselves against the ground and stay quiet, eyes following the Matre's back until she disappears from sight.

Cass drags in a long breath and sighs. "So how do we talk to the Outsider?"

"Well, we know where she's staying for now." He points toward the Admin building.

"That's also where all the Matres' offices are."

"They're only there during the day. They sleep in their quarters at night. You saw Matre Selene leave. If we catch the Outsider in there by herself, we can talk to her."

"Right now?"

Bastian looks to be in thought. "Not yet. Let me think up the best way to approach her so she'll help us."

"Alright. Let's go back to the dorms then. I'm sleepy," she says.

"Let's go see what's behind the ivy wall first."

"Right now?"

"Just real quick. I want to see where they disappeared into earlier. Maybe we can find out something that'll help us."

They crawl out of the bush and run toward the Gate of the Six Bells. From there, they turn off the trail and weave through the overgrown landscape to the giant wall of ivy. They've passed it thousands of times before on their way to the forest but never thought anything of it. During the day it looks like any other wall, just with ivy growing on it. But now, in the dark, it looks like the gate to the netherworld.

Bastian pushes against it. "It's solid."

The CDL has more than a few secret passages—the knowledge has been passed down among the students for generations. But Cass has never heard of the ivy wall being one, not even an inkling of gossip.

"Can you find me a stick?" Bastian asks. "A long one."

She kicks around the ground and finds a piece of dead wood. "Here."

He holds one end against the wall and begins walking.

"What are you doing?" Cass whispers.

"Shhh."

She sits on the ground and watches her friend drag the stick across the ivy. Her eyes are droopy, and she wants her bed. It's probably two by now. They are only six hours away from the breakfast bell. She yawns and wipes her eyes.

"Cass!" Bastian calls.

"Huh?"

"Come over here. I found something."

She gets up and walks over. He steps to the left and suddenly disappears.

What?

"Bastian?" She walks closer.

His arm reappears and tugs at her sleeve, startling her.

"There's a small passage," he says.

She steps closer and sees it in between two walls. "A secret passage?"

She squeezes in behind him. It's dark inside.

"This is amazing!" Bastian says.

They walk almost the length of the wall and come to a door. He twists the knob. *Locked.* He growls in frustration.

"Where do you think it goes?" she asks.

"I don't know, but we're going to find out," he says.

CHAPTER FOURTEEN

SCYLLA

February 28, 2233
(20 days before Tabula Rasa)

Callisto's west side is bustling with the sound of life. It's Gift Market Day. Here, people leave the items they no longer want, and anyone can take whatever catches their eye. The last purge before Tabula Rasa.

Scylla meanders along streets lined with tables. Some eye him as he passes. They know he's not one of them. His uniform—the fedora, the long coat—make him stand out.

He passes a few clothing stores. In one, translucent mannequins in suits of various colors stand in poses. Another has them in black jackets of different lengths and sizes. One displays hats of all kinds on transparent stands, making them appear as though floating in space. He wonders what it would feel like to try on something different from what he's been required to wear since he took his oath.

He shakes the thought from his head. Policemen are meant to stand apart from the citizens of the Four Cities. Unlike the other created children, he and his brothers did not grow up at the CDL. They were raised by retired policemen at a rambling adobe in the middle of the desert, isolated from the Four Cities.

The Planner does not want them commingling with the rest of the population. As officers, they are not supposed to develop personal connections with those they are meant to protect.

Everything in its place.

The restaurants on both sides of the street are filled with people out enjoying the day and each other. It is a time for celebration, a time for reminiscing, a time for forgiveness. *See you in another life.*

He searches from table to table. Here, a carved bookend shaped like a woman carrying a child. There, green and blue stones made into necklaces. Everywhere in this graveyard of memory are things looking to be reborn.

He sees it—a table of jewelry. He walks over and scans through the items. There it is, what he's been looking for. The silver ring sits on a small plate with a delicate rose pattern. He picks it up and brings it closer to his eyes. It has a design in the middle—a spiral drawing of an intricate nine-point mandala with an indented square at the center—at once chaotic and orderly. The symbol for the Dreamers and the Resistance before them.

He has seen this ring on Metis. On some of those in the Elara mass suicide. *Dreamers.* This ring is going to help him get to them before they even think of leaving the Four Cities. Twenty more days to go before Tabula Rasa, and he *cannot* lose any more people to the desert.

His watch beeps, and he picks up. "It's Scylla."

"You're needed back at Police Station One. We found another runaway," Gordon's voice comes through his earphone. "This one is alive."

"I'll be right there!"

"Meet me in Medical Room 1A."

"Okay." Scylla hangs up.

Alive.

Relief floods through him. Alive means one less body to the morgue and one less child plucked from College to fill in for the dead.

He pockets the ring and decides to also take the plate before hurrying back to the nearest station. The next train comes within minutes, just as scheduled. By the time he arrives at his destination, he is the only person left on the train. Police Station One is located at the end of the line of the intercity train on the edge of Callisto. No one comes out here but officers—not because they can't but because they never need to. There is nothing else out here.

He takes the elevator up from the train platform and arrives in front of the doughnut-shaped building. The glass sliding door opens into a vast lobby flooded with light from windows that run along the interior and exterior peripheries.

He glances up at the wall in front of him. On it is a quote:

> Peace is the only battle worth waging.
> —Albert Camus

Turning right, he takes the ramp up to the medical rooms. From this pathway, he can see through both the inner and outer windows of the building. A mountain with parallel layers of strata to his left and a leafy courtyard to his right.

The door to Medical Room 1A is closed. He knocks, and a moment later it opens. Gordon's face peers out.

"Hey, thanks for coming right away."

Scylla slips into the room and closes the door. "Who is it?"

"Gia of Callisto. She had disappeared at the same time as Cole of Elara."

Cole they found dead at the bottom of a ravine eighty miles outside of Elara. The medical examiner determined he had died from a skull fracture, most likely from slipping and hitting his head on a rock as he was trying to make his way across.

"Our drone spotted her. She was found dehydrated and malnourished deep in the desert near Elara, but her vital signs are good now that we've given her an IV drip. Once she's stable, we'll transfer her to the main hospital."

Scylla walks to Gia. She is sound asleep. Her curly hair looks matted with dirt, and there are small cuts on her face and arms, probably from tree branches and thorns. His eyes travel down to her hands. On the third finger of her left hand is a silver ring with the Resistance symbol, the same one that was on the ring Cole was wearing at the time of his death.

His throat tightens. They were trying to escape Tabula Rasa so they could stay together. If they had stayed in the Four Cities, at least there would have been a chance they'd meet each other again in the next cycle. Now that possibility is gone forever.

"I think we have a mass exodus on our hands," Gordon whispers, saying aloud for the first time what everyone knows to be true. This must be why he wanted Scylla here alone.

Scylla sighs. "I know."

"What are we going to do?"

With the Planner refusing to acknowledge this as a systemic problem, there is nothing they can do but patch the leak. He pulls the silver ring from his pocket.

"Run the symbol on this ring through the surveillance system. When the CCTV picks up this symbol, add the people associated with it on a watch list. They may be a flight risk. We need to figure out if this is an organized effort or just individuals acting on their own."

"And then what?" Gordon asks.

"If they try to run away, pick them up and keep them here until the next Tabula Rasa."

"What if it keeps happening in the next cycle?"

Gordon knows as well as he that the issue is deeper than what the police can handle. These people are trying to escape Tabula Rasa, and they will continue to leave.

"I don't know," Scylla says. "We just need to buy time so we can figure this out."

CHAPTER FIFTEEN

METIS

February 28, 2233
(20 days before Tabula Rasa)

In the dark, the metal gate looks a part of the night sky. Metis would have walked past it had he not been here before in daylight. He tilts his neck up at the real sky. No drones. At least for now.

Ignoring the No Trespassing sign, he jumps and grabs the top of the gate with his right hand, finds a foothold, and climbs. From the top, everything below is hidden in the deep shadows of the overhanging trees. He hops down and lands on soft ground. An old worn path lies ahead. He follows it until he reaches another gate—this one in a crooked wooden picket fence.

Beyond it awaits the dilapidated cottage from his dream. He unlatches the gate and enters the overgrown front yard. It leads to a crumbling porch laced with white climbing roses, their sweet scent perfuming the air with melancholy. He steps up, and the floorboards creak under his feet.

"Hello to you too," he whispers.

He turns the knob of the peeling front door and pushes. The swollen wood resists. He leans his weight against it and forces it open.

The interior is lit only by the pale light of the moon seeping in through the cracks in the roof and windows. The smell of dampness permeates the air. He closes the door, and the grayness of the walls deepens. A strong sense of déjà vu hits him in the gut. He has been here many times before.

Walking toward the back of the cottage, he finds a ladder to a loft and climbs up. The loft is the width of the entire cottage and is lined on three sides with bookshelves. The silvery moonlight shines through the back window, giving him some visibility. He walks to the shelf on the right side of the room and sits on his haunches. A book, faded and pale, stands out from the rest.

"Hi again," he says, and pulls out the book.

He opens it to a page bookmarked by a blue origami crane. Somehow, he knows exactly what to do. The same way his fingers remember the piano keys. The same way he knew how much Aris meant to him the first time he laid eyes on her.

He reads the passage and light pours from the pages. But he is not afraid.

A glowing form appears. Her ancient face ripples like a reflection in water. "Hello, Metis."

"Hello," he says, awed. "How do you know my name?"

"It's always been your name, because of your music."

"I've been seeing you in my dreams."

She smiles. "And you're still in one."

"I am?" He looks around. The cottage has an ethereal quality, but so does the figure in front of him. "So you're not real?"

"Not in here, but out there I am."

"Why do I keep dreaming you?"

"Perhaps your brain is trying to tell you something."

"What?"

"That, Metis, is what you have to figure out."

Pain hits him squarely between his eyebrows. He attempts to raise a hand to massage the spot, but his arm will not move. He tries again, and again it refuses to obey his brain.

What the fuck is going on?

He commands his eyes to open, but his lids are too heavy. Every part of him feels weighted down, locked in a prison of darkness. He recalls his last memory, of the black night pressing in. Panic clutches him.

"I can't put him back into the simulation. He's fighting it now that he's aware," a woman's voice speaks, just an arm's length away.

His spine tingles. Is she talking about him?

"Keep trying," a man says. The voice has a strange quality, like someone talking through a speaker. "Find another way if you must."

"What can I do? You won't let me leave this cramped room. You won't let me use Dreamcatcher to explore his dreams. Why can't I transfer him to the Interpreter Center?"

"You will make do, Apollina. There's no safer place than Police Station One."

Metis's heart drops to his stomach. He is in a police station with the Interpreter!

How did I end up here? Where's Cole?

"At least let me look inside his dreams," she asks.

"After you neglected to report the side effects of Dreamcatcher?"

"Is that what Scylla said in his report?" she asks. "Let me remind you that correlation does not imply causation. Not everyone who went through Dreamcatcher killed themselves, and those who did were unstable to begin with."

"The fact is, you broke protocol. I told you from the beginning: your use of Dreamcatcher is to be only per the protocol

I established. And it *cannot* be used on an artist, especially not one like Metis. I don't want to chance damaging his brain."

"How was I supposed to know he was your pet?"

"Don't be ridiculous. He's the most acclaimed musician in the Four Cities."

"But he's a danger to them as well. He helps your wife make Absinthe!"

Absinthe. Wife.

Metis's chest tightens, and he finds it difficult to breathe. He is trapped somewhere in the middle of a police station with not only the Interpreter but the Planner himself. Even worse, they both know he's a Sandman. How is he going to escape this?

And how did he end up here? He searches his brain for answers, but where the knowledge should reside, he finds only emptiness. The only explanation that makes sense is that he must not have escaped the drone as he thought he did. He must have been arrested and brought back to Police Station One.

"I'll be the decision-maker on what is or isn't dangerous to the Four Cities," the Planner says.

"How can you not think Absinthe is dangerous?" Apollina asks. "It's addictive, and addicts are dangerous when they're desperate. Your wife created the very thing that works against Tabula Rasa, and you're letting her continue to make it. Not only that, you're allowing her to recruit Dreamers. Why let her ruin the peace we work so hard to maintain? I don't understand." Her voice becomes louder as she speaks.

"It's not your job to understand." The Planner's tone is as hard as ice. "Your one job is to serve the Four Cities. It has always been the Interpreter's responsibility to follow the protocol I've established. Your predecessors have always been up to the task."

"Well I'm not like them. Perhaps you shouldn't have kept cloning me."

"It's not your DNA. Whatever faults there are lie only with you, Apollina."

Silence stretches on.

"If you can't do your job anymore, all you need to do is say so," the Planner says.

"I apologize," she says quickly. "I can do this. I can start another simulation, one that might be easier for him to assimilate."

"Do it."

Cole was a simulation? Cold washes through Metis. *But it felt so real. The meals, the house, the man himself—everything.*

No, not everything.

Footsteps come toward him. He feels something hard and heavy on his head.

"It'll take me a bit to set up," Apollina says. "I have to warn you there's a risk he will reject it right away. But it may also be the quickest way to get him to talk."

"I need to know what he and Eleanor were planning," the Planner says. "And I need to know where she is."

Panic rises.

I don't know anything. I don't know anything. I don't know anything, he repeats to himself. *Metis, you don't know anything.*

Sharp pain stakes the middle of his head, and—

CHAPTER SIXTEEN

ARIS

February 28, 2233
(20 days before Tabula Rasa)

"We're in the year 2233," Selene says.

"In the Four Cities, we only go by day and month," Aris says. Presumably so no one can figure out a way to track the cycles and mourn what they have lost.

Two hundred and seven years after the Last War.

The knowledge hits her with a strange mixture of awe and sadness. Often she wonders what that world was like. The old movies she saw at the theater have given her glimpses of it, as fictional as they may be. The people looked like her, talked like her, and even dressed somewhat like her. Yet, they had continuous memories and long relationships. They used words like "forever" and had an entire lifetime to attempt realizing it. What would it be like to be them?

"This section is from almost a hundred years ago," Selene says as she places a piece of paper with *2150* on it in front of books with sunny yellow covers.

In the adjacent bookcase, *2149* leans against lime-green books. Next to that, *2148* sits before those with fuchsia covers. Then come *2147, 2146, 2145*—on and on.

When the Matre told her there are exactly 250 children in every grade, Aris had speculated that the colors of the covers stand for each class and the binary numbers on the spines represent each individual child. After Selene found the calculation to convert binary to decimal in an old math textbook, they spent all day yesterday and most of today deciphering them—beginning with the sections nearest the black-and-white mosaic and fanning out from there.

They confirmed her guess. The first set of numbers—the constant within each group—stands for the year the children were born. The second set—with numbers ranging from 1 to 250—is a child's place within the class. Together, they make up one's unique ID number.

The Crone's voice returns to her: *To hide memory books among those who have no use for them in a place no one outside can remember. Very Eli.*

The secret of these books would have stayed hidden had she and Metis not searched for Mem. Now she just has to determine which book is hers.

"How far do you think they go back?" Selene asks.

They've made a good dent at converting the binary numbers on the books into years, but with all the hundreds of thousands in the library, they are nowhere near finished.

"The Last War was in 2026," Aris says. "Based on historical records, the survivors struggled for a long time after. The nuclear fallout had partially blocked the sun and shifted the weather. They were basically starving for a few years. Then came cancer and stillbirths caused by radiation and biological and chemical toxins released during the war."

"What's stillbirth?"

"That's when the child is dead at birth."

Selene's face pales. "We've never had that with the created children. They are all born healthy."

Had it not been for the desperate effort of the scientists in the Four Cities, their species would have died out.

"My guess is the scientists started as soon as they were able," Aris says. "And I think I know where the oldest books may be."

During the hours stuck inside the labyrinthine library, she has had more than enough time to familiarize herself with it. There was one section in particular where the books were different. She leads Selene through the maze of cases and stops at a section where all the covers are pale silver, like the surface of water glittering in the sun. There are tens of thousands of books here. All of them have the same first set of numbers—11111111001.

Selene runs her finger across those on one shelf. "So many."

"My guess is they had to produce more created children at the beginning," Aris says. "If many people were dying, two hundred and fifty a year would not be enough to replace them."

She does a quick calculation to convert the number. "This entire section is from the year 2041. Fifteen years after the Last War."

Selene walks the entire aisle and eases out a book. Its spine reads *11111111001-1*. Birth year 2041, Child 1. "This is the first created child who went through Tabula Rasa. One hundred and sixty-seven years older than me."

"I wonder what year I was born. I think I'm older than you are."

"Not by much, I don't think. I'd guess five years at most. I was born in 2208 and I'm twenty-five, so you may have been born somewhere between 2203 and 2208."

The problem is that even if they get the right year, Aris cannot possibly take all the books from it back with her—not alone. With food and water, she can fit only two books at most in her pack. One for her, one for Metis.

"I wish we could use our records, but they won't have your

name—not as Aris," Selene says. "Each child gets a new one after their first Tabula Rasa."

"And every cycle after," Aris adds. Another fail-safe the System puts in place to make it nearly impossible to track one's old life. Except Metis. He always has the same name because of his music. Could he have been Metis at the CDL?

"We have to find a Matre who remembers you while you were here," Selene says, pulling her from her thought.

Aris's heart jumps. A Matre who knew her as a child?

"But who?'

"That's the big question. We go into service at the age of twenty and retire at seventy. That's fifty years of service. With two hundred and fifty kids in each year, each Matre is exposed to twelve thousand five hundred students—at least. Who we need is your counselor."

"My counselor?"

"Someone like me. Each child is assigned to one. I'll talk to Head Matre Hera and see what she recommends. Right now, no one will talk to you without her approval."

"Is that why you're the only one I see?"

"Yes. The Head Matre is—"

"Protective of those at the CDL, I know."

Selene smiles. "You're included in that too, you know, now that you're here."

Aris swallows. She knows. Her stay, while restrictive, is that of a well-treated guest. Three delicious meals a day. A walk in the forest at night. A helpful Matre by her side. Selene has proven herself trustworthy and an ally, and Aris has been feeling guilty about keeping from her the entire reason for her being here.

It's time.

"Will she also let me see the records?" Aris asks. "I think my husband's name may be on there."

"But names are ch—"

"I know names change, but he's always had the same name in all the cycles he can remember."

The Matre's brow furrows. "What do you mean 'he can remember'?"

She meets the eager eyes of the Matre. "We belong to a group of people who are able to recall some of our memories. We call ourselves Dreamers, and there are many of us."

Selene's eyes widen.

Aris reaches into the pocket of her jacket, where she keeps her last vial of Absinthe. She pulls it out, the green liquid dancing under the bright light of the room.

"This drug makes dream memories more vivid. It's called Absinthe. Dreams are how some memories leak through. But only the emotional memories, and only the strongest. This is how Metis and I remember we were lovers in the past cycles. All the Dreamers take this."

The Matre's jaw slackens. "How does it work?"

"A dream of a memory lights up a chain or cluster of neurons in the same pattern as the memory itself. Absinthe induces this same pattern of neuron firing, enhancing and strengthening the dream memories."

"So your dreams feel like a memory?"

"Your dreams *are* memories."

Selene shakes her head. "So this isn't just about love?"

"It *is* about love," Aris says. "It's always been about love. But it's also bigger than just me and Metis. With the books and Absinthe, we can give memory back to everyone who wants it. The people of the Four Cities will be able to remember their entire past."

Selene looks from the book in her hands to the vial of Absinthe that Aris holds. "This is too much. You're talking about a complete change to how things have always been done—on a grand scale. You need to tell the Head Matre everything."

Aris's stomach sinks. "What if she kicks me out?"

"She won't, not when your life will be at risk if she does. She's protective of *everyone* at the CDL."

"What if she doesn't want to help—not in the way I'm going to ask her to?"

"What I can tell you is most of the things you need to do won't get done without her approval."

"But it will put her and the CDL in direct line of fire."

"It's too late to stop that. We are already helping you." Selene's voice is hard.

Aris can hear the hurt in it. Until now, the Matre did not know she has been inadvertently helping a freedom fighter overthrow an existing regime. It really was not fair to have kept this from her—the one person who has been selflessly helping. Guilt wrenches her gut.

"I'm sorry I didn't tell you this sooner. I just didn't know if I could do what I needed to do, or how. But now that I'm close to achieving our goal, I— I wouldn't have been able to do any of this without you."

Selene's eyes turn gentle. "I understand. You were in a tough position. But now that I know, I'm obligated to tell the Head Matre everything. We won't know what she will do until we ask. But we have to give her that respect and courtesy."

Aris nods. She knows this.

They take the elevator up to the Head Matre's office. Selene steps out into the small space between the elevator and the panel and knocks.

"Come in," a voice says.

Selene unlatches the lock and pulls the panel. The Head Matre is sitting on the other side of her gleaming desk, the dusk sky outside the window behind her. Her direct gaze falls on Aris, making her feel as if she is being dissected.

"Sorry for disturbing you, Head Matre," Selene says. "We have an important update for you."

Hera raises an eyebrow. She points to the chairs across from her. "Sit."

They both take a seat. Aris's mouth feels like sand.

Selene turns to her. "Aris made an important discovery regarding the books in the library."

She feels her heart in her throat and clears it. "I actually have Selene to thank for this. With her help, we've determined the binary numbers on the spines are ID numbers for each child. The first set of digits being the year they were born, and the second set their place in each class. With this, I'm closer to determining which book is mine. And as soon as I can do that, I will be able to leave."

"What do you need from me?" the Head Matre asks.

"Access to the Matres who may remember my name when I was a child here. That way I can cross-reference it with your records and find my ID number."

"Selene told you we have records of the children?"

Aris swallows. She does not want to get the Matre in trouble. "She's just trying to help me figure this out."

"She's very helpful," the Head Matre says.

Aris is not sure whether that is a good thing in Hera's eyes. "Whatever she's doing has been to get me out of the CDL."

"We do align in that."

Here comes the really tough part. "There's more." Aris braces herself and pulls out the vial of Absinthe. "I'm a part of a group called the Dreamers, and we take this drug called Absinthe to help us remember our pasts. But it only helps us access our strongest emotional memories."

Hera sits straighter. The lines between her eyebrows deepen.

"With this drug and the memory books, we can get our pasts back entirely," Aris adds.

The Head Matre springs from her chair. "How dare you! Do you have any idea what the Planner will do if he discovers we're supporting a rebellion?"

Her stomach drops. This is exactly the situation she did not want to be in. "I didn't know I was looking for the CDL when I came looking for Mem. I just want us to have a chance at life."

"You do have a life, a safe one inside the Four Cities! It's one thing to risk your own survival chasing a pipe dream, but to risk all of us at the CDL," Hera yells. "You are not welcome here!"

"Head Matre, please," Selene pleads. "All this time, I thought once we'd lost the children to Tabula Rasa, we'd lost them forever. We've never known how they all fare after they leave here, whether they're happy or well. We've just assumed they were happy." She places her hand on Aris's. "Now, one of them has returned and is telling us she isn't happy—that Tabula Rasa isn't the right path and that there are many like her. That she's willing to risk her life to come here, crossing the dangerous desert to find a way to get her memory back. And we're going to turn her away?"

"She has put the life of everyone here in great peril," the Head Matre says.

"Then let's help her get out of here with the memory books for those who want them."

"How are we going to do that?"

"I may have an idea that will work," Selene says.

CHAPTER SEVENTEEN

CASS

March 1, 2233
(19 days before Tabula Rasa)

A glimmer of light dances behind her closed eyelids. *Is it morning already?* Cass opens her eyes to a figure standing by her desk. Her eyes gaze out the dark window. Her form is wispy and translucent, the edges of her silvery gown feathery as if about to be blown away by a nonexistent wind. But it is her face that Cass cannot look away from. It's as ancient as time itself.

Am I dreaming?

Cass sits up on the bed. "Hello."

The figure turns to her, blue eyes curious. "Hello."

"Who are you?"

"My name is Eleanor. Many call me the Crone. What's your name?"

"Cass. Are you a ghost?"

In all her seventeen years here, she has never seen a ghost. But maybe ghosts wait until one is about to leave the CDL to make themselves known.

The Crone smiles. "Close, but no."

"What are you then?"

"The closest thing I can describe myself as is a consciousness without being."

"I've never met one of those. What are you doing in my room?"

"I've seen you hiding in the bushes."

Is that an answer? It doesn't seem like an answer. "But how does that lead you to my room?"

"I was curious, because you were curious."

"That's not an answer either."

She laughs, her voice sounding like the wind. "You remind me of someone I used to know. You look a bit like her. Her name was Anya. She lived here too."

"I don't know any Anya."

"She was here a very long time ago. She was the youngest survivor of the Last War."

Cass feels her mouth gaping. This dream is becoming more interesting. "How did you know this?"

"I'm from the time before."

"You mean the Old World? You're from the Old World?"

"Yes."

"You're over two hundred years old? That's as old as the Four Cities!"

"I was one of the creators."

"I've never heard of other creators but the Planner."

"You wouldn't. He doesn't allow mention of me in any history book."

"Why not?" Cass asks.

"Stories are told a certain way to make you think a certain way. They're the result of decisions made by the storytellers."

Ugh, what's with the non-answers? "Why doesn't the Planner want people to know you exist?"

"Because he thinks I'm dangerous."

Cass sits back. "You don't look dangerous."

"I'm only dangerous to him."

So many questions go through the girl's mind. Why is the Crone only dangerous to the Planner? What is she capable of? And—

"Who are you to him?" Cass asks.

"Aren't you clever."

Okay . . . "So are you going to tell me?"

The Crone smiles but does not reply.

"Why are you here?" the girl asks another question. She decides she'll keep asking until the Crone answers.

"I'm looking for a solution to a problem."

"What problem?"

"An age-old problem that seems less significant now that I'm here."

Another nonanswer.

"How did you get here?" Cass asks.

"Through the train tunnel."

Finally an answer!

"You took the train? The police brought you here?" She can't imagine why the police would bring someone the Planner thinks is dangerous to the CDL.

"No. I didn't take the train, I walked the tunnel."

"How long was the walk?" Maybe she and Bastian can leave through there.

The Crone tilts her head, studying her. "Too far."

"Where did you come from?"

"A cottage."

"Where's your cottage?"

"Not here."

Cass sighs. They are back to the nonanswers.

"Why have you been hiding in the bushes?" the Crone asks.

The girl considers not answering to give the old woman a taste of her own medicine, but that would end their conversation, and she doesn't want to end it just yet.

"Bastian wants to run away from the CDL. He wants to talk to the Outsider to find out how. So we've been stalking her. Wait, did you two come together?"

"Is Bastian the boy you were hiding with?" The Crone asks, again not answering her question.

"Yes. We've been best friends since we were five."

"How old are you now?"

"Seventeen."

"And next year is your first Tabula Rasa," the Crone says, her voice sad.

"We're going to separate after. I'm going to College, and he's going to the Four Cities."

"That's why he wants to run away?"

"We thought we were going to College together. We have similar propensities. But the Planner changed our assignments last minute."

The lines on the Crone's face deepen. "He's making changes?"

"He also took the seniors earlier. They were supposed to be here until the day before Tabula Rasa. But he just took them."

"He doesn't like change." The Crone looks in thought. "Unless . . ."

"Unless what?"

"It hurts more to stay the same."

"But nothing can hurt him. The Planner is all-powerful."

The glowing woman reaches out and touches the bracelet on Cass's wrist. Her fingers do not feel like anything. "No one is."

That's not what Cass knows to be true. But maybe this

Crone knows more about him. After all, she is from the Old World.

Cass yawns. She leans back on her bed and closes her eyes. "You may be the strangest dream I've ever had."

"And you're the first child I've met in two hundred years."

CHAPTER EIGHTEEN

METIS

March 1, 2233
(19 days before Tabula Rasa)

In the valley below, downtown Lysithea sits against the blank canvas of the desert. Past the barren land, towering mountains surround on all sides, hiding the beyond. The sight is majestic and terrifying in equal measure. Metis turns away from it and sees the familiar robin's-egg-blue house with a white wraparound porch. The sight of it makes him smile.

He opens the gate and takes the flat stone walkway to the porch. A few short steps and he is at the front door. As soon as he enters, a combination of scents hit him at once. Wood oil and dried flowers. Tea in the morning and red wine in the evening. Candlelight dinners and roasted vegetables in the oven. Books.

All the curtains along the front windows are drawn shut. He opens the ones closest to him and light floods in, warming the wood-paneled walls and floor. He weaves past a round wooden table in the middle of the entryway under an ornate glass chandelier and turns right, toward the sitting room.

The couches and chair are empty. The coffee table is clear of half-read books and used mugs. No discarded sweater or throw.

Where's Aris?

He moves farther into the house—passing a spotless kitchen, a dining room with a long wooden table and chairs, and a library with wall-sized shelves and an electric fireplace. All empty of her.

She could be in the solarium, he thinks. He makes his way to the backmost room of the house. Here, daylight pours in through naked French doors and tall windows. All around, Cyathea ferns in giant pots stand almost as tall as the high ceiling. In the middle of the room under the parasols of lacy leaves—in its place of honor—is a shiny black piano.

Metis has always thought of this house as the piano's house and he and Aris as its cohabitants. The grand piano is as massive as the one he plays on the stage at Carnegie Hall and even better in pedigree. On the bench in front of it sits Aris, her back to him. He has never seen her sit at the piano without him.

She looks over her shoulder and smiles brightly. "There you are."

She gets up and walks to him. He wraps her in his arms and kisses her with all the longing in his body. She tastes of everything good and right in the world.

She giggles when they separate. "It's nice to see you too."

He sighs contentedly. "I've missed you."

"Did you have a good day?"

"It's better now."

"I was wondering when you were going to come back," she says. "It's almost dinnertime."

"Do you want to go out to eat?" he asks. "I can wear my watch."

"Actually, I was about to make dinner. Wanna help?"

"I do." He pulls her in and squeezes her once more before letting go. "What is it?"

"I got mushrooms today."

"Well, that's exciting." He laughs. He knows how much she loves them.

They walk into the kitchen, and she pulls out a pan of roasted mushrooms from the oven. The delectable scent fills the kitchen. Why did he not notice it before?

"I thought you said you needed help," he says.

"But you already did, silly. Here, pour yourself a glass of wine."

He sits at the small table in the kitchen, and Aris places a beautiful plate of mushrooms drizzled with sauce in front of him.

"Yum," he says.

She sits across from him and sips from her glass. "Do you want to tell me about your day?"

He cuts the mushrooms into pieces and forks some into his mouth. A sense of déjà vu overwhelms him. *Aris loves mushrooms*, he tells himself as he pushes down a nagging feeling in the pit of his stomach. They have had so many meals together just like this.

"Sound check for the concert was less than stellar," he says.

"I'm sure you were great. You're too hard on yourself."

"Where's your food?"

She does not answer. Instead she gets up and comes to stand behind him. He feels her soft hands on his shoulders, massaging.

A satisfied sound rises from his throat. "That feels amazing."

"What did you do before Carnegie Hall?"

"I went to the cottage."

"And what did you do there?"

"More planning."

"Planning what?"

He looks up but cannot see her face. She is behind him. "The usual. More Absinthe. More cranes. More Dreamers."

"Sounds busy."

"It's getting closer to Tabula Rasa. The Crone wants to make sure everyone who wants to remember can," he says.

Aris squeezes his shoulders, hurting him.

"Ow."

"Oops, sorry."

"If you're going to be rough, can you go up my neck? There's a spot on the side that's killing me."

Her hands move up. "You're tense."

"It's my jobs. Both of them."

"Here, this will help."

"What?" He looks down and sees a white pill sitting by the glass.

Has it always been there?

"It's for the pain," she says.

He takes it with the wine. "When are we taking our next vacation?"

"Whenever you're free. Where do you want to go?"

"You know where I want to go." He closes his eyes.

> *On the edge of a cliff,*
> *hidden by jagged peaks*
> *and a northern forest of pine,*
> *lives Old Mem.*

"Tell me anyway," she says.

"Mem."

"Where's Mem?"

"Just a place." He grabs her hands and brings them to his lips. "It's strange, I miss you so much, and you're just right here."

"Well, you haven't seen me all day."

The desire to see her face overtakes him. He gets up from

his chair and comes to stand in front of her. His hands reach out and touch the sides of her face, cradling it. He leans down and gently places his lips on hers.

"I must just love you so much," he says.

Her expression shifts—becoming warmer, gentler—reminding him of the oncoming of spring.

So very much.

CHAPTER NINETEEN

ARIS

March 2, 2233
(18 days before Tabula Rasa)

"How do you think these books work?" Aris asks.

The Crone turns from the shelves and glides to her, the edge of her glow touching her feet.

"I've been trying to figure that out. The fact that memories can leak through dreams leads me to believe Tabula Rasa doesn't destroy the actual memories themselves, but the initiation points of targeted memories. Once it disrupts the first few neurons in the chain, it disrupts everything downstream. But the heart of the data—the memory—is still there."

Aris feels her mouth gaping. "So we still have all our memories, we just can't access them?"

"Unless by accident. That's what dreaming is—a stumble into the heart of a memory. These then become the dream memories that Absinthe can affect. My theory is the memory books contain neuronal patterns of the initiation points of memories. It would require too big a space to hold years of memories outside the brain."

"Why is it blank then?" Aris asks.

"Is it blank or does it only look blank to your eyes? The

world that we see is a small fraction of what actually exists. Think of all the things you cannot see with the naked eye. Air, sound waves, radio waves, UV light. The human eye is but one tool."

"So, what tool do we use to transmit these patterns of initiation points from my book back into my head?"

"There's only one technology I can think of." She pauses. "Dreamcatcher."

Her stomach drops. "The dream killer?"

"I know it sounds counterintuitive, but if it's able to delete the initiation points of dream memories, I believe it can also 'undelete' them by fixing the initiation points, rearranging the neurons into the pattern of a memory in the book."

"Then I can access the heart of my memories," Aris whispers.

"And those memories can trigger associated and similar memories, creating an avalanche of remembrance," the Crone adds. "Also, since the Dreamcatcher is designed to translate dream memories into images . . ."

Aris gasps. "I can watch my own life and remember!"

A smile spreads across the Crone's ancient face. "Yes."

She feels so light the wind could carry her away.

"The problem is getting inside the Interpreter Center," the Crone says.

The words are like an anchor around her legs, pulling her down. "How do we get through security?"

"There's an old service entrance behind it not on any architectural plan on record."

"How do you know this?"

"I used to live there."

An unexpected laugh escapes. "You did?"

"Yes, it was once mine and Eli's house."

Aris recalls the modern white stone building—all hard lines

and cold glass—surrounded by a green lawn. "It doesn't look very homey."

"Because it really was built to host events for Eli's company and investors. There's a private wing, but with the many parties and events there, even it didn't feel so private. I hated it."

"You are full of surprises."

"Or perhaps you knew but forgot."

"You told me this before?"

"No."

Aris sighs internally. The enigmatic Crone's personality is one she still finds confusing no matter how long she knows her. The woman can vacillate from one mood to the next like the shifting of weather, and her words can be just as puzzling—that is, if she even answers her questions at all. Is this what happens when one lives as long as she has?

"Anyway, first things first," Aris says. "I need to find the Matre who used to be my counselor and can remember my old name. The Head Matre set up some meetings for me."

"When?"

"My first one is this morning before the breakfast bell." She leans in and whispers, "In the garden."

"I thought you're not allowed to leave the library during the day."

"Apparently, this Matre doesn't do late nights."

"You seem thrilled," the Crone says.

"Of course I am. I'm going to meet someone who may remember me as a child. No one else in the Four Cities has ever done this. Besides, I was cooped up in here all of yesterday translating numbers."

She misses the outside, walking and breathing fresh air.

A small smile touches the corner of the Crone's lips. "I'm looking forward to hearing all about it."

"What are you going to do today?" Aris asks.

"The usual," she says though she has never once told Aris what "the usual" is.

While she is bound to her book like a genie, the Crone's diaphanous form means she is also not restricted to four walls. Once she's released, as long as she is close enough to her book, she can travel. That was how she had wandered into Central Park from her cottage, was seen by people strolling at night, and became the folkloric Crone.

The glowing woman tilts her neck. "Someone is coming." Then she glides away.

It's Selene. Aris is so excited to see her that she almost pulls her into a hug.

"Are you ready?" the Matre asks.

"Yes!" Her chest is fluttering with a thousand butterflies she is ready to release.

She notices a lantern in Selene's hand. Before she can ask, the Matre leads her down an aisle different from the one they usually take to the elevator. The books in the cases here have cobalt-blue and sunset-orange covers, the colors reminding Aris of the sky at different times of the day.

"We're going to take another way," Selene says. "The one the police use."

All this time, Aris thought the way they had been using was the only one in and out. "Do they know about the one through the Head Matre's office?"

"No," Selene says with a tiny smile.

The CDL is full of secrets.

The aisle ends at a wall. Selene walks to it and disappears. Aris follows and finds a concealed entry, just like the one in the ivy wall. She enters the passage. At the end of it is a door, and behind it is a tunnel.

The air inside is damp and cool, smelling musty like wet leaves and dirt. Selene turns on the lantern in her hand, and a globe of diffused warm orange light blooms.

"This tunnel was built a long time ago—we suspect during the time of Prohibition, when alcohol was illegal in Old America."

The width of the tunnel is wide enough to bring in trolleys of alcohol—and memory books. Aris touches the wall and finds it rough and hard. Below her feet is a smooth stone floor. This passage was carved out of the earth. It slopes up at an angle, reminding her she is deep below ground.

The Matre is quieter than usual. Maybe she is still upset with her. Or maybe she doesn't like being in the tunnel either. Aris reminds herself at the end of this seemingly unending hole is the other side. There is always the other side.

Almost there.

"There" eventually comes in the shape of a wooden panel. Instead of a door handle, there's a metal bolt holding it shut. Selene slides the bar from the socket and pushes the panel to her right. It makes a heavy sound, as of wheels gliding on a track, and reveals a surprising sight.

"We're inside the Grand Hall," Selene says. This is the last place Aris expected the tunnel to lead.

There are seven large stained-glass windows—three on either side of the building and a large round one in the front. Rows of wooden pews line a central aisle all the way to the large carved door. She cranes her neck toward the soaring ceiling with chandeliers that look like clusters of stars.

"Wow."

Selene seals the entrance behind her. And Aris now sees that what had looked like a panel on the other side is actually the back of an elaborate gilded altar. Selene's golden hair blends into the backdrop of statues casting their gleaming flaxen eyes down at her, an image from a dream. Aris notices a piano on the right side of the stage, and her heart squeezes from missing Metis.

We'll see each other again, she promises.

A long yawn comes from Selene.

Guilt rises. "I'm sorry you have to be up so early for me."

"It's not you. I didn't sleep much last night."

"What happened?"

"I was sick all night. Must have eaten something that didn't agree with me."

The Matre should be resting instead of out here chaperoning her.

"Don't worry," Selene says as though able to read her mind. "I'll rest after I drop you off. Come, we need to return you to the library before the breakfast bell, and we still need to get you dressed properly."

"Dressed?"

"It's just a precaution."

They exit the Grand Hall to crisp air and a plum-purple sky with just a thread of pink at the horizon. Selene turns off the lantern, and they walk until they reach a white stone building with tall windows, wrought iron balconies, and climbing vines. It has the romantic air of a bygone era.

"The Matres' quarters," Selene says. "Where we live."

Selene places a finger on her lips before leading her into the building. They make their way down the hallway until they arrive in front of a door with her name on it.

"This is my apartment," she whispers.

Inside is a high-ceilinged room with warm white walls and dark wood floor. In the middle of it stands a four-post bed with white bedding. In one corner are a dark mahogany desk and chair gleaming from use. In another, sit a small beige couch and a side table topped with a vase of pale pink roses and a book. The title reads *R. S. Raviya's Love Poems.*

Aris walks to the window. Outside is a rose garden laden with new blooms. Its scent sweetens the air, making her feel things she cannot describe. She mouths a silent *wow.*

"I keep thinking I'd get used to how beautiful this place is, then you show me something like this."

"One of the many wonderful things about the CDL is its history," Selene says. "This place was once the most opulent inn in California. People used to come from all over to vacation here. When the Planner acquired it from the original owner, he bought it with all the artwork and furniture to keep the history of the place intact."

She opens the door to her closet and pulls out black tights, a black tank top, and a white dress. "Here."

"You want me to dress like you?" Aris asks.

"Just in case we accidentally run into a student along the way." Selene points to another door. "You can clean up and change in the bathroom. Use whatever you want."

The gleaming white bathroom has another vase of roses on the counter, their scent sweetening the air. Aris stares at her own reflection in the mirror. Her brown hair is disheveled. Her brown skin has patches of sunburn. Her brown eyes look exhausted. She sheds her clothes, turns on the shower head, and steps under it. Warm water pours down her hair, and she sighs. Since she left home, she has kept clean by washing herself in freezing cold creeks and the sink in the library bathroom. This is her first proper shower.

Home. The only one she has now is with Metis, wherever he is.

She washes every inch of her body, scrubbing off the grime accumulated over the month of traveling. Running the ring on her third left hand finger directly under the water, she rubs it until the silver shines and the grooves of the mandala design are free of dirt.

She notices there is no timer on the faucet. Still, she does not linger. An old habit. As she dries herself, her eyes wander to the items on the counter. Lotion. A brush. Various trinkets with rose designs. Someone has a love affair with the flower.

The black tank top fits fine, but the tights and white dress are a few inches too long. Between that and her complexion and hair, she cannot possibly pass as a Matre. But who is she to argue with Selene. She exits the bathroom and finds the Matre lying on the bed with her hands on her stomach.

"The shower was much needed," Aris says. "Thank you."

Selene opens her eyes and sits up, her blond hair a tangled mess. She rubs a palm on her face and Aris notices a veil of purple under her eyes.

"You look exhausted."

"My stomach is making me woozy."

"Are you sure you can go?"

"Yeah. I'll be fine. I'm just dropping you off."

She gets up from the bed and grabs a white scarf from the closet. "Here, put this around your head to cover your hair."

Aris does as asked and studies herself in the mirror. She still looks nothing like a Matre, but at least she is wrapped in white.

"Now you're ready."

The meeting place is conveniently next door. They walk down a stone path in the rose garden until they reach a vast area separated into sections. A green lawn. Flower bushes exploding with scarlet red, pale pink, deep lavender, piercing yellow, and bright orange. An area where glass buildings line up in neat rows—holding tall hydroponic pods laden with vegetables and fruits. Surrounding on all sides are brick walls, protecting the area from the threat of passing students.

A lone Matre is in the glass building, meticulously clipping long green beans hanging off a vine. Her hair is pure platinum, and her back has acquired a gentle curve like a long blade of grass. She looks old enough to have seen several generations of created children come and go.

"That's Matre Demetria," Selene whispers. "She's retired but still likes to garden. She was a counselor her entire career."

Aris takes a deep breath to calm the erratic strumming of her heart. They walk forward and enter the glass building. Matre Demetria looks up from the plants as they approach.

"Good morning," Selene says. "I brought Aris to meet you."

Though of the same blue, Demetria's eyes do not have the steeliness of the Head Matre's or the sweet gentleness of Selene's. Instead they remind Aris of the calm surface of a lake—and of something familiar she cannot put a finger on.

"Good morning, Matre Demetria," Aris says, her voice shaky.

"Good morning, child." She smiles, and the lines on her face crinkle like balled up paper.

"I'm going to leave the two of you to chat. I'll be in the kitchen once you're done, Aris. It's through that large door." Selene points to it.

Aris sees a clipper on the rolling basket next to the Matre. "Can I help you with the harvesting?"

"Do you know how to pick beans?"

She walks to the hydroponic pod. She has never before harvested plants for eating. Until they left the Four Cities, all their food had been delivered by drones, bought at the store, or found at the farmers' markets that dot the cities. She looks at the bright green beans hanging off the plant. It can't be that hard.

"Just cut them at the tip, where it meets the plant," the Matre says. "Make sure the bean is at least the length of your palm."

Aris holds a bean with one hand and clips it off with another.

"Try it," Demetria says and takes a bite off a bean.

Aris bites into one and finds it crispy and sweet. "It's good. I've never eaten them raw before."

"Did you know you're the first student to have ever come back?" the Matre asks as she chews the rest of the bean.

"That's what I've been told."

"Hera said you came here for the books in the library."

"I didn't know they would be books or that this place would be the CDL. I was looking for a place called Mem from an old legend."

The Matre raises a brow. "I suppose the best memories survive in tales. Hera also said you've discovered the meaning of the books in the underground library."

"Only that they're memory books belonging to the citizens of the Four Cities. I don't know how to read them or know which one is mine."

"And you think I may be able to help you."

She nods. "I need to figure out my name while I was here. Was I one of your students? I mean one of those you counseled?"

"I've seen tens of thousands of students in my long years. Faces do change over time—some more significantly than others. Look at mine. Once I was as youthful as Selene. How old are you now?"

"I don't know my exact age, but I think I'm somewhere between twenty-five and thirty-five."

"If you're thirty, you would have left the CDL twelve years ago. I'm eighty-two now, so I was seventy when you left. I may have just retired. I was a middle school counselor during my last decade of service, but I don't recall being yours."

Aris's heart deflates. "You don't?"

"But I do recognize your face."

Her stomach flutters. "You do?"

"I don't know your name though."

"Oh." Without a name to look through the records, she is as lost as before.

The Matre's eyes gentle. "May I ask what you're hoping to gain with your book?"

Aris tilts her head, confused. "My memories, Matre."

"But why?"

"Because—" No one has ever asked her this before. "Because they can help me understand myself better."

"Memories can be a burden to self," Matre Demetria says.

"But can't they also be lessons? Or a reminder of what once was?"

A smile curls one side of Matre Demetria's lips, making her look all the more familiar.

"Lessons tend to be objective. I'm not sure what lesson you would learn from memories. They aren't fixed and finite. There isn't one truth to the past. It's marred by our own experiences and perceptions. The memory of your past viewed at different moments in time becomes different—and one can negate the other. A memory isn't innocuous. The present is much lighter."

"My present doesn't seem very light." Her eyes burn.

"I'm very sorry for what you're going through. But I hope you can find some peace at least in this moment."

She cannot argue with that. "I can."

"Then why leave it? If you want something from me, here is my best advice—find peace in every moment, no matter how minute, and extend it for as long as you can."

"I'll try my best," Aris says.

"That's all each one of us can do, child."

"Thank you for speaking to me." Her chest feels like there's a stone sitting on it. "I'm going to find Selene. I have to return to the library before the breakfast bell rings."

Demetria smiles. "Good luck finding what it is you're looking for."

Aris drags her feet toward the large door to the kitchen, her steps heavy. The space is a gleaming image of white on white, its brightness highlighting every speck of dirt on her shoes. It smells of fried potatoes, roasted carrots, creamy pasta, curry, maple pancakes, stir-fry, vegetable stew, corn bread—all the meals that had come and gone and those that are still to come.

At one of the long metal tables in the middle of the room, she finds Selene sitting in front of a food basket with a steaming cup in her hands. When she notices Aris, she looks up. Her face is ashen.

"Hi. I'm drinking some ginger tea. Want some?"

"No, thank you." Aris sits on the stool next to her. "Do you think you're not feeling well because you've been up late every night since I got here."

"No, it's something else. How was your meeting with Matre Demetria?"

"She recognizes my face in passing but doesn't remember my name. She wasn't my counselor."

Selene places her hand on Aris's. "I'm sorry."

Aris shrugs, too despondent to reply in words.

"We still have two more Matres to meet," the Matre adds.

Aris nods.

"Okay let's go back. The food-prep team will arrive soon. And once the breakfast bell rings, this big door will close." She points to the one leading to the garden. "And that one will open." She points to the one opposite. "That one leads to the Food Hall, where the students eat."

Selene grabs the basket from the table. "Breakfast."

Aris takes it from her and they exit back to the garden, passing Matre Demetria, who is still in the glass structure, harvesting greens. There is more pink in the sky, bleeding into the purple.

"Matre Demetria asked me why I wanted my memory book," she says. "No one has ever asked me that before."

"What did you answer?"

"The obvious. My memories. All the Dreamers want the same. But she thinks memories are a burden."

"Matre Demetria has lived a long time, and with her years comes wisdom. But it's the wisdom that came from living *her* life, not yours. Only you can tell you what's important to you."

Aris realizes they are not heading toward the Grand Hall but the Administration building.

"I'm going to take you to the Head Matre's office," Selene says. "I don't think I can handle the long walk down the tunnel. Can you take the elevator down by yourself?"

"Of course. I hope you'll get some rest."

She gives her a small smile. "Your next appointment is in the afternoon in the Head Matres' office. I'll come get you before then."

CHAPTER TWENTY

CASS

March 2, 2233
(18 days before Tabula Rasa)

"I've been having the weirdest dreams," Cass says.

Bastian forks a piece of pancake into his mouth, staring ahead as if he did not hear her.

"Hey!"

He looks up. "Huh?"

"Did you hear anything I just said?"

"What did you say?"

She rolls her eyes. "Never mind. What were you thinking?"

"I've been wondering where that locked door could go. The fact that it was near where we found the Outsider means it must lead out. And that's probably why none of the students knew about it. All the other passages just loop around the CDL."

His effort to pick the lock has led nowhere. For a simple looking thing, it seems to be impenetrable.

"We need the key to it," he says.

"And who do you think has it?"

"The Head Matre has a key on her necklace."

A laugh escapes. "So you think it's *the* key, and you're going to go up to her and ask her for it? I'd like to see that."

"I'll figure it out." He leans back on his chair. "The Outsider didn't come out last night or the night before. Do you think she's left?"

"I don't know. I haven't seen Matre Selene either. I went by her office yesterday, and her door was closed." She yawns as she chews her oatmeal.

"You think the Outsider is staying in her office?" he asks.

"There's nothing in there but a desk and some chairs. She'd have to sleep on the floor if she is."

Sleep. Cass wishes she could do that right now. They had stayed under the bush in front of the Administrative building for hours each night, Bastian insisting the woman and Matre Selene would show up at any moment. Their amateur sleuthing is going to be the end of her.

"It's probably still better than sleeping outside," he says, then gasps, fork pointing up in the air. "What if we're waiting in the wrong place? What if they've moved her somewhere else?"

"Where?"

"I don't know. The Matres' quarters? The cottage in the forest they use for vacation? The Grand Hall? In a tent, a cave? I don't know."

"Breathe before you pass out," she says. He is in his obsessive mode. "I'm not hiding in the bushes in front of all those places."

"Hey Castian," a voice calls.

They both turn their heads. It's Ori, their classmate and one of the Matre's Assistants. Cass thinks she's interested in Bastian, having overheard her describing him as "dreamy" and "cute" to her friends. It doesn't seem to matter that he's not interested in her—or in anyone for that matter.

"Hey," he says.

"Matre Selene is looking for you."

Cass's stomach drops. "Both of us?"

"Yeah. What trouble did you two get into?" Ori asks.

"Nothing."

"Then why do you look worried."

"I'm not worried."

"Uh-huh sure." Ori redirects her attention back to Bastian. "A group of us are going to the lake tomorrow. Wanna come?"

"Yeah," he says.

Cass feels her eyes growing. He never says yes to Ori. The girl looks just as surprised.

"Great!" she says in a high-pitched voice. "We're leaving after breakfast."

"Okay. We'll see you tomorrow," Bastian says.

Ori returns to her group of friends who look eager to hear whether she'd succeeded.

"Are you done yet?" He takes Cass's bowl, not waiting for an answer. "Let's go see Matre Selene."

Cass drinks the last of her juice and follows him. He deposits his plate, her bowl, and their drinking glasses on a rolling pushcart and exits the Food Hall.

"Why did you say yes to Ori?" Cass asks as soon as they are out of earshot.

"Because I want to go to the lake."

"For what?"

"Foraging."

"What?"

"We need to learn to forage."

"I think this is from the lack of sleep." She yawns, this time a drawn out one. "Let's not go out tonight."

"No! We have to go tonight. She's still here."

"How do you know?"

"Matre Selene would not ask us to see her unless the woman is still here."

"And what logic are you using?"

"She knows we haven't said anything to anyone."

"How does she know that?"

"Because I haven't said anything, and I know you haven't said anything."

"We know that, but how would *she* know?"

"A Matre always knows."

Cass would argue, but he is right. All Matres seem to have a sixth sense when it comes to the students. "But what does that have to do with the Outsider still being here?"

"There are two reasons she'd summon both of us. One is if she thinks we talked, but we didn't, and she knows we didn't. So, the only reason left is to do with the Outsider."

In a weird way, his logic makes sense.

They cross the cobblestone path, passing the younger Matres tending to the flower garden. In their white dresses, they look like cabbage butterflies among the colorful blooms.

Her mind returns to her strange dreams of the glowing woman. Her nightly visitor seemed to be content with hopping from one random conversation to another, mostly about life at the CDL. Cass heard dreams are a way for the mind to process things. Are these dreams her brain telling herself she will miss life here? She turns to her best friend and feels the loss that has yet to happen.

"Don't be nervous," Bastian says. "It's just Matre Selene. She's nice. It could have been the Head Matre."

"I'm fine."

Finally they arrive at the Administrative building. Matres weave around them, bustling from one office to another. Cass and Bastian head down the hallway to Matre Selene's. Her door is open this time.

"Hi Matre," Cass greets. "Ori said you wanted to see us?"

Matre Selene looks up. Her skin and lips are pale and her eyes glassy. She should be in bed instead of working.

"Come in, and please close the door behind you."

They do as asked and sit on the chairs in front of her desk.

The Matre leans forward and closes her eyes, looking as though she is about to throw up.

She swallows and opens her eyes. "I have a favor to ask. It's regarding the woman you discovered in the bush. Her name is Aris."

Cass and Bastian turn to each other, the look on his face mirroring the surprise in hers.

"Since you already know of her existence, you two are the only ones I'm able to ask this of. But know that you do not have to agree to this."

"Where is she from?" Bastian asks.

"The Four Cities. She's here because she got lost."

He deflates. Cass knows he's been hoping she came from the north.

"She needs to return home," Matre Selene continues. "In order for her to do so safely, we will need the train. But the train is controlled by the police, and we can't let them know she's here."

"How come?" Cass says.

"She will be arrested, and I don't want that to happen."

"So how did she get here?"

"She walked the tunnel."

The tunnel? That was how the glowing woman from her dream came too.

"What do you need us to do?" Bastian asks.

"The train can be summoned if a child has a medical emergency."

"You want us to be those children?" Cass asks.

The Matre nods. "I know it's a lot to ask, and like I said, you can say no."

"I'll do it," Bastian says.

Cass jerks her head to him.

"But *you* don't have to if you don't want to," he says to her.

They have always done everything together.

"Can we talk about this first?"

"We can, but I've already made my decision."

"But how are you going to fake a medical emergency?" Cass asks.

They both turn to Matre Selene.

"We're still figuring it out," the Matre says. "It has to be something we can't easily fix here but nothing life-threatening."

She doesn't even know yet? They must still be putting all the pieces together. How desperate must they be to involve two children?

"Would a broken arm work?" Bastian asks.

Cass's jaw drops. "What? No!"

"What about food poisoning?" he says. "No . . . that'll go away on its own. A cut? Wait, the Health Center can do stitches for that. It has to be something that needs what we don't have here."

"You're too eager for this," the Matre says, worry on her face. "Let me and Matre Galena figure it out. Meanwhile, do not tell anyone."

"We won't. We promise," Bastian says.

"Thank you." Matre Selene pushes herself up from her chair. Then she tilts. By the time Cass realizes what is happening, the Matre has collapsed on the floor.

Bastian is on her side at once, shaking her. "Matre! Matre Selene!"

"What's wrong with her?" Cass asks.

"I don't know, but she's burning up." He looks over his shoulder to her. "Get help!"

CHAPTER TWENTY-ONE

SCYLLA

March 2, 2233
(18 days before Tabula Rasa)

The tracks sit atop an embankment overlooking a volcanic field of black rocks on one side and a forest of stunted pines on the other. The landscape appears as if from a different planet. In a way it is. Along with ending most lives, the Last War had also shifted the weather. More precipitation allows more plants to grow, and there is enough water from the snowcapped mountain range to fill streams in the spring. But it is still the high desert, and the plants—those that manage to live here—look unsure whether they can trust their existence.

A group of officers are gathering around the recently discovered footprints on the volcanic soil. Two sets. None of them are adept at examining footprints, having never had to do this before, but they are trying. No one wants to risk upsetting the Planner.

Scylla sighs. It matters less what they learn from the analysis. They already have the most important information: the owners of these footprints know about the train tracks, and they are heading north. Gordon and another officer climb up the embankment and come to stand next to him.

"Evan is the one who saw the footprints from the photographs taken by the drone," Gordon says.

Evan is one of the youngest officers. He's a recent arrival from 'the Camp,' the house and police training facility where they all grew up. He stands rod straight, and his gaze focuses on a point in the distance—the way he was trained. Scylla was this way too when he first arrived at the Four Cities fifteen years ago. Living among the citizens has smoothened his edges, but it does not affect all the officers the same way. Some of his brothers, despising their shared existence, turn more callous toward those they were meant to protect. Most tolerate them, seeing them as dull, docile beings they share the Four Cities with.

"Good job finding the footprints," Scylla commends. It is like finding a needle in a thousand-square-foot haystack. "I will mention this to the Planner."

A wide smile spreads across the young man's face. They all live to please the Planner. Quickly he returns his expression to neutral.

"Thank you, sir."

"You may return to your work."

Evan nods and climbs back to rejoin the others. Gordon steps closer to Scylla.

"This is the first time we've ever found evidence of runaways this far north. What are we going to do?" he whispers. Like Scylla, he probably ran all the probable scenarios in his mind and ended up at the worst one.

"This doesn't have to mean more than it looks—footprints in the desert. Getting to the CDL without the train is a suicide mission. The place is well hidden in the mountains and is hundreds of miles away from civilization." He points. "And to get there, you have to cross this desert."

Temperatures here can swing upward of a hundred degrees

Fahrenheit in the summer and below freezing in the winter. It is an extreme environment that ill-prepared city dwellers would struggle to survive in.

"Do you think, whoever they were, they have the Book of Crone?" Gordon asks.

"Not sure how we'll know, since she doesn't leave footprints. We'll continue to follow protocol. Set a perimeter of twenty miles from this spot and comb the area. Concentrate efforts near sources of water."

"What are you going to tell him?"

"What we've discovered so far. I don't know what he will do. All I know is he will be furious."

Gordon pales. He knows from past lead officers what happens in these meetings. Since he is currently second-in-command, he will most likely take over after Scylla.

Lead officer is both an enviable position and a terrible one. Selected by the Planner himself, the person has a lot of responsibilities and power, and direct access to him. But there is no quitting. The only way out is time—eight years.

Four more years to go. The thought saddens Scylla. Despite all the awful parts, the good—the *only* good—outweighs everything.

He looks to the north. How did the owners of the footprints even get here? The tracks are nowhere close to any intercity or intracity train stations. They cannot be seen from anywhere near the Four Cities. To get here, the people would have had to cross high mountains and dangerous deserts. This was not a random accident. Whoever they were or however they came across the information, they were determined to find these tracks.

A wave of cold runs through his body.

This could be the beginning of the end.

CHAPTER TWENTY-TWO

ARIS

March 2, 2233
(18 days before Tabula Rasa)

Something is wrong. Selene never came with lunch or to take her to meet the other potential counselors. The woman is usually like clockwork.

How sick is she?

Aris looks toward the direction of the wide mezzanine, where a hidden door leads to the elevator to the Head Matre's office. She has never gone up by herself before. Maybe she should. This seems like a good enough reason to leave the library.

What if the police are up there?

Can't be. If the police were at the CDL, someone would come down to warn her or hide her. She gathers her things from the bed and the table and puts them in her backpack just in case she needs to leave in a hurry. At least she is familiar with the library and, thanks to Selene, now knows two exits.

She settles back on the bed, backpack by her side. Time, compounded by her worry for the Matre and her fear of the unknown, comes to a standstill. She is close, so close to having what she and Metis have sacrificed everything to find. She sinks her head into her hand and screams all her frustration.

"What's going on?" the Head Matre's voice calls from the direction of the elevator.

Aris springs up. A moment later two women walk down an aisle toward her, surgical masks covering half their faces. Relief washes over her. Selene is feeling better. But why the masks?

"Was that you screaming?" the Head Matre demands.

"Sorry, I was just letting out my frustrations."

"I thought I had another emergency on my hands."

What emergency?

"This is Galena," the Head Matre says. "She manages our Health Center, and she needs to run some tests on you."

She takes a step back. "Why? What happened to Selene?"

"She's been in the Health Center all day, and her symptoms are only getting worse. Galena has been trying to help her but hasn't had much success."

"She was feeling ill this morning, saying she must have eaten something bad," Aris says.

"Now she can't keep any food down and has a fever. Galena ran all the tests we have available and still doesn't know what it is. We need to determine whether what she has comes from you."

Her heart drops to her stomach. "From me?"

"You traveled through the wilderness. You could have contracted something and passed it on to her."

That explains the surgical masks.

"Are you feeling ill too?" Aris asks. "And how about Matre Demetria? I just met her this morning but—"

"No. We're fine for now. Selene had more exposure to you."

"I'll do whatever is necessary."

"Good. You can sit at the table, and Galena will take some of your blood."

She walks to the table and sits on the chair.

Galena comes to sit across from her. "Have you ever done this before?"

"No. Not that I remember."

"Can you roll up your sleeve? I'm going to take some blood from a vein at the crook of your elbow."

"Will this hurt?"

"Just a little."

Galena wraps a rubber tie around her upper arm and wipes a small area at the bend of her elbow with a small cold cloth. Then she takes out a metal needle and presses it into her skin. It feels like a sharp pinch. She watches with fascination as red liquid pools into the glass vial. Once the Matre has three vials, she withdraws the needle and puts a bandage on the spot.

"All done."

The Head Matre places a basket on the table. "This is what Selene had packed for you. I'll see about your other meals."

"What about my meeting with the potential counselors?" Aris asks.

"You'll not meet anyone else until we've determined you're safe."

She nods.

She waits until the Head Matre and Galena leave before walking to the food basket. Among the meal is a container of soup.

Porridge for cold nights. Soup for stress at its height. Tea for heartaches.

She picks up a roll and bites into it. A tear drops onto her hand. If she is the culprit for Selene's illness, how will she live with herself?

Her resolve to stay strong falls away. The tear turns into a deluge, and she hiccup-cries into her sleeve until it turns soggy. Until now the threat of her was only theoretical. There was always an "if." *If* a student saw her. *If* the police found out. The repercussions would be severe, of course. Still, those threats live somewhere in the imaginary future she has been doing her best to avoid. But this is the present. It is now, and it is frightening.

CHAPTER TWENTY-THREE

METIS

March 2, 2233
(18 days before Tabula Rasa)

The sweet scent of lavender touches his nose. He rolls to his side toward the fragrance and feels the warm softness of skin. His eyes open to a mess of brown hair . . . a shoulder . . . the gentle curve of an arm . . . a body rising and falling with gentle breathing . . . honey skin glowing in the morning sun as it peeks through the curtains.

The familiar image stirs a need inside him, urgent and visceral. He traces a finger along her arm to her waist, gliding up and down its valley before moving forward to the hill of her breasts, eliciting a murmur.

"Awake?"

"Maybe," she says, her voice raspy from sleep.

He gathers her to his chest and breathes in, filling his lungs with her. She nuzzles against his hardness.

"And good morning to you too," he says.

She giggles.

Turning her over, he kisses down her neck to her right breast and wraps his lips around her nipple. *So warm, so soft.* He alternates between lapping and sucking. Her hands tug at his hair.

"You like that?" he asks.

"Mmm . . . don't stop."

He continues until she writhes beneath him. A moan escapes her lips, tugging at the string of his need. His hand travels to the concave of her stomach, to the warmest part of her, finding her ready. He rolls atop her, turning her onto her stomach. He kisses down the nape of her neck. She reaches behind and the tips of her fingers touch his hardness, and his entire body feels like live wire. Her hand wraps around him and guides him into her—every movement, a natural extension of the last.

They groan in unison. He pulls her toward him and thrusts deeper.

"You feel so good," he hears himself say.

She moans back in reply and sinks onto the mattress. Her face is turned to the side, her smiling lips tempting. He needs to kiss those lips. He pulls out and turns her over—an image of tangled brown hair and golden honey goddess. Their lips meet. He dives in, exploring the heat of her mouth with his tongue. He reenters her, and their bodies ebb and flow to a rhythm that takes him to a place he cannot name.

"I love you," she whispers.

His entire being expands to envelop the enormity of those words. His heart feels as though it is growing out of his chest and living outside of him in the form of this woman. He wipes her long hair off her face.

"I love you so mu—"

Icy blue eyes stare up at him. Have her eyes always been so blue? He pulls back, but her hand reaches behind his neck and draws him toward her. She crushes her lips against his, and all his thoughts float away.

CHAPTER TWENTY-FOUR

SCYLLA

March 2, 2233
(18 days before Tabula Rasa)

The two chairs are still there, as are the two people. Their eyes are closed, copper helmets on their heads. What is Apollina seeing inside Metis's mind?

For as long as he's known of her, she has been a constant figure in the Interpreter Center—as much a part of it as the Dreamcatcher. Like the policemen and the Matres, she keeps all her memories every cycle. But unlike them, she is alone. No brothers, no sisters, no connection with the citizens outside of the work she does as Interpreter. Her existence makes his seem like a reward. He wonders why she deserves such punishment.

He walks to the large screen and places a hand on the wall. The screen blinks, and the Planner—their Creator—appears.

"Scylla," he says.

"Hello, sir. I have an update."

"Go ahead."

"Evan, one of our officers, found footprints near the train tracks by the volcanic field up north. We are now sweeping the immediate area."

The lines on the Planner's face deepen and his jaw tightens.

"Why— It's all desert. There's nothing out there but . . ." His voice trails to an oppressive silence.

Scylla braces himself.

"They must have known. Eleanor must be involved!" the Planner yells, his booming voice rattles.

His eyes flit left to right.

"There's only one reason anyone would travel that far north. But how did she find out?" he mumbles to himself. "I never told her where it is."

He turns his flinty gaze back to Scylla. "I'm sending you back to the CDL. Find out what they know and if the Matres are hiding something . . . or someone."

"I will call them and let them know."

"No. Go now and don't let them know you're coming. Catch them off guard in case they're helping Eleanor."

The Head Matre will not take kindly to this surprise disruption. This trip is outside Scylla's regular, scheduled visits, and they are already on shaky ground with the CDL after what the Planner did to the graduating seniors.

"If I leave now, I'll get there in the middle of the night," Scylla says. "This will be taken as disrespectful, and the Head Matre will send me right back. If I wait until morning, I can get there with daylight left. It'll be easier to conduct an inspection when I can see."

"Are you more concerned about your standing with the Head Matre or with me?"

"My loyalty is to you and the Four Cities, of course."

The Planner looks off-screen, most likely recalling all the times Head Matre Hera had sent other lead officers back on the train without allowing them to perform wellness checks. At least Scylla has never been sent back before.

He turns back. "Fine. Since the Head Matre seems *fond* of you, we'll do it your way. But do not give her a warning."

"Yes, sir."

"And bring Evan with you."

"But he's brand new." Twenty, barely out of his teenage years, and with no experience.

"He proved himself to be useful. He saw what the rest of you missed. Maybe he'll spot something else there. Besides, the more senior officers are still on their assignments."

"But that means he'd need clearance to the library and the lab." Only the current and past lead officers have that access.

"Then give him clearance!" the Planner says brusquely.

This is a break in protocol. The Planner must be desperate to find the Crone.

"Yes, sir," Scylla says.

"Report to me anything out of place."

"Yes, sir."

The Planner looks to the two figures on the chair. "Apollina is taking too much time with Metis. We're going to need a different strategy."

Scylla turns to the dark-haired man in slumber or whatever state of unconsciousness the Interpreter put him under. This is not the first time the pianist has been in the hands of this woman.

The Crone materialized from her book. She did not always appear, not for his brothers. Since they were all created in the Planner's likeness, they reminded her of him—all the good, all the bad, and everything in between. But she always appeared for Scylla.

He had always looked forward to their interactions. Most of the time, they would talk of the Old World—music, art, books, the places she'd been and the people she had known. Sometimes the talk would turn philosophical, and they would exchange ideas on the future of the Four Cities. Though they did not always agree, she seemed to enjoy talking with him just as much as he did with her. He regretted today was not going to be one of those visits.

"I need your help," Scylla said.

Her eyebrows folded together. "Why?"

"We found Metis and Aris."

"What does that have to do with me?" she asked.

Her face was a neutral mask, but he knew she must be hiding her true feelings. Metis was no ordinary man to her.

"Apollina has him at the Interpreter Center. You know what she's been doing to Dreamers."

"You mean forcibly erasing their dreams, which has led some of them to kill themselves?"

He swallowed. "Yes. The Planner believes you sent Metis and Aris to the cave, and now he thinks they know too much. He authorized the use of Dreamcatcher on them today."

"Why don't you tell your *Planner* its side effect?"

"I can't prove the deaths were caused by Apollina and her machine. He won't listen to me without proof."

"You think I should care about this, why?" the Crone asked.

His heart dropped. "You don't care about Metis?"

She studied him with her keen eyes. "The real question is, Why do you?"

Heat flooded his cheeks.

"If you're not going to answer me, I see no point in continuing this conversation." Eleanor moved to return to her book.

"Music," he blurted.

"What about it?"

"Have you heard Metis play the piano?"

"I regret to say I haven't."

"His music is beautiful. Extraordinary, really. I worry..."

A look of understanding crossed her face. "You think Dreamcatcher might take his music?"

"Yes."

She looked at him with bemusement. "You're less like him than you are like Viv."

"Who?"

"Eli's mother. She was a kind soul."

Metis will always end up here as long as there is Tabula Rasa. His music, the thing the Planner cultivated, both saves him and traps him in this repeat pattern. It coexists alongside Absinthe, the Crone, and his love for Aris—the making of the perfect storm. But there will be a day when the Planner will lose his patience, Scylla knows. That day he will decide a pianist, remarkable though he may be, is not worth trading peace for.

A field of dead bodies in white, paired up like doves. Glasses drained of poison littering the floor. A ghost of a smile on Seraphina. Benja, face ashen, lifeless on his bed. Mila and Willow, lying side by side on the sandy ground, hands clutching. Cole, a broken bone protruding from his neck, hope gone from his eyes. Milo. Ellen. Penny, Rin, Cinta...

All the names forever etched in his mind.

"I also have an update on the runaw—" The Planner hates that word. To him, the idea of running away from the utopia he painstakingly created is ludicrous. "—the missing. We now have all the drones concentrated around the desert surrounding Elara."

"As long as it's not taking away from the search for Eleanor."

"No, we're doing both," Scylla says. "And Gia, the one we found in the desert near Elara, woke up this morning."

"How are her vital signs?" the Planner asks.

"Strong, considering what she's been through."

"What information did you get out of her?"

"She's still too weak for TBT128."

The truth serum and Subdue Bracelet—a police tool used to handle unruly citizens—make for a powerful combination that acts to relax the subject, ease their anxiety, and loosen their consciousness and tongue. But the effects can be unpredictable. Metis, instead of confessing, had continuously hummed the third movement of Beethoven's *Moonlight* Sonata and almost passed out. That was why Apollina had to be brought in.

Had they had Aris, Metis would have confessed without the drug. *Like the last time.*

"We need to know what she knows. Why she left. Who's involved," the Planner says.

"Of course, as soon as she becomes stronger. Right now we're dealing with her refusal to eat."

The Planner's raises a brow. "I thought she was starving."

"She is severely malnourished."

"So why is she not eating?"

"She went into hysterics after she remembered Cole, her lover, had died."

"If she's still not eating by tomorrow, order the medical droid to force her. We just have to buy eighteen more days. Once she goes through Tabula Rasa, she will be fine."

"I will check on her once more before I leave for the CDL."

"You may leave."

Scylla exits the room and sends a generic message from his watch to Evan to clear tomorrow's schedule. If the Planner doesn't want the CDL to know they are coming, he cannot risk word spreading among the ranks.

7:27 p.m.

He's starving but needs to get to Gia before she falls asleep for the night. He walks to the intracity train station. Three stops, and he arrives at the main hospital.

Located on Fifth Avenue next to Central Park, the forty-story building is a behemoth of glass and steel. A prominent sign—HOSPITAL—sits on its facade. This is also where the citizens of Callisto report before Tabula Rasa.

Scylla enters through the sliding door and takes the elevator up to the highest floor—the restricted area. Here is where they keep all the patients who need to be watched twenty-four seven. Those who had become mentally unstable after Tabula Rasa. The ones who lost function of their body. The survivors they found in the desert. They will be reassessed after the next Tabula Rasa, and those fit enough to rejoin society will be released. It's like a big reset button for humans.

Eighteen more days.

He exits the elevator and finds Gia's room. Nobody here questions him—not the medical droids, not the patients wandering the hall, not even the volunteers who come here to keep the patients company. All policemen get full access to anywhere in the Four Cities.

The door to Gia's room is open. She is lying on the bed, but she is not asleep. Nobody is in here, but the camera in the corner is watching to make sure she is safe. He knocks on the door, and she turns to him. The white in her eyes is bloodshot.

"Hello, Gia. I'm Officer Scylla, the lead officer of the Four Cities."

"We met before." She looks back up at the ceiling.

"Yes."

"Are you here to talk me into eating? I already told the others I'm not hungry."

"I'd hoped you'd consider changing your mind. We need you stronger."

"Why? There's no point."

He walks to her bedside. "There's always a point."

"If you'd ever been in love, you would understand," she says.

"Wouldn't Cole want you to stay alive?"

Her face crumples. "I thought so. That's why I kept going. But now I can't see the future." Tears run down her brown cheeks and disappear into her curly hair. "There's too much pain. He wouldn't want me to suffer this much pain."

"Tabula Rasa is eighteen days away. Just hang on until then. Your pain will be gone, and you can start over."

She shakes her head, eyes brimming with tears. "That's the misconception. The pain, like the love, doesn't disappear. The only thing we forget is the reason. And that's a thousand times worse."

CHAPTER TWENTY-FIVE

ARIS

March 2, 2233
(18 days before Tabula Rasa)

All day, Aris has been imagining the possible diseases she may have contracted in the desert and given to Selene. *Valley fever.* No, that's from fungus. *Lyme disease.* That's transmitted by ticks. *Pneumonia.* But she hasn't been coughing. What if whatever she had given Selene had spread across the entire campus and everyone up there is either dead or dying? A scene from a nightmare.

Maybe she is stuck inside a nightmare that never ends. Every time she takes a step forward, something happens to pull her back. With each passing day, her hope of seeing Metis dwindles. Loneliness drags her down into its dark pool, and she struggles against it.

She distracts herself by searching through the library for the book that could be hers. Based on her estimated age, within a space of ten years, there are 2,500 books. Too many to make her feel any better. She decides to busy herself by cleaning. She straightens up her living area, makes her bed, and wipes down the table. Then she begins dusting the bookshelves. She is Cinderella in the bowels of the CDL.

Just as she is about to get ready for bed, the Crone appears.

"Where have you been?" Aris asks, trying not to feel forgotten by her traveling companion.

"Around. This place is quite big. Have you seen the children's dorms? It's a wondrous place full of old artwork."

"I haven't. I'm not allowed near the students." The flood of tears restarts.

"Are you okay?" the Crone asks, worry on her face.

"No! I'm so far away from okay I don't even know how to get back. Selene is sick and it may be my fault. I'm running out of time to return to Metis," she says in between sobs. "I'm not even allowed to see any more counselors and I can't bring twenty-five hundred books with me."

The Crone places a hand on her shoulder. It feels like light, like nothing. "One thing at a time. What's wrong with Selene?"

"Yesterday she complained of nausea and said she didn't sleep the night before. Now she's running a fever and can't eat. Matre Galena at the Health Center ran tests but still can't find what's wrong. She thinks Selene may have contracted something from me, so she took my blood for testing too. But there's been no word for hours, and I have no idea what's going on up there."

"I can go check on her to see how she's doing," the Crone says.

"Would you?" She wipes her eyes.

"And is their thinking you might be contagious the reason they're not letting you see more counselors?"

"Yes."

"Well, all we can do about that is wait to see the blood test results. They will determine the next step."

Aris sniffs.

"You are doing everything within your control right now to get back to Metis," the Crone adds. "And that's all you can do. Your best."

Something clicks inside her. Maybe it's the cadence of the

Crone's words. Maybe it's the calm expression on her translucent face. Maybe it's being in this very room, at this very moment.

Faces do change over time—some more significantly than others.

"These Matres . . . they're you!"

"Not exactly me, but my DNA."

"When did you know?"

"The first time I saw them. I do know my own face."

"Why didn't you tell me?"

"Would it have changed anything? It's my burden, not yours."

The fire of anger burns inside her stomach. "Your husband did this? He not only enslaved you inside a book, he made replicas of you and imprisoned them here? This is wrong!"

"Right and wrong do not matter in the face of necessity."

Shock rings through her. "You're excusing him?"

"I'm merely stating a truth."

"How are you able to forgive him after what he did—what he's continuing to do?"

"Why would you think I've forgiven him?" the Crone asks.

"The way you talk of him . . . You admire him. You understand his flaws."

"To defeat the System, you have to defeat Eli. And to defeat Eli, you must first understand him. To begin to understand him, you have to see all of his bad next to all of his good. He believes what he's doing will save humanity."

"But it isn't fair!"

"Would you think it's fair if you knew he does it to himself too?"

"What do you mean?"

"He, too, is a consciousness without body. But instead of a book, he's inside the System."

"But the Matres—they're his slaves."

"So are the police officers."

Aris recalls the identical men with dark hair and eyes. Her stomach clenches. "They're his clones?"

"Yes."

Aris feels as if she is treading water in the middle of the ocean, no shores in sight. "Is there no hope?"

The Crone glides around the black-and-white mosaic floor, reading the words embedded in its border. "There's always hope. That's why we're here."

She looks up and smiles. "Now, go to sleep. I will visit Selene and let you know how she's doing."

CHAPTER TWENTY-SIX

CASS

March 3, 2233
(17 days before Tabula Rasa)

The glowing woman from her dreams did not visit last night. Maybe because Cass barely slept. Yesterday, after Matre Selene collapsed and Cass shouted for help, the usually tranquil Administrative building turned into a scene of chaos. All the Matres in the vicinity came into the tiny office and tried to help, but nobody knew what to do. Matres—like students—rarely get sick. Once the Head Matre arrived, she quickly ordered them to move Matre Selene to the Health Center and to say nothing to anyone.

A knock comes at the door. It's Bastian. He's here to take her to breakfast as usual.

"Hey." He sits on her bed. The skin under his eyes is pale purple. He didn't get much sleep either.

"You look awful," she says.

"Ditto."

"Do you think Matre Selene is okay?"

"She'll be okay," he says.

"What do you think is wrong with her?"

"I don't know. I've never known the younger Matres to get

sick." He looks at his palms. "Do you think it's because of the Outsider?"

"What makes you think that?" she asks.

"Remember when the Europeans came over to the Americas and brought with them diseases that killed a lot of Indigenous people?"

"If it's that, we were both exposed. All the Matres in the Administrative building too, including the Head Matre. Is that what you've been thinking about?"

"Do you feel sick?" he asks.

"No, I'm fine."

"Me too."

"Well, if we go down, we'll all go down together," she says.

"There's that."

"Hey, Castian!"

Ori is standing at the door. She holds up two bags in her hands, her face beaming.

"Your breakfasts and lunches—I asked the Kitchen Matres to pack them for us, so if we leave now, we can get to the lake before noon—this is so exciting!" she says without a pause.

Cass and Bastian exchange a glance. They had completely forgotten about the excursion to the lake. In his eyes, she reads, *Might as well.*

He gets up from her bed and grabs the bags from her. "Thanks."

"Where's your backpack?" Ori asks.

"Mine is in my room," he says.

"I'll go with you." She must really be worried Bastian would change his mind.

"Actually, we'll meet you down there," he says. "I'm still helping Cass with something. We'll be quick."

She pauses then shrugs. "Alright. I'll be in the courtyard waiting with everyone."

"How do I keep getting roped into things?" Cass says after Ori is out of earshot.

"It might be fun," Bastian says in his typical optimistic way, though Cass is not convinced. "Besides, this will be our first time going to the lake without Matres as chaperones."

It is one of the privileges of being a senior.

He stands up. "And it'll keep our minds off things."

Just as he is about to leave, he turns back. "Don't forget the plant book."

"You're still on that?"

"Foraging is a good skill," he says. "I'll see you down there."

She grabs a backpack from her closet and throws in a jacket and a water bottle, together with the food Ori had given her. The plant book she had borrowed from the library sits on her desk. She picks it up and studies its red cover. *Edible and Useful Plants of California.* Is she being a supportive friend or an enabler? Does she even know the difference anymore? She shoves the book into her pack.

Ori is waiting in the courtyard at the bottom of the spiral staircase with her best friend, Naya, and two other boys from their class, Hilden and Celo.

"Let's go!" Ori says eagerly.

The dawn sky promises a clear day. The air is a pleasant temperature. *Good weather for a hike*, Cass thinks begrudgingly. They walk past the Gate of the Six Bells, following a trail into the forest. Once they reach a fork where it splits into three, they take the rightmost path. It runs along a narrow ridge that drops straight down on both sides—accessible only in fair-weather months. She keeps her eyes straight, afraid she'll lose her bearing if she looks down the deep gorge. This section of the hike is the reason only seniors are able to go without chaperones.

Once the path opens, the landscape again becomes a forest

of pine backdropped by the jagged sierras. Cass breathes in the cool air and the majestic scene. Around her, laughter and chatting ensue.

"I heard a senior said three years back that they saw a huge animal footprint in the woods—they said was a bear print," Celo says.

"How would they know?" Naya asks.

"I don't know, but they said it was broad with big toes."

"A lot of extinct animals had broad feet with big toes," Cass says.

"We should keep our eyes open, just in case," Ori says, and glances left to right.

As if everyone had made an unspoken pact, they continue to only talk of small and light things. There is no mention of Tabula Rasa, the police, or the Four Cities—as if not doing so means they do not exist. It's play pretend. Like reliving their younger days, before they knew anything about memory erasure. But she knows now and that knowledge changes everything.

"Look! A blue mountain jay!" Hilden says.

Cass follows his pointing arm to see an iridescent blue bird with a triangular black crest standing on a pine branch.

"I wonder what it was called in the Old World," Ori says.

"Steller's jay," Cass says. It's one of her favorites. She likes its color. Blue like the sky. Like freedom.

"How do you know that?"

"I saw it in a book."

"Cass reads everything," Bastian says.

The blue jay flies off toward the north and Cass wants to follow it. But she doesn't have wings.

CHAPTER TWENTY-SEVEN

SCYLLA

March 3, 2233
(17 days before Tabula Rasa)

Last night Scylla slept fitfully, his mind running through different scenarios he could encounter at the CDL. An angry Head Matre ranks high in probability. A few weeks ahead of his next regular visit, this will be a complete surprise. The lack of advanced warning will cause her already simmering anger to boil over, especially after what he had to do the last time he was there.

He sighs. How is he going to tell her he needs to search the CDL for the Book of Crone without her thinking the Planner suspects her of hiding, and possibly conspiring with, his wife? Scylla will have to convince her that, among all the police officers, he is still the best one, from her perspective, to lead this investigation.

He enters Police Station One and makes his way to the storage room. In it, he finds new clothes still in their packaging and throws them into his duffel bag. With the long working hours, he hasn't had time to do laundry. He notices the Subdue Bracelets in his bag and removes them. They are not allowed at the CDL. He's not sure whether it was the Planner or a Head Matre who put that rule in place.

He takes the elevator up to the dorm floor. Police Station One is still asleep. He's glad he no longer has to stay here. Having his own room at an assigned police station, despite it being not much bigger than a cell, is infinitely better than having to share space with his younger brothers. Fresh off the "Camp," they are not the easiest bunch to live with.

He knocks on Evan's door.

"What?" a sleepy voice says from the other side.

"It's Scylla." He hears scrambling, and a moment later the door opens to reveal Evan's surprised face—identical to his own but for its youth.

"Good morning, sir," he says. "What can I do for you?"

Scylla walks into the room and closes the door. "I need you to pack now, enough for four days. We're going to the CDL."

Evan steps back. "What?"

"The Planner wants us to look around the place."

"He thinks the Book of Crone is there?"

"It's just a precaution."

"And he wants me on this case?" he asks, awe written all over his face.

"Yes."

Evan grabs a bag from the closet and begins shoving things into it. "This is incredible. I'm so honored the Planner entrusted me with this assignment. I won't let him down."

Fifteen years younger than Scylla, Evan still worships the Planner and believes in everything taught to him at the Camp. He hasn't lived long enough to know that dissatisfaction is their beloved creator's constant state and that the knowledge acquired from the Camp will not prepare him to understand the true complexity of life.

"You did good discovering those footprints," Scylla says.

"Thank you, sir."

They take the elevator down to the first floor. Scylla can feel Evan's nervous energy bouncing inside the small metal box, making his own worse.

"Go to the kitchen and get us some food for the ride," he says. "I'm going to let the Planner know we're leaving, and I'll meet you at the train station to the CDL."

Evan nods, and they split up once the elevator door opens. Scylla makes his way to the small room and is about to enter when he hears shouting coming from the other side.

"We don't have time for you to dawdle inside his mind! The predictive model projects the longer Eleanor is missing, the higher the probability of a total System collapse. I need you to work faster."

"I'm going as fast as I can," Apollina says. "Using Metis's lover in a simulation is risky. Because of their close relationship, it's easier for him to catch on. If I don't set up the simulation correctly, I could lose the entire thing and we'll be back at square one."

"Do not talk to me as if I don't know how this works. You have plenty of information from their bracelets and probability models to go off of."

"They both took off their bracelets early on in the cycle, and I've had to reconstruct their lives based just on the clues they left in their house."

"Work faster!"

"I have been working day and night! You're being unreasonable."

"I have been more than reasonable. You've yet to give me anything concrete. Not where Eleanor is. Not how Metis learned where the CDL is located. Not what he planned with her. Nothing! If you can't do this . . ."

"No, I can do it." *Is that panic he hears in the Interpreter's voice*, Scylla wonders.

"Then do it! It's not that difficult. I only need him to believe the simulation until I have the information I need."

"You don't care if it'll traumatize him after?"

"I've never known you to care about your subjects, Apollina," the Planner says.

"I don't. I just don't want to get in trouble for doing something you don't like. Again."

"Tabula Rasa is seventeen days away. He'll be reset and won't remember any of this. So the next time you go inside his brain, get me something or I'm going to find a different strategy."

This is only going to make the Interpreter more desperate, Scylla thinks. And a desperate Apollina is a dangerous Apollina.

A long minute of silence follows. Scylla decides their conversation is over. He knocks.

"Come in," the Planner says.

He opens the door to see Apollina standing in front of Metis, adjusting the helmet on his head. The larger-than-life Planner looks on from the screen behind them. With his eyes closed and his face pale, the pianist looks so vulnerable.

When Apollina sees Scylla, she scowls. Since their altercation last cycle that led to him outing her unauthorized use of Dreamcatcher, the Interpreter has been treating him with open hostility.

"What are you doing here?" she asks, loathing in her voice.

Scylla looks past her and addresses the Planner, "I just wanted to let you know Evan and I are about to leave for the CDL."

"If Hera pushes back, let her know I'm prepared to send reinforcements."

His stomach drops. The relationship between the Head Matre and the Planner has been contentious since she took office eight years ago, and their conflict has escalated over time. As much as the Planner does not want to accept it, the Head Matre holds more power over the CDL—and the future—than he does. This threat is only going to make things worse.

CHAPTER TWENTY-EIGHT

ARIS

March 3, 2233
(17 days before Tabula Rasa)

She stares into the dark subterranean passage leading to the Grand Hall. This is the fastest way out of the library and to the train tunnel. The Crone has not returned from checking on Selene. It must be really bad out there. Plague-level bad.

"Aris? Where are you?" the Head Matre's voice calls.

She rushes back to the black-and-white mosaic area. Head Matre Hera is standing by the table, her face no longer covered by a surgical mask.

"Your tests came back clean."

Relief floods through her. *It's not me.*

"I know breakfast is late, but I couldn't come earlier," the Head Matre adds, her voice gentler, but only slightly. "There should be enough here to keep you full a while."

"It's okay. How's Selene?"

The worry lines between her eyebrows deepen. "Worse than before."

"Can I visit her?"

"No, you can't go out during the day."

"What about at night after everyone is asleep?"

"I can't let you wander around here alone."

"Can you at least tell me what's wrong with her?"

"I would if I knew."

"If you can't help her here, why don't you send her to the hospital in Callisto?"

The Matre shakes her head. "If there's one rule we can never break, it's never leaving the CDL."

"Not even when you're sick? I thought the kids can."

"The children are assets to the System."

Aris cannot believe her ears. "As are all the Matres!"

Her face tightens. "We're not a part of the System."

"But what if she dies?"

"I'm well aware!" Hera yells.

They both glare at each other, silence sharp as stinging nettles.

The Matre sighs impatiently. "I have other matters to attend to. I'll see you next meal."

"Wait. Am I not being assigned a new Matre?" Aris asks.

"No. I don't want to involve more people than necessary."

"And the two other potential counselors? When can I meet them?"

"Soon. I'll arrange it. I haven't had time, as you can imagine."

Aris feels the fire of resentment inside her chest growing, traveling up to her cheeks.

"Look, I know you're frustrated. I'm frustrated," the Head Matre says brusquely. "I know you need your memory book before you can leave, and no one is more invested in seeing you leave than me. You'll just have to be patient. Can you do that?"

Aris knows the Head Matre does not want her here, but to hear it expressed so clearly feels like a punch in the stomach.

"Of course." The words taste bitter on her tongue.

"I really need to go," the Head Matre says, and walks off.

"Thank y—" Aris says to her back.

She sighs. Again she is back to being stuck waiting in the library, forgotten by the world. A delicious scent from the basket draws her attention, reminding her she is starving. She opens it to find three blueberry muffins, a canister of oatmeal with dried fruits, and some fresh berries. There is even a thermos of coffee. These are better than the usual cereal and rolls Selene had given her for breakfast. Aris wonders why the Head Matre would ask the kitchen to make special food if she doesn't want anyone else to know about her being here.

She wouldn't.

A realization dawns. Despite being the Head Matre, she doesn't have the same access to the kitchen as Selene. Her presence there would cause a stir. So this must be her own breakfast.

Head Matre Hera is really a kind person, Selene's voice reminds. Gratitude and guilt clutch her.

There is nothing she can do now but be patient. She thinks back to Matre Demetria's advice to find peace in every moment, no matter how small. She breathes in the muffin and sinks her teeth into it. Juicy blueberries pop in her mouth. She washes it down with the coffee she hasn't had since she left Lysithea. With stomach full, her mood improves significantly.

"Aris!" The Crone appears out of nowhere, startling her out of her skin.

"You scared me!"

"We need to speak to the Head Matre right now," the Crone says.

"What? Did you see Selene?"

"Yes, I watched her all night, and this morning I was able to sneak a look at the test results Matre Galena left on the table. I know what's wrong with Selene."

Aris's heart drops. "What is it?"

"I'll explain everything. Hurry, we don't have much time. If we don't fix this, she will die."

Aris runs as fast as she can to the elevator, the Crone beside her. She pushes the button for the Head Matre's office. A moment later the elevator door opens, and she leaps out and pounds against the panel.

"I asked you to be patient!" The panel pushes in, revealing the Head Matre's furious face.

Aris stares at her, not knowing what to say. She hadn't thought that far.

Hera's eyes fall on the glowing figure and blood leaches from her face. "W-what? Who—"

"I'm Eleanor, some call me the Crone. I'm from before the Last War and a creator of the Four Cities."

"But—"

"The Planner is my husband and he's not really into telling people about me. Especially not those he created using my DNA without my knowledge."

The Head Matre's eyes widen.

"We need to talk." The Crone slips through the door, grazing against Hera, who jumps back.

"Wait, what are you doing here?"

"To give people choice."

"What people? We're fine at the CDL."

"You're not."

Hera blinks, returning to herself. "What are you talking about?"

When the Crone does not answer, she whips to Aris. "Did you bring her here?"

"Yes," Aris says. There's no point in lying.

"You're working together to overthrow the System." Anger lights up Hera's eyes. She advances her tall frame towards Aris.

"You've kept this important information from us all this time after we've been more than helpful to you. How dare you!"

The Crone comes to stand between them. "Don't blame Aris. It was my decision not to tell you."

"You both need to leave right now. Take your things and go!"

Aris's heart drops to her stomach. "But I don't have my memory book yet."

"I don't care! I shouldn't have let you stay so long. Do you know what will happen if both of you are found here? You've put all of us in great peril."

"We're not going," the Crone says.

"Excuse me?"

Aris wonders if anyone has ever defied Head Matre Hera before.

"There will be time to be angry, but it isn't now," the Crone adds.

She leans in and Hera winces but does not step back this time. "There've been several changes lately, seemingly out of nowhere. Am I right?"

The Head Matre stills. "How do you know?"

"Eli doesn't usually make changes. Not lightly. Not without empirical data. It means things aren't usual in the Four Cities. But that's another conversation. What's more important right now is Selene. She will die if I don't help her."

Hera's hand comes to her chest. "You know what's wrong with her?"

"Yes." The Crone's form brightens.

"She's pregnant."

CHAPTER TWENTY-NINE

METIS

March 3, 2233
(17 days before Tabula Rasa)

The Crone's glowing figure stands surrounded by a field of light green hypnos flowers on tall tapering spikes. She appears to be twirling, hands grazing over their tips like dragonflies skimming over water. A full moon—rounder and brighter than he had ever seen—hangs low in the sky.

Her lips are moving, but he cannot hear what she is saying. He walks closer and realizes she is not talking but singing, so softly he can barely hear it.

> "On the edge of a cliff,
> hidden by jagged peaks
> and a northern forest of pine,
> lives Old Mem.
> Her face,
> empty of lines,
> holds secret lives within.
> Her soul,
> stolen in slumber—"

She notices him and stops.

"What's the song?" Metis asks. "I've never heard it before."

"It's a poem."

"What is it about?"

"Old Mem."

"Who's that?"

"Someone who lives faraway. Far, far away from the Four Cities."

He is used to her cryptic ways. She never gives anything easily to him, not even how to make Absinthe. Everything is a maze to get through and a puzzle to solve.

"What does Old Mem do?" he asks.

"She keeps memories safe."

"Like you?"

"No. I do not keep memories. I merely exist to remind." She moves to pluck a bell-shaped flower from the stalk, but her hand comes up empty. She is no more solid than light itself. "You know it took me decades to perfect Absinthe? I almost gave up many times."

"I'm glad you didn't. We would never have known dreams are memories."

"You know why I never quit?"

"Why?"

"Words."

"Words?"

"They came from a college professor. She said, 'Eleanor, tenacity is the thing that separates failure and success.' Every time I felt like quitting, I thought of that. It's also the quality I look for in my Sandmen."

Suddenly her face is an inch from his. How did she move so fast?

"So why are you quitting, Metis?"

He steps back. "But I'm not quitting. I'm still Sandman."

"Your fire, the one burning inside your chest," She places her translucent hand on it. "It's dying."

"What do you mean?"

"Our purpose is more than what we do. It's the one thing our soul calls to. The answer to life. What does your soul call to, Metis?"

"Aris," he says automatically. It is the name, the word, constantly perched on the tip of his tongue—

"Then fight for her."

He opens his eyes and immediately turns to his left. Aris is lying next to him, asleep. He sits up and takes account of his surroundings. Under him is a bed—their bed. Across from him is a painting of two oak trees standing next to each other in the middle of the desert. He and Aris are in their bedroom inside their house in Lysithea. Everything is just as it should be.

Cold wind blows in, fluttering the curtains. Aris must have left the window open before bed last night. He looks out it. The indigo sky warns morning is still hours away. Wide awake, he quietly eases himself off the bed. He is being careful not to disturb her; she wakes at the slightest of sound. Aris does not stir.

He gently closes the bedroom door behind him before tiptoeing downstairs. The house creaks with each step, the way old houses do. In the kitchen, he makes himself a cup of tea. Earl Grey, as usual. He breathes in the scent, chasing away the disquieting dream. He can't quite remember what it was, making it all the more unsettling. He always remembers his dreams.

In the solarium, he picks out the piano's shiny body from the shadows and walks toward it. He turns on the lamp next to it, revealing a half-written sheet of music on the stand. He has been composing a new song for Aris, something for her to remember their time in this house. Something to draw her back in.

He sits on the bench and plays what's on the page. As his fingers trail along the keys, he realizes something is missing—what it is he isn't sure. He plays it again, and again he feels that same lack. He stops and studies the notes. They appear exactly as he had written them, but why do they not make the melody he remembers?

A rustling sound comes from behind him. He looks over his shoulder and catches movement in the garden.

What's that?

He gets up from the bench and peers through the glass door. It's too dark to make out anything. His left palm feels cold all of a sudden. He looks down and sees it holding the door handle, about to turn it. How did it get there? He yanks his hand back and grips it with another against his chest.

"What are you doing up?"—a question followed by the warm softness of skin pressing against his back. Two arms wrap around his chest.

"Did I wake you? I'm sorry," he says.

"It was lonely in bed without you."

He reaches behind him and finds only bare skin. "I couldn't sleep."

"Why are you at the door?"

"I thought I saw something in the backyard."

"What was it?"

"I don't know. It was just a quick movement. A streak of light."

"Is it the Crone?" she asks.

He stares out. "It can't be her."

"Why not?"

He opens his mouth to answer, but the reason, like the dream, is out of reach.

"Why not, Metis?" she repeats.

"I don't know."

"How can you not know? Aren't you her Sandman?"

"I—" *Why is Aris being like this?*

"Where is she?"

A wave of cold rushes through, and the hair on his arms stands up. The arms around his chest tighten, pressing out air. He tries to move but cannot. The back of his neck prickles.

"What are you doing?" He struggles. The vice-like grip holds him fast.

"Where is the Crone, Metis?"

"On the edge of a cliff," he blurts.

"Where is the cliff?"

"I don't know! Aris, you're hurting me."

"Why did she go?"

"To find Mem."

"Where's Mem?"

"I don't know."

She comes to stand in front of him. "Do you want me to beg?" Her voice drips with a mixture of lust and desperation. His throat dries, and he swallows.

Her hand moves down from his chest and disappears below the waist of his pajama pants, stirring needs within. Her fingers hook the elastic band of his pants and tug. The fabric slides down and pools around his ankles. With a small smile, she lowers to her knees. His stomach clenches.

"Aris, I really don't—" Her lips wrap around him, warm and moist. Electricity pulses through his entire body.

He winds his fingers around the strands of her hair, noticing the blond streaks mixing in with the usual brown. His eyes shift to the outside. The light is still there, dim but dancing among the trees. In it is a form. No, it's not the Crone. The face . . . it's

Aris. What is she doing out there? It's his mind playing a trick on him, he tells himself. Aris is here. Warm. Soft. Loving. She is here with him, and he's never letting go.

"Don't you love me, Metis? Because I love you," she says.

"Of course I d—"

He looks back down and their eyes connect.

Blue, so blue.

CHAPTER THIRTY

CASS

March 3, 2233
(17 days before Tabula Rasa)

After three hours, they reach a meadow of wildflowers and a mirror-clear lake, the first of a series of lakes on the same mountain as the CDL. The sight distracts Cass from the pain in her back and knees. The descent from the crest has been wearing. Everyone spreads out—some to the grove of pines, where it is the shadiest, some to the edge of the lake. Bastian points to a lone pine near a boulder.

She releases her pack onto the needle-carpeted ground and massages her neck. Bastian uncaps his water bottle and drinks deeply. They'll refill the water later from the ice-cold lake. In the branches above them, birds chirp in various tempos and pitches. This is their territory, and they want it to be known.

"Do you have the book?" Bastian asks.

She pulls it from her backpack and hands it to him. Around them are plants that sprung up after the winter thaw. She knows some from the book and has seen them around the CDL—magenta penstemons; bright, sunny buttercups; orange-red Indian paintbrushes; purply-blue sky pilots; ivory columbines.

By their feet is a field of dandelions. She pulls one out by the root.

"We can eat this one," she says. "The plant book says the whole plant is edible."

"Flowers too?"

Bastian pinches off the dirt-encrusted roots and puts the entire thing in his mouth. "Not bad."

He begins picking those near him.

"Are you eating grass?" Ori asks.

"Dandelion. Try some." He gives her a piece. "You can eat the whole thing, but the leaf is best."

She makes a face but takes it, likely not wanting to disappoint him. She takes a tiny bite and chews. Her face unclenches. "It tastes like salad."

"See! Not bad, right? These will be a good addition to our lunch," he says.

"Let's collect them," Ori says.

Together, they gather two handfuls each.

"Lunchtime!" Naya says from the trees.

They join her and Hilden at a table-shaped rock under the shade. Covered by red and yellow lichens, the rock looks feast ready. On it are the things the Kitchen Matres had given them: carrots, pieces of oat cheese, tubs of hummus, muffins, bread. They place the harvested dandelions on the rock and add the food from their lunch bags to the mix. The meal looks good enough to be an offering to the forest gods. Cass wonders if Bastian could be right—this could be a way out if they can somehow survive the harsh winter.

"What else can we eat out here?" Hilden asks.

"Cattails," Cass says, pointing to a patch growing at the edge of the lake. "You can grill or boil the roots. Or if you harvest them when they're still green and hidden in the leaves, you can boil them and eat them like corn on the cob. The shoots can also be eaten raw, and the pollen is full of vitamins."

"How do you know so much?" Ori asks.

"Just books."

"We could live out here like the birds." Bastian wraps a dandelion around a piece of cheese before popping it in his mouth.

"I heard after the break we're going to learn how to cook. Doesn't that sound so fun?"

"I have to eat my own cooking?" Hilden shudders. "No thanks."

"I wonder what specialty I'll be assigned in College," Naya asks. "Cass, you'll probably be in biology."

"Maybe." It's where she most excels. "Do you think it's weird they're splitting up best friends?" Bastian says, obviously annoyed. Cass and he both thought the two of them would go to College for science.

"Are they?" Ori asks, looking uncomfortable.

"Come on, you haven't noticed? Besides us four, there's Eugene and Linus, Rhode and Suri, Cleo and Tia."

"Morgan and Stan," Hilden says.

"Why do you think that is?" Celo asks.

"It's pretty obvious to me," Bastian says. "They separate us so they can more easily control us."

Silence drapes. They begin to look uncomfortable. Even Ori is pretending to look at something in the trees instead of at Bastian like usual.

"And don't you ever wonder why there are only two tracks?" he continues. "Why not a third track—for a task force to explore the outside world?"

"Probably because it's a destroyed world out there," Naya says.

"But it's been a few hundred years. Whatever killed everyone is probably gone by now. We could leave."

"And go where? And live off of what?" Ori asks.

"We have all this," Bastian says. "We can live out here."

"I don't think we should be talking about this," Ori says, and heads to the lake. A nervous Naya follows.

"Hey, you want to see which of us can hold our feet in the water the longest?" Hilden asks Celo.

"Yeah," Celo says, and they both walk off behind Naya.

Cass taps Bastian's shoulder with hers. "They don't seem to like the idea."

He shrugs. "It doesn't matter. It'll be harder to leave with more people anyway."

"It's going to be hard to live out here in the winter."

"Maybe the weather will be better if we go lower?"

"We've never been farther than this lake."

"What if we just go?" he asks.

"Like right now? I don't know how far the other lakes are from here. I doubt the others want to keep walking since we've walked all morning."

"I'm not talking about going to the lakes."

"Bastian . . . We're nowhere near prepared."

"But we have wild edibles. We have water."

"We don't have medicine if we get sick. And we'll freeze at night. We don't have a blanket, not even a thick jacket. Where are we going to sleep."

He looks down at his feet.

She reaches out and touches his hand. "Why are you in a hurry. Tabula Rasa for us is still a year away."

He sighs. "Ever since the police came to take the seniors early, I've been getting this strange feeling that something really bad is going to happen. And now with Matre Selene being sick . . ."

"Those two things are not related."

"Still, I don't think we should be at the CDL." He shudders.

Maybe he's right. Bastian has always had a strange intuition about him. Years ago, in the middle of nowhere, he started shaking in class. A moment later, an announcement came through the intercom that Matre Elizobeth had passed. He did the same thing on the day Agan died.

CHAPTER THIRTY-ONE

ARIS

March 3, 2233
(17 days before Tabula Rasa)

Hera sticks her head back into her office. "I sent everyone to lunch. We can leave."

She takes Aris and the Crone up the second story and down a long hallway to a nondescript door. She opens it with the gold key hanging from her necklace—the same one Selene used to get into the train station.

The door leads down a dark passageway, the glow of the Crone blending with the lantern in the Head Matre's hand. At the end, there's another door. On the other side of it is a large bathroom.

"No one uses it, don't worry," the Head Matre says, more for herself.

The Health Center has an eeriness that makes Aris's spine tingle. A cavernous space with a curving vaulted ceiling supported by a row of columns on each side, it smells of history dipped in disinfectant. She keeps hearing footsteps behind them, but when she looks over her shoulder to check, no one is there.

At the intake desk is a Matre. She looks up from her book, sees them, and springs from her chair with terror on her face.

Her book drops to the ground, sending echoes bouncing around the room.

"Where's Galena?" the Head Matre demands.

The name tag on her coat reads *Lydia*.

"Uh . . . um . . . she's with Selene. What—"

"Do not, under any circumstance, let anyone else through while we're here," the Head Matre orders. "And you are forbidden to speak of this. I will answer your questions later."

Lydia nods. She eyes both Aris and the Crone with a mixture of distrust and curiosity, but she says nothing.

The Head Matre leads them through a vast room with two long rows of empty hospital beds and tall windows along one wall. The commingling scent of antiseptic and bleach is strongest here. It seems to live in everything—the sheets, the floor, even the privacy curtains between the beds.

"Selene was complaining about the strong smell, so we moved her into her own room," the Head Matre says. In her tone, Aris hears affection.

"You don't have any other patients?" she asks.

"Created children are generally healthy. They were made that way. With cells resistant to cancer and screened for any congenital diseases, they typically only get hurt by accident and—" Hera stops herself.

"Tabula Rasa," Aris says. "I know about it."

Hera makes an indecipherable sound in her throat. They exit the room and continue down another hallway of doors lined up on the left side.

So many hallways, so many doors.

They enter the last room on the left, where they find Selene and Galena. Aris's chest hollows at the sight. The Selene on the bed—eyes closed and hands folded on her stomach—looks different from the one she met the first time in the

Library of Memory. Her pale skin has become sallow except for the feverish pink coloring the knolls of her cheeks. Her concave chest is moving up and down with shallow breaths. Her collarbones . . . They look as though one wrong touch would break them.

"What's going on?" Galena stares at them, mouth agape.

"This is Eleanor, who also goes by 'the Crone,'" the Head Matre says. "I'll have her explain who she is later. What's more important is she believes she knows what's wrong with Selene."

"I've seen these symptoms countless times," the Crone says. "Hypertension, elevated liver enzymes, high fever. These symptoms all appeared when the survivors were beginning to get pregnant again after the Last War."

A gasp comes from Galena.

Pregnant has no place in this world. Aris only knows of it from a book she read long ago with a title she cannot remember.

"How is that possible?" Galena asks. "Our bodies are not supposed to procreate. The scientists who worked on the DNA of the created children turned off that gene because of the pregnancy defects."

"Life finds a way," the Crone says. "Somehow, Selene's genes have reverted. But her body is unable to handle it. We need to first control her hypertension. We can begin a preliminary treatment plan."

She turns to the Head Matre. "We need an antihypertensive, an anticonvulsant, and corticosteroids to promote the baby's lung development before delivery—if she does want to keep it."

"We don't have any of that," Galena says. "We can try to use what we have as makeshift but we will need more medicine and equipment."

"We have to get them from the Four Cities," the Crone adds.

Aris's heart skips. She looks over at Hera and sees her

shoulders sagging. This is too much weight even for a person as tough as the Head Matre.

"Our other problem comes once Eli finds out about Selene," the Crone says. "She's an anomaly, and he will want her as a test subject."

The Head Matre lifts her head, eyes flashing. "That won't happen. No one here will ever breathe a word. We Matres are nothing if not loyal to each other."

"My experience with secrets is that they always come out. One this big will not stay hidden forever. Say she is able to carry the baby, then we will have to do a preterm delivery. That will require a surgical team. And after that, how will it live?"

"Like the other children here. We will house it, educate it, and love it like we do the rest."

"And what happens once the child reaches eighteen? Are you going to send them to the Four Cities, where they will be among those who forget? Sacrifice them to a world where their ability to remember is a threat? Where no one they care about will be able to remember them? How long before the police realize the child doesn't belong, before they hunt them down for Eli to experiment on?"

Hera's expression tightens. "The Planner will not have them!"

"If this can happen to Selene, can it happen to others?" Aris asks.

"It's a possibility," the Crone says.

"Her child, will it have the Tabula Rasa trigger?"

"No. Matres and Officers, being clones, do not have the Tabula Rasa trigger built into their DNA," Galena says. "So their child wouldn't either."

They all turn to her.

"Makes sense, doesn't it?" Galena adds.

"How about us created children, would our children have the Tabula Rasa trigger?"

"We wouldn't know, would we?" Galena shrugs. "None of you have ever procreated to our knowledge, so we don't know if it's inheritable. What we do know is we run DNA screenings of all the embryos from the lab before we put them into the artificial womb, to ensure there are no inherited defects."

"The lab is here?" Aris asks.

"Yes. It's on the far side of the CDL."

"You not only raise the children, you grow them from conception too?"

"Do you have any idea of the power you have here?" the Crone says to the Head Matre. "You have more power than even Eli—more loyalty from your Matres. You have the future in your hands."

The Head Matre narrows her eyes. "I'm not interested in your revolution. My responsibility is to protect everyone in this place. I will not let you use the CDL as a pawn in your revolution."

"*My* revolution? In the little time I've been here, I've never seen a place more ripe for one. Are you telling me you're happy with all that is happening? That all the Matres are?"

"All that is secondary to the children!"

"Tell me, are you able to protect them from Tabula Rasa? From the Planner? Whatever security you think you're giving them is false."

"What choice do I have? This is our purpose."

The Crone drags in a long breath. "*You* have all the options in the world, if only you could see beyond your fear."

"Can we please go back to Selene?" Galena says. "I need to know right away how to keep her from dying."

Her words refocus them on what is most important.

"I'm sorry," the Crone says.

"We'll leave you to it. Aris, I'll take you back to the library," the Head Matre says.

Suddenly the door bangs open.

"Head Matre!" Two Matres stand in the doorway, faces bleached of color.

"What's the meaning of this?" Hera says sternly. "I told you not to let anyone through."

"I'm sorry, Head Matre, I couldn't stop Amira. Once she knew you were here, she insisted she speak to you at once."

Amira looks from Selene to Aris to the Crone with wide eyes. "Who are these peop— Is she a ghost?"

"Questions later. Why are you looking for me?" the Head Matre says.

Amira composes herself. "Athena spotted a train in the valley heading our way from her post up the mountain."

Fear prickles Aris's spine. There is only one train heading here, only one group who controls it. A thousand questions ricochet off each other in her brain. Why are the police here? Is it because of her?

"There's no scheduled visit for weeks yet! Why are they here?" Hera says.

Aris turns to the Crone. "Do you think they're here for us?"

"Eli must have sent them," she says.

"He's been actively looking for you?" Hera roars. She looks about to burst. "Why didn't you tell me this?"

"We thought we had more time," Aris says.

"What do we do?" Amira says, her voice shaky.

Hera turns to her. "It'll most likely be Scylla. Take a team to the station and bring him to me."

Scylla . . . Scylla . . . Aris knows the name.

"I also need him to answer for Selene," the Head Matre says.

"He's responsible for her condition?" Amira asks, eyes on the Matre sleeping on the bed.

"I have my suspicion." Hera turns to Galena. "Can you confirm since you and Selene are close?"

The Matre looks down at her feet.

"I take your silence as an answer. Hera turns to Amira. "How much time do we have?"

"Twenty minutes, tops."

The Head Matre bows her head and closes her eyes. A moment later they snap open. "We need to minimize interactions with the police. Send the children to their dorms, and keep them where we can see them. No hiking in the forest until we figure out what this is about."

Hera turns to Lydia. "Scylla will want to look at the library. The books are what Aris came here for. Send a group to clean every trace of her from that place."

"Yes, Head Matre," Lydia and Amira say.

Hera turns to Aris and the Crone. "Eleanor, you will work directly with Galena to treat Selene. Aris, you will stay here for the time being. The police will want to search this entire place, so we will need to keep moving you."

She takes off her necklace and hands it to Aris. "This is the master key to all the doors at the CDL. Do you remember the secret passages Selene showed you?

"Yes."

"Your job—your only responsibility for as long as the police are here—is to not be seen. Can you do that?"

Aris's chest tightens. "Yes, Head Matre."

"Amira, Lydia, walk with me to the Food Hall. I'll update you on the way. We need to get everything ready before the train gets here."

CHAPTER THIRTY-TWO

SCYLLA

March 3, 2233
(17 days before Tabula Rasa)

The train slows, its high-pitched hum reducing to a purr. They are almost to their destination. Scylla stands up and walks to the front, where he can look out the large window. The headlights illuminate the tunnel to a warm gray.

Evan comes to stand next to him. The entire trip, he has been asking questions about the CDL, and Scylla has answered as much as he has been able to. He's told him of the identical-faced Matres, the campus of majestic old buildings, the snowcapped mountain range, and the many children in one place. Still, Scylla knows there is nothing to prepare the new officer for the experience of being there.

The station comes into view, an image of pristine white. On the platform, a line of Matres awaits. They'd probably seen the train coming. Scylla expected this given what happened the last time. This visit is outside his monthly wellness check, outside scheduled field trips, outside protocol.

"Do they always give you this reception?" Evan asks.

"No. They're here because we're not supposed to be here." He buttons his coat and straightens his fedora. Evan mimics him. "Let me do the talking. I don't want the Matres to think we're accusing them of harboring a fugitive."

"What if they are?"

"I've never heard of anyone succeeding in finding this place. The train is the only safe way in or out, and no one but us has control of it."

And even if one could get in, how would they get out?

"But it's possible, isn't it? Isn't that why we're here?" Evan asks.

Of course it's possible. When one deals in probability as the Planner does, anything is plausible. But that possibility leads to a consequence Scylla cannot accept.

The Planner may appear omnipotent, but the Head Matre holds the future of the Four Cities in her hands. Without the people at the Center for Discovery and Learning—the children to replace the yearly dead and the Matres to raise them—the Four Cities cannot continue to exist.

If the CDL chooses to break free, their Creator will find himself up against a wall. He knows it, and Scylla knows it. What saves them all is the Matres' love for the students. All of them have always had the children's interests at heart. The Head Matre will not do anything to hurt them—Scylla is sure of it.

"Our job is to get information. With the CDL, I've found tact and diplomacy work the best. Our job is not to accuse or dole out judgment. The Planner will be the one to make decisions. Be very sure the information you bring him is correct. He does not tolerate errors."

Evan nods.

The train eases to a stop. The sliding doors open, and they both exit. The line of Matres steps forward.

"What are you doing here?" a Matre says, voice like flint.

He looks at the name tag on her dress. "Hello, Matre Amira. It's me, Scylla."

Her posture relaxes, but only slightly. "Your usual wellness visit isn't for a few more weeks."

"I apologize for our unexpected visit. This is my partner, Officer Evan."

She glances quickly at Evan. Scylla is usually alone on his visits.

She focuses back on him. "Why are you here?"

"If I can just speak to Head Matre Hera, I may better explain our needs."

"Are you here to take more children?" There's fear in her voice.

"No." He smiles to reassure her. "I know there've been many changes lately. But this visit has nothing to do with the children."

"So why didn't you send us word?"

"We had to leave as soon as we received the request from the Planner," he says. It was almost the truth.

Her lips purse. After a long minute she says, "If it's by the Planner's order, I suppose we'll have to comply. I'll take you to the Head Matre."

"Thank you for your understanding."

Amira turns, and the other Matres part to let them through. He and Evan follow. Behind them, the line of Matres trail— their footsteps soft and barely audible.

They exit to the outside, and the Grand Hall stands before them, startlingly majestic in the midday sun. Despite the many times he has seen it, he never ceases to be in awe of its beauty— ever growing because of what this place has come to mean for him. All curves and colors, it is the opposite of the modern station, the opposite of the glittering steel and glass skyscrapers in Callisto, the opposite of his bare-bones sleeping quarters inside the police station.

"Wow," whispers Evan. His face has the open excitement

of a child riding an elevator for the first time. When he notices Scylla looking, he composes himself.

Amira leads them down the main cobblestone walkway across the campus. There is no one out and about, unusual for this time of day.

"Where is everyone?" Scylla asks.

"The children are working on a special project with the teachers."

"Aren't they still on break?"

Amira does not reply.

Their walk takes them past another of Scylla's favorite places—the flower garden. Right now it is laden with blooms of all colors and types, their scents sweetening the air. He inhales it, filling his lungs. The flowers are not yet blooming in Callisto. He doesn't know what the Matres do to get theirs to produce almost all year round.

They turn left after the garden toward the Gate of the Six Bells—the boundary where the manicured landscape gives way to a pine forest. Just before they reach the gate, they turn right toward a circular approach with a dry fountain before heading up the steps to the Administrative building.

The foyer is empty—another anomaly.

"Wait here," Matre Amira says.

Scylla watches as she walks down the long hallway with the line of Matres behind her. He has no idea how the Head Matre will react to his visit. When he was first assigned the position, the previous lead officer had warned him how difficult it could be working with the Head Matre. At the CDL, she has the last word in all matters.

At first, she had lived up to her reputation. But over time, she had somehow softened in her view of him and made his life a bit easier than that of the previous lead officer. Now, he needed to investigate her. He feels as though he is betraying her kindness, but there is no way around it.

"What do you plan to say?" Evan asks.

"Only as much as I need to without getting us thrown out of the CDL," Scylla says.

"She can do that?"

"She has done that. Not to me, but to other leads."

"She's allowed to?"

"The CDL operates independently of the System. We have to be delicate with our investigation. It's not as straightforward a procedure as when we investigate issues in the Four Cities."

"What do you mean?"

"We can't use any truth-extracting technology on the Matres."

Evan's mouth gapes. "So how do we know if they're telling us the truth?"

"We don't."

"How is this going to work?"

"Just follow my lead."

"If they even let us see her," Evan says. "We've been waiting quite a while."

"They will."

Eventually Amira and her line of Matres return.

"She will see you now." Amira takes them down the long corridor.

The Head Matre's office is the last one at the end. Amira knocks on the door.

"Enter," Head Matre Hera says.

He and Evan enter and find her seated behind her large desk. Her back is straight, her penetrating eyes heavy on them. He swallows.

Amira closes the door behind them. The Head Matre points

with her open palm to the chairs in front of her desk. He and Evan take their seats.

"Thank you for receiving us," Scylla says. "This is Evan, my partner on this assignment."

"And what assignment is that exactly?" she asks.

"We've been asked to search the CDL."

"Why?"

"We have reason to believe it may be a target for infiltration."

"What is your evidence?"

"We found footprints near the train tracks leading here."

She frowns. "How far away?"

"Far enough from the Four Cities to be worrisome. We're here to ensure you're safe."

She leans back in her chair. "We're very safe here. No place is as secure as the CDL. Your Planner has made sure of that."

"While I don't doubt that, this request came directly from him. You understand I'm in no position to refuse."

Her face tightens. He feels sweat trickling down his back.

She crosses her arms. "It seems I'm in no position to question it either."

"We hope to stay no more than a few days," he says. "Your help will make our work go faster and . . . require fewer people to be involved."

Her eyebrows fold in together, understanding in her intelligent eyes.

"You may stay at the cottage by the edge of the forest. It's our vacation house, so it's already set up for the next Matre. We'll have to move some vacations around."

Right. Unable to leave the CDL, the Matres take their vacations only in the vicinity.

"You will eat all your meals there," she continues. "We'll have them delivered to you."

"We can eat at the main hall if that would be easier. I'd hate to be a bother."

"Well, you are a bother, and I don't want you disturbing the children's routine."

"Of course. We'll keep a low profile these next few days."

"What will you do during this *visit*?" she asks.

"We'll start by examining the library, the lab, the main buildings. We'll check to make sure the way in and out of the CDL is secure. And we will also need to speak to some people to find out if they've seen anything."

She narrows her eyes. Her expression reminds him of Matre Amira, despite their many years apart. "Who?"

"Other than you, a few Matres and some students."

Her lips press into a fine line. "The children are not to be interviewed."

"It will just be a casual chat with a selected few. Of your choosing, of course."

"Whatever information you think you need will not come from the students." There's finality in her voice. "While I couldn't stop you earlier from taking the seniors, since your Planner considers them adults, under no circumstance will I allow you to bring outside concerns to the children still under my care."

Evan leans forward. "That's not going to work. The Planner requires th—"

"Officer Scylla." She does not even look at his brother. "Please ask your partner to leave the room."

Evan's jaw drops.

With the time constraint, Scylla needs her cooperation. He looks at Evan. "Step out for a moment."

"But—"

"Step out."

Evan presses his lips together and leaves the room. Whatever he needed to say will have to wait until later.

"I assure you we do not intend to create any disturbance to your daily life," Scylla says.

She laces her hands on the desk. "You may only speak to me and the Matres. And you must keep away from the children. Do we have an understanding?"

"Yes."

Her posture relaxes. "I will assign you a guide."

"Alright." He's no stranger to having a guide since the CDL is vast enough to get lost in.

"Though I'll have to find someone new since Selene is not feeling well," Hera adds.

His stomach drops. "What's wrong with her?"

"We're not sure yet, but we're keeping a close eye on her."

Though her words are controlled, he can sense a heavy strain on the Head Matre. And to not know what it is Selene has . . . No Matre is ever sick—not really, not until they are close to death. Their DNA, like everyone else's, was created to withstand diseases.

How sick is Selene? His insides roil. "I can take her to the hospital in Callisto," he says. "They have a great facility and diagnostic tools."

"Scylla, you know that cannot happen."

"But I'm sure the Planner can make an exception."

She leans forward. "We have tried to petition your Planner in the past, but he has always said the same thing. There are rules in place that make it impossible for any Matre to leave. Period."

"Can I visit her then?"

Her eyes soften. "I appreciate your concern for Selene. But we can take care of our own. We always have."

She stands, letting him know his time is up. "I'll have Amira take you and your partner to the cottage. Wait for your guide there."

"Thank you for your cooperation," he says, feeling defeated.

He opens the office door to see Evan grimacing next to the stony-faced Amira and her group of Matres.

"Amira, take them to the cottage," Hera says.

"Yes, Head Matre."

They leave the Administrative building, again trailed by Matres. There is no escape. The campus is still eerily devoid of children. Through the Gate of the Six Bells, they exit into the forest. Evan scans his surroundings with great interest, but Scylla can only think of Selene.

What does she have that the Matres here cannot figure out?

The main trail forks into three. They take the leftmost path and find themselves surrounded by a thicket of trees. After a while, they come to a clearing. In the middle, alone among the pines, stands a cottage.

"This is quite a walk from the main buildings," Evan says.

"It's our vacation house. It has to be far enough from the busyness of the CDL." Amira and the Matres stop in front of the door. "There are two bedrooms and one bathroom inside. I trust you'll find this place comfortable."

"Thank you, Matre Amira," Scylla says.

She nods and leaves with her group of Matres.

Inside, the cottage smells of woodsmoke and cookies. The cozy living room has a comfortable couch, full bookshelves, and a small fireplace—all the makings of a perfect retreat. But instead of feeling relaxed, Scylla is burning with worry.

"May I speak freely, sir?" Evan asks.

Scylla nods.

"Why are you allowing the Head Matre to assign us a guide? I don't think she should have that much control over our investigation. She is a part of what we're investigating."

"I understand your concern, but we need her to grant us access."

"But this place belongs to the Planner. Shouldn't he and, by extension, we have free access to this place like we do the Four Cities?"

"Check your watch," Scylla says.

"Sir?"

"Check your watch."

Evan frowns but does as asked. A second later he looks up. "How come my watch doesn't work?"

"The CDL is a tech dead zone."

His mouth opens. "What?"

"All advanced technologies are prohibited here. No droids working the kitchen. No drones flying the sky. No AIs to help with homework."

"So we can't use our watches?"

"No."

"Not even to contact Station One?"

"There are two ways to contact Station One. The first is how we got here—the train. The second is through an ancient technology called the analog telephone. There are only two phones that can do that—one is in the Head Matre's office, and the other is at the station itself."

Evan scowls. "But that's ridiculous."

"The Planner wants the CDL to be cut off from the Four Cities. It's completely off the grid and doesn't exist in any database."

Evan blinks repeatedly. "So when we're here, we're at the mercy of the Matres."

"You got it."

CHAPTER THIRTY-THREE

METIS

March 3, 2233
(17 days before Tabula Rasa)

Metis woke in a mood. He doesn't know where it came from. Maybe his dream. But he cannot remember his dream. All he knows is he opened his eyes, saw Aris, and felt unsettled. She hasn't been herself lately. No, that's not true. It's more like she's pretending to be herself.

He slices into the mushroom and takes a bite. It tastes good. Like the time before. Like the time before that.

The same damn meal.

Aris is sitting across the table from him. He eyes her cautiously.

"I'm going to the cottage today," he says. Maybe the answer is there.

"What did you talk to the Crone about the last time you were there?" she asks.

"The usual. More Absinthe. More cranes. More Dreamers."

The same damn conversation.

Maybe they've just been together too long. With years of interactions, things are bound to repeat. How many cycles now? But that can't be true. He cannot imagine loving anybody more. What's wrong with him?

"I'd like to go with you next time," she says.

He pauses mid-chew. "Why?"

"Am I not allowed?"

"You've never asked before."

"And if I had, what would the answer have been?"

"Our meetings are private."

She drops the fork and knife in her hands. They clang against the plate. "I thought we weren't supposed to have secrets."

"This is a part of my job. You knew that from the beginning."

"Maybe I'm just jealous of the special relationship between the Crone and her Sandman."

He's not sure what she's getting at. "What are you worried about?"

"She's taking you away from me!"

"No one can take me away from you."

She looks down. "Everyone always leaves."

His heart drops. Perhaps he has been neglectful.

He walks to her and sits on the balls of his feet by her chair. "I won't go willingly."

"You will when you don't love me anymore."

"I'll always love you. This is forever." He takes her hand. It feels fragile. "What's going on? This isn't like you. What's really bothering you?"

She turns her head away. "I'm just stressed at work."

"Why, what happened?"

"My boss wants me to do something I'm not sure I can do."

"What is it?"

She shakes her head. "It's just this new project. The tool I've been told to use is not suited for the task."

"Have you told them that?"

"Yes. But they're unreasonable."

"What if you just tell them no?"

"But I want to work on the project."

"Well, then I know you will succeed. You can do anything you put your mind to. I believe in you."

She leans down and kisses him. "I love you."

"How about we take a vacation? It might help with your stress."

She turns to him, blue eyes digging. "To Mem? The place you told me about. The one on the cliff."

His heart does a pirouette. "No!"

A shooting pain hits him. His hand goes to the spot on his forehead. "Ow!"

Aris turns his palm up and puts a white pill in the middle of it. "This is your last pill."

He takes it, and the pain subsides.

She sighs. "I really wish you didn't fight me so hard. Don't you know it hurts you to do so, Metis."

CHAPTER THIRTY-FOUR

CASS

March 3, 2233
(17 days before Tabula Rasa)

"I want to meet her," Bastian says from beside her as they make their way back from the lake to the CDL.

"Who?" Cass asks.

"The Outsider. The Aris person."

Cass looks over her shoulder to see where the others are and finds them trailing a bit farther behind.

"I think we need to talk to the Head Matre about her since Matre Selene is sick," he continues. "We need to know if the plan is still going to happen. Either that or talk to the Outsider ourselves."

"Why do you want to meet her so badly?"

He looks at her strangely. "So she can teach us how to survive in the wild."

"But she wants to go back to the Four Cities."

"We don't have to go all the way there. Or leave from Callisto. All we need to be is not here."

"But we're not ready to leave."

"We're never going to be ready, Cass!" He raises his voice, then remembers they're not alone. He leans in closer. "Not if we keep waiting instead of doing."

"I know how much you want to go, but this is a big deal."

"I know it's scary," he says, his eyes far away. "But this is the only way we can stay together."

Footsteps come from behind. It's Ori. It appears she has forgiven Bastian for almost ruining her hiking expedition with his dark conversation.

"Hey! That was fun, wasn't it?"

"Yeah. Thanks for inviting us," Bastian says.

"Of course! We're going to be doing more things together over the break if you want to join us. Since you, me, and Hilden will be in the same program, and Naya, Celo, and Cass will be in a different one, it'll be good to get to know each other better."

Cass realizes Ori has been trying to make new friends for both herself and Naya, for when they go their separate ways. She *is* aware the System is separating best friends. But while Bastian's answer to it is to run away, hers is to make the best of the situation. It makes Cass like her more.

Just as they approach the ridge, they see a Matre standing there, a worried expression on her face.

They look at each other.

"Are we in trouble?" Cass asks.

"Can't be. I signed all of us out this morning and let them know where we'd be." Ori quickens her steps to the Matre. "Hi, Matre Florence, is something wrong?"

"You six hurry and come with me."

"What happened?" Hilden asks.

"The police are here," Matre Florence says.

"What? Why?"

"Are they here to take more of us?" Naya asks, her voice shaky.

"No. It's not about you kids."

"Then what?" Celo asks.

"They're here to do some inspections."

"Why?" Bastian asks.

"I don't know why, but the Head Matre ordered all children to stay in their dorms for the time being."

"How long are they staying?"

"A few days."

"I don't think the police ever stayed overnight before," Ori says, eyebrows furrowing. "Have they?"

"Okay, enough Q and A. Let's cross over," Matre Florence says, and leads them in a single line up the ridge toward the CDL.

This must have been a surprise visit if the Head Matre ordered all the children to stay inside. The only reason Cass can think of is that they are looking for Aris. Matre Selene said she's here because she got lost. But what if she did not get lost but was looking for this place?

Why would she come to the CDL? There's nothing here but children and Matres.

They arrive back to a dorm bustling with speculation and gossip. The first floor is so jam-packed with students there's barely enough room for them to walk in. Matre Florence has to fend off a few more questions before she leaves, looking thoroughly harassed.

"Did you see the policemen on your way back?" a student two grades below them asks.

"No," Ori says.

"I hear they're staying in the forest," another says. "That's why we're not allowed out there."

"Are they going to take more students back with them?" one asks.

"Matre Florence said no," Naya says.

"Maybe she just said that because she doesn't want us afraid."

"No, she wouldn't lie about something like that."

"What if she doesn't really know?"

"But I don't want to leave." The girl looks to be in her first year in high school, her eyes wet with fresh tears.

Cass leans down. "They won't. And they're not going to be here long. Matre Florence said just a few days. You'll be safe in here. Do you have a best friend?"

The girl nods and points to a boy standing next to her, looking just as lost.

"Alright, you two stay together, okay? You'll be extra safe if you stay together."

"Okay," the girl says, and takes her friend's hand.

Cass looks at Bastian and knows—against all the logic she has been throwing at him—that leaving the CDL is the only way they will make it together.

CHAPTER THIRTY-FIVE

ARIS

March 3, 2233
(17 days before Tabula Rasa)

Matre Galena breathes a sigh of relief after she removes the cuff from Selene's arm. "Her blood pressure has come down."

"She does look better," Aris says.

After the first treatment, Selene began showing signs of improvement. Her color is less pallid, her breathing less shallow.

"It won't last," the Crone warns. "We're going to need medication."

"If you don't mind, I'd like to hold on to this good feeling for a bit," Galena says brusquely. "I'm going to check our inventory," she adds, and leaves the room.

"I used to be that way when I was younger," the Crone says. "Insisting on turning a blind eye to what is obviously wrong in front of me."

"She's just worried about Selene," Aris says. "They look about the same age, so they probably grew up together."

"I wouldn't know what that feels like. I was a single child."

"Was it lonely?"

"I was often alone, but that was what I knew. In a way, it prepared me for solitude later on in life."

"I wonder what it was like for me growing up here, being surrounded by Matres and classmates all the time," Aris says.

"It can be easy to get lost in a place this big with so many people. It helps if you have a best friend, someone who you can always count on."

Aris looks at her. "How do you know this?"

"A student told me."

"A student! How were you able to talk to a student?"

"One of the benefits of being me is people think I'm not real—that I'm just a part of their imagination or a dream. You can get quite a lot of information from people when they think they're just talking to themselves."

"Well, I guess it's still working." She looks out the window at the clear blue sky. "I've been thinking. I can get Selene some medicine when I go to Callisto for the Dreamcatcher."

"Getting the Dreamcatcher is going to be tough enough. The hospital isn't somewhere you can just waltz in and steal medication. There are medical droids everywhere, and each of them is connected to the System. In either case, we won't have time for you to walk all the way back. We're going to need the train."

"Okay, name a better option."

"Scylla."

Aris is unsure if she heard her correctly. "The policeman? But he works for the Planner."

"He's not like the others."

"What do you know?"

She does not answer.

"Eleanor . . ." Aris says. "We agreed before we took this trip—no secrets on things that directly affect us."

Knowing how the Crone can be, it was one of the stipulations Metis put in place when she asked to come with them to Mem.

"Scylla asked me not to tell you. This can never get out."

"Who am I going to tell?"

"You can never mention this—not to Metis, not even to Scylla. You have to understand—policemen are supposed to maintain objectivity and never interfere with the lives of the citizens. It's one of their commandments."

"I won't say anything to anyone."

The Crone glides to the window, and for a moment Aris worries she will drift away. "When you and Metis were arrested in the last cycle and the Interpreter was about to erase your dream memories, Scylla came to me for help to get you out."

Her stomach squeezes. "He helped us? But why?"

"He loves Metis's music. He was afraid it would disappear."

"Scylla did that?" Her chest feels as though something is blooming inside.

"Without his interference, you and Metis wouldn't have been placed in the same city at the beginning of this cycle and wouldn't have found each other so quickly. Without that, you wouldn't have had the time to discover what Mem is, and you, Aris, wouldn't be at the CDL this very moment."

She cannot believe her ears—a police officer of the Four Cities had a hand in putting her on the course to Mem. "This is surreal."

"One never knows the things one sets in motion with an action. That's why the rule is in place." The Crone turns to look at Selene's sleeping face. "But if he loves her as much as he loves Metis's music, he will help us."

"His actions will go directly against the System," Aris says. "He's not going to do it. The moment he sees you and me, he's going to bring us to the Planner."

"It's a risk we're going to have to take."

"That's a big risk."

"Name a better option," she says, turning Aris's words back on her.

The problem is, unlike the Crone, she doesn't have an answer. She notices her edges have grown faint. "You're going to need to rest soon."

Her power source, though efficient, is not infinite. While Aris does not know how the technology works, she knows the Crone needs to periodically retreat into her book.

"Will you be okay alone?"

"I'm not alone. I have Selene."

Aris brings out the Book of Crone from her backpack, which the Matres had brought to her after cleaning up the library. How something that looks like it's about to fall apart can contain the most advanced technology in the Four Cities, she will never know.

After the Crone disappears into it, Aris settles on the chair next to Selene's bed. It's hard to relax with the police around, but the Matre watching the entrance of the Health Center will ensure she has enough warning to run to the bathroom, where the secret entrance to the Administration building is.

"Aris?" Selene's groggy voice says. "Why are you in my room?"

Aris gasps. "You're up! How are you feeling?"

"Terrible." She lifts her head and looks around. "Where am I?"

"The Health Center."

"Why?"

"You're very ill."

"What's wrong with me?"

Aris swallows, unsure whether it should be her to break the news. "You're—um—you're—"

"I heard—" Galena says from the door. When she sees Selene sitting upright, she rushes to her side. "You're awake! I thought we were going to lose you."

"Tell me what's wrong with me."

Galena takes her hand and holds it. "You're carrying a fetus, and your body isn't able to handle it."

She blinks, takes back her hand, and places both primly on her lap as though what Galena said has not registered. "That's not possible. Our bodies aren't meant to do that."

"I know. But it's true."

Her eyes turn red. "Galena, it isn't funny. You should never joke to someone like that."

"Look at me. I'm not joking, Selene."

"But I—I just ate something bad."

Galena takes her hand again and holds it tighter this time. "Don't be afraid. We're going to find a way to take care of you. The Crone has already taught me how I can ease some of the symptoms. And once we have medication from the Four Cities, you'll be fine."

A deluge of tears pours down Selene's face. Galena wraps her arms around her, and they both cry into each other's embrace. A knot forms in Aris's throat.

Selene lifts her head from Galena's shoulder and wipes her eyes. "Galena, who's the Crone?"

CHAPTER THIRTY-SIX

SCYLLA

March 3, 2233
(17 days before Tabula Rasa)

Evan paces back and forth in the tiny living room of the cottage.

"Where's the guide?" he asks. "Why are they keeping us waiting?"

"To give us a guide, they have to first find one. We did come here without warning. We're lucky they didn't turn us away," Scylla says as he flips through a book to occupy his own racing mind.

He needs to find out what's wrong with Selene. She must be at the Health Center. How can he get inside it without anyone suspecting?

"Sir, may I speak freely?" Evan asks.

Scylla puts the book down and looks up. "Go ahead."

"The Planner gave us a mission to search this place, and the Head Matre is preventing us from doing it. Either this is a power play, or she's hiding something."

"I warned you not to throw accusations around without proof."

"I think being easy on the Matres isn't a good strategy. That's why they feel like they can do whatever they want. I think we should request backup from the Planner."

"You're telling me you want to go back to the Planner empty handed and request more policemen based on the fact that our guide is late? Have you not heard anything I've told you?" Scylla asks.

Evan's lips press into a straight line.

"Since this is your first assignment here, I'm going to repeat what I said in case you didn't hear it right the first time," Scylla adds. "The Head Matre is not someone to trifle with. We follow her rules, or she will make it impossible for us to do our job."

"But isn't she already doing that?"

A knock comes from the door, and Scylla nods for Evan to open it. A Matre is standing on the porch, a lantern in her hand.

"Hello, I'm Mona. I'll be your guide while you're here."

"I'm Evan. We've been waiting for you awhile."

Annoyance plays across her face. "I have other responsibilities besides this one. If you had given us the courtesy of informing us about your arrival beforehand, we could have been better prepared."

Scylla sighs internally. "Thank you for being here, Matre Mona."

"Officer Scylla, where would you like to go first?"

"We'll start with the big one. The library."

She nods.

The sky is in layers of orange, pink, and purple. A flock of dark wings flies by, accompanied by the sound of squawking. They trace their footsteps back to the main campus through the forest, passing through the Gate of the Six Bells and crossing the grounds. There are still no children around. The Head Matre must have everyone on lockdown because they are here. She has not forgiven them for taking the senior students early. She may never.

They turn a corner and arrive in front of the Grand Hall.

Instead of going through its massive front doors, Matre Mona leads them to a small one on the side. The place is shrouded in shadows. The pews are empty, the long aisles stretching into black. The sweet scent of incense from years past still lingers in the wood. Matre Mona flips the light switch on the wall. The chandeliers above twinkle and light up the large stained glass windows. Evan's eyes widen.

"You've been granted special access to the library," Scylla says to him, "You will not breathe a word about it, or I and those who guard its secret will make sure you never get promoted your entire career."

"Yes, sir. I won't say anything to anyone, sir."

"Good."

"Is *this* the library?" Evan looks around, probably trying to figure out why a place with no books would be called a library.

"No, this is the Grand Hall."

Mona takes them up to the gold altar embellished with statues of saints from a dead religion.

"It's through here," Scylla says to his partner and pushes the altar sideways. It moves on tracks, revealing a dark tunnel.

The air inside is damp and cool. He shuts the door from behind, and darkness entombs them. The lantern in Mona's hand turns on, enveloping them in a globe of orange light.

The secret of the library is unknown to all but a few. Only a special operations team the Planner handpicked from a list of past lead officers is allowed access, aside from the Matres, who do not know that the books contain the memories of the citizens of the Four Cities.

He was first told of this place after he became lead. Once a year, he accompanies those in the special operations team as they bring books from the newly reset graduates. And once every four years, after every Tabula Rasa, he helps them bring in a machine to transfer the erased memories of all the citizens to their respective books—a long and tedious process.

She leads them downward, the lantern swaying to the rhythm of her steps. The sound of their shoes bounces off the stone walls. *Clack, clack, clack.* His mind drifts back to the last time he was with Selene.

Pale morning sun flooded through the stained glass windows, painting the air with colorful light. The glass chandeliers glittered, the wooden pews gleamed. Everything an image of perfect peace.

"Welcome back to the CDL," came a voice from one of the pews.

His heart skipped, and he rushed toward Selene. In one fluid motion, he pulled her in and crushed her against his chest. A sigh escaped them both.

"I've missed you," he whispered into her hair.

"I've missed you too."

He breathed her in. "I've been wanting to do this since I saw you in the Head Matre's office."

She giggled. "Can you imagine the look on her face?"

"She'd throw me out of here so fast."

"Maybe she wouldn't. She doesn't seem to mind you as much as the others."

"I doubt it. I'm still an outsider."

His lips trailed from her hair to her cheek. She smelled of roses. He found her earlobe and began nibbling. Her moan sent electricity to his groin. He kissed down the curve of her cheekbones to her lips. The warm softness of her mouth and tongue sent shudders through him.

His need became too much. He gathered up the fabric of her dress, his hands traveling along her smooth skin, higher and higher.

He was pleased to find she was completely bare underneath. He caressed her heated core, and another moan escaped her lips.

"I've missed you," he said. "So much."

"I've missed you." Her voice was dripping with desire tinged with the pain of distance—the same one he had been living with in between their meetings.

"I wish I'd never have to leave."

"I know."

He closed his eyes, and everything was reduced to sound. Wood dragging against the stone floor. The clinking of a belt unbuckling. The weight of bodies pushing against the pew. Skin rubbing against skin. The suppressed moaning of two voices in unison. The whispering of loving words, of devotion. Moans rising in steady rhythm until they reached a muffled crescendo. Then silence.

He opened his eyes. Selene's face was flushed and dewy. Hers was the most beautiful he had ever seen.

"That was wonderful," she said, breathless. "You're wonderful."

"I love you."

"As I love you."

They exit into the massive space lined with books in all the shades on the color wheel.

Evan's eyes widened. "This is bigger than the Central Library."

"We'll split up and look around," Scylla says. "You can take one side of the library, and I'll take the other."

He turns to Mona. "Matre, we may be here for a while."

"The Head Matre asked me to wait. It's fine. I brought a book."

"We'll start from the black-and-white mosaic over there," he says to Evan, and they both walk to it.

"What are these books for?" his partner asks.

"That's classified."

"It's a maze in here. Would be a good place to hide."

"Go aisle by aisle. Look for anything that doesn't seem to belong."

CHAPTER THIRTY-SEVEN

METIS

March 3, 2233
(17 days before Tabula Rasa)

Metis runs his fingers along the keys of the piano according to the music on the paper. He repeats. Still, it does not sound the same as what he had written before.

"What are you playing?" Aris asks from behind him, her arms wrapping around his chest.

A feeling of unease sinks in his stomach. "Just a song I'm composing."

He had begun it with her in mind, but somehow, he does not want to tell her that. Why doesn't he want to tell her?

Maybe I want it to be a surprise? Right. That must be it.

"I want to apologize for how I've been behaving," she says. "I know I've been acting strange."

He softens. "You're under a lot of stress."

"I am."

"Maybe we can go for a walk in Central Park. Just to clear our heads."

"Not Central Park."

"Why not?" It's one of her favorite places.

"It's too big."

The reason seems strange.

"I've been thinking about your boss. The unreasonable one," Metis says. "What if you just request a change of job from the Labor Council?"

"I can't do that."

"Why not?"

"There's no one else that can do my job," she says.

"That can't be possible. There are other scientists."

"He only trusts me to do this particular project. I was created for this."

"We were not created for specific jobs."

"The most special of us were." She unwraps her arms from his chest. "Do you think you'd be able to do anything but be a brilliant pianist?"

"I'm sure I could also be a brilliant baker if I put my mind to it."

"That's interesting." She comes to sit next to him. She presses her right finger on a C key.

"What's interesting?" he asks.

"The power of the illusion of choice."

"Excuse me?"

Her finger moves to a D. "It's a cognitive bias that makes people believe they have more control of their own choices than they actually do."

"You don't think we have a choice in our profession?" he asks.

"Created children are created."

Her finger walks to the E note. Everything around him blinks into black.

What?

The F note rings. The world returns.

"Are you okay?" Aris asks, her blue eyes curious.

He's not sure if he is—he's not even sure what just happened. His eyes blur. He wipes them with the back of his hand.

"I'm tired. I just need to rest, I think."

"Okay. I'll wake you before dinner."

He makes his way to the stairs and climbs to the second story. From the threshold, his bedroom looks as it always does. *Exactly* as it always does. There is nothing out of place. No jacket draping the back of a chair. No stray pillow lying face down on the floor. No half-finished book on the side table.

Suddenly he wants more than anything to tear apart this perfection. He walks to his desk and picks up the chair. He decides it now lives in the bathroom. The desk he drags to the side of the bed. The side tables he moves to the foot of his bed. He throws all the pillows on the floor and pulls all the books from the bookshelf. From the closet, he takes out his clothes and throws them around the room, ripping some of them in the process. Satisfied with the mess, he climbs into bed and closes his eyes.

CHAPTER THIRTY-EIGHT

ARIS

March 3, 2233
(17 days before Tabula Rasa)

"You and I," Aris reads from Selene's poetry book,

> "our souls intertwining banyan roots
> Powerful, tangled branches
> shadow dancing.
> Heart leaves follow the sun
> like prayers
> collecting rain drops and starlight
> beating as one."

A soft smile appears on Selene's colorless face. "Isn't it amazing we can wear the memories of another person from hundreds or even thousands of years ago through their books?"

"I've never thought of it that way before," Aris says.

"It's one of the most beautiful things about our humanity when I look at a book. I don't think of it just as lines written on paper, I think of it as somebody's memory, a memory they had carefully crafted and put into a delivery vehicle that I can then take into myself—consume and understand. And because of that, I feel like memory is—it's magical." Selene sits straighter. "Oh, hello, Head Matre!"

Aris looks over her shoulder to see the Head Matre standing at the door with two other Matres behind her.

"How are you feeling?" Hera asks.

"I feel better. I'm sorry for worrying everyone. I didn't—I didn't—" Selene looks down at her hands.

"There's nothing we can do with regret. What we need to do is find a way out of this, and to do that, we take it a step at a time. For you, that means staying healthy. And you"—she turns to Aris—"need to find your memory book."

She steps aside. "These are Matre Sonya and Matre Eleni. They both were high school counselors around the time you may have been here."

Aris's heart jumps. She springs up from her seat. "Hello."

"You look exactly the same," Matre Eleni says.

"You were my counselor?"

She nods. "You were Aimilia then."

Aris walks toward her, feeling as if she's gliding on air. This must be how the Crone feels when she moves.

"I'm very happy to see you again," Matre Eleni says, and brings her into a hug. "I never thought I'd ever see a student once they'd left the CDL."

A knot forms in Aris's chest, and tears gather in her eyes. "You have no idea how happy I am to find you."

"With your name, we can find your place of birth within your year in the record. And with that, we can get your book!" Selene says.

"There's a problem with that," the Head Matre says. "The police are now going through the library."

Selene covers her mouth with her hands.

"Has no one told you?" Hera asks.

"We didn't want to worry her, with her high blood pressure," Aris says.

Hera sighs. "Must I do everything?"

She turns to the Matres. "Sonya, Eleni, I'm going to need privacy with these two."

"Yes, Head Matre," they both say, and leave the room, closing the door behind them.

Aris looks at the closed door wistfully—there are still so many questions she has for her counselor. But now is not the time.

Hera walks to Selene's bedside. "I'm going to tell you some things, and you can stop me anytime to ask questions. Are you ready?"

Selene nods.

"Two policemen are here. They were given an urgent order to search this place because footprints were found near the train tracks miles from here. But that's all they have to go on."

"Do they belong to Aris?" Selene asks.

"Most likely yes, but we don't know for sure."

"What are they looking for?"

"They say they're here to check our safety, but they've asked to see the library and the lab. So I think they're looking for signs of Aris and the Crone."

"Who are the officers?"

"Scylla and his partner, Evan. Evan looks like he's barely older than our seniors."

Selene's eyes shift to her hands on her lap.

"Is it Scylla?" the Head Matre asks.

"Yes," Selene says.

"Do you love him?"

She nods, eyes brimming with tears.

"Does he love you?"

She nods again.

"Does he love you more than he loves the System?"

She chews her lips and a tear falls. "I don't know."

"Well, we need to figure that out before we let him know about your . . . condition. I did tell him you're ill, and he has offered to take you to the hospital in Callisto."

"But Matres can never leave the CDL," Selene says.

"Exactly. So we know he's not above breaking a rule—a pretty big one—to save you. Still, I can't risk him taking you to the Planner once he learns of your pregnancy."

"The Crone knows him," Aris says. "She says he's different from the other policemen."

The Head Matre wipes the tear from Selene's face. "Maybe she can help us figure out whether he loves you enough to challenge everything he has been taught his entire life."

CHAPTER THIRTY-NINE

SCYLLA

March 3, 2233
(17 days before Tabula Rasa)

"I found something," Evan yells. Scylla's stomach drops.

He runs to his brother and sees him standing in front of a bookcase of lavender-colored books. In his hand is a piece of paper.

When he sees Scylla, he hands it to him. "I saw it peeking out from under one of the shelves. It must have fallen from somewhere up here."

Scylla stares at the number. *2206.*

"What do you think it's for?" Evan asks.

"I don't know, but we'll bring it back with us for analysis." But he does know. A feeling of doom clutches him.

"Good work," he says to Evan. "I've looked pretty thoroughly and haven't seen the Book of Crone or signs of an intruder."

"Me neither." Evan's stomach growls.

"Sounds like you're ready for dinner," Scylla says.

"No, I can keep going."

"You're not getting extra points from me by starving yourself. We can eat and rest. Tomorrow we can finish here and do the lab and the other buildings."

Matre Mona appears behind him. "What did you find?"

He folds the paper and puts it in the pocket of his pants. "Sorry, we can't share. It's protocol."

"Are you done then?"

"For now."

"You must want dinner. It's late. Your food should be waiting for you at the cottage."

Outside, the indigo velvet sky is pocked with stars. Scylla looks at his watch. They have been here for over three hours.

Mona is leading them with the lantern in her hand. The forest at night is another world from the one in daylight. The bright green pines are now black against a dark sky. The afternoon meadow that was bursting with colorful wildflowers is now a swath of gray. The air is calm and cool, wrapping him in melancholy.

Thoughts of Selene have been swirling around his mind. He hurries to Mona's side. "How is Matre Selene doing?"

"I'm sorry, I'm not at liberty to share. You should talk to Head Matre Hera about it."

He nods, his chest tightening. He had expected her answer. Still, disappointment clutches.

In front of the cottage, Mona turns to them and says, "I'll meet you here at ten in the morning."

Entering, they follow their noses to the dining room table. On it are two covered bowls and a plate of freshly baked bread. Evan lifts the cover, and a delicious scent wafts out.

"The food looks good." He takes a seat and spoons a bite into his mouth. His eyebrows shoot up. "Tastes good too."

Scylla sits on the chair opposite and uncovers his bowl. "Most of the mushrooms are from their garden, but some they harvest from the forest."

He knows the varieties of mushrooms the kitchen uses by

heart. The meatiness of cremini. The chewy shiitake. The intense porcini broth. The buttery crunch of oyster and chanterelle garnish. He spoons it in, and the stew travels down his throat and warms his insides.

"Who's Matre Selene?" Evan asks as he chews. "You were asking Matre Mona about her."

Scylla looks up. "She's usually assigned to deal with us officers."

"She's sick?"

"That's what the Head Matre said. That's why she had to find us a new guide."

"I still don't think she should be allowed to assign us a guide." He raises a hand. "Before you reprimand me again, I know what you said. I heard it. I still don't agree with it."

"You don't have to agree. You just have to obey orders."

"She has too much power," Evan says.

"That's between her and the Planner."

"But aren't you worried?"

Scylla knows what's coming. It's the same worry he's had since the beginning. He keeps his face neutral, composed. "About?"

Evan leans in. "Treason."

Smart kid. But then again, he does have the genes.

"No Matre would ever put the students in danger," Scylla says. "They care for and love them very much."

It's the truth.

Evan leans back on his chair. "Do you think we'd be different if we grew up here? Among all these trees and raised by women instead of retired officers?"

"Perhaps. We're also the product of our environment."

"Glad we didn't then. The citizens . . ." He shakes his head. "Most of them don't have a unique thought in their heads."

"Kind of difficult when they get the equivalent of a brain injury every four years," Scylla says.

"You feel for them."

"They're humans just like us. Only we have the privilege of a continuous memory and they don't. If we were in their shoes, we would want some empathy too."

Evan taps a nail against his bowl. "I must admit I don't have much empathy for them."

"It'll come with time. You just started. You learn through interactions and experience."

"There's so much I don't understand," Evan adds. "For example, why didn't the Planner remove the Crone from her cottage and keep her somewhere safe? Why does he allow her to see the Dreamers? And now she's out there, a threat to peace."

"Their relationship is complicated."

"But why does it have to be? He has the power to do anything. She's just a consciousness inside a book."

"Because he loves her."

Evan spears the last mushroom and puts it into his mouth before wiping his lips with a napkin. "It's a good thing the citizens get Tabula Rasa. The world would be in chaos otherwise."

He takes his dish, and Scylla hears water running in the kitchen. A moment later it turns off, and Evan reappears in front of him.

"Permission to retire for the night, sir."

"Of course. Take whichever room you want."

After he hears the bedroom door close, Scylla finishes his food and takes his dirty bowl to the kitchen. He washes it in the sink as he stares out the window. The field, the trees, and the sky all blend together—making one big black hole.

There were three little white boxes this time. Their names were Alexander, Nico, and Harper—names he knew, having taken them

on field trips to Callisto. Today was his first day as lead officer, and just as the Planner had done with his predecessor, his first assignment was to bring them back to the CDL.

He almost threw up while waiting for their ashes outside the morgue. No one had warned him about standing downwind while the gray cloud was spewing out of the metal smokestack. It was nothing he had ever smelled before—nauseating, sweet, and putrid all at once. The droid that worked there had told him it took the crematorium burning two to three hours at 1,750 degrees Fahrenheit to turn a body into ash. But it did not tell him anything about the smell.

He was feeling sick all day—through the hours-long train ride into the CDL, through the Ceremony of the Dead, through the tear-filled speeches by the Matres and students. So when he was invited to dinner afterward at the Food Hall, he declined and chose instead to sit staring out at the valley below.

He felt wetness on his cheeks. He looked up at the sky. It was still clear and bright blue. He touched his cheeks and saw the water was not rain but tears. He wiped them off and felt more hollowed out than he had felt all day.

"Hello," a voice spoke.

He turned to see a young Matre. The tag on her dress said Selene. In her hand was a bowl.

"May I sit?" she asked. "I brought you something."

"S-sure. I'm afraid I'm not good company right now though."

"Neither am I. We can just sit here while you eat this stew."

"I'm not very hungry. My stomach has been feeling . . ."

"Queasy?" she said.

"Yeah."

"It happens to the best of us. That's why we make stew on a day like this."

"What kind is it?"

"Mushroom. It's a recipe we've been using for generations. There are five types in here, and I bet you've never had at least one of them. Some are wild from around here."

"Well, then I must taste it." He took the bowl from her and one spoonful from it. The flavors exploded in his mouth, making him feel better at once. "The queasiness is gone."

"You should eat more."

They settled into a comfortable silence as he quietly finished the stew. When he was done, he let out a satisfied sound.

"I'm glad you liked it," she said.

"It may now be my favorite food."

She smiled. They sank into another stretch of silence that felt like a long exhale. He watched as birds flew by, flock after flock. They were among the few species left after the Last War—at least from what he had seen. But unlike humans, they seemed to have thrived. He saw she was watching them too.

So beautiful . . .

"Does it get any better?" he asked.

"Any better?"

"The queasiness on a day like this."

"No, I'm afraid not."

"How do you continue to do it?"

She leaned back on her hands and dragged in a long breath. "You hold on to the love."

"How?"

"I think of the students' smiling faces. I imagine a happy life for those who survive. I read poems about love."

"Like what?"

She tilted her head in thought, her eyes glittering.

> "When I leave the nest of my body,
> ease me gently into the wind

as I lift my unfolding wings
to soar and begin again."

"Whose is that?"

"R. S. Raviya. She was a poet who lived a long, long time ago. But she was just like us. She wrote of love and the magic of life."

Scylla decided the poet might also become his favorite.

He dries his hands and pulls out the paper from his pants pocket—*2206*. It's the first part of an ID number that identifies a citizen—the year they were born, the same number as the one etched on the back of the watch they wear. Either the Matres have realized what the books in the library are and have been deciphering the binary numbers on the spines, or someone else has. Either way, this is not good. The secret of the library is no longer safe.

The moment he hands this piece of paper in, the Planner will know what it means. What will he do with the CDL then?

CHAPTER FORTY

CASS

March 4, 2233
(16 days before Tabula Rasa)

Cass moves the oatmeal around the bowl with a spoon, no appetite even for low-effort food. Bastian takes a bite of his pancake and stares into space as he chews. Aside from two hours of free time this morning, today is going to be another long day stuck inside the dorms.

"We need to get into the Health Center," he says. "I've been thinking it's the best way to see both Matre Selene and the Outsider."

"You think they're together?"

"I think so, and even if they're not, at least we can see how Matre Selene is doing."

Cass has not seen her around. *How sick is she really?* An image of a tiny white box flashes in her mind, and her heart drops to her stomach.

"The problem is *how*," he says. They have never been sick a day in their lives.

"What are you thinking?"

His eyes flick to the knife on the napkin next to his plate. *Why does he have that?*

"Remember what happened to Hector last year?" he asks.

Before she can recall, Ori and Naya join them at their table.

"This isn't a break!" Ori waves around a piece of paper in her hand. "I have planned a full schedule for the next sixteen days. And now we only have two hours a day—*two hours*—before we have to go back to our dorms? The police are ruining our break!"

"What do you think the seniors they took are doing?" Bastian asks. "Do you think they're allowed to walk around Callisto with their full-memory brains?"

"Is that supposed to make me feel better?"

"No, I'm just saying nobody is having a good break. Or life, for that matter."

Naya touches Ori's hand. "We'll do what we can. Here, let me see your schedule." She studies it. "We can still walk around the garden. Maybe just the flower garden with the time we have."

"Alright," Ori says, and turns to Bastian. "Do you want to come with— Aaargh!" Her high-pitched shriek rings through the Food Hall.

Cass is about to ask what is wrong, when a scream also bursts from the root of Bastian's throat—the pain in it too real to be made up. The tip of the knife in Bastian's hand is dripping red. He holds his cut hand in the air, bright red blood running the length of his arm and branching out like newly formed streams. She feels her own blood leaching from her face.

"What happened?" a Matre yells from somewhere behind them.

"My finger—ow—my finger!" he howls. "I cut it. My finger is gone!"

Kids rush over to get a closer look, forming a wall around them. Then Cass hears a thud.

"Ori fainted!" Naya says.

"Stop crowding. Give them room!" the Matre hisses. At those words, the students around them back away.

"Let me see your cut," the Matre says to Bastian, her voice anxious. She sighs. "Your finger is not gone. But it does look like you're going to need stitches. Here, press this cloth on the wound."

She turns back to Naya. "How is she?"

"She's waking up, Matre."

"Good. Get her back to her seat, and give her some water. I'll take Bastian to the Health Center."

Cass stirs. "I can take him."

"Alright." The Matre walks to Ori and checks on her.

Cass gathers Bastian from his seat, and together they leave the Food Hall. Once no one is around, she jabs him with her elbow.

"Ow! Careful. I have a cut on my hand," he says.

"Idiot! Why did you hurt yourself like that?" Her eyes burn.

"I'm fine," he says in a weak voice.

"Stitches are a big deal! I can't believe you did that!"

"We needed a way to get into the Health Center. I didn't think it would hurt this much. It didn't seem that bad when it happened to Hector."

Cass realizes that, until now, Bastian had never known how much pain a cut can cause. Sure, he's had a scrape here or there, but he's never been seriously injured before. She eyes the cloth wrapped around his finger. The circle of blood is growing—so red it looks unreal.

Her stomach coils. "Let's get you fixed before I faint like Ori."

They rush toward the Health Center. The skinny structure is tucked away near the Administrative building. It's taller than it is wide, with windows rising up all the way to the ceiling.

They step into it, and a Matre appears out of nowhere, startling them. "What are you doing here?"

"Bastian accidentally cut himself, Matre."

She examines his hand. "Alright, you may go in. See Matre Lydia at the front, and she'll fix you up."

"Thank you."

They enter the light-filled space. The sound of their footsteps echoes in the long corridor, mimicking her hammering heart. At the end, they reach the intake desk, with Matre Lydia behind it. She sees them, and a worried expression crosses her face.

"What happened, children?"

"Can you please take a look at the cut on Bastian's hand?"

"How did it happen?"

"I wasn't looking. It was an accident," Bastian says.

"Let's go to the back."

Matre Lydia leads them to a large room with two long rows of beds with curtains drawn between each of them. A strong scent assaults Cass's nose. The Matre points Bastian to a bed. He sits on it, and Cass takes the chair on his right.

"Let me see the cut."

Bastian presents his injured left hand. The bracelet he made—identical to the one he gave her—dangles off his wrist, blood coloring the stones. The bravado he had earlier is gone.

Matre Lydia picks up a thin square packet from the medical cart next to her and rips it open. She pulls out an alcohol swab and dabs it around the cut, wiping blood away from skin. Bastian sucks in sharp breaths through his teeth.

"This will need stitches," she says.

"Will it hurt?" he asks, his voice small and face leached of blood.

"Yes. I'll numb the skin before I put in the stitches—it'll help. And until it's completely healed, we'll have to watch for infection."

"What happens if he gets an infection?" Cass asks.

"Usually, we can treat it with antibiotics. But in the worst-case scenario, you can develop gangrene."

"What's that?" he asks.

"It's when the skin dies and decomposes. If that happens, we'll have to cut the infected skin off."

Bastian's eyes widen, his mouth hanging.

The Matre stands up. "Let me go get the anesthetic."

"I told you it's not nothing," Cass whispers once the Matre is out of the room.

He whimpers. "I don't want to lose my hand."

Cass's stomach roils. "You won't."

He drags in a breath. "Now go look for Matre Selene and the Outsider. This is the only time Matre Lydia will be busy."

"Where am I supposed to look?"

"We didn't pass anything coming here, so go that way." He points to the right beyond the large room they're in.

"What are you going to tell Matre Lydia if she asks about me?"

"I'll just tell her you left."

She hesitantly stands up, heart beating like a drum inside her chest. Distant footsteps are approaching. Matre Lydia is coming back with her medical kit to stitch up Bastian. Cass has to leave now. She gives Bastian one last look and darts to the right in the opposite direction.

She finds herself in a long corridor. There are doors on the left side, all closed. She has no idea which one would have Matre Selene in it.

Suddenly a door clicks open next to her. She sees an alcove down the way to her right and leaps into it. It's barely big enough for her. She presses her body flat against the wall and closes her eyes, willing herself invisible.

"Let's talk out here so we can let Selene sleep. What's the latest, Galena?" It's the Head Matre. Cass's insides turn to stone.

"It doesn't look good," Matre Galena's voice shakes with emotion. "Her blood pressure is beginning to climb again."

"What we've been doing is only a temporary fix. Selene is not going to make it if we don't get her the medicine soon," another voice says. "Every minute we can't treat her is a minute she's closer to death."

Cass feels cold all over—not only because of what was said but because of the voice itself. The familiarity of its strange whispery quality is straight from her dreams. But how can that be? The Crone isn't real.

"Aris, how soon can you be ready to leave?" the Head Matre asks.

The Outsider!

"As soon as I have mine and Metis's ID numbers. Then we just need our memory books," she says.

What memory books? There are memory books?

"I've put the request in—records should have that to me shortly. The police should be done with the library by today. Our problem—as if we need another one—is Mona said they found a piece of paper they're bringing back as evidence."

Aris's heart drops. "My translation!"

"It must have fallen when we were rushing through cleaning the library. I'm seeing Scylla today. My guess is he won't say more than he can, but I'll see what I can glean from him."

"We also have to persuade him to take Aris on the train," Matre Galena says. "And it's going to be tough with his partner around."

"I'm aware."

"He will do whatever it takes if he truly loves Selene," the Crone says.

"But how can we know for sure?" the Head Matre says.

"Bring him here. You'll have your answer the moment he lays his eyes on her. He won't be able to hide his first reaction."

"That's too big a risk. What if he doesn't love her?"

"From what I know of him, he sincerely cares for others, so at the very least he will help get us the medicine," the Crone says. "What we don't know is whether or not he will tell the Planner once he learns of her pregnancy. He may perceive the child to be a threat to peace."

"But it's *his* child," Matre Galena says.

"Do you know what their motto is? 'Peace is the only battle worth waging.' The police were raised to protect peace at all costs."

"Then why are we even going to him?"

"Because we need the train and him to get the medicine. And, like I said before, if he truly loves Selene, everything else becomes secondary. But what we need to understand is that all of these fixes are only temporary. Even if we have Scylla on our side, he's just one person. The ultimate problem—the root cause of everything—is the System itself, and the one permanent fix is to bring it down."

"I already told you I'm not involving the CDL in your revolution," the Head Matre says. "You and Aris—and your Dreamers or whoever—can do whatever you want to get your memories back. That's your prerogative. But I cannot risk the safety of the children."

"What guarantee do you have that your children are safe? Do they seem safe now that the police took the senior students? Yes, I know. I heard the children talking to each other. I heard them crying in the night. There's no real safety. The System will always want to exert control. That's the one constant. If you keep reacting to that same constant, nothing will ever change."

"What do you suggest we do then?" The Head Matre's voice is terse.

"Not play by their rules."

"And what? Not take care of the children? Not teach them? Not love them? For as long as children are born, someone has to take care of them."

"These are not your only options."

"What choice do we have?"

"You have all the choices. All of the paths are yours to take. Realizing that is your first step to freedom."

The Head Matre scoffs. "Easy for you to say, when you don't have all these lives depending on you."

"Just because they left this place, it doesn't mean they no longer need you," the Crone says. "There are people in the Four Cities struggling against the System. They're all our children. Today it's Selene and Aris who need help hiding from the System, tomorrow it could be anyone. As long as the System exists, as long as Tabula Rasa exists."

"You mean as long as your husband exists," the Head Matre says. "You keep saying 'the System' as if it were separate from the Planner. He designed the System. He thought up Tabula Rasa. They exist because *he* exists."

Husband. That's why she did not answer Cass's question— *Who are you to him?*

"You say I'm more powerful than he, that I hold the future of the Four Cities in my hands, but that's just deflecting your own responsibility," the Head Matre continues. "You have the power to change him—more so than anyone."

All voices fall silent.

"I have to attend to other matters," the Head Matre says eventually. "Let me know of any updates, and I'll do the same."

Cass clutches at the wall, her heart pounding inside her ears. Her brain is fraying at the edges. She needs to find Bastian. She needs to get to him now.

CHAPTER FORTY-ONE

METIS

March 4, 2233
(16 days before Tabula Rasa)

A sloping ceiling. Rafters. A chandelier of round capiz shells that dance softly in the wind with a tinkling sound.

He sits up. Under him is a blue leather and cherrywood chair. Next to him is a full bookshelf. In one corner is a wooden desk, and on it sits a distillation kit. Ferns and orchids in bloom are sprinkled throughout the room.

The front door opens, and through it appears a blond woman in a white T-shirt and jeans, barefooted.

"Oh, hello," she says. "It's nice to see you again."

"Do I know you?"

Her eyebrows crinkle. "I'm Eleanor."

"Eleanor?" He springs up. "The Crone?"

He goes to her "But you look—"

She looks down at her body. "I suppose so."

He notices in her hand is a bouquet of light green flowers—hypnos. "Are you going to make Absinthe?"

"Yes. You know, I'm very close to making it perfect."

"It will be." He looks around. "What's this place?"

"A prison." She points to the outside, but instead of a lawn,

Metis sees a white room. On the far wall hangs a large computer screen, and on it is the ancient face of a man who's not a man.

"He said he found a way for us to live forever," she says. "As digitized consciousnesses, we are no longer bound to the blood bags that were our bodies. I didn't agree to it."

"Why would he do that to you?"

"The Four Cities need him, and he needs me. He said it's for the good of all."

"But why am I here with you?" he asks.

"You're his prisoner too. You need to get out, Metis. Before it's too late."

He sits up and wipes his eyes, feeling as if his brain is made of clouds. The sun is setting outside the window. How long was he asleep?

"How was your nap?" Aris asks from the door.

"Fine." But it's not true. He isn't fine. There's an odd feeling growing inside his stomach. But why? He is on his bed in his room in his house in Lysithea. Aris is here. Everything is just as it should be. Exactly as it's always been.

But that's not right.

He casts his eyes over the room. He remembers the chair should live in the bathroom, not with the desk. The bedside tables should not be on either side of the bed but at the foot of it. All the pillows should be on the floor, not neatly stacked behind him.

"Where are all my clothes?" he asks. They were supposed to be on the floor.

Aris gives him a strange look. "In the closet, where all the clothes are."

She comes to sit on the bed next to him. "Are you okay?"

Her hand is on his cheek, her blue eyes digging. But that's not right either. These eyes are not the familiar brown he'd lost himself in countless times—why didn't he see it before? He pulls away.

"Metis?" She leans in to kiss him.

He scoots backward.

"Metis?" she calls, blue eyes following him.

Suddenly the bed disappears from under him. He falls backward and drops down, bracing himself for an impact, but the floor never comes. He keeps falling, caught in an unending plunge into nothingness. A scream builds inside his chest and travels up his throat, but no sound comes. His fear is trapped behind his mouth. He is going to die, and no one will ever know.

Something grabs him and yanks him forward. He feels a jolt, and a piercing brightness shocks his vision. The source of light comes from above. He blinks, and his surroundings come into focus. White walls. White ceiling. White floors.

Sitting on the chair across from him is a woman with pale blond hair and icy blue eyes. The Interpreter. Apollina. She removes the helmet on her head and springs up in one quick movement.

"No, no, no, no, no," she says.

What the fuck is going on?

He tries to lift his arms, but they are rigid by his sides. He tries to stand but cannot. He looks down and sees his arms bound to the armrests by bands of metal around his wrists. His legs, too, are immovable—attached to the chair he's sitting on. Grazing the side of his face are colorful tendrils. He traces their path down his arms, alongside his leg, to a white box with lights in various colors blinking at random intervals. Panic grabs his insides. He shakes his head, the only thing he still has control of.

"No, you'll break it," she says and lifts something heavy from his head and puts it on the table next to the white box. He sees now it's a copper helmet with colorful wires running from it.

"Help!" he screams at the top of his lungs. "Anybody out there? Help!"

"Stop screaming, Metis. I need to check if you're okay," She grabs the sides of his face and stares into his eyes. Her icy blues are the same pair he saw on Aris, that he saw on Cole.

"Clear. Good," she says to herself.

Cold runs up his spine. He had been romantic with her, thinking she was someone dear to him. He feels nauseated.

"Where am I?" he asks.

"You're in Police Station One."

"But I— What's happening?"

"I need to put you back in twilight," she says.

"No, please no. Tell me what's happening. Please."

She touches his cheek. "It's too bad we lost that simulation. It may be my best one yet."

A throbbing pain hits him in the back of his skull, blinding him. "Ow!"

"Are you experiencing pain?"

"Yes, a headache. Can I have the pill?"

"What pill?"

"The white pill."

"Oh. There's no white pill. It doesn't exist in reality."

"Then what was it? It helped with my headache."

"A relaxant. Every time the machine detects you are not being truthful, it sends you a headache. Then I administer a small dosage of TBT128 to help relax you, but not enough for you to become incoherent, the way the police use it." She rolls her eyes. "They don't know what they're doing. The trick is to use consent so the subject doesn't fight it so hard."

"You manufactured a headache? Is that what this is?"

She looks worried. "No. You're not wearing the helmet. I'm going to need to scan you to see if everything is okay. You've been through more simulations than I've ever done on one person in such a short period of time."

"Why are you doing this to me?" he asks.

"We're trying to find out what you and the Crone have been planning."

"I don't know anything."

"That's what you've said. But we know you're lying." She points to the machine. "It knows."

He realizes she's telling him more than she needs to. The only reason she would do that is if he won't remember it when she puts him into the next simulation—just as he did not remember Cole when he was with Aris.

"It's too bad I can't take you to the Interpreter Center," she continues. "Though less precise, the device there makes it easy to see directly into your dreams. Simulations are more complicated and require me as a conduit, but . . ." She gives him a shy smile. "It has its benefits."

Warmth rushes to his cheeks.

"You and Aris have quite a special connection," Apollina says. "I've never seen such a love. The spectrum of the emotions is so expansive."

"I don't want you inside my head!" he yells.

Hurt crosses her face.

"You don't have to do this," he pleads.

She shakes her head. "I have to. It's my job. It's my purpose."

CHAPTER FORTY-TWO

ARIS

March 4, 2233
(16 days before Tabula Rasa)

"I'm sorry, it's a strange place to meet," Aris says, and gestures to the vast bathroom around them. "The Head Matre thought it would be the most convenient."

They have been using this secret passageway to go between the Administrative building and the Health Center so no one could detect their movements from the outside.

"It's fine. I understand," Matre Eleni says.

The Matre looks about the same age as the Head Matre, but instead of looking severe, she wears her expression with the same gentleness as Selene. Aris wonders if they also assign jobs here based on propensity models.

"Was this place the same when I was growing up here?" she asks.

"The CDL itself doesn't change, so what you see now is what you saw when you were a child. And we Matres, well, we've looked this way since the beginning. The children are what change."

"What was I like?"

Matre Eleni smiles. "That's quite a big question."

She laughs. "I know. I guess whatever you can remember would be great."

"Let's see. I remember you were an inquisitive child and excelled in the sciences."

"I became a scientist."

"You did go to College."

"How long were you my counselor?"

"All four years of high school."

"What did we talk about?"

"The usual things mostly—classes, preparing for College, relationships. As I recall you were worried about Tabula Rasa—I'd say more so than most children. You were especially worried about losing your best friend, understandable since you two were inseparable."

"What was their name?"

"Belen. He wasn't one of mine, but I know his name very well. He came up often in our sessions. Quite a mischief-maker, that one."

"He was?" Her heart squeezes around the missing shape of someone she cannot remember.

"He was always in trouble with Matre Elizabeth, who was the Head Matre at the time, though he was quite popular with everyone. Once, and I remember this vividly, he performed a poetry reading on the stage while dripping clay on his entire body, making a big mess."

Aris could almost see him now, covered in brown earth with a big smile.

> *I live in between dreams*
> *Traversing from one plane to another*
> *Sirus beside me*
> *Our desires blending like fire.*

She doesn't know why she thought of the poem or even if it is the same one. But that is less important, she decides.

"Though you were yourself a well-behaved child, you'd get in trouble quite often," the Matre adds. "I assumed it was Belen who roped you into things."

"What did we do?"

"You'd run around the CDL late at night, scaring students."

"Scaring them?"

"You were pretending to be ghosts. Belen wanted to leave a legacy."

They both laugh until they cry.

She wipes her eyes. "Thank you, Matre."

"The pleasure is mine." She reaches out her hand and touches Aris's. "Being Matres means we have to make peace with never seeing our children again, but that doesn't stop us from missing you all. Every time we have to let each of you go, we lose a part of ourselves. But with you here, a little bit of who I was also came back."

Aris feels the exchange. From the center of her chest, something of hers is being drawn out, traveling through a string connecting them. In return, through that same thread, she is receiving something of Matre Eleni. Memories.

> *On the edge of a cliff,*
> *hidden by jagged peaks*
> *and a northern forest of pine,*
> *lives Old Mem.*

She realizes Mem isn't just the library. It is also all the Matres, who have been waiting here, holding a trove of memories like jewels.

A part of the wall opens, and the Head Matre steps out. "Aris, I have your ID number. Oh, hello Eleni."

"Hi Hera."

"Good catching up?"

"Yes. It's been a special time. I'll leave you two be." She embraces Aris and exits through the false wall.

Head Matre Hera hands Aris a piece of paper. On it are two sets of numbers: 2200-11 and 2196-111.

"The first one is yours, and the other is Metis's," she says. "Just as you had suspected, his name was Metis while he was here too, which made it easier for Records. Though they still had to look through ten years of ledgers since they were not sure which year he was born in. That's why it took so long."

"Thank you." Aris stares at the numbers, hands shaking. She cannot believe she is finally holding the key to her memories.

She does the calculation to convert these numbers to binary.

2200-11 = 100010011000-1011.

2196-111 = 100010010100-1101111.

"I have them." New tears begin to form. Happy ones.

Before this, she didn't often cry. Not after the first time she woke from an Absinthe dream. Not on the day she left their house in Lysithea. Not even when she said goodbye to Metis. Being here—surrounded by memories—has changed her. Something has happened to her heart. She feels it. Freer. Lighter. She feels . . . everything.

CHAPTER FORTY-THREE

SCYLLA

March 4, 2233
(16 days before Tabula Rasa)

A knock at the door comes promptly at ten. It's Mona. Her face, identical to that of Selene, is a needle to his heart. The worry that began the moment he learned of her illness has only grown to fill his entire chest, leaving little space for much else. He is no longer fit to be on this assignment, yet he cannot leave. Leaving means he will be even farther from her.

"Good morning. Did you eat breakfast already?" she asks.

"Yes, the kitchen delivered it at eight. Thank you." He takes a step closer and lowers his voice. "I need to speak to the Head Matre today."

"Well, you're in luck. She has asked to meet with you. I can take you to her before I take Officer Evan back to the library. Will that work?"

"Yes."

Evan appears behind him. "Thanks for being on time today, Matre."

Scylla sighs. On top of being inexperienced, the younger ones can be so exasperating. Why did the Planner decide to send Evan? Was he worried about Scylla's ability to stay objective when it comes to the Matres? The thought rakes him.

I'm the lead officer of the Four Cities. This is my job. This is my purpose.

Scylla tries to clear his mind of Selene and focuses instead on the task at hand. The crisp morning air has a distinct scent of pine, helping to ease the heat of anxiety within. In no time, they are back at the Gate of the Six Bells.

Inside the Administrative building, Matres walk the hall. Still, he does not see any students. The Head Matre is still hiding them away. Mona leads them down toward her office.

"These rooms, are they all offices for the Matres?" Evan asks.

"Yes."

"This place is so big. And very . . . unique."

"It has a long and interesting history."

"I've never heard anything about it."

"It's very well hidden, isn't it?" she says.

"How can I learn more?"

"There are several books in the main library. All of us study the history of this place extensively, seeing as we're not allowed anywhere else." There's resentment in her voice.

"Where is that?"

"In the same building as the students' dorms."

"Let me guess, I'm not allowed there."

"Not when it's being used by the children."

Evan is doing police work the way he knows how and has been trained to. But he has so far worked only with the citizens of the Four Cities, and with the help of the Subdue Bracelets. He knows nothing of the Matres. They are notoriously private and loyal to each other. An outsider will never be able to break that bond. Police work here will not be accomplished through the questioning of Matres.

The door to the Head Matre's office is open. She is standing by the window, her back to them. The morning light illuminates her, reminding him of the Crone.

"Good morning, Head Matre Hera," Scylla says.

She turns around. "Come in."

He nods to Evan and Matre Mona before he closes the door.

"Would you like to sit down?" she says.

He takes a seat, and so does she. She laces her fingers together on the desk, her face grave. The silence is heavy with unspoken words. He will let her begin this conversation. She is the one who called the meeting.

"I've always liked you," she says, surprising him. "You seem to care about us here at the CDL, unlike your predecessors, who only saw us as means to an end."

"Please forgive them. They're just a product of their training."

"You had the same training, the same upbringing, the same people raising you."

"So have the Matres, yet you're all different."

"I suppose the same DNA does not result in the same people. There lies the defect in the Planner's idea of cloning us."

The Planner had told him that the Matres are from Eleanor's DNA, just as all the policemen are from his. They are the only two people he trusts to run the Four Cities—the only two in the whole world. Scylla never knew what happened to the Planner to make him so distrustful. But none of this has anything to do with the reason the Head Matre has asked him here.

"How was your investigation yesterday? Mona said you spent most of your time in the library."

There it is. "We did."

"You found something," she says, not as a question but a statement. *Mona must have told her. Of course she did.*

"We did. Evan found it."

She nods but does not ask what it is. Either she knows what

it is, or she's not worried about its existence. But she should be worried.

"Has anybody been in there lately?" he asks.

"We don't have many reasons to go into the library except for cursory cleaning after the police officers are done with it."

"So, the last time was at the beginning of this cycle?"

"Officer Scylla," The Head Matre leans forward. "Over the past two hundred years, the library has been the police officers' domain. You have spent significantly more time in it than us Matres combined. We have no idea what you do in there, yet we do not question you—the books are of no use to us. So, whatever you may have found would more likely come from one of the officers."

Smart. With one sentence, she presented a plausible reason for the evidence to be dismissed.

"I know, Head Matre. Still, I have to question you. It's protocol."

She leans back, looking too calm to be guilty. "What else do you want to ask me?"

"Has anyone removed anything from it?"

"No. Why would we? And what does this have to do with keeping the CDL safe?"

"We can never be too careful."

"So, you think someone from the outside might want these books? What's in them?"

She just asked the one question he cannot answer.

"That's classified," he says.

She narrows her eyes. "If there's anything I need to know pertaining to the safety of the children . . ."

He cannot risk her sealing off the entire CDL. "No, Head Matre. This does not concern the children."

She relaxes. "When do you think you'll be done with the investigation?"

"In two days, I think. We still have the lab, this building, and a few others, as well as the boundaries."

"And you will not go near the students."

"We won't."

"Yesterday you offered to take Selene to the Four Cities for diagnostics and treatment."

At the name of his love, his heart jumps.

"Will you allow me to ask the Planner?" He eyes the analog telephone on the shelf behind her.

"No. She's to stay here where she's safest."

"I will personally guarantee her safety while she's there."

"What she needs—what you can help her get—is medication."

"I can do that. Have you determined what's wrong with her?"

"Yes."

Relief fills him with gratitude. "Just give me the list of what you need, and I'll get it as soon as I return to Callisto."

"You cannot let anyone know that she's sick or about the medication."

"Why not?"

The Head Matre does not answer.

"What's wrong with her?" he asks.

"I cannot tell you. All I can say is without the medication, she will die."

He couldn't have heard her correctly. "I'm sorry, what?"

"Selene will die without the medication."

His entire body feels as though it has fallen through ice into a freezing river.

"How is that possible?" he asks.

"Matres do die, Officer Scylla. We are not immortal. But at least our deaths belong to us."

He feels a crack in his heart. "May I see her?"

The space between her brows folds together. "Why?"

He should not have asked it so recklessly, so desperately, but he cannot take back what he has already said. "It's just—she's just been so kind to me."

"I don't think that's a good idea," she says. "She's not in a state to receive guests. Just know she's well taken care of by Galena."

The love of his life is dying, and he is unable to see her, to be by her side and hold her hand. Pain hits the middle of his chest, and he wants to scream. But he cannot.

He swallows it down. "I will do what I can for Matre Selene."

"I'm glad to hear it. The sooner you can get her the medicine, the better."

He nods. "Is there anything else you need from me?"

"No, I know you're busy. I will take you to join your partner and Matre Mona at the library."

CHAPTER FORTY-FOUR

CASS

March 4, 2233
(16 days before Tabula Rasa)

"Whoa..." Bastian says after she told him what she heard in the Health Center. He looks at his thickly bandaged hand. "Thank you for your sacrifice."

Cass rolls her eyes. "How much painkiller did Matre Lydia give you?"

"I watched her put the stitches in."

"Maybe it's a good thing you're calm right now."

He leans back on his bed. "There's a Crone who's made of light, and she's the wife of the Planner. Matre Selene is pregnant. All of this is so surreal."

"And Officer Scylla is somehow responsible, even though Matre Galena said no one is supposed to be able to get pregnant."

"So they're going to blackmail him to take the Outsider on the train back to Callisto and get Matre Selene medicine."

"Not blackmail. They just need to find out whether he loves Matre Selene. And if he does, he'll do it for her without a fight."

"That's the exact definition of blackmail."

"But it's *his* child," she repeats what Matre Galena said.

"That he doesn't know about or want."

"How do you know he doesn't want it?" she asks.

"Because why would you want something you never thought you could have? It's like wanting two extra arms—handy, but didn't think I could have them."

A laugh escapes. It makes her feel better.

"Also, what's with the Crone from your dream being real?" he asks.

"She was always real. I guess they weren't dreams."

"Do you remember what you talked about?"

"All kinds of things. Mostly she asked me about life here and told me about the Old World. She's one of the creators of the Four Cities."

"I thought only the Planner created the Four Cities."

"That's what I thought too. But the Planner doesn't want people to know about her because he thinks she's dangerous."

"She does want to overthrow the System."

"And the Head Matre said the Crone has the power to change the Planner. She said the System and the Planner are one and the same."

"She's not wrong."

"Shhh."

"It's just the two of us."

"But this is huge. They—the Crone and the Outsider—they mentioned Dreamers, whoever they are. They want their memories back."

"They want a revolution," Bastian says the last word so quietly she almost can't hear it.

It makes her think of the American colonists fighting to break free from the British hundreds of years ago. People fought in over 230 battles—big and small. Will there be battles? Her heart drops to her stomach.

"What do we do?" Her voice is shaky. She hugs her legs close to her knees.

"I don't know."

"The Head Matre said she doesn't want to involve the CDL, because of us kids."

"But next year we won't be kids, and we'll have to go through what those in the Four Cities have been going through," he says.

"What are you saying?"

"We can wait for the revolution to come to us, or we can leave."

"But the Head Matre said—"

"I know, but she can't control everything. Once the Planner finds out about her involvement, he's going to get rid of her. Maybe all the Matres. Maybe the entire CDL. You know that strange feeling I've been getting that something bad is going to happen, I think it's this very thing."

She feels a quake starting at her core. "What are you saying?"

"We have to leave, Cass. It's the only way we can stay together. First to the lake, then farther. Maybe to the other side of the mountains."

"I don't know if I want to do this."

"What choice do we have?" Bastian closes his eyes, his brows furrowing.

She looks at his bandaged hand. "How are you feeling?"

"Amazing. Just terrific."

"I'm serious."

"My entire hand feels like it's going to fall off. I think my painkiller is wearing off."

"Why don't you rest? I'll wake you up for dinner." She gets up from his bed, feeling a thousand miles away from okay herself.

"Cass?"

"Yeah?"

"Do you think she'll lay an egg like a bird?" he asks.

An image of a mini Matre Selene pushing its way out of a cracked egg enters her mind. A laugh escapes. She needed that laugh.

"Humans don't lay eggs." But then again, what's real anymore?

When Bastian does not say anything else, she tiptoes off. She opens his door to find Ori leaning against the wall across the hall.

"Hey. Have you been out here long?"

"Kind of."

"Why didn't you go in?"

"How is he?" she asks.

"Resting. Matre Lydia stitched up his cut and gave him pain medication."

Ori leans in and whispers, "It wasn't an accident."

"What?"

"I saw it happen. He picked up the knife and was looking directly at his hand before he sliced it."

"What?"

"Why would he do that? Why would he hurt himself on purpose?" Ori asks.

"I-I don't—"

"Has he done this before?"

"No! Of course not."

Ori's eyes water. "He can't be like that senior we held the Ceremony of the Dead for last year."

"Agan . . ." Cass says.

He was a solemn-faced skinny boy in the class before them. He was supposed to go through this year's Tabula Rasa but had died late last year from a fall. Rumors had it his neck was broken so badly the bone protruded out of his skin.

That morning of the ceremony, Cass stood with her class between Bastian and Caylyn—the same two she had been standing next to her entire childhood. Her friend was shaking like a leaf as they listened to people saying nice things about the dead boy. Later she couldn't remember any of the words and realized it was because they were all generic. No one really knew him.

Agan was quiet, kept to himself mostly. The one thing that made him standout was his piano playing. They said he was created for it. He was quite good and would sometimes play in place of Matre Selene. Once Cass accidentally walked in on him crying at his piano. These details didn't seem connected at the time, but now . . .

"You think Agan hurt himself on purpose?" she asks Ori.

"Yes. I thought you knew. He did it because he didn't want to go through Tabula Rasa."

CHAPTER FORTY-FIVE

METIS

March 4, 2233
(16 days before Tabula Rasa)

Outside the small room Apollina keeps him in, Police Station One is a study in contrasts. Curved walls and hard concrete floors. Severe white on the inside and sunset-drenched desert out the expansive windows. Neutral-faced droids and angry-faced policemen.

He is in a wheelchair, being pushed by one of the droids. Apollina is next to him. She's told him he is being moved up to the medical floor to get his head checked out. As much as he hates the idea of there being something wrong with his brain, this is a respite from the mindfuck of the simulations.

Eyes stare at him as he passes—not in the least bit friendly. He shifts his gaze to the ground.

"Don't worry, you're perfectly safe," Apollina says. "No one will hurt you. Planner's orders."

Strange that his well-being has been guaranteed by the one keeping him against his will.

"Metis!" a voice calls. "Metis, is that you?"

He looks up and sees a familiar face coming toward him. "Vic?"

Like him, she is accompanied by a droid. She stops in front of him.

"They got you too? No . . ." she says.

The droid tugs at her.

"They arrested us for no reason," she yells as she is being pulled away. "I didn't do anything."

Us. She could only mean other Dreamers. *Why?* Operating in secret, they have been keeping themselves under the radar. There is no list of members, no regular meeting places. They do not cause trouble. All they want are their dream memories.

"A Dreamer friend?" Apollina asks.

"No, I—"

"Don't bother lying. The police finally figured out a way to identify them."

"How?"

"They're under quite a lot of stress trying to find those missing and keep more people from disappearing."

Not the answer to his question but an answer nonetheless. There must be enough Dreamers running away for the System to decide to preempt it.

"Did you know some of them even died trying?" she adds.

He gasps. "They died?"

"Quite a few, actually. The desert is an unforgiving place."

"How do you know all this?"

"When you have to be here twenty-four seven, you hear things. Did you all plan this out?"

"No! Why would we do that?"

"I'd like to believe, but unfortunately, I have no idea if you're lying or not."

"But I'm telling the truth." He is. Aside from Aris, he never planned or mentioned going north with anyone. They were not even the first people to have left.

The droid pushes him up the ramp to the second floor and

takes him into a small room dominated by a large cylinder-shaped tube. The sight of it terrifies him.

"Take your ring off," Apollina says.

"What? Why?"

"Depending on the metal, the machine could rip it off your finger."

He thinks of Aris's face and hesitantly removes it. It feels like a finger is missing. He hands it to Apollina.

She points. "You're going to lie on that long table, and it's going to move you into that machine. It will scan your brain. I will be in the other room, and the droid will be outside. Do not try to run away, because it will stop you."

He gets up onto the table and lies down. A mechanical sound whirs, and he is now inside the narrow tubelike space. He finds it harder to breathe.

"It's an old technology, but that's what we have" she says. "Try to relax. But do not move, or we won't get a good image."

"How long is it going to take?" he asks.

"As long as it takes. *Don't* move."

A minute passes, and a loud clanging rings through the room, rattling his skull. He shuts his eyes tightly, hoping this passes soon.

The light flickers on. He knows this place. It's the cave on the edge of Elara. He sees a figure walking toward him. It's Eleanor—not as young a version as he last saw in the cottage but still in her pre-Crone form. She does not appear to see him.

She pulls a bag from her shoulder and tips it over the table. Things tumble onto the wood surface. He walks closer and peruses the items. A bag of hypnos blossoms, three tomatoes, ten strawberries, and a handful of greens.

Pulling the chair in behind her, she sits down. She opens a notebook on the table. Her hands are visibly trembling. The skin on them papery thin—the bumps and grooves a topographic map of her years.

"Hello, Metis," Eleanor says.

He is sitting across from her, and she is looking straight at him. She slides the notebook in front of him. On it is a diagram.

"What is this?" he asks.

"The answer."

"What answer?"

"To how you can save everyone. You've known it for a while. You saw it once, and you knew what it was then."

"Where did I see it?"

"The Interpreter Center."

"You're all done," Apollina's voice stirs him.

What was it he just saw? It couldn't be a dream, he's not asleep. It was not a simulation—he's out of it. Or is he? Was it a hallucination?

His bed slides out of the machine. Apollina is peering down at him.

"We have the result. There's some trauma." She sounds genuinely concerned.

His stomach drops. "What's wrong with my head?"

"I'm not sure if it's from the simulations or something else. I'll send it in for further analysis. The Planner is not going to like this."

A brain injury. Cold washes through him.

My music.

The droid replaces Apollina. It helps him up and guides him back into the wheelchair.

"I can walk. Why can't I walk myself?" Metis asks.

"Not a good idea after days of simulations and now the trauma. I can't risk you falling," Apollina says. "Come. Let's have dinner before we break the news to the Planner. No point being hungry while doing it."

They go back down to the first floor and the room. Inside it he sees a new addition—a table and two chairs. On top of the table is a basket.

"Sit," she says. "I had food delivered. It's the one luxury they've afforded me while I'm here. I can't stomach their uninspiring food."

He moves from his wheelchair to the chair across from her. The droid walks the wheelchair to the corner of the room and stands there, looking like a piece of avant-garde furniture.

"Why is the droid still here?" he asks.

"It stays while you're not in restraints. Police Station One rule." She rolls her eyes. "It's the safest place in the Four Cities."

She unpacks the basket and brings out container after container. "If only the Planner would let us work at the Interpreter Center, we'd have better facilities." She looks over her shoulder at the large screen on the wall. "And a better view."

She places a plate in front of him. "First course. Heart of palm and radish carpaccio with lemon vinaigrette. It's from one of my favorite restaurants, near the art museum. Right now they have a menu celebrating the brightness of spring."

"The second is saffron risotto with cherry tomatoes stuffed with basil puree," she adds. "And the main is chanterelle casserole with stuffed zucchini flowers."

The carpaccio tastes amazing. As he forks more into his

mouth, something occurs to him. All the simulations contained a mealtime with beautifully presented foods.

He studies her as she eats. "How often do you eat out?"

"I don't eat out. All of my meals are brought in. I'm not allowed to mingle with the populace. None of us with continuous memories are."

"So you don't talk to anyone?"

"Of course I do. I talk to those that come for my help at the Interpreter Center."

"Are you friends with any of the policemen?"

She sneers. "No thanks."

She cuts a lonely figure. These gourmet meals are her one pleasure in an otherwise one-dimensional life. But it isn't just the food she craves—it's the company. The domestic scenes she built into her simulations were a way for her to connect with another human.

"But at least I'm not hidden away like those Matres at the CDL," she adds. "What a terrible life that must be."

The door opens, and a police officer comes in. He is tall and thin, wearing a long khaki trench coat and a fedora.

"Don't you know how to knock?" Apollina says.

"I didn't know you were"—he studies the scene—"having dinner with the prisoner. I need to update the Planner."

Her eyes narrow. "You're not Scylla."

"No. I'm Gordon, second-in-command while Scylla is out." He walks to the wall and places a hand on it next to the large screen. It flickers on, and a face appears. The man's ancient skin makes him look as though he is made of tree roots and the earth itself.

The Planner.

"Gordon," he says.

"I'm here to give you your daily report, sir."

"Go ahead."

"We've searched all the libraries and bookshelves in the Four Cities, and there's still no sign of the Book of Crone, sir."

"What! Is the entire force incompetent?" he yells.

Gordon appears as if he has shrunk to half his height.

"What is your purpose?" the Planner asks.

"To keep the peace, sir."

"The predictive model forecasts the longer she is missing, the more dangerous she becomes to the System—to peace. I want the entire police force searching for Eleanor twenty-four seven. Double, triple the shift if you must. Until she's found, no one rests."

He looks around the room, and his dark brown eyes—dark like his own—catch Metis's. Fear prickles his spine.

"Apollina, why is he awake?" the Planner asks, his voice as icy as her eyes.

She puts her fork down, appearing unconcerned by his question. "He rejected his last simulation. Afterward he complained of a headache. I took him up to get a head scan and found signs of brain trauma. I sent the scan to the hospital for further analysis and can't put him back into another simulation until he's clear. Now we're having dinner because . . . well . . . I'm hungry."

"Brain trauma? Why? I thought the simulations were safe." He sounds worried.

"I won't know why until I get further analysis."

"How's his musical ability? Can he still play?"

"We'll have to test him."

"Do that."

"Also, I know you've rejected this request before, but I'd be doing you a disservice if I didn't bring it up again." She laces her fingers together. "The Dreamcatcher may be the only way, right now, to look inside his mind."

"The side effects—"

"I will be extra gentle, I promise," she cuts him off. "I won't touch anything. I'll only look."

"The Interpreter Center isn't safe."

"With all due respect, the Interpreter Center has one of the most advanced security systems in the Four Cities. In all my years, no one has ever broken in."

"I will run a predictive model on it." The Planner turns back to Gordon. "Any word from Scylla?"

"Nothing, sir. But we are monitoring the analog phone system and will alert you as soon as we hear something."

"Where is she?" the Planner says to himself.

CHAPTER FORTY-SIX

ARIS

March 4, 2233
(16 days before Tabula Rasa)

"He's a man at war with himself," the Head Matre says, her eyes on Selene's sleeping face.

"How so?" Aris asks.

"I could see he cares for her, but I couldn't get a clear read on whether it's more than just sympathy. At times he appeared burning with worry. But in the next breath, he cooled. Perhaps it's my own insufficiency. I've never known romantic love."

"Don't blame yourself," the Crone says. "Policemen are trained to turn the emotional part of themselves off because it interferes with their objectivity."

A knock comes from the door, and it opens. Galena steps into the room with another Matre. *Amira.* Aris is becoming quicker at identifying the Matres without using their name tags.

"The police are done in the library," Amira says. "Mona is now taking them to the lab."

"All day in there. They must have combed the place after the evidence they found," the Head Matre says. "How are the children?"

"Restless, Head Matre."

She drags in a long breath and exhales. "Make sure they get exercise indoors."

"It's kind of difficult with all the irreplaceable art around, but we'll do our best."

"Thank you, Amira."

She nods and leaves.

Galena walks to Selene's side. "Has she woken up yet?"

"She's stirred but hasn't woken up," the Crone says. "Her body is trying to heal itself. But it's losing."

"I increased the dosage per your instruction."

"We're going to have to keep doing that until the medication comes. But we're just mitigating her symptoms."

"That's all we can do right now," the Head Matre says, and stands up. "Aris, are you ready?"

She nods. She has been ready ever since she left Lysithea. She grabs her backpack—always by her side now—and follows the Head Matre out. They make their way to the bathroom and through the tunnel to the Administrative building. It's nearly empty after dinner, most everyone back at the children's dorms or their own quarters.

"What are your plans once you return to the Four Cities?" the Head Matre asks.

"First thing is I need to break into the Interpreter Center and see whether Dreamcatcher will work with the book."

"And if it doesn't?"

"Then we look for whatever will. The books must be readable with the right tool—why keep them?"

"What if the Planner is the only one who can read them?"

She hasn't thought of that before. What if, like his old record collection, these books exist only for his own personal satisfaction?

"I don't know." She steels herself. "But I still have to try."

The Head Matre nods. She enters her office and walks to

the map on the wall. She places a hand on it, looking poised to open the secret passageway. She does not.

"I want to show you something," she says. "I have reason to believe that the CDL is located somewhere on this map of the Eastern Sierra, though I don't know where exactly. We're at the top of a crest between valleys surrounded by a forest and near some small lakes. But the lakes may be too small to have made it onto the map."

The topographic map displays a swath of brown, flat land and mountain ranges with green forests and a series of blue lakes in the crevices between peaks.

The Head Matre wipes a hand above a raised green area. "Somewhere around here, maybe." Her hand trails to a similar-looking area. "Or here."

"Where're the Four Cities?" Aris asks.

"The train comes from the south. It takes several hours to get to Callisto, so I think it's beyond this map."

She points to a tiny number on a long white line—395. "I'm guessing that this used to be a traveling route of some kind. I don't know if it's still there after all this time."

Aris follows it south to the beige-brown area of the map. The nearest blue patch is far away. There is no green anywhere.

"How did I survive coming here?" she murmurs.

"You were extremely lucky to find us."

And with sheer will and stubbornness. She looks back up to the green patches the Head Matre pointed to earlier.

"You said you're near small lakes?"

"Yes. The closest is about a three-hour walk away. But we never go beyond that."

"Enough to support life." She stares at the land north of the mountains. "Do you think anyone else out there survived?"

"If they did, they would have found us by now." Hera pushes

the panel, revealing the elevator. They step into the small antechamber and she presses the elevator button. A ding, and the door opens. "Be quick."

Aris gets into the elevator. The door closes, and she descends.

The library looks the same but feels different. The aromas of the food and flowers Selene brought to her no longer linger. Instead, the place smells of cleaning products and city shoes. Of little plastic evidence bags and rubber gloves. Of an invasion.

She treks forward cautiously, feeling as if someone is going to appear from behind one of the shelves at any moment. Every time the air conditioning clicks on, she jumps and looks behind her only to find nothing.

Without the signs she and Selene put up after painstakingly deciphering the binary numbers, the spines again appear overwhelming. She looks down at the paper in her hand.

2200-11 = 100010011000-1011
2196-111 = 100010010100-1101111

In a library of hundreds of thousands of books, how will she find hers and Metis's?

Start at the beginning.

She runs to the section of silvery gray books. The oldest part. All the books here are from 2041, fifteen years after the Last War.

Metis was born 155 years after this first batch of created children, and she was born four years after him. The books are shelved in chronological order. She begins counting until she reaches the section she thinks could be for the year 2196. The books here are reddish orange, the color of a pomegranate flower.

She looks down at the paper—*2196-111 = 100010010100-1101111.*

She looks up at the book in front of her—*100010010100-1.*

Her heart leaps. She counts to book number 111. There it is. She eases it from the shelf and hugs it to her chest. These are all of Metis's memories—everything the System has taken away from him. She puts it into her backpack.

My turn.

Four sections later, she is standing in front of a swath of aqua blue, the color of sky-reflecting water. She counts to eleven and finds her book. *100010011000-1011.* Slowly she eases it out and holds it with both hands.

"Hello, Aimilia," she says with reverence. "It's nice to meet you."

Sobs roll out of her in waves. She hugs the book—her entire childhood, her first love, her first kiss, all her moments with Metis, every meaningful and mundane thing that has happened in her life—tightly to her chest.

Welcome home.

CHAPTER FORTY-SEVEN

SCYLLA

March 5, 2233
(15 days before Tabula Rasa)

It's midnight. Scylla puts the book down and walks to Evan's bedroom door. He places an ear against it and cannot hear anything from inside. His brother is asleep.

He puts on his coat and opens the front door with a gentle hand. The sound of crickets and winged things comes from the forest. He trots toward the main path, and once he reaches the Gate of the Six Bells, he turns left.

Across the circular approach and a dry fountain is the Administrative building. And next to it is the Health Center. The two-story annex is long and skinny, with tall windows on three sides. Behind one of these has to be Selene.

He hides behind a tree, his eyes focusing on the entrance. Someone is guarding it—not in the front but just inside it. The shadow moves back and forth, the rhythm of a meditative walk. Why would there be a guard? Is it to prevent someone from leaving or from coming in?

He runs to the next tree, closer to the building, and waits there until he's sure he hasn't been seen. He continues to the one after and the one after that until he reaches the low shrubs around the perimeter of the building. Dropping to the ground, he crawls under.

These shrubs are a security risk, and if he was a better policeman, he would ask the Head Matre to get rid of them the next time he sees her. But right now, he is glad to have them. He crawls on his hands and knees—and in places, his stomach—from one window to another, listening for sounds.

So quiet.

Selene must be here somewhere. She has to be. The Head Matre said Galena is taking care of her, and this is where she works. He continues forward, ignoring the scratches to his exposed skin from the branches.

"How is she?" comes a Matre's voice from above, and he freezes.

"Her blood pressure is elevating again," another says. They are not talking to him.

"We'll keep an eye on her tonight."

"What else can we do?"

"There's not much more we can do without the medicine."

The crack in his heart deepens, and he finds it difficult to breathe a lungful.

"Come, let her rest," the voice says.

He waits until he is sure they have left the room before crawling out of the shrubs. He looks through the windows. They and the curtains are partially open. On the bed inside the room is a sleeping form, her face lit by a sliver of light coming through the door.

Selene is a ghost of herself. Her face bears the signs of bone-deep fatigue and malnutrition, reminding him of Gia, the survivor they found in the desert. She looks as if she could disappear with the morning light. His eyes blur.

Without another thought, he swings one of the windows

wide and climbs in. His feet are as heavy as lead as he takes a tentative step forward. Once he reaches her bed, something inside slides into place. He picks up her limp hand and holds it to his lips.

"You need to hold on. I'm going to get the medicine soon. I promise," he says. He presses her hand to his cheek, the way she does after they kiss. A torrent of tears pours down his face.

Her eyes flutter open.

"Scylla," she whispers. "You're here. How are you here?"

His heart stutters. He gulps in air and wipes tears from his eyes with his sleeves. "Hi, love."

She smiles. "Hi."

"What's wrong?" he asks.

"It's . . . it's the most wonderful, magical thing," she says.

How can something that makes her look at death's door be wonderful? Maybe she's not thinking clearly. Maybe she is even sicker than she looks.

"I'm so happy you're here," she says. "I've missed you."

"I've missed you too. So very much."

He wipes her stray hair from her face and kisses her. Her lips feel like they're on fire. "You're burning up."

"I don't feel so good."

"The Head Matre said you need medication. I'm going to get it tomorrow. You can wait until tomorrow, right?"

"Everyone is doing all they can to make me feel better. The Crone, Galena, you . . ."

He blinks. He could not have heard that correctly. "Did you say the Crone?"

"Everyone, so wonderful."

"Is the Crone here?" She can't be. This is too far from her cottage in Callisto. No one could have walked all the way here through the desert. That's not possible.

"Yes," a whispery high voice says from behind him.

He whips around and sees Eleanor and the Head Matre standing by the door. His heart jumps. "Eleanor!"

"Hello, Scylla," she greets.

"You're here! How did you—"

"I came here with Aris."

Her words feel like a punch to his stomach. This means one thing.

"You came here for the memory books." He turns to the Head Matre. "And you helped them?"

"Inadvertently. But yes," she says.

His mind jumps from scenario to scenario, calculating probabilities. Every single one led to disaster. The most likely is the worst. Once the Planner learns of this, he will tear through the CDL and remove all the children from the Matres. He will imprison the Head Matre and everyone involved, including Selene. The Four Cities will be in turmoil.

"This—it's not—it's going to throw everything into chaos." He takes a step toward Eleanor but doesn't let go of Selene's hand. "We've been looking everywhere for you. The entire force. You weren't supposed to leave the cottage. Where's your book? You need to go back."

"I will go back. But only with Aris."

"But the memory books will destroy peace."

"No, they won't. They're someone's history. History needs to be learned. Destroying it doesn't preserve peace, just ignorance."

Panic clutches him. "I'm sorry. The Four Cities are my responsibility."

"The Four Cities belong to all of us. We're all responsible for it. Have faith."

"I can't—this—it can't happen."

"What are you going to do, Scylla?"

He deflates. He is standing between love and loyalty, pulled apart by both.

"I-I don't know."

That's the truth.

Wait. "Why did you show yourself? You could have stayed hidden, and I wouldn't have known."

"For love." Eleanor looks at Selene.

"You knew I would come in to see her?"

"We were hoping, but we didn't know," the Head Matre says.

The glowing woman glides toward them. She places a hand on Selene's cheek. "You're awake. How are you feeling?"

"Better now that Scylla is here." Selene smiles weakly. She is struggling to keep her eyes open. She's not better.

"What are you treating her for?" he asks.

"She should be the one to tell you," the Crone says.

Selene squeezes his hand. A slight pink fights its way through the white of her cheeks.

"I'm carrying a child inside me," she whispers.

His heart stops beating—he's sure of it. When it restarts, every drop of blood in his body rushes up to his head and pounds in his ears. All at once, he feels lightheaded, cold, feverish, tingly—his insides rearranging themselves to fit his new reality.

"How?" Humans cannot procreate. Not without the artificial wombs.

Eleanor smiles. "I don't know. It's a mystery."

"But why is she so sick?"

"Without a thorough analysis, I can't tell for sure. What I do know is that her body can't handle it. Some of the symptoms are similar to those in the women I treated after the Last War, so we've been using the same treatment plan with some modifications, but it isn't foolproof. And without the right medication,

I'm afraid"—she looks at Selene—"our only other option is to remove the fetus."

Selene squeezes his hand. "No, I already said no. Our child has to exist. It will be the first one not created in the lab in two hundred years. It'll be free from Tabula Rasa, from the System."

The words "our child" fill his heart to the brim with feelings he didn't know he was capable of. He wants—*needs*—the child to exist too.

He squeezes back. "I can get the medicine tonight. I will leave right now."

"What of your partner, Evan?" the Head Matre asks.

While younger and less experienced, he is no less intelligent. They are, after all, clones of the Planner. Once he sees Scylla and the train missing, he will ask questions and investigate. He will put things together.

"I don't know. I'll lie."

"And what about after that?" the Crone asks. "What happens after Eli finds out about Selene?"

A knot forms in his chest. "I don't know."

"But you *do* know, don't you? Once he learns of her condition, he will do every experiment possible to figure out why this anomaly happened."

Eleanor is right. Panic grips him.

"We have to hide her and the child," he says. "I will find somewhere safe for them to be."

"Selene is not going anywhere," the Head Matre says. "She and the child will be safest here. Just as we've done for generations, to raise and nurture humanity, we—all of us here—will protect this new beginning. It's our purpose. It's *been* our purpose. And it will always *be* our purpose."

Eleanor turns to her. "I know, but there's only so much you and everyone here can do to protect them."

Scylla looks back at Selene. Around her, his world contracts and expands, becoming clearer than it has ever been. His entire purpose shifts to her and the life inside her.

"I will protect them for as long as I'm alive. I'll do anything to protect them."

"But you won't always be lead officer. You won't always come here every month to make sure they're safe. The ultimate problem she has, that we all have, is the Sys—" Eleanor pauses. "Is Eli. He has taken too much. From me, from you, from everyone. None of us should have to keep sacrificing our hearts, our memories, life itself for his idea of peace. We can't keep being fine with walking around with half our souls. We don't have to let this continue. We can change things."

"But how? It's been this way for two hundred years."

"We have an idea, if you'd be willing to listen," a voice says from the threshold.

He turns and sees the woman he has been searching for.

"There's Aris," Selene says, beaming.

She tentatively enters the room. "Hi, Officer Scylla."

A part of him wants to put her under arrest, but another part—one that is growing, demanding more space—wants her to have all the answers to their conundrum.

"What's your idea?"

"To change the way things have been but not in a way that will overthrow everything into chaos. There are things that work in the Four Cities, and there are things that don't—and we only need to change the things that don't work. Right now, what doesn't work is Tabula Rasa. Taking away the memories of the people we love is not the way to real peace. Until we can remove the Tabula Rasa trigger from our DNA, we can remember our past with the help of the memory books and Absinthe."

"How do you plan to do this?" he asks.

"I have my memory book. Mine and my partner's, Metis. I've figured out what the numbers on the spines mean, and we can match them back to every citizen using the CDL records. Then, we just need to get the books to those who want them. We can operate the same way we did as Dreamers—in secret and without causing trouble."

"But how are you and the others going to access the books?"

"The Crone thinks we can use the Dreamcatcher."

"That won't be easy. You won't get past the security at the Interpreter Center."

"We have a plan," Eleanor says.

"What plan?" he asks.

"I have another way in."

"You're really going to do this?" he asks.

"Yes," Aris says. "There's no other choice. We, all of us, want to stay with those we love." She looks to Selene, and the two women smile at each other. "Can you imagine a world where we won't have to lose them over and over? Where we won't need to fight to be together anymore? We can have that world."

He wants that world.

"Will it stop people from wanting to run away?" he asks.

"We run because it's the only chance we have to stay together forever," Aris says.

"Have there been more people leaving?" Eleanor asks.

"Many more. And many have died," he says.

Aris's mouth hangs open. "Died?"

"They couldn't survive the desert, but they tried anyway. We've been collecting the Dreamers and keeping them until the next Tabula Rasa."

"That won't matter. They will keep trying. Metis and I will never stop wanting to be together."

"Aris is right," Eleanor says. "It'll keep happening every cycle. I've seen it for over two hundred years. They'll keep leaving, trying to break free."

Scylla knows the problem has always been there. He used to blame Absinthe. But the drug is only fuel to an existing firestorm. Falling in love with Selene made him realize that.

He turns to the Head Matre. She needs to know what else is coming. "Most of the graduating class heading for College did not go. We put them into the Four Cities to replenish the missing and the dead. If more people keep running away and dying because of it, there's a high probability the Planner will ask the lab to create more children."

The Head Matre's eyes widen, her entire body shaking. "No! I will not allow it. To bring more children into a world that doesn't work for them. I can't."

"This will solve that," Aris says.

"But how will that help Selene and our child?" He immediately feels selfish for asking.

"I will negotiate with Eli using the memory books as leverage," Eleanor says. "If we can take a chunk of the memory books and get them into the hands of their owners, he will not have a choice but to loosen his iron grip. Once the word is out, more people will want to come here. We will need to manage the security of this place. I will ask him to let you stay at the CDL permanently for that purpose."

Would the Planner give in that easily? While the Planner has listened to Eleanor before, Scylla isn't so sure he will let go of the Four Cities without a fight. But this is the best plan they have. If it does work, he will get to see their child grow and to be with Selene every day. It is the best option he has—the only option he can see himself taking. Nothing else matters.

Scylla takes a deep breath to settle himself on his new path.

He turns to Aris. "There's an easier way to match up the books to their owners."

"There is?"

"The watch each of you wears. The ID number is on the back. Then you can just convert it to binary."

Aris grabs him into a hug, surprising him. "Thank you, Officer Scylla. I can't wait to tell Metis all of this when I see him again."

Her body is vibrating. She's crying.

His heart drops. She doesn't know. Of course she doesn't. How would she if she's been here?

"Where do you think he is?" he asks.

She releases him. "Elara. He's supposed to be waiting for me there, after we separated in the desert."

"I'm sorry, Aris, but he isn't."

Fear replaces the excitement in her eyes. He doesn't want to tell her, but she needs to know.

"Metis is at Police Station One, with the Interpreter."

CHAPTER FORTY-EIGHT

CASS

March 5, 2233
(15 days before Tabula Rasa)

She wakes up to Bastian's face.

"I think we should go tonight," he says.

She sits up and wipes her eyes. "What? What time is it?"

"Six."

"This is too early."

"I'm hungry."

"The breakfast bell is not for another hour."

"We have a few things to do before then."

"What things?"

"The things to get us ready for our escape tonight."

Her stomach does a flip. "Tonight? Why tonight?"

"This is the best time to leave. The Matres are too busy with everyone being stuck inside. I heard some freshmen broke a marble bust last night with a volleyball. And once the entire police force descends, we won't have the opportunity."

"The entire force! Why?"

"That's what will happen once they know what the Outsider, your Crone, and the Head Matre are planning."

"I told you the Head Matre isn't planning anything."

"She will," he says. "She won't have a choice. The revolution is coming."

She shudders. "I hate when you say that word."

"Revolution?"

"Ugh, stop it."

He pulls a piece of paper from his pocket. "This is what we need to get today."

She reads from it. "Food, lanterns, blankets, more books on edible plants, change of clothes, first aid kit, painkiller, bandages, sunblock, toiletries, forks, a knife, something to cook with."

"We have blankets and clothes already," he says. "The lanterns we'll have to steal from the storage room. The books from the library. Food and utensils from the Food Hall. Something to cook with will have to come from the kitchen, but I'm not sure how to get in yet. We can get the first aid kit from a classroom and bandages and painkillers from the Health Center."

"How are we going to fit everything into our backpacks?" she asks.

What she really wants to say but doesn't is, "How are we going to survive?"

"We'll wear all our clothes," he says. "Put all the food in one pack, since that'll be bulkier, and the rest in another. Blankets are going to be a bit tough. Do you think we'll need them in the spring? We're more likely to survive with food than a blanket. Maybe we can share one."

"Should we delay it a little?" she asks. "Just to give us more time to get things?"

"If we don't leave now, we won't leave," he says, determined. He folds the list and puts it back in his pocket. "Get changed, and let's go. We can start with the books before breakfast."

The library is empty. She breathes in the combined scent of old books and wood oil—her second favorite smell after the pine forest. Morning light shines in through the windows, bathing the wooden tables with its warmth. They make their way to the botany and horticulture section. The floor-to-ceiling shelves intimidate.

"Here—*Foraging for Survival*—that sounds useful." Bastian pulls it from the shelf.

"How many books should we bring?"

"Maybe three? You already have one, so two more."

She spots a title and pulls it out: *Edible Wild Plants, Mushrooms, Fruits, and Nuts*. "I think we have our three."

"What are you two doing?" a voice says.

They both jump.

"How are you so quiet?" Bastian asks Ori.

"You two just weren't paying attention," she says. "I'm on my way to breakfast. What's that?" She cranes her neck. "Edible plants . . . Going harvesting?"

"Just want to see what else we can find," Cass says.

"Ooo! We can go back to the lake!" Ori says.

Her heart drops to her stomach. She looks at Bastian, who does not appear in the least bit worried.

"Sure," he says. "Where's Naya?"

"She's not feeling well. I'm going to grab some food for her."

"We'll go to breakfast with you."

Bastian signs the books out at the desk and puts both in his backpack. How is he able to be so calm, while she feels like an entire colony of butterflies is pollinating flowers inside her stomach?

"I heard the Matres saying the police may leave tomorrow," Ori says. "We can go back to the lake the day after. It'll be a good way to stretch our legs. I feel so cooped up, don't you?"

"Yeah," he replies. "We can have another picnic. How did you get all that food last time? The muffins were delicious."

"The Kitchen Matres know me. I've run some errands for

them before, and they always have a batch of muffins going in the oven. The Head Matre likes them with her breakfast and tea."

"You've been inside the kitchen?" he asks.

"Loads of times."

"Didn't think they let students inside."

"Only the MAs. They can't possibly do everything themselves. It's a full-time job feeding us kids. Sometimes they're so busy they even let us MAs harvest vegetables from the garden."

"Where's that?"

"In the back. On the other side of that giant door that you never see open. They only open it outside of mealtimes and when the door to the Food Hall is closed."

"You like volunteering?" Bastian asks.

"Yeah." She shrugs. "They do so much for us, and we won't even remember them."

Guilt clutches Cass. She has not really done much to help the Matres, and now she's going to make more trouble for them. But what can she do? Leaving is the only way for her and Bastian to stay together.

On their walk to the Food Hall, she looks at everything with renewed appreciation. The CDL is the only home she has ever known. If she stays and goes through Tabula Rasa, she will not even remember to miss it. If she leaves, she will always reminisce about a place she can never return to. Lose-lose.

They enter the Food Hall just as the breakfast bell rings.

Bastian grabs a tray with his good hand. "Cass, can you give me two of everything?"

"Hungry, are we?" Ori asks.

He holds up his bandaged hand. "Didn't eat dinner last night."

But he did. Cass brought it to him and watched him eat the entire thing.

"Actually, this is good. I won't look like a glutton when I take two of everything too," Ori says. "Not all for me. For Naya."

Cass grabs herself a tray and puts two of everything on it as well. "For snacking later."

They sit down, mounds of food on all three trays. Luckily, no one is paying too much attention to them.

Bastian eats two pancakes, his usual, but leaves the rest.

"I thought you were hungry," Ori asks.

This girl notices everything, Cass observes.

"My hand is starting to really hurt. I need pain medication."

Impressive.

He looks at her.

Oh. "I'll go with you to the Health Center," Cass says.

"Here, put all the leftovers in my backpack."

"I'll carry it," she says after putting everything in. With the two books, the pack is now almost full.

Food—check. Books—check.

Next will be medicine and bandages. They are moving through their list quickly and still have plenty of time left before their two-hour curfew.

"Thanks. Will you be okay, Ori?" Bastian asks.

"I'll leave with you. Have to drop off food for Naya."

They say bye to the girl at the door and take off to the Health Center.

"Ori is going to be crushed after you leave," Cass says. "I'm surprised she hasn't tried to sleep in front of your door, she's so worried about you."

"Why?"

"You have to promise you won't act differently around her."

"Out with it," he says.

"She saw you stab yourself and thought you were, you know, trying to hurt yourself. She was afraid you'd be another Agan."

"The senior who fell and broke his neck?"

"She said he did it on purpose."

"So, she thinks I'm going to do the same?"

"I mean, I can't blame her for thinking it."

"Do you—uh—think that?" he asks.

"No! No. I never did."

"Good, because I wouldn't. Though I can understand why someone would. It sucks to not have hope." He looks down at his bandaged hand. "Doesn't it make you wonder how many of what we thought were accidents actually weren't?"

"I don't know what to think anymore."

He nudges her shoulder with his. "We will be okay, you know?"

She's reminded of the way he was on graduation day. How optimistic and sure he was they'd both go to College and have four more years together before Tabula Rasa separated them. Was that really just eleven days ago?

She doesn't believe him, but she nods anyway. Truth is, she needs for them to be okay.

A white rose bush they pass makes her think of Matre Selene. Her counselor always has the flowers in a vase in her office.

"Wait," she says to Bastian, and he halts.

She looks around, sees there's no one, and plucks a flower. "I want to say goodbye to Matre Selene—if she's alone."

As they enter the Health Center, a Matre appears in front of them. This time, Bastian only has to show her his maimed hand to be let through. This place is as empty as before.

At the intake desk, they find Matre Lydia.

"How are you feeling, Bastian?"

"It hurts, Matre. And the spot feels like it has its own heart."

"That's just it throbbing. Let me take a look. We'll go to the back."

She puts Bastian on the same bed and unwraps his hand. "Looks red and swollen."

He really has been in pain.

"Let me get some antibiotics and pain medication." Matre Lydia leaves the room.

"Are you sure you want to leave tonight?" Cass whispers. "Shouldn't we wait until it's healed?"

"Yes. It's tonight or never."

"What if it gets worse out there?"

"Not if I steal enough medicine. You need to hurry before Matre Lydia comes back."

Cass hurries to Matre Selene's room. The door is partially open. She listens for any sound coming from within, and when she doesn't hear it, she sticks her head through. Matre Selene is lying on the bed, eyes closed, and alone.

Cass walks in and stands next to her. The Matre looks frail. If pregnancy does this to a person, Cass isn't sure how Matre Selene is supposed to endure it much longer.

Eleven days.

How can everything change so quickly in such a short amount of time?

"Good morning, Matre," Cass whispers.

She does not stir.

"I just wanted to say thank you for everything you've done for me. For all the hours you spent listening to my problems and offering solutions. You never once blamed me, not even when it was obviously my fault. I'm sorry I never did anything for you in return. And I'm sorry I'm going to have to say goodbye."

She lays the flower on her side table. "We'll be okay though, so don't worry about us. I'll miss you."

CHAPTER FORTY-NINE

METIS

March 5, 2233
(15 days before Tabula Rasa)

Ahead stands a blue house with a white wraparound porch. Their house. Metis walks inside, passing rooms with wood-paneled walls, a bookcase, paintings—making his way deeper until he reaches the back room, where a black piano stands, surrounded by Cyathea ferns.

"Play," a voice whispers.

He sits down in front of it and places his fingers on the keys. They feel like an extension of himself. He begins playing. Luce trickles out like a brook—cool and clear, traversing over sharp rocks and smooth pebbles, meandering through desert and mountains and forest—rushing, slowing, carrying him along, tugging him forward. Always forward.

He had written it for Aris back before she was Aris, before she became Althea and went back to being Aris again. Did he know her even before their first meeting? She feels as though she has always been in his life, always a part of him.

"Sounds like you can still play. The Planner will be pleased."

He turns to his right and sees Apollina sitting on the bench next to him. "How did you get in here?"

She casts her eyes around the room. "Your dreams are so vivid.

The brightness, the tone, the atmosphere—so lifelike. I've seen other Dreamers', but none compare to yours in quality."

Her eyes return to him. "If all dreams are like this, I wouldn't mind being here. To tell you the truth, I like the dreamworld more. Unlike in the real world, we're our most honest selves here."

She leans in. "I can even tell you that I like you without a care."

He ignores her last comment. "Why are you in my dream?"

"Doing my job."

"But how? I thought you could only look."

"My predecessors and I have been perfecting the Dreamcatcher technology for almost two hundred years—ever since the first of us realized its potential. Looking through and erasing dreams are just a few things it can do. We haven't even touched its full capability yet. The mind is a wondrous place."

She drapes an arm around him. "But don't worry. Going through dreams is much gentler than the simulations. Your brain is doing most of the work, and I'm only along for the ride."

She moves her hand to his cheek. "Now, tell me where you're hiding the Crone."

He flits his eyes to the entrance.

"Are you expecting her? You must have been dreaming her. Well, this should be interesting." Apollina smiles.

No, she can't be here.

He inhales deeply and poises his hands over the keys. The notes race out of him fast and furiously. He sinks his entire self into the third movement of Beethoven's Moonlight *Sonata*. In defiance. In anger.

And repeat.

He opens his eyes to Apollina standing beside his bed, the pale blue of her irises sharp like ice. Above them hangs a copper machine the size of the ceiling. From it rain hundreds of wires in different colors, all coming to a single point—the helmet on his head. He is at the Interpreter Center.

"I'm not sure what that was all about," Apollina says. "Do you always dream so . . . intensely?"

A mechanical whir, and his bed tilts up, propping him into a seated position. Apollina removes his helmet.

"Maybe we jumped in too soon," she says. "Perhaps a day of rest is needed. What do you think? What would you like to do for fun? We can't leave, of course."

He does not answer.

"Are you angry with me?" she asks. "You are, aren't you?"

"You went inside my dreams. I don't think anyone would be okay with that invasion."

"But it's my job. That's the entire purpose of the Interpreter. We look at dreams and interpret them. And we erase the dangerous ones."

"That can't be your entire purpose," he says.

She looks up. "This place is why I was created. Why *you* were created." She shifts her gaze back to him and touches his face, the way she did in his dream. "If you're worried I will erase your dreams, don't be. Planner's orders."

"Why does he care about my musical ability?"

"He believes music and art are the best humanity has to offer. He said they're 'soul work.'" She smiles. "I used to not know what that means."

She helps him up off the bed, and he realizes he hasn't had restraints on the entire time. But there's a new weight around his left wrist. He looks down. It's a silver bangle.

"Oh, don't worry, that's not the Subdue Bracelet," she says. "That thing *will* mess with your brain. It's just your watch."

He looks around. No droids. "You're allowing me to walk freely?"

"Of course. I told you this place isn't like Police Station One. It's not a prison."

He notices his empty finger. "Where's my ring? The one you took."

"Oh, I left it at the hospital."

His heart sinks. "But it's mine. I need it back."

"Why? Tabula Rasa is coming soon, and they're going to remove it anyway."

It's his fault. He had forgotten to ask for it right after his brain scan, distracted by the possible brain injury. It's his one physical tie to Aris.

"I just need it back. Please, Apollina."

The Interpreter softens. "I'll ask for it."

They leave the room and enter a long hallway with glass windows on one side and a wall of black-and-white photographs on the other.

"These are images from when they were building the Four Cities," she says as they pass.

He sees photos of construction sites made beautiful by the photographer's artistic eye. The lake in the middle of Central Park as an empty hole in the ground surrounded by trees. High rises in progress. Half-built brownstones in Europa. A pristine speed train in its pristine station. A row of Victorian houses—a few still with scaffolding. One of them is his home in Lysithea.

"Fascinating, isn't it, to see the origin of things?" she says. "It makes you realize this place wasn't always here. That its creator, immortal as he may be, was once just like us—human."

The hall opens to a large space with a modern kitchen, a dining room, and a living room.

"This is where I live," she says. "Make yourself comfortable. I'll make you tea. Earl Grey, is it?"

He wants to run away, but something inside warns him to stay. A successful escape needs a good plan. He walks into the living room and sits on a couch, feeling as unsettled as he was in the room with the Dreamcatcher—perhaps even more so because of the atmosphere of domesticity.

He hears her in the kitchen. The clinking sound of cup and saucer. A minute later, she places a cup of tea on the coffee table in front of him.

"Your propensity model says you like it with cream but no sugar," she says with a shy smile. "I've never made tea for another person before, so I hope it's okay."

"Uh, thank you." He picks up the cup and sips from it. It tastes exactly how he likes it.

She sits on the chair across from him. "You know, that was the first time I've ever heard you play live—well, if dream-playing counts. I've only heard your music through the Metabank. I've never been to your concerts."

Right. She's not allowed to mingle with the populace. The thought saddens him.

"That music you were playing, it's not in your repertoire. I haven't heard you play that before. Why did you play it over and over again?"

"You're asking *me* why I did something in my dream? I have no idea why I dream what I dream."

But that's not the truth. The music is a conjuring, from the first note to the last. Him standing inside the cottage, the Crone next to him. Him making Absinthe, the green liquid dropping into the flask. Him writing secret words on pieces of blue paper and folding them into origami cranes. Him giving them to the Dreamers to recruit others. Through its *presto agitato* tempo, life happens in blinks of eyes and gasps of breaths. Maps, books, poems, conversations. Everything about Mem. *Secrets*.

He does this because, as Sandman, he is the weakest point. Inside his head is the recipe for Absinthe, the names of all the Dreamers, all his talks with the Crone. With TBT128 and the Subdue Bracelet, he could easily expose them all. That's why the Crone never gave anything to him freely, never an easy exchange. She made him work for everything, effectively absolving herself and removing her involvement as much as she could from his memory.

I once read about a prisoner of war who helped save the lives of two hundred and fifty-six other prisoners by memorizing their detailed information using a song as a mnemonic device, the Crone had said.

That's all she had to mention to set him down a path. If music could hold so much information for the man, Metis figured it could hold information for him too. After all, they were both prisoners.

Over time, he learned how to use music as a container for his own memories. He chose the third movement of the *Moonlight* Sonata because of its complexity. Like velvet stage curtains, there are so many hiding places—tuck things here, pin things there, fold over, layer one on top of the other, fold again.

He plays it in place of the words he cannot say. Apollina and the police can ask, and he will tell, but they will never understand.

CHAPTER FIFTY

ARIS

March 5, 2233
(15 days before Tabula Rasa)

She packs and repacks her bag so many times she's lost count. When she tastes blood, she realizes she has been pulling at the skin of her cracked lips with her teeth. All her limbs feel like they're going to vibrate off the ground if she isn't careful.

Today is the day.
Today is the day.
Today is the day.
Hang on. I'm coming.

Metis is detained at Police Station One with the Interpreter. Though the Planner doesn't want to destroy his ability to create, if they're desperate enough, nothing can be guaranteed. Her eyes burn.

What has she been doing to you?

"Aris," the Crone calls.

She looks up. The glowing woman is standing next to the Head Matre and Amira. In such close proximity, it's easier to see their similarities. The deep-set melancholic eyes. The high cheekbones. Pale, long hair. The sight gives her the unsettling feeling of looking at a person throughout their entire existence—from vibrant to faded.

"Hera is asking you a question," the Crone says.

"Oh, sorry. I've just been . . ." She sighs. "All over the place."

"I know you're worried, but we're doing all we can to prepare," the Head Matre says.

"We're almost there," Amira says. "All two thousand five hundred books have been packed and are ready to be moved to the train."

All night, she and her crew have worked to decode binary titles into decimal numbers for ten classes—Aris's, Metis's, and those in between and around theirs. They chose them in hopes Aris and Metis can identify and recruit the owners once they regain their own memories.

The team will also come with them on the train to help move the books into the dilapidated building near the tracks, the one she and Metis hid in the night before they separated. The books will later be distributed across the Four Cities with the Dreamers' help. That's the plan. But as Aris is painfully aware, plans have a way of going off the rails.

"How far do you think the building is from here, Aris?" Hera asks.

"I'm not sure exactly. It was uphill the whole way, and I was trying not to be seen. It took me eleven days to get here."

"That sounds far," Amira says.

None of the Matres have ever left the CDL before.

"How's everyone feeling about leaving?" Head Matre Hera asks.

"Most are pretty excited. The rest are a bit apprehensive—to be expected."

"Make sure you have enough food and water to last a couple of days while you wait for Aris and Scylla to come back with Metis."

"Yes, Head Matre."

"Now we all should rest in preparation."

They had not slept much last night, waiting for Scylla to come visit Selene and, later, to craft their plan.

"Just make sure Scylla and his partner will be nowhere near the library today," she says to Amira.

"Of course."

"Aris, you can stay in here. I'll instruct that no one disturb you except to deliver meals," Head Matre Hera says. "You'll want to eat your breakfast before it's cold."

She has forgotten about it. The plate of pancakes on the Head Matre's gleaming desk gives off a delicious scent, but there is nothing in her that wants them.

"I'm not hungry."

"At least drink your tea before it gets cold. It'll help."

She sips from the cup. The liquid is lukewarm from sitting too long, but it does make her feel better.

"I'm going to the lab for our next phase," Hera says.

CHAPTER FIFTY-ONE

SCYLLA

March 5, 2233
(15 days before Tabula Rasa)

Scylla is standing with Evan and Matre Mona in front of a large door with *Embryology* printed on it. On the left side of the door is a keypad. Mona places a card against it, and it clicks. The lock unlatches, and the door slides open.

They enter a bright room containing neat rows of tables with white boxes on them.

"These are the incubators," Mona says. "They're the primary housing units, where the embryos are stored. Temperature and gas-regulated, they keep the embryos safe from environmental changes."

This is the only high tech the CDL is allowed to have.

"So this is where we all began," Evan says.

"Well, this is where the *children* begin. We are grown separately—and only one of us a year."

"How many children are created a year?"

"Two hundred and fifty."

Evan's brow furrows, and Scylla wonders if he has figured out this is the same number as each block of color-coded books in the library.

They continue walking down the middle aisle and come to another large door, this time with the word *Exowomb* on it. Mona again places a card on the keypad, and the door opens.

Evan gasps. Scylla has seen this place before, but the sight of it still stuns him. The massive room is at least three stories tall with two giant cylindrical structures in the middle. From it radiates platforms that angle up like stadium seating. On each row are glass pods atop machines with digital displays. Inside each oval pod is a growing child—naked and bald, eyes closed in slumber.

"They will be ready to come out in fifteen days," Mona says. "This is pretty much how they will look at birth. Be glad you didn't see them when they were younger. They can look quite frightening, with skin so thin you can see into their beating hearts."

Scylla walks to a pod and peers through the glass. The child's skin is wrinkly, its lips moving in a sucking motion. He hopes his and Selene's baby will look much better, though he'll love it no matter what. He already does.

"What are those for?" Evan asks, and points to the two structures in the middle of the room.

"Those are bioreactors," Mona says. "The first contains amniotic fluid rich with nutrients and oxygen, which supplies each pod through artificial umbilical cords. You see the tube that goes into the belly button? The second bioreactor eliminates waste produced by the children and recycles it back into nutrients."

"Fascinating."

"As you can see, the security in this place is tight. It would be very difficult for an intruder to get in."

"Unless they somehow get hold of the key." Evan walks around the structure.

"Only the Head Matre and the Matres assigned to work here have keys. The Head Matre's key is locked inside her office when it's not being used. Besides, why would someone else want to come in here?"

"To destroy them."

"But why? There's no reason to. They're just children."

"I don't know. But it's a possibility."

"Well, the CDL is the safest place for them to be, with only one way in and out. Isn't that why the Planner puts them here?" Her voice is annoyed.

"Once the children are birthed, where do they go?" Evan changes the subject.

"To the nursery. It's located farther down the way. The Matres there raise the children from birth until their fifth birthday before transferring them to the elementary school."

"This has been very educational. Thank you," Scylla says.

"Anything else you'd like to see here?" Mona asks.

"I think we're good."

They leave the facility by the same doors they came in through. Outside the lab, Scylla sees the Head Matre approaching.

Right on time.

"Officer Scylla," Head Matre Hera says.

"Hello, Head Matre."

"I wanted to ask you for a favor. One of our Matres is very sick, and I need some medication from the hospital in the Four Cities. Is that something you can help with?"

"Of course. That doesn't sound difficult. I will get it after we're done with our assignment here. We should be done by tomorrow, and I can come back in a day or so."

"I'm afraid she will need it sooner than that. If you could, I would very much appreciate you bringing it by tonight."

"I'm not sure about tonight. We have several places to see

still. How about this? I can leave after dinner and get back before tomorrow morning. Officer Evan can stay behind here and start the morning without me."

Hide lies in truths.

"I would really appreciate that," the Head Matre says. "Come by my office later, and I should have the list of medications by then."

"I will."

"We won't forget your help."

"Glad to," he says.

The Head Matre turns around and leaves.

Matre Mona continues ahead.

Evan pulls him back, leans in, and whispers, "Is this for Matre Selene?"

"I assume so."

"She must be really sick for the Head Matre to ask you for help."

"We've built a good relationship because we help each other. It's important to extend a hand whenever it's needed."

"But why did she ask you now? Why not call you into her office later?"

"Maybe she just wanted to save time."

"Maybe she just wanted to see what we're doing." Evan leans in closer, his voice lower. "I know everything looks fine on the surface, but something is going on here, sir. I can feel it."

CHAPTER FIFTY-TWO

CASS

March 5, 2233
(15 days before Tabula Rasa)

After dinner in the courtyard of their dorms, Cass and Bastian fight their way through the congested hallway as students return to their rooms. Slipping into a hallway bathroom, they hide there for what feels like hours.

"I don't hear anything anymore," Bastian says and sticks his head out the door. "We're good to go."

They tiptoe down the hallway—Cass nodding goodbye to her favorite painting of the ocean as she passes—and out the building. From under a nearby bush, they pick up their backpacks and the stolen lanterns they hid there earlier in the day. They sneak across the grounds, keeping to the shadows of the trees until they reach the Gate of the Six Bells. Then they run.

They head toward the forest, following the path familiar to them since childhood. Silhouettes of trees whiz by. The darkness around them feels more oppressive. The pines appear bigger and more menacing, every rustling a possible threat. She increases her pace, faster and faster, and Bastian matches it until they are running at full speed. In no time, they are deep in the forest—the CDL far behind them.

"Can we stop?" Hands to her knees, she tries to catch her breath. Her heart is beating as fast as a hummingbird's wings.

She cannot believe she just ran away. Her cheeks feel both hot and cold. Her stomach roils, threatening to push out her dinner. Bastian sits on the ground, and she does the same. Her heart begins to slow.

"Look!" He points.

She shifts her gaze and catches a shooting star flying across the night sky.

"Let's make a wish," he says.

In the old days, people used to make a wish on one. She knows it's not real of course. Stars cannot grant wishes. They're just huge glowing balls of hot gas. But in this moment, she does.

Please let us make it together.

"Did you make your wish?" he asks.

"Yeah."

"Me too. Are you ready to keep going?"

"Sure."

They get up and continue at a fast pace along the path through the pines. The cool scent helps to calm the worry within. The moon is a waning crescent, and the sky twinkling with stars.

"It's not so bad, right, being out here?" he asks. "Not that different from us walking around at night after curfew."

She makes a sound in her throat.

"We should make it to the lake with time to sleep for a few hours," he adds. "People won't notice us missing until after the breakfast bell."

"Maybe."

"I know you're scared," he says. "But I really feel it's all going to work out. Do you believe me?"

She wants to. "I do."

"We'll feel better once we reach the lake."

The fork in the path, where it splits into three, is not too far ahead, and after that, the ridge. It's going to be scary crossing it at night, but they have the lanterns, and they'll go slow—foot by foot if need be.

"What do you think is out there?" he asks.

"Planets, stars, dark matter, black holes."

"No, not in space. Out on the other side of the mountain range."

From his tone, she knows this isn't one of their games. He is not looking for a fairy tale.

"I'm assuming more of this—forest, lakes, a valley of desert." And as long as there's water and food, they should be okay.

"When I thought the Outsider was from there, I got really excited, you know. I thought, here's another way to be. And even though I don't know if it's better, it's better than Tabula Rasa."

"What if there's no one else out there?" she asks.

"At least we'll have each other."

The wind picks up, rustling the trees around them. She hugs her jacket to her chest. Hopefully, it will keep her warm enough come winter.

They arrive at the fork.

"Once we go down the hill, we won't see the CDL anymore," he says.

They both stop and turn around. From here she can see the bell tower glowing in the distance. But she also sees something else—another shadow among the closest trees, its eyes glinting. Ice touches the small of her back.

"Bastian," she whispers. "There's something out there."

"What is it?"

"I saw a shadow moving. Something with shiny eyes."

"Are you sure it's not just a big owl?"

"No, it's something bigger."

"Let's keep going." He pulls her forward.

She moves to turn on the lantern in her hand.

"Leave the lantern off so it can't see us," he says.

"But the ridge."

"We'll go slow."

They take the rightmost path. The wind is picking up now, its sound high in her ears, reminding her of the Crone's laugh. But instead of making her feel good, she has never been more terrified. All she can do is focus on her footsteps—one in front of the other. From her memory, the ridge should be coming up soon.

She looks behind her. The shiny eyes are still there—and coming closer.

"Bastian! It's coming!"

They take off running as fast as they can. The ground slopes down. They're almost to the ridge now, but they don't know where it is exactly. Everything to their right is dark gray. They could just as easily fall to their death as make it across to the other side.

Bastian is ahead of her, the thumping of his pack against his back the same rhythm as the beating of her heart. Something grabs at her pack and yanks. Her hand separates from Bastian's as she stumbles backward onto the ground. She screams.

A shadow looms over her. It stands erect like a human, but its head is deformed. Where the eyes should be, something protrudes. Its hands reach down toward her.

"No!" She kicks up and flips over, trying to right herself.

"Stay there!" a gruff voice says.

It speaks her language!

Something crashes into it, sending it off balance. It's Bastian. They are both on the ground, wrestling. She flips onto all fours and crawls to where they are. From the shadows, she can see Bastian with his backpack on top. She scrambles up and starts kicking the figure on the ground.

"Stop! I'm a police officer of the Four Cities. You're both under arrest!" the voice says.

The police!

The order halts both her and Bastian. The officer flips Bastian onto his back and holds him down. The motion sends Cass falling back onto her hands. All of a sudden, Bastian stops struggling and lies still. Doom clutches her. Bastian would never stop fighting to free himself. Something is wrong.

She crawls forward and tries to pull the officer off her friend. His hand grabs her wrist like a vice.

"You are persistent!" he says, his tone irritated.

She feels something hard and cold on her wrist. A click, and all of a sudden, her brain feels as if made of cloud—floaty and diaphanous. Her limbs are heavy. She cannot remember why she had a need to move them in the first place.

The officer sits on his bottom, arms on both knees. "Good, now we can talk. First, tell me your names."

"Bastian."

"Cass." She didn't mean to tell the officer, but it slipped out anyway.

"I'm Officer Evan. What city are you from?"

She doesn't understand the question. What does he mean?

"Have you seen the moon? It's not very bright today," Bastian says.

"What. City. Do. You. Live. In," The officer repeats, slowly emphasizing each word.

"We. Live. Here," Bastian replies, delivering each word in the same slow cadence.

"Live here? You mean at the CDL?"

"Yes."

"Shit! You're students! Your Head Matre is going to have my head."

She giggles. "You said a bad word."

"What are you doing out here? Aren't you supposed to be in your dorms?"

A small part of her tries to push against the question, but the rest of her doesn't seem to agree.

"We're running away," she says.

"Why?" Officer Evan asks.

Her friend lifts his arm and stares at the metal bangle on it. "What's this?"

"A Subdue Bracelet. It helps you help me."

She looks at her wrist and sees she has the same thing. "Is that why I feel woozy?"

"Now answer me," the officer says.

"A revolution is coming," Bastian says.

The officer jerks and leans forward. "What do you mean?"

"The Outsider, the Crone, and the Head Matre." He laughs. "Doesn't that sound like the beginning of a really lame joke?"

"Wait, did you say the Crone?"

"Crony, Crony, bo-bony, bonana-fanna fo-fony, fee fi mo-mony, Crony" Her friend laughs, triggering her own giggling.

"Focus, Bastian!" Officer Evan's voice is angry. She doesn't like it.

Bastian swallows. "The Outsider, the Crone, and the Head Matre are planning a revolution."

"What are they doing?"

"We don't know."

"Tell me what you do know."

"The Outsider and the Crone are going back to the Four Cities with memory books. The Head Matre doesn't want her here."

"The Crone's book must be with her," Officer Evan says to

himself. "And the Head Matre has been helping them. This is going to be bad for her."

"Only because she needs their help."

"For what?"

"Matre Selene."

Cass is vaguely aware Bastian should stop talking to the police, but the clouds inside her brain are so thick she cannot see beyond it.

"What's wrong with Matre Selene?"

Her friend turns to look at her. His face is vacant, but his eyes show a struggle within. She wants to make him feel better, but she doesn't know how.

Officer Evan grabs his shoulders and shakes. "Bastian! Tell me what's happening,"

He yelps. "Matre Selene is pregnant, and the child is Officer Scylla's."

Officer Evan's arms fall to his sides. He sits so still Cass wonders if he has turned into stone. Or maybe he has lost interest in them. Maybe he can let them go to the lake. It'll be so nice to wake up next to the water.

"Fucking Scylla. I knew something was up," he says sharply, his words cutting the thickness of the night into ribbons.

"Stay here!" he orders, and runs off.

CHAPTER FIFTY-THREE

SCYLLA

March 5, 2233
(15 days before Tabula Rasa)

He does not want to wake Selene, but he cannot leave her without saying goodbye. He leans down and kisses her forehead. Her eyes flutter open, glassy from the fever that has returned.

"Hi, love," he says.

She smiles. "Hi."

"I have to go back to Callisto. There are a few things I have to do, but I'll be back as soon as I'm done."

"It was raining stars last night. Did you see? I swallowed one. You know the one I like? The blue one?"

His heart sinks to his stomach. He looks back at Galena. "She seems worse."

"I'll take care of her, don't worry. Just get her the medication and come back," she says.

A knot forms in his throat. He picks up Selene's hands and kisses each one. "I love you."

"I love you." Her lids gently close.

I swallowed a star . . .

What if her condition not only affects her body but her

mind? Guilt twists his insides. He cannot fail her. Failing means she will die.

The thought sends pain to the middle of his palms. He balls his hands into fists, holding himself together. All he can do right now is focus on the tasks at hand. Hide the memory books, sneak Aris into Callisto, get medicine. He kisses Selene's forehead again and peels himself from her.

A scream rings out, rattling the night. It came from outside. He and Galena rush to the window. In the circular approach between the Gate of the Six Bells and the Administrative building is the shadow of a figure.

"Help! Please help!" The voice is that of a girl.

Galena runs out of the room, and he follows.

"Lydia, stay with Selene," Galena yells as they whiz past the intake desk.

They arrive at the circular approach and another Matre—the one who stands guard in front of the Health Center—is already there, her arms on the girl's shoulders.

"What's going on?" Galena asks. "Ori! What are you doing out?"

"It got Bastian and Cass!"

"What got them?"

She sees Scylla and hesitates. "What's a policeman doing here?"

"Ori! Look at me," Galena says. "What got Bastian and Cass?"

"I don't know!" The girl is frantic. "I was looking for Bastian and saw him and Cass running toward the forest, so I followed and tried to catch up with them. I heard a struggle and saw something or someone tackle them to the ground."

"Where?" he asks.

It has to be Evan. He has been wanting to look around the grounds without supervision.

"Out in the forest. Near the ridge."

"Show me!"

Ori runs and he follows her, the Matres behind them. The forest is dark. The kids and the Matres know the terrain, but how did Evan see? He must have brought the night-vision goggles!

Finally they reach a fork in the path.

"There!" the girl says and points to the right. Ahead he sees a shadowy shape on the ground.

Scylla sprints toward it. "Evan, stop!"

As he gets closer, he sees the one big shadow split into two. But where's the third?

"Bastian! Cass!" Ori rushes to them. "How come they're not moving? What's wrong with them?"

"Looks like they have lanterns," one of the Matres says. Two small clicks, and the round globes light up, setting the area aglow.

The two children stare fixedly ahead. They don't appear to be hurt. He sees the metal bangles on their wrists. *It* is *Evan*. The heat of anger climbs up his neck.

Idiot! Evan must be feeling bold without him there to supervise.

"Evan, my partner, did this. He used the Subdue Bracelets on them. Don't worry, they'll be fine." He swipes a finger across the bangles. They unlatch and fall into his palms. He puts them in his coat. Evan has broken a lot of rules, and he will be punished—hopefully, enough to satisfy the Head Matre.

"Where's the other policeman?" he asks.

The boy, Bastian, begins to shake uncontrollably. "I told him everything."

"What do you mean?"

Sobbing comes from the girl next to him. "We know about Aris, the Crone, and Matre Selene, and now *he* does too."

Scylla feels as if he has tripped and fallen down a gorge. He cannot believe the speed in which everything has turned. One decision. One act. One twist of fate, and everything comes tumbling down like a tower of dominoes. Evan interrogated two students. Those children happen to know their secrets. And now Evan knows everything.

If he gets on the train and reports what he learned to the Planner, it will be the end of the CDL. Without hesitance, the Planner will take Selene in for experiments. Their child—once born—will become the property of the System.

Scylla's eyes blur. He cannot let it happen. He will die fighting to stop it.

His entire vision shrinks to a single point. *Evan.* He needs to stop him. He springs up and races back toward the CDL.

CHAPTER FIFTY-FOUR

ARIS

March 5, 2233
(15 days before Tabula Rasa)

The Head Matre's desk looks as though it would fit in perfectly at the art museum in Callisto. The reddish-toned wood desk is reminiscent of Roman marble furniture, with carved drapes, radiating leaves, and lion's paws for feet. Aris spreads her arms across the top and places her cheek on its surface inlaid with a constellation of mother-of-pearl stars. She has been staying in the Head Matre's office all day, waiting. Her lips are practically raw from her picking at the dry skin.

What time is it now?

The Head Matre, Amira, and Scylla are supposed to join her here before they all go down to the library and the train station together.

"I think they forgot," she says to the only other person here.

The Crone turns from the map of Eastern Sierra and glides to her. "They haven't forgotten."

"I *feel* forgotten. Can time move any slower?"

She hears the sound of feet striking against the floor from the hallway. Who's running at this hour? The door bangs open, startling her. It's Scylla.

She gets up from the chair. "Is it time?"

He looks from her to the Crone. He pushes the door closed. It crashes against its casing, rattling the room. He advances toward her. His face is a mix of rage and betrayal. She steps back.

"Officer Scylla? What's going on?"

"I know your face. You're Althea, the Sandman's partner. Today must be my lucky day," he says through gritted teeth. "You are under arrest for plotting to revolt against the System and undermining Tabula Rasa. I'm not going to let you ruin our peace."

Confusion turns to terror when it begins to sink in that the man in front of her is not Scylla but Evan.

"You're—you're not Scylla."

"Do not call me that traitor's name!" he screams and whips his head to the Crone. "And you! The Planner lets you keep your Absinthe and the Dreamers, and still you betray him."

She floats toward him and places a hand on his cheek, startling him. "You look like him on the first day we met, but you are not him. Don't you dare speak for him."

Then she glides away and disappears through the door. Aris feels as though she herself has been betrayed.

A cruel smile touches the corner of Evan's mouth. "Looks like your savior has abandoned you."

He continues toward her. "You're lucky I don't have another Subdue Bracelet. But you're not going anywhere. We're going to have this place on lockdown so tight you won't be able to even move a finger without us knowing."

Aris walks backward until she hits the wall. She feels faint, her hope of returning to Metis crumbling to pieces. Evan walks to the table next to her. His eyes are focused on the object atop it. It looks like an old telephone—the kind she has seen somewhere before but cannot place.

He stops in front of it and picks up the receiver. He stares at it.

"Hello?" he yells. He doesn't quite know how to use it. "This is Evan calling from the CDL. I need to report an emergency. Hello?"

No sound comes. Maybe it does not work.

"Damn it! How am I going to get on the train with all those Matres there?"

He looks at her. "Maybe I can trade you. Will they care for you more than they do themselves?"

"Hello," a voice says faintly from the other end. "This is Officer Gordon. Who is this?"

"This is Evan. I'm requesting backup at the CDL."

The police!

"What's going on over there?"

"Scylla has been compromised. I've found—"

With all her strength, Aris slams into him, sending the phone and Evan to the ground. Before she regains her balance, his leg sweeps under her, and she is airborne. She hits the desk with a heavy thud. The impact strikes her dead center in the stomach, knocking the air out of her.

He twists himself, crawls toward the phone lying nearby, and picks up the receiver. "I've found—"

Gasping for breath, she scrambles forward, grabs his leg, and pulls. He kicks at her.

"—the Crone and the Sandman's partner at the CDL," he yells. "Request backup."

No!

The sound of the door striking the wall pulls their attention. On the threshold is another police officer and a Matre. *Scylla and Amira!*

When Evan's eyes land on Scylla, he looks as if he wants to tear him into pieces. "Traitor!"

Scylla flinches.

Amira rushes to Evan. She straddles his back and wrestles his arms behind him.

"How could you?" Evan seethes. "You're the lead officer of the Four Cities! How could you side with these people? We're supposed to protect peace. You're supposed to be on our side."

"Not at all costs." Scylla puts a metal bangle around his wrist, and Evan stops struggling. "Not anymore."

He puts the receiver back on the phone. "Aris, are you okay?"

Sobs roll through her. "He called the police. He talked to someone named Gordon. Now they know we're here."

"What's going on?" the Head Matre says from the threshold. Next to her is the Crone.

"Evan used the Subdue Bracelet on two of your students," Scylla says. "Somehow, they knew all about Aris and Eleanor and confessed to him. I went to the train, thinking he would be there to take it back to Police Station One. I saw Amira and her team instead. But then Eleanor came and told us he was with Aris in your office. I realized he had decided to call for backup. Did I get that right, Aris?"

She nods.

"Now what do we do?" Amira asks as she climbs off Evan.

"It appears we need a new plan," the Head Matre says, eyeing the man on the floor. "Starting with what we're going to do with him. Once the two children get examined by Galena, bring them to me. I need to know exactly what they know and what they told him."

CHAPTER FIFTY-FIVE

CASS

March 6, 2233
(14 days before Tabula Rasa)

The Head Matre is sitting with her chair facing the window. It's still dark outside, with not a single thread of the coming dawn. For almost an hour she questioned them, then silence. A sigh comes from her. The chair turns around. Her face is heavy with worry and fatigue. Her eyes are rimmed red.

Cass looks down at her hands on her lap, feeling like the worst human in the world. Bastian is next to her, quietly sniffling.

"You could have gotten really hurt," Head Matre Hera says. "Running away in the middle of the night, attempting to cross the ridge without light, thinking you could survive the wild with nothing but a few stolen items. Bastian, you still with an unhealed cut on your hand. One infection, and you'd be dead."

"We're very sorry, Head Matre," he says.

"We're very, very sorry," Cass adds.

"Tell me how you came to learn about Matre Selene?" the Head Matre asks.

"I—um—cut my hand to get inside the Health Center," Bastian says.

"And I snuck in and hid by her room and overheard you talking," Cass adds.

"So it was a team effort. What possessed you to hurt yourself?"

"I didn't think it was going to hurt that badly."

"For a smart child . . ." She shakes her head, exasperation in her voice.

"It's all my fault, Head Matre," he says. "I pressured Cass into it. Please don't punish her."

She can't let him take all the blame. "No, I did it because I wanted to. We just wanted to stay together. If we escape, we won't have to deal with Tabula Rasa."

"Oh, child." A tear falls down her cheek, and she wipes it. "You can't escape Tabula Rasa. It's built into your DNA."

Cass's entire heart feels as though it has fallen from her chest onto the ground and broken upon impact. "It'll always happen?"

"The trigger is inside your brain."

"There's no escape?"

Head Matre Hera shakes her head.

"Why didn't anyone tell us before?"

"Because we didn't want you to be afraid."

"But Matre, we *are* afraid," Bastian says. "All of us are. We've always been afraid, and we will always *be* afraid."

Cass looks over at her friend, and her thoughts flit to Agan. Somehow, the boy knew. That's why he left. He couldn't live his life without hope. In a year she and Bastian will separate, and there is nothing more they can do. She squeezes his hand, and he squeezes back.

Head Matre Hera laces her fingers together and drops her head. The sadness that emanates from her wrenches Cass's gut. She'd rather the Matre yell at them.

She hears the sound of a drawer opening. She looks up and sees the Head Matre pulling out a piece of paper and a pen.

She scribbles something onto it and folds it. Then she puts a wax seal on it.

"Give this to the Head Professor at College," she says, and slides it across the desk.

Cass looks at it, not understanding. "What?"

"I'm sending you to College tonight."

Her stomach hollows. "No! Please Head Matre! I'm very sorry for what I did. I'll do detentions. I'll make atonements. Please let me stay. I can't just leave Bastian. You don't understand. He's been my best friend since we were five. I've known him for twelve years. We can't separate."

A sob escapes and she swallows it. "He's *my* person—the one who always has my back, the one I can tell everything to. Please don't take our last year together away."

She looks frantically at her friend and sees the same desperation reflecting back.

"Calm down, Cassiopeia," the Head Matre says. "I'm sending *both* of you."

"Wait, we get to stay together at College?" Bastian asks.

Relief washes through her.

The Head Matre studies them with her hawklike eyes. "Do not mistake this as a reward. The police will come here and will be looking for evidence. You are evidence."

The Head Matre picks up one of the lanterns they had stolen and walks to the large map on the wall. She pushes against it. The map opens, becoming a door. Cass feels her mouth hanging open.

Behind the door is another door. It's metal like the elevator doors she's seen during field trips in the Four Cities. The Head Matre steps into the small space between the two doors, pushes a button on the wall, and the metal door slides open. It *is* an elevator!

"Come," she says. "Bring your things."

Cass and Bastian pick up their packs and follow. The door closes and they descend. They're heading underground. A dinging sound, and the door opens to a mezzanine overlooking a vast space filled with shelves that fan out in all directions.

She cannot believe her eyes. "What's this place?"

"The Library of Memory." The Head Matre leads them down the stairs onto the library floor. "This is where the System keeps all the erased memories of the citizens of the Four Cities. They are collected and maintained by the police."

Cass wonders why she is showing them this place.

"I want you to see this so it's not just *our* secret," the Head Matre says as if she can read her mind. "Just in case."

"Just in case of wha—?" Cass stops, realizing what the Matre means.

Once the police storm the CDL, there may not be any Matres left to keep the knowledge of this place. The thought sends a tremor to her chest.

"These zeros and ones translate to year and order of birth—a person's ID number," she continues. "The numbers are also on the watches the citizens wear. Each block of color is a class of students. The Crone thinks these books can be read using a machine called 'Dreamcatcher' located at the Interpreter Center in Callisto."

They come to a wall. Head Matre Hera turns on the lantern. "Through here is a tunnel the police use when they come in to transfer memories and bring in books. This leads to the Grand Hall and the train tunnel."

She walks them into it. It's dark inside but for the lantern light.

"We're underground?" Cass asks, looking around at the rock wall.

"Yes."

Her skin prickles. Her heart thrums, the sound filling her ears. Sweat begins to drip down the nape of her neck. She wants to run back to the safety of the library and take the elevator. It's an irrational fear, she tells herself. The tunnel has been around for hundreds of years, it is not going to collapse now. She focuses all her attention on the Matre's back. Her white gown, aglow with the lantern light, reminds her of the warmth of the sun.

"I will ask Officer Scylla to divert the train to College before they head into the Four Cities. College is run by Head Professor Thalia. I haven't seen her since she took the post ten years ago, but I trust her implicitly. Hand her the letter I gave you, and she will take you in."

The Head Matre continues talking—about the lab, the process of creating humans in the artificial womb, and even Matre Selene's pregnancy and how her body cannot handle it without medical help. Cass feels like she and Bastian are the memory books the Head Matre is downloading her secrets into.

At the end of the tunnel is a wooden door. The Head Matre slides it open, and fresh air rushes in. Cass exhales in relief and steps out. They are standing on a stage. She realizes that what she thought was a door is actually the back of the gilded altar. From this angle and in this light, this place looks a world away from the exotic fairy-tale castle of her childhood. But it's not just the hall. The entire CDL feels like a friend she thought she knew but never did.

They exit the hall, cross to the station, and make their way down the ramp. A group of Matres uncharacteristically clad in black pants and tops stand in stark contrast next to the white train. Their gaze falls on them, making Cass feel paper thin.

"Amira, is everything ready?" the Head Matre asks.

"Yes, we have everything on the train."

What things?

"Where's Scylla?"

"Inside."

"You all come with me. You'll want to hear this."

The Head Matre leads them aboard, and they find Officer Scylla standing with the Outsider and the glowing form of the Crone. Though Cass knows he is not Officer Evan, their similarity is enough to make her shudder.

"Hello, Cass," the Crone greets.

"Uh, h-hello."

Head Matre Hera looks from one to the other. "How do you— Never mind. I don't have time for this. Scylla, I need you to drop these two children off at College. Only to Head Professor Thalia. Cass will give her a letter from me. We need to hide them there."

He wrinkles his brow. "We're already short on time."

The Head Matre glares at him, her eyes icy. "We stayed up all night making a new plan, and I'm exhausted. I'm keeping a policeman hostage. One of my Matres is dying. Two of my children will be hunted down by the System for the knowledge they possess. I'm aiding a fugitive and the Crone. And once the Planner knows what is happening, he will bring his wrath down on the CDL so fast we won't know what's coming. So you will *make* time—and this is not up for discussion."

A stillness drapes over the room.

Officer Scylla swallows and nods.

Head Matre Hera whips her icy eyes back to them. Cass feels her blood leaching out of her.

"Children, you won't have a graduation ceremony or spend your last year here to prepare for adulthood. Your adulthood starts now."

Bastian's eyes redden. "I'm so sorry for causing all this trouble. Because of me, you're all in danger."

The Head Matre' expression gentles. She wipes his cheek.

"The danger was always there, Bastian. The real danger isn't what we're about to do, it's Tabula Rasa and this way of life we've come to accept as inevitable. Because of you, we've finally found enough courage to enter a long-overdue fight. Because of you, we've realized this path is the only one that makes sense. You did not put us in danger, you reminded us what it is."

She wraps him and Cass in a hug. "Remember you are stronger together. That's why the Planner wanted to separate you, and that's why I'm keeping you together. Try not to get yourselves in too much danger, or if you do, make it count. Find a purpose worth fighting for."

She turns to the Crone and the Outsider. "I wish you luck. While I may not like how it happened, I'm glad we met. I hope we'll see each other again under better circumstances."

She walks to the other Matres. "Take care of each other. It's going to be difficult, but the future of the Four Cities depends on your success. I will see you back here."

"Yes, Head Matre," they all say in unison.

"Scylla," she addresses him. "Get what we need, and get out. Don't try to be a hero. Selene and your child need you."

He hands her an object. A silver bangle. "It's my watch. The System might try to track it."

She takes it and casts one more look at them before turning and exiting the train.

Cass and Bastian move toward the front and sit in the first row, where they can see out the large window. She watches Officer Scylla walk to a control panel on the wall. He presses his right hand on it and enters their first destination: College.

The doors slide shut, and the train eases itself from the station. Bastian's eyes are on the gray tunnel wall, his knee bouncing like a ball. The Outsider is sitting at the window seat across from them. She looks smaller than Cass imagined.

For all the waiting under the bushes to see her, it seems of little importance now. If only the old Cass knew what she should have really been worried about.

The sound of Bastian's shoe tapping against the floor adds exclamation points to what they have experienced in the last few hours. She feels changed by it, or not so much changed but broken off. Like a cracked rock or a branch from a tree. Like there is a "before" version of her—whole and undamaged—that she had left behind in the forest.

A thought comes—faint at first but growing brighter. She turns to her best friend.

"Hey. You were right!"

He turns toward her, confusion in his tear-filled eyes.

"You said we'd be together at College," she says. "You said everything would work out. Remember?"

"Yeah."

"We will be okay," she says, relief flooding her. "We're going to stay together. Our wishes came true!"

He smiles through his tears.

CHAPTER FIFTY-SIX

METIS

March 6, 2233
(14 days before Tabula Rasa)

The Interpreter Center was once the residence of the Planner and his wife, Apollina said. It was originally designed to have private and public wings, separated by a long walkway—the one with the black-and-white photographs. The private side is where the Interpreter now lives. The public side is where she treats patients, the rooms repurposed to house Dreamcatchers. But before it became a place that murders dreams—before the Last War—they used the space to host parties for the Planner's investors. The exit is through there.

From the outside in and the inside out, the Interpreter Center appears porous. Big windows. One story. No fencing. But Metis remembers what Apollina had said to the Planner: *With all due respect, the Interpreter Center has one of the most advanced security systems in the Four Cities. In all my years, no one has ever broken in.*

But has someone broken out?

He gets up from bed and goes to the window. Outside, the vast lawn is a dark pit of shadows. It's too exposed to not have some kind of a perimeter alarm. But if he can get across it and to the line of trees beyond, he can make his way deep into Central Park. There are plenty of places to hide there.

He slides his fingers under the window casing and lifts. It does not budge. He checks around for a lock but cannot find one. A dot of red light on the casing blinks a warning. The security alarm! This is not going to be his way out.

He creeps slowly to the door. Stretching out a hand, he reaches for the knob. The silver watch around his wrist catches light. He stops. Apollina and the police will be able to track him in no time.

He swipes a finger on the band to unlock it. Nothing. He swipes again. The click of its catch does not come. Why can't he remove it?

Panicking, he tries to wrench it off. The metal scrapes his skin but will not slide past his wrist bones.

Breathe.

This will complicate things but does not make escape impossible. Until he finds a way to take off the watch, he can still test the security of this place. He turns the doorknob and finds it unlocked. At least he can leave his room.

Across the hall is Apollina's bedroom. He tiptoes past it. No sound comes from behind her door. She is asleep. Dawn is still hours away.

Earlier he had noticed a sliding door connecting the living room to the deck. Quietly he makes his way toward it. The door is locked. Another red dot of light blinks on the casing. An alarm here too.

He checks all the windows and doors in the vicinity and finds alarm indicators on all of them. Maybe he will have better luck in the public wing. He makes his way out the living room—past the kitchen, the hallway, and a row of doors to Dreamcatchers—and out to the reception area.

The space is vast enough to host a gathering of a hundred and was designed to impress. From the vaulted ceiling hangs giant modern chandeliers and on every wall are large-scale artworks.

He sees the exit just across the room. His heart beats so hard against his ribs that he can hardly breathe. He steps forward, first tentatively, then quickly. He's almost there.

"Good morning," Apollina's voice comes from behind him.

"Lights on," she commands, and the pendants above glow, bathing the space in light, revealing a droid beside her.

"I see you're enjoying a night stroll through the building. There's a lot to admire, I agree. But I forgot to warn you that any attempt to leave—like trying to open a window in your bedroom or the door in the living room—will set off an alarm. Good thing it woke me up and I turned it off. The police would have descended on this place in mere minutes."

"You-you have a droid," he says.

"Of course I do. It came with the house. I don't keep it out and about, of course, but it does come in handy. His name is Stevens." She walks to him, a cup in hand. "Also you can't take off your watch by yourself anymore. It was actually my suggestion to the police. An entire force full of big brains but they missed the most obvious thing. I find that's true of geniuses, you know. Intelligence does not equal shrewdness."

She hands him the cup, and he doesn't know what to do but take it.

"The runaways were able to leave because they were not being tracked," she continues. "All of them removed their watches, including you. If we make it so watches cannot be taken off by their owners, then it'll be easier to track and find them. Sure, psychologically it's a bit scary for people to be constantly reminded they're stuck. That's what the Planner was trying to avoid. But it's better than having people running off and dying in the desert."

Cold washes through his entire body.

"Say all you will about the Planner, he was a patron of the arts," she says as if they had not been talking about his imprisonment. "Come, I'll show you the pieces he had commissioned before the Last War."

Feeling dazed and defeated, he follows her. The droid does not move.

"You should drink it before it gets cold," Apollina says. "I'll have to order more Earl Grey. I'm not sure if I have enough for the next fourteen days. I'm a coffee drinker myself."

He sips from the cup. Again, the tea tastes exactly as he prefers.

She stops in front of a painting. "I really like this one."

It is an image of a four-legged animal the color of the desert sand surrounded by overgrown grass and wildflowers backdropped by a pitch-black forest. The animal has a pointy face with a dark brown nose—its pointy ears on alert, its tail curling over like the limb of a tree. It looks almost approachable except for its eyes. They're dark and stare straight out at him with an expression that unsettles.

"I was told it's called a dog. *Canis lupus familiaris*," Apollina says. "A species descended from the gray wolf, *Canis lupus*. Those are long extinct too."

She walks to the next one. "This one must have taken the artist forever to do."

The colorful painting, almost the height of the wall, is made up of a series of raised dots that someone looks to have painstakingly placed one by one onto the canvas. He cannot tell what it is exactly. It could be many things—a roiling seascape, the windblown desert, a close up of a giant's skin, or an abstract representation of what was in the artist's mind. Like the secrets he hid in the *Moonlight* Sonata's third movement.

"It was Kade's favorite," she adds, her voice laced with longing.

"Who's Kade?" he asks.

"Someone I used to know."

From her tone, he knows the person was more than just someone she used to know. It was someone dear to her.

"Where is he now?" Metis asks.

She walks to the next painting, ignoring his question.

"The Planner never told me what this one is supposed to be. But it gives me a headache when I look at it. So let's move on."

It looks like a mess of intersecting lines overlaid with complex mazes. But Metis knows what it is. *The answer.*

The Crone's voice comes to him from a memory he cannot quite place. *You've known it for a while. You saw it once, and you knew what it was then.*

He had seen a crude version of it before in one of the Crone's notebooks in her cave, and he had seen it here when he was brought in to have his dream memories wiped last cycle.

A map. Not just any map, but the most important one of all. It is the schematic drawing of the train and water pipe systems. He had seen a part of it in the train tunnel to Elara last cycle. The memory is faint, but it's there.

Everything is connected.

If he can find exactly where he is on the map, he can plot the path to Elara or anywhere the train will take him. Even Mem.

CHAPTER FIFTY-SEVEN

SCYLLA

March 6, 2233
(14 days before Tabula Rasa)

The train picks up speed, and the tunnel wall becomes a gray blur. He looks over at Aris. Her hands are fiddling with the silver ring on her finger. The one with the Resistance symbol.

He walks over and sits next to her. "You will want to take off the ring."

She looks at him, her eyes glazed as though waking from a dream. "What?"

"That ring. It has the Resistance symbol. The CCTVs have recently been trained to scan for it to identify Dreamers." *Because of me.* Guilt eats at his stomach.

Her eyebrows scrunch together. "It's my wedding ring."

"And it's going to get you picked up by the police."

"We found this one and another in the house we now live in."

"I know. I put them there."

She blinks repeatedly. "Why?"

"They were yours. The droids would have taken them away at the hospital before Tabula Rasa. Protocol."

"Why are you telling me this now?"

"I figured we should learn to trust each other, and to do that, we should get to know each other."

She looks down at her ring. "The Crone told me you saved us from Dreamcatcher last cycle. But she told me not to tell you."

"As policemen, we're not supposed to meddle. But seeing as I'm no longer fit for the title . . ." A lump forms in his throat.

"Selene loves you. That can only mean you're a good person. That's what matters." Aris twists the ring off and puts it deep in her pants pocket. "How long have you been together?"

"Four years. We met on my first assignment as lead officer."

"How often do you see each other?"

"Once a month for the wellness check."

"Seems so little."

"Ninety-six days."

"What?"

"We'll have a total of ninety-six days together. Once a month for eight years. A lead officer is assigned the post for only two cycles. Afterward, a new officer will be taking over my responsibilities, and I won't be coming to the CDL as often."

She raises her eyebrows. "What were you going to do?"

He looks down at his hands. "We haven't talked about it. We've actually been actively avoiding it."

"What do you think the Planner will do once he finds out about Selene?"

"Like Eleanor said, he will want to experiment on her and our child, to learn how our DNA changed, how we were able to procreate when we weren't supposed to be able to. He'll want to know whether it will happen to others. And once he knows what we're planning, he'll declare a state of emergency. I'll be arrested along with everyone else involved. He'll replace the Head Matre. Or worse, get rid of the CDL, replacing Matres with droids or police officers to raise the children. He will want complete control."

Aris shudders. "Well, we can't let that happen then."

"We can't." His eyes return to the front window and the oppressive gray of the tunnel. "It must have taken you days to walk through this."

"It did."

"Were you not afraid of being hit by a train?"

"I was."

"How did you do it then?"

"By putting one foot in front of the other. It was the best option I had at the time."

A pinpoint of light appears ahead. It's finally dawn. They are approaching the end of the tunnel. All the Matres make their way from the back of the car and gather around the large window.

A whoosh, and the gray walls transform into a green forest. Gasps come from all around them. This spot marks the boundary between the CDL and the rest of the world. It's the farthest the Matres have ever been.

Tall mountains loom to both the east and west. The ones in the west are still snowcapped.

"How did you know to come north?" he asks.

"An old poem."

"What?"

She recites its beginning for him:

> "On the edge of a cliff,
> hidden by jagged peaks
> and a northern forest of pine,
> lives Old Mem."

"How did you know it'd lead you to the CDL?" he asks.

"We didn't. We were looking for Mem, a place where memories reside. Not the CDL."

"How did you come across the poem?"

"Metis told me about it. I don't know how he learned of it. But it's not just the poem. The clues are in paintings, books, songs."

He shakes his head in disbelief. "You followed a myth and found the CDL."

"It's not a myth if it's been proven true. I think these are memories. Before there were Dreamers, there was the Resistance. The Crone thinks they found the CDL and left their memories of it all over the Four Cities. On walls and jewelry, in secret messages on pages of books, in music. One memory may not mean much, but together they make a tapestry of knowledge that stretches back generations. And that's how we have the poem."

"But how did you find the train tracks? They're nowhere near a town and run independent of other tracks."

"About twenty miles from downtown Elara is an old underground military bunker. Connected to it is a decommissioned train tunnel. We followed it until it ended in the desert. But we kept walking—call it stubbornness or stupidity. Eventually we found these tracks heading north."

"Unbelievable."

"It wasn't easy. There were so many drones flying out in the desert at random hours of the day."

"We were looking for runaways. How did you not get spotted?"

"We hid in ghost towns along the tracks. Old gas stations. Broken-down churches. Run-down storage buildings. At least that's what their signs said."

All the places they no longer need.

"But the farther north we traveled, the fewer towns there were. And drones were circling closer. Then Metis and I decided to separate because he wanted to draw the drones away from me." Her eyes brim with tears. "And now he's with the Interpreter."

"We'll get him back." He can see the man now, strapped to a chair in the small room with a helmet on his head.

"What do you think the police are going to do now?"

"The CDL's location is its best strength. Drones can't fly that far. And without the train, the only way in is what you did—go by foot. Another thing the police could do is send droids, but they're not equipped for fieldwork. They might break down, and that'd be a waste of assets. Their best strategy is to use Metis. They know you will try to rescue him. He's your weak point."

"And we also have the Planner's weak point," Eleanor says from behind them. "Me."

He turns to see her with Amira and the other Matres. "What he wants most is my book, and me inside it. That's why we're going to make a trade."

"I still don't know if I like the idea," Aris says. "We need you."

"You need me less than you think," Eleanor says. "And it will only be temporary. Eli and I have a standing agreement. Since he insists on me existing, he is—as we said in the Old World—'in a bind.'"

Aris nods, though she does not look completely convinced.

"Officer Scylla, can you tell us about College?" Amira asks, looking at the two kids across the way. She must think they want to know but are too afraid to ask.

"Sure," he says. "I've never been inside, but I'll tell you what I know."

"How come you've never been inside?"

"It operates under secrecy, and no outsider is allowed in."

The kids turn their attention to him but stay in their seats. They seem uncomfortable, understandable since someone with his face just attacked them and mind-controlled them into confessing.

"It's much smaller than the CDL," he continues. "There are only five hundred students in the undergraduate program, a hundred in the graduate program, and fifty professors. Head Professor Thalia manages the place and a team of professors."

"Some of us are sent there," a Matre behind Amira says. "It's a prestigious post, but no one ever comes back."

"They wouldn't," he says. "The knowledge gained and discovered at College becomes the property of the System. Their lab created some of our best innovations. Them leaving would be a breach."

Another way the Planner keeps everything neatly separated and in its place.

"They have a lab?" Eleanor asks.

"Yes, the students work directly with their professors as part of their studies. After they graduate, they're transferred to the Four Cities and assigned jobs based on their area of focus."

College's purpose is to deliver 125 graduates every year. The best minds are sent by the Planner to work in Research & Intelligence to create new technologies and medicines for the Four Cities. Scylla is not sure how Cass and Bastian will be accepted into it with nothing more than a letter from the Head Matre—powerful though she may be.

The trees outside grow smaller and sparser as they descend into a barren valley. A vast dusty-brown landscape of desiccated grass and shrubs flies past.

"You walked through all of this?" Amira asks Aris.

She nods.

"How did you survive without water?"

"There are streams with melted snow from the mountains. But I imagine in the summer it would be impossible to cross on foot."

"And food?"

"Packets of camping foods and—" She pulls out a book from her pack. "Wild edibles."

"We have that same one," Bastian says from across the way, book in hand.

"There's a good section on berries," Aris says, leaning over Scylla.

"I'm Bastian, and this is Cass."

"I'm Aris."

The boy smiles. "We know who you are. We were the ones who found you collapsed near the Gate of Six Bells."

"Oh!" She blinks. "Thanks for finding me."

"You're welcome."

The lightness of this moment makes Scylla smile. He needed it.

The train reaches a fork in the tracks and veers left, the way to College. The tracks become curvier as the terrain changes to rocky hills in shades of brown. Once the train bends around a large boulder that looks like a hammer, a building on a hill comes into view. He has only been here at night. In daylight, it looks the same color as the dry land surrounding it—perfectly camouflaged.

Scylla sees the train station ahead. Like the building on the hill, it's the same color as the surrounding land. In his past visits, the platform was filled with professors and students to greet the new arrivals. Today it's empty. The train slows and comes to a stop.

The children get up. The Matres follow suit.

"Do you have the Head Matre's letter?" he asks Cass.

She pulls it from her jacket. Its contents he can only guess. Scylla pushes the button next to the door, and it opens. A scent of dry sage hits his nose. He steps forward, and the kids and the Matres follow him out the train.

From down the platform, a group of women approaches. He looks behind him at Bastian and Cass. Their faces are ashen.

"What's going on here?" the one in front asks.

Her name tag says Head Professor Thalia. She holds herself with the same authority as the Head Matre and appears about the same age.

She looks from him to the six Matres and the two children. "This isn't a planned visit. And why are there Matres?"

"The Head Matre sent us here with a letter," Scylla says.

"From Hera?"

Cass steps up and gives her the sealed envelope with a shaky hand. The Head Professor takes the letter and cracks open the seal. As she reads, her expression shifts from curiosity to fear to anger to wonderment.

When she finishes, she looks up, her eyes glistening. "Is it true about the pregnancy? Our bodies can now create life?"

He nods. "But Selene is very ill from it. We need to get medicine in Callisto to help her."

"And those books underneath the CDL are memory books?"

"Yes. We have some of them, which we will be distributing."

Thalia rubs her forehead. "You're waging a war against the System?"

"No, not waging a war," Eleanor's voice says from behind him. "We're merely giving people another option."

He didn't see her exit the train. In the sunlight, her gauze-like appearance is even more translucent. All the professors' mouths hang open.

"You're the Crone Hera mentioned," Thalia says.

"Yes."

"How are you still alive? Hera said you're from before the Last War. You're over two hundred years old!"

"Eli, your Planner, has imprisoned my consciousness inside a book."

"He isn't my Planner when he decided to take the children

meant for College and forced them into the Four Cities prematurely," the Head Professor says, defiance in her voice.

She reminds him more and more of Head Matre Hera. Perhaps they were childhood friends.

"My name is Eleanor. And this is Aris." She points to the woman beside her. "She's a Dreamer. She wants her old memories, and there are many others like her in the Four Cities. The memory books, together with Absinthe, will allow them to remember those they love forever. We can finally have a real chance at true peace."

"What's Absinthe?" Thalia asks.

Eleanor gestures to Aris, who steps up and hands the Head Professor a small glass vial filled with green liquid.

"This is Absinthe, a drug I created to make dream memories more vivid," Eleanor says. "It's from hypnos, a flower of my own creation."

Head Professor Thalia brings the vial to her eyes and studies it. "How does it work?"

"A dream of a memory lights up neurons in the same pattern as the memory itself. Absinthe induces this same pattern of neuron firing, enhancing and strengthening the dream memories."

"Fascinating." She hands it back.

"Keep it," the Crone says. "It has more potential than I was able to discover when I had a physical body. Perhaps you and your students can study it and find other uses for it."

The Head Professor puts it in her jacket pocket.

"Will you be able to take in the children?" Scylla asks.

Her eyes go to Cass and Bastian. "Of course. We will care for them and keep them safe."

The Matres form a line, and each hugs the children.

"You're very brave," one says. "We're so proud of you."

"You're going to be safe here. Listen to the professors, and do your best," another says.

"Take care of each other."

"We will miss you."

When it's her turn, Matre Amira places her hands on both their shoulders. "You both are very loved by all of us. No matter what."

The kids nod, tears in their eyes. "Yes, Matre."

Aris hands them two blue birds, folded from paper. "In the Old World, this was a sign of good fortune and happiness. Thank you for finding me, and I hope to be back here for a visit."

The Crone glides toward them, her glow muted by the sun. She looks like a faded photograph. "Remember what your Head Matre said. You are stronger together."

They nod and walk to Thalia.

"Head Professor?" Cass asks in a small voice. "Will we be with the College students?"

"Yes, you'll be in the dorms with everyone. This place isn't big, and there's nowhere else for you to be. All the students will be excited to see you."

"Us?"

"Yes. They miss everyone at the CDL very much."

The girl's eyes widen. "They remember us? Weren't they reset by Tabula Rasa?"

"No."

"But how?" Aris asks, eyes bulging. "I thought everyone gets Tabula Rasa at eighteen. It's a trigger in the brain."

"We have a drug to delay it," the Head Professor says.

"Wait, what? Since when?"

"We've had it since the beginning. When College was set up, it was determined to be easier for the students to learn with unbroken histories."

CHAPTER FIFTY-EIGHT

ARIS

March 6, 2233
(14 days before Tabula Rasa)

Aris leans her head against the window. Its cool surface helps to calm. The desert blurs by in streaks of buttery yellow. She feels as though she's in a dream, and if she moves too suddenly, she'll startle awake.

No more goodbyes.

With the drug, she and Metis can have a life where they do not have to keep rebuilding atop the ashes of old ones. No more counting down to a reset. No more chasing the past.

A life of continuity.

"Did you know about it?" the Crone asks Scylla.

"No. College keeps everything a secret. There's not even direct communication between it and the CDL. And this isn't the kind of information you can easily relay without jeopardizing the safety of both places."

"Eli must know about it."

"But why does he let it exist?" Scylla asks.

"For the same reason he lets Absinthe exist," the Crone says. "He feels he has to."

She glides back and forth on the aisle. "Between the drug,

Absinthe, and the memory books, the System is vulnerable. That's why he separated the CDL and College and why he isolated both from the Four Cities. We have all the puzzle pieces. We just need to put them together."

"We have two of those pieces already," Scylla says. "The memory books and Absinthe."

"We just have to convince the Head Professor to give us the third," Amira says.

"Aris," the Crone asks. "You've been quiet. What are you thinking?"

She peels her eyes away from the landscape and to the glowing woman.

"As soon as the Planner realizes what we know, he's going to destroy all three," she says—less a thought than an absolute truth. "The only way to succeed is to create a wave of change so monumental he can't control it."

"Agreed," Scylla says.

She turns back to the window. These miles that took her days by foot, she is passing in minutes. Each step she made was a hope toward a better life. She is closer to that life than she has ever been, yet she feels nothing but terror. It wraps its arms around her chest like a vice, squeezing, making it hard to breathe.

"We have to," she adds. "There won't be another chance."

Sitting cross-legged on the dirt, she scratched the wall with a sharp rock. She felt hands on her cheeks, pulling her long hair behind her. Lips on the crook of her neck.

"Hi."

"What are you doing?" Metis asked.

"Leaving a mark. I want those that come after us to know we got at least this far."

"It's a beautiful mark."

"Hardly. It's no Luce. You know, I've always been a little jealous of artists and your ability to create."

He made an indecipherable sound, stood up, and walked off without a word. She followed and found him leaning against the oak tree growing out the side of the building. His eyes were faraway.

"Are you okay?" she asked.

"Yeah," he said, but did not look at her.

"Do you miss playing music?" she asked—the question she had been avoiding, mainly because he had been actively avoiding the topic himself.

"I've made my choice."

"I know, but do you miss it?"

He dragged in air through his nose and emptied his lungs. "Yes. But there's no point dwelling on it."

"It was your life."

He turned to her. "You're *my* life."

"I'm sorry you had to give it up."

For a fraction of a second his face crumpled, but he composed himself. "It's not for nothing. Now I do *this*."

"This isn't much more than just surviving. It's a means to an end."

"What we're doing is important. It isn't just for us."

She touched his cheek. "Have you done anything just for you, Sandman?"

He grabbed her hand and kissed it. "Loving you. That's just for me."

She leaned against him. "Maybe we can disappear once we've found Mem."

"Disappear?"

"After we help get people's memories back to them, you can retire from being Sandman. Have someone else make Absinthe. We can live a quiet life. I'll find a hobby. You'll play the piano, just because you want to."

"With what piano?" he asked, his voice sad.

The only way to touch one was to be in the Four Cities. As much as they liked to pretend they could return to their home in Lysithea, they both knew deep down there was no going back. Absinthe was protected because of the Crone, but whatever they'd find at Mem would be forbidden.

The land outside begins to change from barren brown to a field of small black rocks. In the distance is a group of buildings—the last ghost town before all traces of civilization give way to nature.

"We're almost there," Aris says. "We need to slow down the train."

Scylla walks to the control panel on the wall. He presses buttons, and the speed reduces to a crawl.

Aris walks to the front window, Amira and the Matres behind her.

She sees it. "There! That building."

The train eases to a stop. Down the embankment is a lone concrete structure with peeling paint. A small oak tree grows out of its side, reclaiming it for the desert. This was where she and Metis spent their last night together.

Scylla opens the door, and the scent of the desert wafts through. Aris steps off the train and inhales a lungful. The arid air is tinged with an undercurrent of fresh spring leaves. The tightness around her chest loosens.

She walks to one side of the building, her eyes searching

the wall. It's faint, barely enough to be noticeable. She lowers to her haunches and touches it. The design is a crude version of the one on her ring. The symbol of the Resistance.

I was here.

Inside, the scent of a burning campfire still lingers. A bittersweet memory rises—her and Metis making love under the starry sky, goodbyes at their lips. This place was where she was last happy.

"The roof isn't in great condition," Amira says. "We won't be able to leave the books here long."

"Hopefully, they won't be here longer than we need them to be," the Crone says.

Amira waves to the Matres on the train. "Okay, let's do it!"

They begin bringing down boxes and stacking them in one corner.

Scylla looks up at the sky as he walks a box in. "I don't know if this is a flying route for the security drones. The sooner we can get inside the tunnel, the better."

"Where is it?" Aris asks.

He points to the southwest. "Where those mountains are."

They work in silence, and before too long, half the boxes are transferred. These will be insurance in case they do not succeed. The other half will go with them to Callisto.

"Let's get back on the train," Scylla says. "Hurry!"

They all pile back in and soon are moving again. The Matres will no longer wait here. The new plan requires that they go into Callisto with the Crone to recruit the Dreamers, a job Aris and Metis were originally supposed to do after they regained their memories. With the Planner now aware that Aris has found the Library of Memory, she will not be able to move easily through the Four Cities. The target will be squarely on her back.

Her main focus is to figure out how to use Dreamcatcher

to read her memory book. Without a way to access it, it is no more special than the empty journal she thought it was when she first saw it. The task of rescuing Metis will fall on Scylla, as will getting the medication for Selene.

Divide and conquer.

"Get comfortable," Scylla says. "Once we enter the tunnel at the mountain, we're going to wait inside it until nightfall before we continue on to Callisto."

Aris finds Amira sitting by herself in the last train car.

"Can I sit with you?"

"Yeah."

"Here." She hands her a box of folded origami cranes.

Before leaving the CDL, she had a Matre collect as much blue paper as she could find, and together they folded them before Aris left on the train in the morning. Each crane contains only three letters written in lemon juice: CDL.

If a Dreamer were to find a crane, they would know how to reveal the invisible message within. If not, it would just be a folded bird.

"Thank you," Amira says.

"Nervous?"

"Yes."

"Me too," Aris says.

"Where's Elara from here?" Amira asks.

"Southeast. I'm not sure how many days away, since we were just stumbling through the desert before we found these tracks."

"The Crone said many Dreamers live in Elara."

"Yes, though there aren't that many people who live there, a high percentage of them are Dreamers," Aris says.

"I wonder why."

"There are a lot of artists there. The community concentrates around the downtown area."

Amira raises her eyebrows.

"It's my personal theory," Aris continues. "Artists have great imagination. They're better equipped at imagining a different life, seeing it as a possibility."

"Was that where you lived?" Amira asks.

"No, both Metis and I lived in Lysithea—in a blue house on a hill overlooking the valley. In the back is a piano and a garden." She feels her face stretching in a smile. "In the summer, we'd leave the door in between open, and I could hear Metis's music while working in the backyard."

There's no going back.

"Here," the Matre gives her a handkerchief.

She looks at it, not understanding what had prompted her to do such a thing.

"You're crying," Amira says.

She wipes her cheek, the wetness glistening in the setting sun.

CHAPTER FIFTY-NINE

METIS

March 6, 2233
(14 days before Tabula Rasa)

Dinner is another elaborate multicourse meal. Apollina had described each course in detail, but he was not listening. His mind buzzes. The Interpreter had someone. It must have been someone she was close to. She must have lost that person to Tabula Rasa. She knows their pain. This could be a way out.

"Are you not enjoying the food?" the Interpreter asks. "You've hardly touched your artichoke."

"I'm fine. It's just, I've been wondering how you know about all these restaurants if you've never been out."

She looks down at her plate and moves her food around. This is not something she wants to talk about. But that's exactly what he needs her to do.

"Does this have anything to do with Kade?" he asks.

Her fork stops moving.

"I know the look of longing when I see it," he adds. "Did you two used to have dinners like this?"

"We're not talking about it," she says.

"I spent the majority of the last cycle eating alone," he tells her. "I didn't reconnect with my wife until the entire four years was nearly gone. I ate mostly at home too. It was lonely, but I was never alone. I always had my thoughts of her. I had the dream memories of our time together."

He cuts a piece of the steamed artichoke heart and dips it in the yellow hollandaise. The tanginess and creaminess of the sauce dance on his tongue.

"In the beginning, I tried to distract myself—with work, with a date here or there," he continues. "But I came to realize there was no escape. I couldn't connect with another person. Not in that deep, visceral way she and I did. Those interactions became empty, and I was wasting that person's time. It wasn't fair to them. Or to me, for that matter. So I stopped."

"It must have been hard," Apollina says.

"It was. But it was also inevitable. I wasn't trying to be a martyr. I just wasn't feeling what I knew I was capable of. And my life was already full of lies. Being a Sandman isn't something you could just confide to people."

"Seems we're not so different."

"In the end, we're just people," he says. "Some with more memories than others."

Apollina sighs. "Kade loved to cook, but all the restaurants are run by droids. So we'd order meals from those restaurants, and he would try to recreate them in my kitchen."

"What happened to him?"

"The same thing that happened to you and Althea, to everyone else. Tabula Rasa. But he never found his way back to me. I kept thinking one day he'd walk through my door wanting to have his dreams erased, but he never did."

"Have you looked for him?"

"No. No matter what I find, it'll be painful."

"How did you meet him in the first place?"

"I was on the lawn. I saw people lying out and wanted

to try. I had a full picnic spread, and that drew his attention. He didn't know I was the Interpreter. Well, until I invited him in."

"That sounds pretty—um—wholesome."

"For a 'murderer of dreams'?" she says. "Yeah, I know what the Dreamers call me."

"You know, we don't have to live this way. Life can be different. Love doesn't have to be limited to a four-year cycle."

"You don't know the Planner like I do. Let's just say I wouldn't be surprised if he knew about Kade and has been diverting him from this place."

"What do you mean?"

"Have you ever used your watch for directions?"

"Of course."

"Have you ever wondered how it decides which route you should take?"

"No. I've always assumed it gives me the shortest, most efficient route."

"Exactly. No one ever questions it."

An alarm sounds. Apollina springs up and runs to her room. He follows. Inside it he sees Stevens the droid standing in one corner, and on one wall are monitors showing images from around the outside the Interpreter Center.

"The police! What do they want?" she mutters.

To his surprise, she returns to the dining room. She sits down at the table and continues eating.

"We don't want the food to get cold," she says.

He sits. Though her face bears no emotions, he notices her sitting with her back straighter and her shoulders pulled back. He realizes then that this performance she plays with the police, with the Planner, is a front. A moment later, a police officer appears in the room.

"Which one are you?" she asks without looking as she meticulously cuts her food into small bites.

"Gordon," he says. "I see you have a penchant for eating with prisoners."

"What am I supposed to do, starve and let *him* starve? Why are you here?"

"Urgent orders from the Planner," the officer says.

"What orders?"

He looks sideways at Metis.

"He's fine. He'll be erased anyway," she tells him.

"It seems the CDL is mobilizing."

"The CDL? They're just Matres. What does that have to do with you disrupting my dinner?"

"Because they're heading here."

"How? The only way here is the train."

"Scylla has turned."

Apollina scoffs. "Your lead officer has switched sides? How did that happen?"

Gordon looks annoyed. "We don't know. We still need to confirm it. Anyway, what this has to do with you is we're going to post officers and droids around your perimeter. So if you don't want to keep getting security alerts, I suggest you turn it off."

"It does more than just alerting," Apollina says. "Why here?"

"Well, because his partner is coming. And once she realizes he's not at Police Station One, she'll come looking for him here."

Metis's heart jumps.

Aris coming here? Has she found Mem? What happened to Officer Scylla to turn him?

"So, what are you going to do, arrest her?" Apollina asks.

"The Planner wants us to let her through," Gordon says.

CHAPTER SIXTY

SCYLLA

March 6, 2233
(14 days before Tabula Rasa)

The brakes screech. Scylla grabs onto his seat, bracing himself. The train comes to a stop at the spot he had reprogrammed it to. They are about two miles from Callisto. This is a part of the new plan. Police Station One will be swarming with officers and droids waiting for them.

He walks around, rousing his traveling companions. It was the middle of the night now.

"Time to go."

Without a word, everyone puts on their backpacks and files in behind him. He opens the door into the pitch-black tunnel. Eleanor leaves first, illuminating the tunnel with her glow. They all follow.

It smells both damp and chalky, like earth that had gone through endless cycles of rain and drought. The temperature is colder down here. Goose bumps raise on his skin. Next to him, Aris buttons her jacket.

"The ladder out should be somewhere around here," he says.

Eleanor glides away and a minute later comes back. "It's that way."

They run until they reach a metal ladder.

"I need to get back inside my book so we don't get spotted out there," Eleanor says.

"Wait," Aris says. "There has to be another way to get Metis."

"This is the best way," Eleanor says. She places her glowing hand on Aris's cheek. "Don't let guilt weigh you down."

"I . . . I can't thank you enough."

Eleanor smiles. "Thank me by helping others find their way."

She disappears into her book inside Amira's pack, and they are plunged into darkness—the blackest black Scylla has ever seen. He and Aris turn on the lights on their jackets, and a dim glow envelops them.

"I'll go first. Aris you go last. Between both our jackets we should have enough light to climb."

Scylla grabs onto the first rung. The metal is freezing under his hands. He climbs until his arms and legs burn. At the top of the ladder is a hatch. He unlatches it and pushes it open. Cool air hits his cheeks, and he sucks it in hungrily. He turns off the light on his jacket and pulls himself out. Aris and the Matres climb out behind him.

The dark desert surrounds. Ahead, the Callisto skyline lights up the horizon. The Matres stare at it with awe and apprehension in their eyes.

"We're north. That way is south," he says, pointing straight at the city. "If you keep going straight, you will hit the north side of Central Park."

He turns to Amira and the Matres. "Central Park is a rectangle. The library and hospital are along its northern edge. The Interpreter Center is in the park, toward the western side. Police Station One is on the east side of Callisto, on the edge of the city."

"Can we go over everything one more time?" Aris asks.

"The Matres and I will be going to the hospital first. Afterward, I'll leave for Police Station One and get Metis."

"And we will be locating the Dreamers to help us distribute the books and cranes," Amira says, and pats her backpack.

"I'm sorry there's not a more efficient way," he tells her. Each time they need more books, they'd have to climb down the shaft to the train and back up to the city.

"We will do what we have to," she says. "The survival of the CDL depends on this."

"You, Aris, will go to the Interpreter Center and figure out how to use Dreamcatcher for the memory book. We'll all meet back here, at this spot, before dawn."

He points to the southwest, toward a swath of land so black it stands out against the night. "That's the solar field. You're going to come back through there. It'll provide cover from drones. From the Interpreter Center, keep heading northeast from Central Park."

"Okay," Aris says. "Good luck. See everyone here before dawn."

She heads toward the west side. He watches her back melding into the night before leading the Matres south toward the hospital.

CHAPTER SIXTY-ONE

ARIS

March 6, 2233
(14 days before Tabula Rasa)

She studies the modern white stone building from a nearby shadowy thicket. It sits sprawling on a vast lawn in the middle of a dense tract of trees that partitions it from the rest of the park. No lights are on inside.

The sky is still dark, but Aris doesn't know what time it is. She wipes her tired eyes. Whatever time it is, it is time.

Tightening the hood on her jacket around her face, she races forward—fatigue and adrenaline coursing through her in equal measure. She will not be using the front door. It's locked, she knows without checking. The Interpreter Center has one of the most technologically advanced security systems in the Four Cities—except for one weak point.

Finally Aris spots it. The service entrance is now covered over with vines and shrubs. If the Crone had not told her what to look for, she would have mistaken it for a part of the foundation.

She looks up at the sky. No drones. She whizzes across the lawn toward the building. The ground—once a driveway for caterers to enter and exit—slopes down toward it. She picks up speed as she hurtles toward the rows of bushes and smacks into them. Tears well up, but there's no time to be in pain.

She dives in between the bushes, branches scratching her exposed skin. Her backpack catches, and she yanks it with all her might. It comes loose, sending her tumbling onto the ground. She covers her mouth with her hands to keep any scream, should one come, from escaping.

The sound of her breathing competes with the ruckus of her heart. She remains curled up on the ground until she calms, then crawls through the bushes toward the side of the building.

The entrance is hidden behind a wall of vines, reminding her of the secret entry to the train station at the CDL. There's barely any space for her to get in. She turns sideways and squeezes through.

Inside, the space is cavernous, with a darkness so thick and velvety it seems to throb to the rhythm of her breathing. She turns on her jacket light and makes her way through the passage. At the end she finds a loading dock. This must be what the service people used to bring in things for parties.

She walks up the ramp. It ends at a door with a lever. She pushes down on it. *Unlocked.* The door opens to reveal a set of stairs and an elevator. They had really forgotten about this place.

A step onto the bottom stair throws dust into the air. She is the first to come through here in two centuries. At the top is another closed door. This one doesn't have a knob. She turns off the light on her jacket, drags in a deep breath, and pushes. It glides open.

She finds herself inside a large commercial kitchen. On this side, the door is disguised as a row of shelves. Quietly she keeps moving forward and enters an open space. The foyer. Large-scale artworks hang on the walls and modern pendants off the ceiling. She imagines this room filled with people in fancy clothes walking around, drinks in hand, talking about Old World things that no longer matter. What must it be like to be them?

From the foyer, turn left toward a corridor of rooms. Inside them, you'll find the Dreamcatcher machines, the Eleanor in her head reminds.

Aris takes a left and walks until she comes to a corridor of rooms. She chooses the first door and enters a small room with a complicated-looking tabletop machine and a chair.

On one wall is a window overlooking the adjacent room. Through it she sees a lone bed, and above it a large machine suspended from the ceiling, raining wires down from it. The wires gather to a single point—a helmet on the bed. The image is at once familiar and not.

Dreamcatcher.

Her heart thuds. She is mere moments from being able to access her past. She exits this room and enters the other. The window is tinted black from this side. A feeling of déjà vu hits her, and the hair on her arms stands up. She has seen this place in a dream memory.

She walks to the bed and picks up the helmet. How does this work? From her backpack she brings out her memory book and puts it next to the helmet. There's nothing to attach one to the other. She thinks back to the tabletop machine in the adjacent room. Maybe it controls the Dreamcatcher.

Book in hand, she walks to the door and twists the knob. The lock catches. She looks down from her hand to the knob. It wasn't locked before. Her heart drops to her stomach.

CHAPTER SIXTY-TWO

SCYLLA

March 6, 2233
(14 days before Tabula Rasa)

The glass-and-steel building stands alone. No droid or policeman guards the hospital entrance. The System does not deem this place to be in danger.

"Are you ready?" he asks the Matres.

Amira makes a sound in her throat he cannot decipher.

"I'm going in first to make sure everything is fine," he continues. "Watch for my signal before you come in. We'll split up at the elevator. I'm going to the storage room down in the basement for Selene's medicine. You'll go to the fortieth floor to gather any detained Dreamers willing to help distribute the memory books. Just like we planned."

The idea came after realizing that because of him, many Dreamers have been collected and brought to either the hospital or Police Station One to be held until the next Tabula Rasa.

"There will be one medical droid on the floor," he says. "It's scheduled to do rounds from room to room in clockwise order. You can't miss it. It's about six feet tall."

The Matres look uneasy. They have never dealt with droids before.

"Medical droids are not dangerous," he adds. "You just have to make sure they don't spot you."

"What happens if they do?"

"They will ask you questions. And if they don't like your answers, well, they might call the police."

"We don't want that."

"Just get in and get out as quickly as you can. After, we'll meet back out here and swap. I'll hand you the medicine, and you'll hand me the Crone's book. Please get the medicine to the train no matter what."

"We will," Amira says.

"You know what to do when you're up there?"

"Whatever *she* tells me to."

A feeling of doom, ignored and suppressed since he left the CDL, rears its head. He brushes it off together with the dirt from his coat. Pulling his shoulders back, he straightens his fedora and walks toward the entrance. The sliding door opens, and he enters.

The silence in here has the rattling quality of an empty drum. There's no one here. He looks out the window and waves. Shadows move from the bushes they were hiding behind and toward the building.

The six Matres enter the lobby, Amira in the front. In their fitted black pants and tops, they could be mistaken for any young Callisto citizen going out on a Friday night. He feels protective of them.

"You'll need to separate so you won't stand out," he says.

"We plan to."

He calls an elevator and pushes the button to the fortieth floor. "Push L for lobby once you're ready to come back down. Maybe I should go up there with you."

"We do know how to use an elevator," Amira says. "We have a few at the CDL. It used to be a hotel, remember?"

"Sorry. I'm just—"

Amira places a hand on his shoulder. "We appreciate your concern. We'll be okay. Don't worry about us."

He nods. "There's a woman up there, a patient. Her name is Gia. Curly dark hair, dark brown eyes, light brown skin. She lost her partner, Cole, while they were trying to run away. She'll be a good recruit. She needs a new purpose."

Amira smiles. "We'll find her."

He steps out of the elevator, and the door closes behind him. He takes the next elevator down to the basement and finds the storage room around the corner.

Like the rest of the hospital, it has pale, smooth concrete floors and white walls. Shelves line it, reminding him of the Library of Memory. But instead of books, there are boxes labeled with long scientific names. At least they are alphabetical. He fishes the list of medication from his pocket.

He finds each quickly. Leaving some for emergencies, he puts most in his backpack. This was so easy he can't believe he was worried about it.

Too easy.

The hair on the back of his neck stands up. That weird feeling is back. This time he cannot ignore it. He zips his backpack closed and puts it on before cautiously, making his way out of the storage room.

He decides not to take the elevator this time and uses the stairs. His steps echo in the stairwell as he ascends, his stomach in knots. What is that strange feeling?

He realizes.

It's easy because it's been allowed *to be easy.*

The knowledge knocks the air out of him. His heart palpitates, and he leans against the wall, bracing himself. They're all in danger. He needs to get to the Matres. They're on the highest floor. He runs up the stairs and yanks the door open. Brown eyes, identical to his own, stare back.

"Gordon!"

"Scylla." There is sadness in his eyes. "Where's Evan?"

He steps back. "Safe."

Gordon does not ask another question, not demanding any explanation. "Hand me your backpack."

Scylla's mind skips to Selene lying pale on the hospital bed at the CDL. Without the medicine, she will die—poisoned by the life he put inside her.

"Someone at the CDL needs this, or she will die. Promise me you will get this to her. Please. She shouldn't suffer because I failed."

His brother hesitates, then nods. Scylla hands him the pack.

"How did you know I was going to be here?" Scylla asks.

"I didn't. The CCTV picked you up. It's been tracking you since you entered Callisto."

"Why didn't you stop me earlier?"

"The Planner wanted to see what you'd be doing," Gordon says.

"Do you want to know what I'm here to do?" he asks his brother. "I'll tell you."

"I'm leaving the questioning to the Planner. You will see him soon enough."

Gordon wants to remain objective. He does not want to understand Scylla. He's afraid to.

"Oh, and we know about the Matres on the fortieth floor too," he adds.

Scylla's stomach sinks. "What are you going to do to them?"

He sighs. "All the medical droids are heading there. Then the Planner will decide their fate. This is really bad, Scylla."

That's why there was no one in the basement.

"Believe me, I'm doing what I'm doing because I don't want things to get really bad," he says.

Gordon's watch buzzes. He taps on it.

"We have the perpetrator. She is inside the Interpreter Center," a voice says from it.

Aris!

Gordon speaks into the watch. "All units, head to the Interpreter Center. I have Scylla. We're taking the car, and we'll be there soon."

All hope drains from him. She, too, is walking into a trap.

CHAPTER SIXTY-THREE

ARIS

March 6, 2233
(14 days before Tabula Rasa)

Suddenly the room brightens. Cold shoots up Aris's spine.

"Good morning," a woman's voice says from a concealed speaker inside the room. "I am the Interpreter. My name is Apollina. We've been waiting for you."

Her heart drops to her stomach. What's the Interpreter doing here? She's supposed to be at Police Station One.

"I see you have your memory book," Apollina continues. "The Planner was right."

"H-how does he know?"

"I suppose this has always been a probability."

Aris looks at the dark pane of glass. The Interpreter must be on the other side of it.

"Where's the Book of Crone?" Apollina asks.

"I don't have it."

"Let's see if you're telling the truth."

Aris braces herself. The door opens, and a droid comes into the room, its expressionless eyes fixed on her. She holds the book tightly to her chest.

"Give the book and your backpack to Stevens," Apollina

says. "If you don't, I can't guarantee it won't damage it."

The thought of her memory book destroyed deflates her. She hands it and her backpack to the droid, and it leaves.

A minute later, Apollina speaks again. "Two books but no Book of Crone. You weren't lying. Fascinating... I've never held a memory book in my hand before. Is the other one Metis's?"

"What did you do to him?" Aris asks.

"I've only heard my predecessor talking about it. She was downright obsessed," Apollina says, ignoring her question. "She wanted to devote her life to studying it, but the Planner wouldn't let her. It wasn't her purpose, he told her. But I've always wanted to try it. What do you say?"

What?

"I'll take your silence as a yes. Lie down on the bed and put on the helmet."

"Wait a minute. What?"

"Lie down, and we're going to see what your memories look like."

"How do I know you won't erase my dreams with it?"

"You don't, but I *am* curious. I've never used Dreamcatcher for another purpose before. Call it professional curiosity. Besides, you're not really in a position to negotiate."

The droid, Stevens, reenters the room and stands in one corner. Aris swallows. "H-how does it work?"

"It's easier to show you. Lie down on the bed, and put on the helmet."

She looks from the gleaming copper helmet to the machine above. Against the screaming voice inside her head, she picks it up and fits it on. She feels it suctioning to her skull, tickling her.

"Now lie down," Apollina says.

Aris sits on the bed. It adjusts to mold to the shape of her body. She reclines, and it cradles her head and the helmet in place.

"Initially created to treat post-traumatic stress syndrome for the survivors, Dreamcatcher does many things," Apollina says, her tone professorial.

"Post-traumatic stress syndrome?"

"Many were suffering from it after the Last War. Being the last of humankind came with an enormous amount of stress—survivor guilt, existential dread—but the scientists eventually discovered a medicinal solution that was easier to administer."

"How did this end up here?"

"The Planner is extremely efficient at repurposing," she says. Aris detects defiance in her tone. "To access dreams, it first takes a dimensional scan of the neural network and what neurons are involved and translates it into images that are then projected up top."

The cloud-shaped copper surface above her is empty.

"It's not showing anything right now because, well, you're not dreaming," Apollina adds as if she could hear her thought.

Maybe she can.

"To delete the dream, it uses multifocal lasers to move the first few neurons in the chain to disrupt the initiation points, removing access to the heart of the dream itself."

"They're not just dreams, they're memories," Aris says.

"That's one theory."

"It's the truth!"

"We need a proper study."

"Not erasing memories would be a good first step." Aris cannot help herself.

"Are you going to keep interrupting me, or do you want to know how this works?" Apollina sounds annoyed. "Maybe it'll be easier if I sedate you."

Aris sucks in a deep breath. "Please continue."

"To look at the memory book, we're going to do the opposite

with it. We'll use Dreamcatcher to look for groups of neurons in the hippocampus that are similar to the patterns found in the memory books. And we are going to move the disrupted neurons back into the right configurations. Hopefully, what it'll do is—"

"Create an avalanche of remembrance," Aris repeats what the Crone had said before.

"Exactly. Though I've never used it for this purpose before. We both will see whether it really works."

Something hard wraps around both her wrists. Aris tries to move, but she's too late. Her arms are now strapped down to the bed. Panic grips her.

"Is this really necessary?" she asks.

"Yes. I don't want you moving around. Alright, give me a moment. I need to attach this here. Okay . . . This should work."

Fear's slippery tentacles grab hold, trying to yank her down into its depths. Maybe this is a very, very bad idea.

"Stay still," Apollina says. "Here. We. Go."

Aris feels an electric current running through her entire skull. The texture of the copper machine above changes, looking more like the surface of water than metal.

An image appears.

The color green fills her vision. A web of new florescent leaves lacing the sky. Black branches stretching up like fingers.

"Hello," a voice says.

Startled, she tilts her head down. In front of her is a pair of dark eyes.

Metis.

"What are you doing? I almost walked into you," she says, her tone irritated.

"I'm sorry. You were looking up, and I was wondering if you needed assistance."

"Can't a person look up for no reason?"

"I suppose." He turns his face to the sky. "It's a normal blue—nothing out of the ordinary. No reason to look up at all."

"I was looking at the leaves."

"Of the trees?"

"What else?"

"Tea for example."

She laughs. "There are no tea leaves up there."

"Would you like to go where you can find some?"

"Oh? And where would that be?"

"A coffee shop."

"You're telling me to go to a coffee shop?"

"No, I'm asking you if you want to go. With me. I know a place with good tea."

"Are you asking me out on a date?"

He runs a hand through his black hair, pink touching the knolls of his cheekbones. "I suppose so, yes. I know it's weird to be asked out on a date in the park by a stranger."

"What's your name?" she asks.

"Metis."

"I'm Avi. Now we're not strangers anymore."

His face spreads into a wide smile. "So, is that a yes?"

"What's the worst that could happen?" she says.

This was the first time they met.

The image changes to that of a lake, the one in the middle of Central Park. The blue house on a hill. Metis playing the piano under the canopy of Cyathea ferns. Him performing on a stage. Sunset in the desert. Gravelly paths dotted by Joshua trees. The pictures flip faster and faster until they stop.

Our bedroom.

Metis is sitting astride her. His fingers travel along the side of her body, tracing its curves like pilgrims traversing sand dunes. He finds her hand and binds it in his own. Their fingers entwine.

"I love you," he says.

"It's not enough." *She untangles her hands from his and covers her eyes. Everything turns black.* "I'm so tired of being afraid every day. Of losing you. Of losing myself. Of losing the last four years like they were just a dream."

He peels her hands off her face and holds them to the sides.

"This pain you're feeling is temporary," he says. "Tomorrow, after they come to collect us, all this will go away. Your mind will be wiped clean of the pain. It will be gone."

This was the night before Tabula Rasa. Which cycle was it?

"And where does the love go?" she asks.

He hesitates. He doesn't have an answer.

"We both know the side effects of falling in love," he says eventually. "We knew it before we went into it. We knew it couldn't last."

She yanks her hands from his grasp. "Was a disclaimer supposed to make it easier?"

"That's not what I meant."

"Then what did you mean? That it's my fault for falling in love? That I should have known better?"

"You're upset," he says.

"Why are you not?"

"How can you think I'm not?"

"Because I'm in pieces, and you're fine," she says.

His face crumples. He lowers himself until their faces are inches apart.

"I'm. Not. Fine," he says through gritted teeth.

"To live is to suffer. Is that it?" she says. "I wish I'd never fallen in love."

Silence fills the room. He climbs off her and leans against the headboard.

"It's never been a choice for me," he says.

She looks at his profile, shadowy but for the light of the moon coming through the windows. "Nor me."

His hand finds hers again. He brings her palm to his lips and kisses it.

"Sometimes I think we were here before," he says. "I've had dreams of us together. In a different life. In another time. It felt too real to only be dreams."

He turns to face her. "What if this was not the first cycle we came together? What if we're just repeating the patterns of our past? What if we'll find each other again?"

"The probability is one in a million," she says.

"We only need one chance."

"You're talking of hope."

"Is that so bad?"

"Hope is dangerous," she says. "It's a parasite that feeds off dreams and romanticism. One day it will burst out of your middle, only to find that it can't survive this world."

"Do you have to be so dark?"

"So you're the yang to my yin? The lightness to my darkness?"

"Can you for once try to imagine? Is it so hard to believe?" he says.

"How? Tabula Rasa is thorough."

He sits up and swings his legs over the side of the bed.

"Are you mad at me?" she asks.

"No, I'm just thinking."

"Can't we just be? There're not many hours left before the sun rises. I can already feel the air changing."

She leans over to the side table. A dot of light from a candle interrupts the darkness. It grows bigger, enveloping the room in its glow.

She wraps her arms around him and kisses his back. Hands

running across the plane of his body, she leaves a trail of goose bumps. Her lips touch the crook of his neck.

The image flickers.

He picks up the candle from the side table and offers her his hand.

"Come with me?" he asks.

He pulls her from the bed—leading her along the hallway, passing a vestibule and closed doors, and down the creaky stairs. The glow of the single candle, though small, is enough to light the familiar path. Soon, they find their way into a room of ferns, where the piano sits.

He finds a spot for the candle on a nearby table and pulls out the bench from under the piano. They sit on it side by side. He leans in and kisses her forehead before placing his fingers on the keys. The first note strikes—high and hopeful.

"Did you know this song came to me from a dream?" he asks. "It was as if it had always been there, having existed even before we met. Yet, I've always known it was yours. This is how we'll find each other. This song."

"How?"

"The same way I know music. My body remembers even if I can't. I think there's a part of our brain Tabula Rasa cannot touch. A secret place overlooked for its primitiveness, for its significance to survival. The part where we hide our dreams."

The music becomes louder.

"From the first time we met, there was a sense of affinity. I couldn't put a finger on it," he adds. "You asked me where love goes after Tabula Rasa. I have to believe it continues to exist, floating around like a spirit, waiting for a body to inhabit. Even if you don't remember me or us, remember this song."

"Can you pause? I can't see anymore," Aris asks, tears blurring her eyes.

The image above freezes. A moment later, Apollina enters the room. The blond woman looks down, her sharp blue eyes chilling her.

The Interpreter releases one of Aris's hands from the lock. "How does it feel to see your past like that?"

"Painful. Amazing." Aris wipes her eyes. "It's so much more than what I expected—everything I never knew I needed."

"Do you want to keep going?"

A door bangs open.

"Let her go!" a voice as familiar as her own yells. "Don't do this. Please. Let her go."

She cannot see him.

"Metis!" she cries.

"I asked you to wait in your bedroom," the Interpreter says.

His arms swaddle protectively over her body. Aris wraps her free arm around him, grabbing on tight.

"Please, Apollina, don't erase her," he says.

"She's not, Metis," Aris says. "She's helping me see my memory. Look up."

He does and looks back at her—confusion in his eyes.

"That's us," she says. "Our first meeting. A night before Tabula Rasa. In our house. You playing *Luce* for me. I found Mem. I have my memory book. I found yours too."

"You found Mem?"

"It's a library underneath the CDL. All the memories are there. All the way to the beginning."

Tears fill his eyes. He leans down and presses his lips on hers, his mouth hot and soft. She sinks into the kiss, filling all the cracks in her heart with his love.

He wipes tears off her face and kisses her forehead. "I've

missed you so much. I didn't know if I'd ever see you again. I'm sorry I left you alone."

"Don't be sorry. We made it."

He looks at the Interpreter. "We're going to change things, Apollina. The Planner's way isn't the only way to be anymore. You can have a life without loneliness, another chance with Kade."

Kade?

"How?" Apollina whispers.

"Use Dreamcatcher for another purpose. You can help people remember instead of forget. You can connect instead of sever them from their memories."

The door opens again.

"What are you doing?" The voice sounds similar to Scylla's. But it cannot be him.

"Don't you knock?" Apollina says, her voice venomous. "Can't you see I'm working?"

"You were only supposed to retain her. And what is *he* doing in there?"

"Do I question how *you* work?"

"Gordon is on his way, and he wants me to tell you the Planner wants to see both the prisoners."

Aris's stomach drops.

"Metis, move," the Interpreter orders.

Hesitantly he steps aside. His face is replaced by Apollina's. She looks down at her, eyes indecipherable. She releases the lock around her other wrist and removes the helmet from her head.

"Get up," the Interpreter says.

Aris does. Metis pulls her into his arms, and they wrap themselves in each other. He smells the same—Earl Grey tea and fresh laundry. She breathes him in, filling her lungs with all the memories she can contain.

"Hurry," the voice at the door says. It's a police officer younger than Scylla.

They walk out the room, Stevens the droid following behind them. They turn down the corridor and enter another room. This one is larger than the other. There is no Dreamcatcher, no bed—nothing but a large screen on one wall. On it is a man who looks as old as the earth itself. The Planner.

CHAPTER SIXTY-FOUR

ELEANOR

March 7, 2233
(13 days before Tabula Rasa)

It's three in the morning. That's what the clock on the wall says. Sunrise is just three hours away. A new day. A day all the days that follow hinge on. Their success or failure here will determine what kind of future those in the Four Cities and the CDL will have.

Mine to protect.

The fortieth floor is quiet, everyone asleep. She leads the Matres down the long corridor. They, too, know how important their work here is. She looks over her shoulder at the identical faces—her own. Their differences give her hope. DNA may govern their appearances, but it does not own who they are.

On each door is a name.

She points. "This one is a Dreamer."

They open the door and find a man sleeping. She walks to him and places her hand on his cheek. His eyes flutter open.

"The Crone!" he gasps. "You're here."

He sits up, his eyes casting about at her and the Matres. "Am I dreaming?"

"No, child. I'm here because we need your help. These women are Matres from the CDL. We found the memory books that contain the erased past of each citizen of the Four Cities. We don't know who they belong to, and we need help getting them to their owners. Will you be willing to help us?"

He blinks. "Yes. Yes! Of course."

"One of the Matres will give you details," she says and leaves the room.

She leads the other five Matres to the next room belonging to a Dreamer and repeats the same message. She continues her walk down the corridor until only Amira is left.

"This one is Gia," Amira says. "Scylla said she lost her partner recently."

The Matre opens the door, and they enter.

The curly-haired woman is sitting on her bed. She turns to them but, unlike the others, does not look surprised. Her eyes are glassy with sleeplessness and defeat.

"Hello, Gia," the Crone says.

"Am I dead yet?" Gia asks.

She glides to her "No. You still have more life to live."

"For what?"

"A new purpose."

"Cole is dead."

Sadness grips her. "I know. I'm so very sorry."

"He didn't want to leave. I pressured him into it," Gia says. "It's my fault he's dead."

"You didn't know it would turn out that way."

"I didn't know a lot of things. All I know is I don't want to live this way anymore."

"And you won't have to," Amira says. "Not if we succeed."

Gia slowly turns her head to the Matre. "And who are you?"

"My name is Amira. I'm a Matre from the CDL."

"A Matre . . . you're the one who raises all of us created children?"

Amira smiles. "Not just me. There are many of us."

She walks closer to Gia. "We have books of memories locked up under the CDL we need to get back to their owners."

"What if they don't want to remember?"

"Then they won't have to," Eleanor says. "But those who do—like you, like Cole did—will have that choice. With these, you can stop those who want to leave because they are afraid of Tabula Rasa. You can help prevent future tragedies."

"Will you help us?" Amira asks.

"I don't want to remember." Tears brim Gia's eyes. "Even though I know my pain won't go away, I will let Tabula Rasa take me. But I will help."

Eleanor nods. She understands the desire to let go.

They make their way out of the room and meet the others waiting in front of the elevator.

"Your job is to spread the word as quickly as you can about the books. Then move as many books as you can from the train and hide them throughout the Four Cities. Each pair of Dreamer and Matre, do what you can."

"We're ready."

Amira pushes the elevator button. It dings, and the door opens. Inside are droids. They step out and slowly advance toward them. The Matres line up in front of the Dreamers, readying themselves for a fight.

"Hello, Doctor Hope."

CHAPTER SIXTY-FIVE

SCYLLA

March 7, 2233
(13 days before Tabula Rasa)

Gordon's police car winds its way up the private drive leading to the Interpreter Center and comes to a stop in front of it. The white building stands harsh against the vast green lawn. Cold lines deprive it of all warmth, the opposite of the CDL. Surrounding it are police officers and droids. Aris and Metis are inside. It will take a miracle to get them out.

"You don't have to do this," Scylla says. "There's another way to be. We can stop people from running away from the Four Cities permanently. We don't have to take more children from the CDL to replace the dead."

Gordon does not reply. Instead he gets out of the car. "Let's go."

"No Subdue Bracelet?"

"I'm not going to dishonor you with that. You know as well as I there's no running from the System, and definitely no point in lying to the Planner."

They cross the lawn, all eyes tracking them. Scylla feels like a target. The front door is open. They enter into the art-filled foyer.

The Planner's room is the last one, past the rooms of

Dreamcatchers. Inside it he finds Aris, Metis, and Apollina. On either side of them stands a droid. On the screen before them is the Creator.

"Leave us, Gordon!" the Planner says, and his brother retreats and closes the door.

The Planner whips his hate-filled eyes to Scylla. "The prodigal son returns. Where's Eleanor's book?"

"I don't have it, sir." Scylla looks at Aris and Metis. "Are you two okay?"

"Do not talk to the other prisoners!" the Planner says. "I will do the questioning here."

He drags in a long breath and releases it. An old human habit. The Planner no longer needs to breathe. "If you don't have it, who does? The Matres? You know I will tear through that place looking for her."

Scylla swallows.

"Tell me everything, and I will know if you withhold!" the Planner demands.

He looks directly into his creator's eyes—not his gaze but his irises. They're dark brown like his own. In magnified detail, the color isn't solid. It undulates lighter and darker as it dances closer to the pupils, with a texture that's difficult to describe. Almost like the surface of water.

He decides the story he wants to tell isn't about him.

"The first death I experienced was of my own. It wasn't me in the literal sense. It was of the man who raised me. His name was Theo. He was a good man, a kind man. A lead officer of peace. As he lay dying, he told me that long ago he had fallen in love with a woman. She was a Matre. Their love was forbidden, but they had eight years together. It wasn't enough, but they both had accepted it for what it was. He told me that love changes everything. That he wished it for me. And until

I had experienced it myself, I didn't know its true power."

"Are you telling me this is about love, Scylla?"

"Isn't everything? All the Dreamers, everyone who tried to leave the Four Cities, Aris and Metis, even you and Eleanor—you all did it for love."

"What's her name?"

Scylla does not reply.

"For her you're going to break the Four Cities and destroy our way of life?" the Planner asks. "How selfish can you be? Your purpose isn't to love. It's to protect peace. And you have failed."

A knot forms in Scylla's throat, and he swallows it. His mind flits to Selene—her smiling, happy, alive. Serenity washes over him. He straightens to his full height.

"Have you considered that maybe I'm just trying to get us to true peace?" Scylla says. "You haven't once acknowledged that we have a mass exodus on our hands. People, sir, have been leaving this utopia, and they're willing to die for it!"

"It isn't a mass exodus. It's just a few people we can replace. I will just make more children."

"More and more people are becoming unhappy. True peace isn't about avoiding risks or making everyone fall in line. It comes from love. From being with someone we love, from knowing we are loved. It's in the love the Matres give to the children they raise. The love friends at the CDL give each other. In the contented moments between lovers. Tabula Rasa takes all of that away."

The Planner scoffs. "True peace? Is that why you brought the Matres here? Why you're helping the CDL and these two with their revolution?"

"This isn't the CDL's fault," Aris says. "They didn't want to be a part of this."

The Planner's eyes tighten. "I am not talking to you right now."

"Aris is right," Scylla says. "The CDL did not want a revolution. You have to let them be."

"Let them be? The Head Matre has been in defiance of me since the beginning. Letting them be has led to this. Letting them be has allowed them to lure you into their grasp. No more!"

"You can't. The children need their love."

The Planner shakes his head. "You are such a disappointment. A traitor. A disgrace to the System."

The words hit Scylla in the chest, and his eyes water. As much as he wants to change the System, he still can't completely turn off his desire to please his creator. He was raised to, trained to—the way of thinking drilled into his mind. Only a force greater than a lifetime of conditioning could change him. For Scylla it's love. He holds on to it like a lifeline.

"It's you who's the traitor," a voice says, high and whispery like the wind. "To love. To life."

Eleanor! Scylla whips around, searching.

Her glowing form appears through the door.

"You're back!" Relief washes through the Planner's face. Just as suddenly, it shifts to anger. "How dare you leave the cottage! We had an agreement! How could you unravel everything we worked so hard for? I gave you everything you wanted."

"Gave me? Tell me, what have you *given me*, Eli? You took away my memories, my freedom, even my right to die."

"I gave you the Dreamers. I gave you back your purpose. I should have erased your memory. I've done it before. I can do it again."

"You would go back on your agreement?"

"You broke yours." His voice is hard as flint. "You led a revolt against me. You said you would never rejoin the Resistance."

"I didn't. The Resistance as it existed back in Elara did not survive. You made sure of that."

"They were dangerous. As is this one."

"This isn't the same resistance."

"It's a resistance none the less."

She tilts her chin up. "A resistance doesn't exist because of me. It will always exist because of Tabula Rasa."

"It keeps peace! It's been keeping peace for over two hundred years."

"Peace manufactured through force isn't real peace. There's no peace in living a life of fear. There's no peace in trading away a precious part of yourself. Not everyone is content in living a lie."

"I don't care! Humanity needs to be kept alive!" he yells.

"You've betrayed everything beautiful about it. Look at you now, so far away from your own humanity you don't even remember why you saved it to begin with. You listen only to your predictive model, and you've stopped listening to your own heart."

"This is ridiculous. Your revolution ends now. Apollina, take them all and erase their memories."

"Even Metis?" the Interpreter asks. "But his music."

"I no longer give a fuck about his music. As long as he can remember, he will continue to want to destroy our peace." He whips to Scylla. "Tell me where Eleanor's book is."

"I don't have it, sir," he repeats.

"Gordon—" he directs off-screen. "Do you have what Scylla was carrying? Is there a book in it?" A pause as he listens to Gordon's answer. "Read me the list of medications."

His face changes as he listens. His jaw tightens, ropes of veins appearing on his forehead. He looks back to Scylla. "How?"

Scylla's spine tightens, and cold washes through him. *He*

knows. He knows, and he will take Selene and their child away.

Eleanor walks to the Planner. "Eli . . ."

"Apollina, remove everyone from this room right now," the Planner says without taking his eyes off Eleanor. "I need to talk to my wife."

CHAPTER SIXTY-SIX

METIS

March 7, 2233
(13 days before Tabula Rasa)

Aris—the real Aris—is here. Metis wants to pull her into his embrace and never let go, but that will have to wait. Apollina is walking between them, and in front is the droid.

Metis turns to look over his shoulder. Trailing behind them is Scylla. His eyes are on the floor, his expression heavy. How did Aris get him on their side?

Their walk ends in the living room. Apollina sits down on a couch.

"What a day. I'm exhausted, and it's not even dawn yet," she says, and leans back. "Stevens, tea for everyone."

The droid moves to the kitchen.

Without the Interpreter and droid between them, Metis pulls Aris to him and crushes her to his chest. "I've missed you so much."

"I've missed you. It's been really hard." Her eyes are red.

"I know, baby. It's been really hard for me too." He wishes he could say everything he needs to say and do everything he needs to do without all these eyes around them.

"We tried," she adds.

"We did. At least we have each other in this moment." He brushes her hair from her face and gazes into her eyes—the beautiful brown he'd sorely missed. He leans down and kisses her.

The droid brings cups of tea on a tray and distributes them to everyone. His tea is again perfect. This should be the only way propensity models are used.

"Thank you, Stevens," he says.

A smile touches Apollina's icy blue eyes.

She sips from her cup. "So Scylla, why did the Planner send us out of the room?"

The officer does not reply.

Apollina sighs. "Look, we can either do this the easy way or not."

Stevens comes to stand next to Scylla.

"A Matre is sick," he says.

"With what?"

"Pregnancy."

Apollina laughs. "Now tell the truth, Scylla."

"I am. And the child is also mine."

What?

She leans forward. "How?"

"The old-fashioned way."

"Don't be vulgar."

"You asked." He laces his fingers together. "But I don't know exactly how. She calls it a miracle."

"You love her?"

"Yes, with all of me."

Metis can see Apollina's entire facade falling. Her eyes softening. Her sharp edges smoothening.

"Life can be different. Love doesn't have to be limited to a four-year cycle," she whispers the words he had said to her.

"Life *can* be different," Metis says. "No one has to be alone."

She drags in a long breath and drains her tea. "Well, drink up. We don't have all day. I'm going to electrocute the police and droids. Not you, Stevens."

He looks to Aris and sees the same confusion on her face.

"The story, if you're caught, is that you forced me to do it." Apollina gets up.

"What about the Crone?" Aris asks.

"This is her plan," Scylla says. "We need to go. The front door! We can take the car."

They spring up.

"Oh, Metis. Here." Apollina hands him his ring without an explanation before walking to her bedroom.

Relieved, he slips it on. He doesn't even want to know why she was holding it hostage.

They run to the front and arrive at the door just in time to see officers and droids falling to the ground.

"All clear," Apollina yells from the back.

They rush across the lawn, snaking around the unconscious bodies, and into the parked car out front.

"Get in! Hurry!" Scylla says.

They pile into the white police car, and Scylla speeds down the drive, leaving the Interpreter Center behind them. Metis has never been inside a car before. Their only use is to transport officers and those they've arrested. He is now a full-fledged criminal.

They drive down the streets of the still-asleep west side at full speed.

"Where are we going?"

"We're heading to the solar field. From there we can get to the train."

"How far is it?"

"Not too far."

The car rolls to a stop mid-block.

"Are we here?" he asks, confused.

"No," the officer says. "The car just stopped working. I think they've realized we've escaped. It's probably tracked. Let's run."

They follow him, zigzagging through the city, keeping to the shadows. Metis's feet and legs—weak from imprisonment—ache against the unforgiving pavement. Aris is beside him, each stride matching his pace. She's wiping streams of tears from her cheeks with her jacket sleeve. He wants to wrap her in his arms and whisper comforting words into her ears but does not. They lost the Crone, but they do not have time to lose.

Head down, Metis keeps his focus on the path in front of him. Block after block they run, heading toward the edge of the city. Forty-story skyscrapers give way to twenty-floor edifices, which eventually become ten-floor towers, then two- to three-story buildings.

It's quiet here—eerily so. In this part of the city, Callisto is no longer a bustling metropolis. There's a wrongness to it that unsettles. The place feels like a stage with no actors. He shudders. Everything about it is a lie.

The sky is beginning to shift. They need to get to the tunnel before they completely lose the protection of the dark. The sound of whirring, faded but ever growing, comes from somewhere behind them. He knows this sound. His heart drops to his stomach.

"Drones! Hide," Scylla hisses and throws himself against the door of the stout building closest to them. It's locked.

Metis peers through the gap between the drawn curtains covering its large glass window but can't see inside. Aris checks the door of the next building. It does not budge. Scylla points to a space between two buildings. They run to it.

The alley has two large metal boxes big enough to fit a few people. They hurl themselves between them and press their bodies deep into the narrow slot.

The whirring grows louder, now coming from right above them. Its sound and the beating of his heart commingle, becoming a strange thrum-hum fusion in his ears. Fear roils his stomach, pressing against his diaphragm, making it hard to breathe. And beneath it, rage. The fire at his core reignites, sending waves of heat through his body. If the police find him, he won't go easily. He will fight. They'll have to be more desperate than he is. Aris's arms are around his waist, and he pulls her in tighter.

The sound of the drone eases, becoming a low-pitched purr. It's moving away. The spring inside him unwinds. He lets out a long-held breath.

Scylla nods, and they leave the cover of the alley. Metis glimpses a tip of the flying machine as it veers off down a side street.

They resume their flight, no one saying a word. Between their silence and the city's, he feels as if he is stuck inside a nightmare.

The street begins sloping up in a gentle incline. His thigh muscles scream for him to stop, but he mustn't. They finally arrive at the top, and he gasps.

Below is the buttery desert, and to its right stands a field of solar panels that stretches as far as the eye can see. Their angled, shiny surfaces reflect the warm, pink glow of the dawn sky. Letting gravity pull him, he trots down the hill—the stiffness in his legs no longer a bother.

At the bottom, they stop. Here, the street fades into sand. There may have been more asphalt at one point that had, over time, lost its battle to nature. It's not as if he hasn't seen the solar field before, but it has always been from the windows of a distant train. Supplemented by geothermal and wind power, these are the main electrical generators for the Four Cities. But from this close, it all feels somehow foreign, not of this earth. His eyes burn.

He turns to Aris and Scylla. "Which way is the tunnel?"

Scylla points. "Beyond the field. There's a manhole to get down. Aris knows."

With a nod, they step forward. The rough sand crunches underfoot. The sound makes his teeth itch. A laugh escapes. They've made it.

Suddenly the whirring sound returns. His heart drops to his stomach.

"The drone! It's back!" Aris yells, looking frantically side to side.

The edge of the city is a hundred feet from where they stand. Ahead, the desert lies flat. The nearest copse of oak trees big enough to provide cover stands near the foot of the mountains—farther than their feet can carry them in time.

"The solar field!" Scylla yells.

They take off toward it.

The whirring gets louder. His legs burn, and a stitch stabs his side. Ignoring the pain, he pushes forward. His eyes focus on the shiny surfaces of the panels, an ombré of pale yellow and blue, reflecting the sky. As much as he wants to, he wills himself not to look back.

The solar panels are bigger than they first seemed. They look like roofs—many, many roofs—a village of roofs. And under them, legs. The whirring grows. He picks up his pace.

He makes the mistake of looking back. There is not one, but a group of drones flying toward them. The image freezes him.

"Metis!" Aris screams.

He feels her hand on his, dragging him.

"Stop where you are!" an amplified voice calls out.

Ahead of them, a line of police officers emerges from the solar field, blocking their way to the train. They can't go forward, and they cannot go back. Metis feels as if his soul has left his body.

"Brothers, listen to me!" Scylla yells. "You don't have to keep doing this. There's another way to be."

"Shut up, Scylla!" an officer says, advancing toward them. "Don't get yourself in any more trouble. Step away from the citizens. Your empathy for them has led you to this."

"No, Gordon. Can't you see the problem isn't them? It's us. We were trained to look at the citizens of the Four Cities as those to be controlled and tamed, not as our equals. That mindset has isolated us, has shut us off from love. It made us forget that we are just like them. We crave love just like they do."

"You will answer to the Planner. Put the Subdue Bracelets on all of them."

Metis grabs Aris, and they both run. Two officers seize them and separate them. He feels the hardness of metal on his wrists. Suddenly he cannot remember why he was so afraid.

CHAPTER SIXTY-SEVEN

ELI

March 7, 2233
(13 days before Tabula Rasa)

"I know these drugs," Eli says. "And I know *you* know these drugs. Did you give the names to Scylla?"

"Yes."

"What's going on at the CDL to make them so desperate to join your revolution?"

"I told you it's not my revolution."

"Fine. We don't have to assign ownership. I still need an answer."

"A Matre is sick, and she needs the medicine."

"Why *these* medicines?" He knows but needs her to say it. It isn't true until he hears it from her mouth.

"Eli . . ."

"I want to hear it from you."

She takes a step closer. "She's pregnant."

The words warm him. "The Four Cities is about to have its first non-created child?"

"Yes."

"We need to find out how her DNA changed, to see if it's systemic. We need to understand why this is happening."

"No, we don't Eli. Not right now. Right now, we need to help her and the child live."

"Understanding the cause will help. We need to bring her to Callisto."

"She's staying where she is. You will not take her from the CDL."

"But how else are we to figure out if it could happen to others or how to insert the Tabula Rasa gene into the child?"

"What? No! You will not do that."

"A peaceful society cannot stay peaceful without everyone following the same rule. How will the Four Cities be if some of them can remember and some can't? How are we going to keep peace?"

"No! Nature is taking its course. You need to let it be."

Eli shakes his head. "Instability will lead to chaos. Chaos will lead to unrest. Unrest will lead to war."

"What is this chaos you're so afraid of? You cannot keep ruling the Four Cities with your own fear."

"The predictive model helps us keep peace."

"It's not a living thing! It can't know what's inside our hearts. Why else would the only solution it offers to keep peace be to separate people—from each other, from their own memories, from their own selves?"

"Because we can't be trusted to not destroy each other!"

She walks to the screen and touches his cheek. "Yes, we can."

"But what happens when another police officer falls in love with another Matre? With a citizen? What happens if all of them do? Who will keep peace in the Four Cities? Who will raise the children?"

"Those who want to," she says.

"They can't. Their memories are not continuous."

"People can choose to get their pasts back. With the memory book, with Absinthe, they now have a choice."

"Memories are dangerous."

"Says who? The artificial intelligence of the predictive model isn't omniscient, Eli. It can't predict everything. That's why it can't comprehend the reason you keep me around or why you allow the Dreamers to find me."

"What's not to comprehend? The Four Cities can't live without me, and I can't live without you," he says. "Besides, that's not relevant to this conversation."

"It is. Who we are, what we do, affects everything and everyone we touch. And you—powerful as you are—affect things the most. Your decisions change lives, take away love, give it. You've changed the course of our civilization. You brought it back from the brink of extinction."

"*We* brought it back," he corrects. She was just as much its savior.

"We did good. But we've outlasted our usefulness."

"No. The Four Cities still need us."

"Not through imprisonment. Like it or not, things are going to change. At this moment, the memory books are being distributed across the Four Cities. People will have the choice to choose to remember their past or not. You can no longer keep other people's memories locked up."

His eyes bulge. "The Matres—it's why they're here, isn't it? I can't let it happen. I won't. Gordon—" he calls.

"The police don't have the Matres," Eleanor says.

"What? The droids—they were sent to get them."

"You had forgotten one little thing. Long ago they were all programmed to know me. To help me."

"But you don't look the way you did."

"I don't. But the Matres do."

He cannot believe this. How could he have overlooked this. It seems when it comes to Eleanor, he will always have a blind spot. "This can't happen!"

"It *is* happening."

"I can't let it."

She closes her eyes, looking like the same exasperated Eleanor he once knew from all the times before, when they were stuck in an endless argument. She opens them again. "Amalthea."

He feels as if his insides shift. "What did you say?"

"This is how she can live again. Scylla and Selene—they're us. But not just us. They're the best versions of who we are—who we could have been had things not gone so wrong. Their child is *our* child. We never had a chance to see Amalthea alive, but we can help this one. Help them, Eli. Help them, and then let them be. We need to let go."

He searches for something hard inside him to hold onto, but he cannot. The name, the one name—Amalthea—has thawed him. "I don't know how."

"We can just disappear from existence. Would that be the worst thing? Would it be worse than living this way?"

He reduces himself until he becomes the same size she is. He is no longer just a face but takes on his full form. They are two glowing entities separated by a thin screen.

"It isn't peace that needs to be protected, Eli. It's love. Without it, nothing is enough. Remember what it was like to be in love? That all-consuming, all-encompassing love?"

"I remember."

"*Hey,*" a voice said.

His head sprang up. An attractive blond woman stood before him with a light smile on her lips. Her face was as colorless as a winter sky, but her blue eyes had the warmth of a summer day. His heart skipped a beat. He felt as if he was looking down a skyscraper.

"You're Eli Anders, right? They said I might find you here."

"Uh—yeah."

"I'm Eleanor Hope. I'm in your Statistics II class. You sit behind me?"

He searched his memory but couldn't recall her face. Truth was, he didn't remember anyone from his undergraduate class at Columbia. He rarely looked around. If he did, he was pretty sure he would have remembered her. She wasn't the kind of girl one would forget.

She stretched out a hand, and he took it. Her palm felt as if she had been keeping it in the freezer.

"Sorry about that. My hands are always cold." She tilted her head to one side. Her eyes dug into his as if trying to excavate him. "They say you're a genius at predictive modeling."

"Who's they?"

"Everyone. Didn't a guy make ten grand using your stock tip?"

So, this is why she's here. A beautiful girl like her wouldn't just talk to a nothing like him for no reason.

"NanoTechX. N-A-T-X." He spelled each letter out.

"What?"

"The stock you'd want to buy now. They're a start-up and the CEO is an MIT dropout. But they're going to be huge."

Her cheeks reddened. "Oh, that's not why I'm here."

He blinked. "No? Oh, sorry."

She smiled. "It's okay. I'm sure you get a lot of people asking. My interest lies more in the sciences."

"Which one?"

"All kinds. Right now, health and the human genome." She eyed the bench. "Can I sit?"

He flicked his eyes from her to the spot next to him, uncertain whether he had heard her right. She continued to look at him expectantly.

"Oh. Yeah. Sure." He scooted to make room for her.

She sat down. His skin tingled, and the hair on his arms stood up. It was as if there was a magnetic field around her pulling him in.

"Thanks," she said, her cheeks colored. She tucked a strand of hair behind one ear. "I was hoping you could help me with a project."

"Health and human genetics aren't really my specialties."

"Hear me out." She smiles. "I'm working with my professor on probabilistic prognostic estimates of survival in metastatic cancer patients and wanted to see if you can help me on the predictive modeling for it."

"Probabilistic prognosis estimates of survival in metastatic cancer patients . . ." He moved the words around in his mouth like a piece of taffy. "That's not something you hear every day. What's your purpose for predicting survival rates?"

"To help doctors better plan treatment."

He studied her. Beyond the stunning blond waif facade were determined eyes and what appeared to be a serious temperament. "So, you're that type, huh?"

The space between her eyebrows folded together. "What type?"

"A do-gooder."

The pink in her cheeks brightened. He could get used to seeing it. He decided to step out onto the ledge.

"Sure, I'll help you," he said. "Let's meet this weekend."

"Okay. Where?"

"I'll text you the place. Say Saturday afternoon around one?"

"Sure."

"It's a date," he said.

She stared at him with her intense blue eyes again, making

him feel as if he was about to slip off a ledge and fall forty stories down to the asphalt below.

"Real or figurative?" she asked.

He was not expecting the blunt question. "Which would you like it to be?"

Annoyance rose on her face. He should not have put the pressure on her to decide. It was not gentlemanly, as his mother would say.

He cleared his throat. "I meant a real date."

She raised an eyebrow. "What do we do on this date?"

He couldn't help but laugh. "You want an itinerary?"

Her cheeks reddened.

"I can promise there'll be food and maybe music," he said.

"So, you're serious?"

"Are you opposed to it?"

"I don't know." She frowned. "It's just, I don't have a lot of time, and I don't know what you're expecting, and I . . ."

He cleared his throat. "I can also promise a lesson on predictive modeling."

She looked thoughtful. Eli felt unstable on that ledge again.

"Okay," she said finally. "It's a date."

"I still love you," he tells her.

A smile graces her lips. "I do too."

Her glow is dimming. Why is her glow dimming?

"You need to go back inside your book," he says. "Where is it?"

"Away."

"What do you mean?"

"I'm not going back in, Eli. I'm letting go."

His entire world tilts and cracks. "No! You can't. You can't leave me."

"Come with me," she says.

"Come with you?"

"Yes. We've been here long enough. We need to go so we can make room for change."

"What kind of change?"

"This child, for example, may not be the only one of its kind. There may be others in the future, and they need to be allowed to exist exactly as they are."

"But it will kill the mothers."

"Not necessarily. I gave the Matres at the CDL instructions on how to keep Selene alive with the help of medication. Then there's the memory books. They will be read, and people will be able to remember their pasts."

"But we will have those who can remember and those who can't. It will be chaos."

"We'll also have people who are allowed to keep their love. It'll stop them from running away. Yes, I know about the runaways. I also know about the drug at College that extends memories."

"How do you know?"

"Secrets have a way of coming out. Aren't you tired of living life this way?"

She touches his cheek, and he wishes with his entire being to be able to feel her hand.

"I can feel it coming," she says, awe in her voice.

"No . . ."

"It's not scary, Eli." Her lips turn up in a slow smile. "It's freeing."

"I can't— I don't—" He's feeling a part of himself breaking off, crumbling into dust.

A beeping sound draws his attention.

"Sir, we have the prisoners," Gordon says.

He gazes into Eleanor's blue eyes. The deep ocean he fell in love with on that perfect spring day long ago now evaporating and paling as she fades. The glow that once illuminated the night dimming. Her edges diffusing, blending with the air.

"Remember, love is what matters," she says, her hand reaching out to stroke his cheek one last time before dissolving into nothingness.

He stares at the empty space. His head, usually buzzing with thoughts, is at once silent.

She is gone. She is gone, and I am here.

He knows at the center of his being that there is no reality in which he will exist long after she's gone from this world.

"Sir?" Gordon says.

"Let them go," he says.

"What?"

"Let. Them. Go."

"Why?"

"Gather your brothers. I have a message for all of you."

He turns off Gordon's transmission.

"I'm coming right behind you," he whispers.

Today is a good day to say goodbye.

EPILOGUE

ARIS

March 19, 2233
(The day before Tabula Rasa)

Aris squints at the brightness above. She shields her eyes with a hand.

"Looks like we're going to need to move again," she says.

Throughout the day, they have been adjusting their position beneath the pine with the changing angle of the sun.

"But it's so comfortable," Metis says. The blanket under them has provided just enough cushion from the pine needles.

"We're going to sweat. Remember we're having dinner at Selene and Scylla's cottage. I don't want to be stinky."

The medicine the officer had brought back from Callisto has improved her condition, and the child inside is growing.

"Fine."

They adjust their blanket and are again under full shade.

"What's tonight's dinner?" Metis asks.

"Mushrooms."

"You must love that."

"She likes me."

"The big dinner on Tabula Rasa night," he says.

They both quiet. The trigger is still inside their brains, built into their DNA.

"Do you think the drug will work?" she asks.

"Yes."

"How are you so sure? They've never tried it on an adult who's gone through Tabula Rasa before."

"We'll find out tomorrow morning."

"It would be nice to not have to restart this cycle a stranger to each other."

"Of course. Though it would also mean we'd get to have another first date. Didn't you use to like those?"

She elbows him.

"If it doesn't work, we have our memory books," he says.

Apollina has been resetting the Dreamcatchers to read the memory books. Aris has received a few sessions since her first. She's learned the past is easier to take in small chunks and not all at once. The Interpreter still offers the dream-erasure service as well. While Aris cannot understand why anyone would want to forget their past, she cannot judge them for it. As long as no one tries to take her memories away, she's happy to let them be.

"But my memory book is missing a bunch of memories," she says. "How was I supposed to know we needed to wear our watch for that?"

"If both fail, we also have Absinthe."

At the word, her thought flits to the Crone. She and the Planner had disappeared—gone without a trace—after the Planner let them go and told his officers his new wishes.

Aris had no idea the Crone had planned her departure until Amira told them all on the train back to the CDL. It was the only way to rid the Four Cities of the System. The System is the Planner, and the Planner could not live without the Crone. Logical. Selfless. Just like her.

"I miss her," Metis says, knowing exactly what's on her mind.

"Me too. I didn't even get to say a final goodbye."

Their fingers lace. She looks up. Through the needles, the sky is bright cerulean with not a single cloud.

"Do you think the lab will ever figure out how to remove the trigger?" she asks after a while.

"I don't know. I hope so, at least on the new batch."

She shudders. "I hate when you call them 'batches'—they're children."

"That place is kind of creepy."

"Yeah, still, they're children."

"Hi, Professor Metis!" A child waves from the path. She's with a group of seniors wearing backpacks.

On top of managing the Library of Mem—the official name they agreed on—the Head Matre has allowed them to stay on as teachers to replace the Matres who are leaving on a much-needed vacation away from the CDL. Metis teaches music, Aris science.

"There's a batch," he says. "Hi, Ora! Where are you going?"

"The lake."

"Have you been practicing the piano?"

"Yes. See you in class tomorrow. If you can remember." She laughs and continues walking.

"Morbid humor, that one," Metis says.

"She's a good kid," Aris says. "She'll be happy Bastian and Cass are coming back tomorrow for the birthday feast."

Everyone will be a year older. She will be thirty-three and Metis thirty-seven. All the seniors will turn seventeen. One surprise is that Cass and Bastian have decided to stay together at College. They've found a purpose working in the lab there to create more ways to help people keep their memories. Though with the train running regularly between the CDL and College, they and others will be able to come back for a visit when time allows.

Head Matre Hera and Head Professor Thalia have also been meeting often for tea to exchange ideas. One they presented to the police force is to have a monthly train to and from Callisto to bring in Dreamers. That way, they hope to prevent pilgrims from risking their lives traveling the dangerous desert to get here. There've been no more runaways.

One disagreement they have so far with the police is over the fate of the graduates they took to Callisto. The officers maintain that these children now belong to the Four Cities and that their lives are governed by their rules, which means they will go through Tabula Rasa.

The police are also keeping tight control of the memory books they brought with them on the train. They will work with Dreamers to identify and locate the books' owners to make sure they only go to those who really want them. Results will be monitored and put into the predictive model. They cannot wean themselves completely from it.

Aris has come to realize that decisions will be a series of compromises. Nothing will be perfect. Everything will be slow. But it's better than what it was.

Still, it amazes her how she and Metis ended up where they are. They could not have gotten here had it not been for everyone they'd met along the way—each a puzzle piece that when put together created an image wilder than her imagination. A community.

"One more nap before we go?" Metis asks.

"Okay."

They kiss, long and lingeringly.

"Maybe we should go back to our room," he says.

She laughs. "If we go back, we'll never come out again."

"Scylla and Selene won't mind if we miss dinner, right?"

"They will definitely mind." She closes her eyes. "See you on the other side."

"Hey," he says.

She opens her eyes and sees his face above hers. "Yeah?"

"I love you, forever."

Forever. She finds she no longer hates the word. It's become comforting in a way. To feel its weight and value. To wear it like the ring that graces her finger.

"I love *you* forever," she says.

ACKNOWLEDGMENTS

There's a sweet sadness that came after turning in to my publisher *Freeset*, the last book in my love triptych set in a world where memories are erased in the name of peace. I've lived in the utopia/dystopia of the Four Cities since 2017. For almost seven years, I've walked alongside my characters. I've come to love each one dearly—for their fierce dedication, idealism, faults, and complexity. Though I created them, they have just as much created me. With each book, I've shifted, becoming more aligned with myself. It's hard not to when the act of writing requires so much inner work—that I lean into instead of away from. And it's hard not to when the stories themselves demand I take apart and analyze our society from different angles, and myself along with it.

    I couldn't have written *Freeset* without my husband. Thank you for your staunch support in every aspect of my writing life. For reading every word. For your honest but kind feedback. For listening. For accepting me as a writer and a human just the way that I am. *Maybe* one day I'll believe "good" really means "good" and stop asking the question (though I doubt it).

My thanks also go out to . . .

My children, for constantly inspiring me to be, do, and write better. Being a parent is an act of hope. So is writing. I'm forever grateful I get to do both.

My twenty-year-old cat and muse, Scooter. We're never cold with each other's warmth.

My extended family in the US, Thailand, Indonesia, and all over the world. I'm proud to be a part of our family tree.

My found family and forever friends: Bobby, Yvette, Laurie, Grace, Carmel. Thank you for always being there through our decades of friendship.

Lauren and Caroline, for tea and sympathy. No one knows the life of a writer like another writer.

Shannon, for your creative eye.

Diana Gill, my editorial editor. Thank you for helping me break the story open. *Freeset* is a much tighter book because of your advice.

My agent, Julie Gwinn. Without you, this series wouldn't be a series.

Rick Bleiweiss, for acquiring the Four Cities series for Blackstone Publishing.

The team at Blackstone for bringing all three books to life: Josie Woodbridge, Ananda Finwall, Alenka Linaschke, Michael Krohn, Rebecca Malzahn, Nicole Sklitsis, Brianna Jones, Francie Crawford, Bella Bedoya, and everyone who worked tirelessly in the background.

Shiromi Arserio, for your wonderful vocal performances on the entire Four Cities series, and a pleasant afternoon in San Diego talking about books.

Dr. Ronald Coleman, for helping me figure out the scientific logic of memory erasure and retrieval. Thank you for making me sound smarter.

Sara Patel, for the name Amira.

Every reader, reviewer, bookstagrammer, and booklover. Thank you for spending your precious time with *Freeset* (as well as *Reset* and *Preset*). Your reviews, kind messages, and posts mean the world to this writer (and all writers). Book people are the best people.

Once Upon a Book Club and Unplugged Book Box, for choosing my books for your wonderful collections. So many thanks for introducing my stories to your readers.

My gratitude to those who speak up when they see injustice. Those who believe in the power of the collective and act to protect it. Those who give something of themselves to lift up the voiceless. The injustices of the world are committed by people who want us to believe that we won't come together as a community. But we know that we are stronger together.

Finally to Freeset, an organization based in the heart of Calcutta's red-light district, offering employment to women who want to escape prostitution. Working with Freeset can provide them and their family with an alternative life—a life of freedom. Please support their cause by purchasing handmade Freeset products at www.globalhandicrafts.org.

Hope is a moral obligation.

PRAISE FOR SARINA DAHLAN

"A vivid, evocative journey...This compelling debut is a story for our current world."
—Kimiko Guthrie, author of *Block Seventeen*, on *Reset*

"A collision of our era's catastrophes fuses a new world, becoming something rich and strange."
—Kim Stanley Robinson, Hugo Award–winning novelist, on *Preset*

"Crisp, stylish prose and a story about love trying to withstand the rigors of time. This is a book subtle in its intensity, lush and beautiful, while carefully exploring what it means to be human and what we are to each other. Evocative and literary, I highly recommend it."
—David R. Slayton, author of *White Trash Warlock*, on *Reset*